Bella
Will Rally

Michael Sedloff

Bella Will Rally
Michael Sedloff

Published by Readable Books

Readable Books
San Diego, California
http://www.BellaWillRally.com
mlsedloff@gmail.com

Cover design by Teri Rider
Publishing Services by www.Sellbox.com

My mother was a loving woman. When I was young, we were very close. It was only as an adult that I learned how little of herself she revealed to me during those early years. I dedicate *Bella Will Rally* to her. Although a work of fiction, I imagine she would have been proud to have her namesake reflected in that of the novel's main character, Bella Krawiec.

Acknowledgements

This novel could not have been written without my sister, **Bonnie Lipton,** whose insights helped form the foundation for my story and characters.

Early on, I was privileged to have been a student of **Marni Freedman,** who urged me to draw from my mother's life and times to create a memorable central character for my novel.

I could not have completed this novel without the love and support of my wife, **Janice;** daughter, **Erin;** and son, **Brandon.**

Sam Spevack, my brilliant father-in-law, provided invaluable input on the accuracy and appropriateness of the use of Yiddish phrases.

My thrice-published Aunt **Harriet Rochlin** both inspired me and gave me the strength to believe in myself, along with providing a clearer picture of how my mother's family lived.

Last, but far from least, the enormous redirection of my work by my editor, **Denise Middlebrooks,** shines through in its readability. I am deeply grateful for her patience.

If you want to, you can move the whole world.

AZ ME VIL, KEN MEN IBERKERN DI GANTSE VELT.

Yiddish Proverb

Chapter 1

I n 1933, when I was twelve, my older brother Solly owned a 1926 Model T Roadster. I called it the Shiny Black Beast. On summer days, while Solly spent his time in green-velvet land at the Brooklyn Avenue Pool Hall, hoping his cue would save the day, or at the very least, make him an extra George Washington quarter, I would run through the kitchen, grab a spoonful of Mama's kosher chicken soup, lather myself with suntan oil and run outside to where the roadster hugged the curb. Solly didn't trust parking it anywhere near the pool hall.

In those days, it seemed I was always in a rush to slow down. Nature and reading calmed me. That summer, I was rolling down the Mississippi with Huck Finn, sharing in his shenanigans with criminals, religious zealots, and the like. *The Adventures of Huckleberry Finn* was my refuge.

It was *shabes*, the Jewish Sabbath, September 11, 1933. This day of prayer and rest would soon turn into Rosh Hashanah, the beginning of the Highest Holy Days. That meant that Pa, the only religious one in the family, would soon begin a period of prayer and self-evaluation that would end in Yom Kippur.

I planned to spend the afternoon reading. My older brother's car was in its usual spot. It was indeed the bee's knees. I wasn't allowed inside his pride and joy, but neither he nor anyone else was around so I pried open the car door and seated myself comfortably inside. It felt good to sit in this forbidden place. The soft leather seat was cool on my backside, even though the afternoon sun pounded down. I didn't intend to stay there long, but certainly I had time to read a chapter or two of my book.

The suntan cream didn't protect me for long. The strong September sunbeams quickly turned my nose to a pinkish crisp. Perspiration rolled from my brow down my cheek and wet the page that lay open before me. From time to time, I looked up and around to see if I was about to be found out. Since it was Saturday, the street was empty.

Solly, who was three years older, was supposed to be at Breed Street Shul with Pa. But he managed to escape hours of praying by lying about his whereabouts. Neither Mama, my sisters Sarah, Kate, Pearl, and Frieda, nor

I were even asked to go to services. We weren't part of the Jewish man's fraternity. Women were outsiders.

If Solly had known I was in his car, he would have had a stroke. As I read, the Santa Ana winds twisted dirt from the empty lot across the street into a whirling dust devil. My eyes became pencil-thin slits as I struggled to keep the dirt out and focus on the pages of my book. My sleeveless sunflower dress attracted a bumble bee, which buzzed my head. I took action "Get out of here, Mr. Bee. Get away! Get away!" I swatted at him so hard, I slapped my forehead with my hand. "Ouch, that hurt!" Unharmed, the bee flew to its next destination, one of Mama's roses. I returned to Huck.

All at once, my reading was rudely interrupted as I looked up and saw Solly and two older guys bickering on the corner. The two strangers were in Solly's face. One pressed a finger into his chest. Not another soul was around. I ducked down behind the steering wheel, hoping they wouldn't notice me. Solly was really getting bawled out. He took a *klap* square in the center of his stomach. He hit the ground with a thump. Asphalt rocks sprayed up. One of the guys said something to Solly, but I couldn't make out his words. Sliding into the passenger seat, I turned the door handle and edged the car door open, hoping to make my way inside the house without being noticed. I made it halfway up the porch steps and froze in place. *Solly needs me. I can't abandon him*, I thought.

Pivoting, I crept back into the front yard. Hiding behind the magnolia tree, I nudged the swing hanging from its limbs, but caught it before the movement got the thugs' attention. That's when I noticed that Solly's Babe Ruth baseball bat, the one he'd won in a game of eight ball at the pool hall, was beneath the swing. I grabbed the bat and let out a war hoop. "Solly, I'm coming. Don't move, I've got your Babe Ruth baseball bat."

There was no response, not a word. The bullies didn't even look up as I ran at them. They were bent over Solly instead. I whipped the bat over my head and sprinted at them. Swinging it like an axe, I chopped the air in front of me. As I got closer, Solly's attackers turned my way. They were truly idiots. The *neveyle* ran for it. One of them tripped on his own cuffed pants leg, almost fell over, but caught himself and ran, without looking back. The other one followed. They didn't seem to have a clue that I was just a wimpy twelve-year-old girl. If they had known, I can't even think what would have happened.

When I reached Solly, I was out of breath, still huffing and puffing. I leaned over him. He lay motionless and his face was covered with blood. In shock, I let the bat go. It clanked on the asphalt and rolled against one of his legs. Solly must have felt it because he came to his senses. He raised one hand to his face, readying himself to respond to another hit.

"Solly, it's me, Bella, I scared them off with your bat." I bent down toward him, pulling out the handkerchief Mama had made for my sixth-grade graduation. I mopped the blood off his face. The pink flowers embroidered with BK, for Bella Krawiec, filled with his blood. "Your lip … the blood … it's gushing! Can you stand up?" I extended my hand. "Grab it, the boys are gone."

Solly probably outweighed me by fifty pounds. Without his help, pulling him up would have been impossible. He pushed against the cement and struggled to steady himself as his short, squat body edged up toward mine. The shear idiocy of what I had just done hit me. I felt dizzy. Solly pinched my cheek.

"Oweeeee! Why'd you do that? That hurt!"

"You saved me so I pinched you before you passed."

Those thugs had pounded Solly good. He was a mess. His tie was flipped over his shoulder and his Hamburg hat was crushed on the ground where he had fallen on top of it. His navy-blue jacket was shredded in several places. His face, that was another story.

"Why'd you do that?" Solly said. "You could have been killed."

I shrugged. "I was kind a brave, wasn't I."

"Look, you don't have to worry about me." Solly touched his lip with his right hand. "This hurts like hell. Damn, it stings. My new suit is shredded. Damn it, those bastards! I didn't see the big one's fist until it was heading right at my eye. They jumped me. I would have broken their arms if only … if only I'd seen them first." He looked at me. "Don't you dare say a word to Mama, you hear. She'll tell Pa, no doubt about it. Then, I'll be in for his stupid moralizing again. Can't believe none of my boys came to help me turn the tables on those guys. They always walk this way on the way home. Wonder if they heard something on the street and stayed away on purpose. Those rats, can't count on anyone these days." Solly's eyes glazed over. "Hey, can I borrow that?"

"What?"

"Your handkerchief, idiot. I need to put pressure on my lip to stop the bleeding."

In the time we stood there, the temperature had cooled and the late afternoon sun had dropped below the horizon, leaving a red glow to temporarily fill the sky. Covered in dried sweat, my teeth jittered. "Why are you calling me an idiot? I didn't deck you. Why'd those guys hit you, anyway?"

Solly's hand waved me off. "It's none of your business, kid. But from now on, I'll take care of myself, okay."

I slapped his shoulder with the palm of my hand. "Okay, big brother, I get it. You're a tough guy. Hey tough guy, you're the one with the bloody lip."

"Look, it's nothing, okay."

I was cold and getting colder. A horse and buggy turned the corner. Solly pulled me out of the way, so the driver could pass.

"God, what's that smell?" I said.

"Horse shit, didn't you see it drop?"

"No, I was too busy listening to *your* horseshit."

"Knock it off, will you. I've got enough going. I owe a few bucks to a guy named Harry. He's the boss of those thugs. I don't have it quite yet. I'll get it from Pa's store. They'll be back, the bastards!"

I looked around. How could he talk so tough when his butt was still stinging from the fall? "Are you worried?" I asked. "Are they coming back? Are we going to see a whole bloody gang of them?"

Solly spit out blood and pressed on his lip again. "Just stay out of their way, okay. Do you understand? Stay out of the way!"

I wasn't about to let that be the end of it. I wasn't walking away from him until I knew more. "How much do you owe him?"

"Not much. Look, don't worry, I've got it figured. Just don't tell Pa or I'll be a dead man. Don't tell anybody! If you keep this quiet long enough, I'll have the time to win the money back. It's really small potatoes, anyway, what I owe. Their boss won't bother to send more than two of them. He's got bigger fish to fry."

"Solly, today is *shabes*, tomorrow is Rosh Hashanah. Does that mean anything to you?"

"Yeah, it means Pa will be *davening* with all the old men at *shul*." I won't have to worry about him coming into the store." He smirked. "Maybe I'll just borrow what I need from the cash register drawer."

It was always about the money with Solly. He'd been in trouble before. Pa often warned him not to crawl in that gamblers' cesspool. I was about to say something when I noticed my sister Pearl walk out onto our porch. She was smoking. My sister embarrassed me. She was wearing a straight-line red silk dress so tightly she couldn't separate her feet far enough apart to get good balance. Standing on the porch, she looked much older than her thirteen years. Maybe it was those three-inch high heels.

Curious, or maybe just happy to give Solly a hard time, she walked over and joined us in the street. With that dress and those shoes, she wobbled like a storm battered her. As soon as she got close to Solly, she reached out and touched his chin with one long, black-polished nail. I stared at her, anxious to see what she would say. Her thickly painted red lips looked like a neon sign ready to pulsate, even before she opened her mouth.

"Hey, sis," I said. "I've got this one under control. You can go back to your smoke if you want."

She ignored me and glared at Solly. "Don't you look pretty. What happened? Some girl slap you? Were you fresh?"

"Stay out of my business," he said. "Who invited you anyway?" He patted me on the shoulder. "Bella and I were just having a little chat. Go away. I don't need your smart mouth. While you're at it, get a dress that actually fits."

Pearl lips opened wide. Her teeth were so white, they could probably be seen halfway across the block. "Wow, nice shiner, too!" Pearl wouldn't back off. "You welsh on a bet?"

"Hell no! Harry's boys got anxious, that's all. They're collectors. My pockets were empty."

"You jackass, you bet again without pennies in your pocket? Will you never learn? Harry would just as soon have killed you as look at you. I've seen him in motion."

Pearl and Solly had started to frequent the speakeasies as soon as she turned thirteen. They were both too young for seedy whiskey halls, but Pearl enjoyed the attention of the older boys and Solly liked the thrill of the wild cards. As Pearl continued to harass Solly, he reminded her that taking a few punches to the gut was no big deal. "Look Pearl, you weren't barking so loudly last night at the club when those thugs barreled you down and carried away that guy who *kibitzed* you up."

Hearing Pearl and Solly talk like that scared me. Just the other morning, on our walk to school, Pearl had told our sister Frieda that she wasn't feeling so well. Frieda, who was twelve, made a face.

"Are you getting the influenza? Ick! Don't touch me. I don't want to be sick."

Pearl struck back. "The flu, no, no, that's not it. Solly and I snuck out and gallivanted to Smell the Roses last night. A stunning guy offered me a gin fizz. You can't go there and just sit on your hands, you know. You've got to play the role. Act just like you know what you're doing. The drink got me tipsy. So our tough-guy brother ushers me out before I finish chatting with the big galoot who bought the drink. Too bad, he was a musician. You know how I love guys who can carry a tune."

"Why do you go to those places anyway?" Frieda asked "I can't even imagine what Pa would do if he found out."

"There's no reason for Pa to know we were there, Frieda. Besides, I'm planning ahead when I talk to guys like that. I'd like to sing and dance in one of those clubs very soon. Getting work is all about making proper connections. You should join us one night if you've got the nerve."

Although I knew Pearl and Solly hung out at the wrong kind of places, like Smell the Roses, I never thought I'd see Solly get beaten up right in front of our house. I doubted if Pearl did either. Now, she turned to me. "Bella, why are you so pasty white?"

"I'm not pasty white," I said. "Anyway, it'll be alright. Solly's going to take a loan from Pa's cash drawer to get the money he needs."

Solly must have realized he'd given up too much about his plans because he turned to me and said, "Kid, let's go inside and get some water. Stop worrying so much. You've got to have guts to get ahead in this world. I'll take care of the collectors and I'll be rolling in the dough before you know it. Sometimes you have to take a punch or two. Don't worry, I can take care of myself. You should stay out of it. This is no game for a little girl."

Pearl stepped onto Solly's toes as he sermonized. "Stealing from Pa's cash drawer, that's not a game, that's crap. Watch out for Pa. He'll undo his belt and give you a swat like those hooligans couldn't have imagined."

Solly stood his ground. "If Pa finds out, then some little bird might just squawk about you sneaking out to the clubs. You know everything happens for a reason. It's *bashert*."

That was a word that Mama always used. I knew it was Yiddish for "meant to be." But Mama never used it to threaten us. With Solly, it was different. He used Mama's words to block Pearl's assault.

While Solly preached to Pearl, some animal roaming the hills yapped loud enough to wake the dead. Pearl scanned the hills, but Solly didn't flinch. I blurted, "What was that?" None of us could see where the sound came from. Solly laughed like a crazy man.

"Those coyotes must have nabbed a pack of rats. Maybe they went after to the two thugs who beat me up. *Zolst du laigen mit dein putz in kayver und mit a loch In kishka* " I looked funny at him.

"It's an old curse," he said. It means *may your penis lie in a grave and may you have a hole in your gut and a hernia.*"

Getting beat up made Solly feel tougher. Feeling his oats, he gave us a plan to handle the thugs if they came back in the morning before he got the money to pay Harry. "If you hear them knock, don't answer, don't whisper. Don't move! They'll just leave."

I wasn't convinced. "What about Mama?"

Solly rubbed his finger with his thumb as he spoke. "I forgot. She might be home. She'll probably be in the back yard picking strawberries or some-thin' for breakfast. If she's in the kitchen, one of you needs to keep her away from the door. The other one ... Pearl, that's you ... just open the door enough for them to hear you. Don't unlatch it. Tell them I've gone and then close ... no ... slam it in their fat faces."

Pearl wanted a better plan. "What if they barge in?"

"After you open the door, speak very softly. Be tight lipped. Tell them I'm not around. It's me they're looking for. They won't dare come inside. Can you do that? They won't know how to react to a soft-spoken woman with a stick up her ass. Tell them I'll have it tomorrow night. Believe me, I'll have the money. Don't worry, I'll give it to them!"

"Worry, I won't," said Pearl. "It's your scalp."

Solly reached up and raked his hair, leaving a streak of blood down the middle.

"Okay," said Pearl, "we'll do our job but you better not delay with those boys for a second longer than necessary. You've really put us on the spot this time."

Solly pressed on his lip. His left eye was swollen shut. It was now early evening. One of our neighbors, Mr. Garfinkle, turned the corner on his way home from work. He looked over at us and waved his arm high in the air. Luckily, he didn't seem to notice Solly's shiner. If he had, it would have been the talk of the neighborhood.

"Look," said Solly, "I've got to go. There's a chick waiting. Does my lip stick out like a sore thumb? Is there somethin' I can put on it?"

Pearl, for some reason, got nicer. She took a closer look. "I'll fix it. There's not much I can do for that shiner. You better come up with a great story."

The three of us walked back to the house. Solly and Pearl waited on the front porch as I opened the front door and slipped inside. Walking calmly to the kitchen toward Mama, I distracted her by bragging loudly about the A I got on my spelling test.

Mama was proud of my grades in school, but demanded humility. "Don't be a *lets*, nobody likes a know-it-all," she said, without looking up from her preparations for dinner. I walked back to the porch and signaled to Solly and Pearl. Pearl took off her black patent-leather high heels, and without a word, tiptoed into the house. Solly unlaced his two-tone oxfords, slipped them off, and followed Pearl. I walked back into the kitchen, where Mama and I *kibitzed* as Pearl and Solly snuck past.

When Mama went upstairs for something, I grabbed a big hunk of meat from the icebox and took it to Solly. Pearl was putting some camphor on his cuts to avoid infection. The odor about knocked me over. His date would know for sure he'd had been in a fight.

Chapter 2

The next morning, long after everyone but Mama and Pearl had left the house, I awoke. Lying in bed, still sleepy, I yawned while stretching toward the ceiling. There was a knock at the front door.

Before I could get to my feet, the door took such a pounding, the whole house rattled. No one pounded on our front door like that. It had to be them. Remembering Solly's instructions, I ran downstairs and sprinted to the door, worried that Mama would get there first. Luckily, I could hear her humming in the backyard. Where was Pearl? She was supposed to do the talking. I couldn't wait any longer. I pried the door barely open, just enough to put my nose through it. It swung wide out of my hands as one of the guys pushed it into me. *Damn it,* I thought. I couldn't believe Solly forgot to latch it the night before. I jumped back to avoid it smashing me in the face.

The first guy to speak was the little one. Solly had told me he was called Tony. The other one, called Eddy, was bigger, with a handlebar mustache and a gimpy eye. He had a cigarette hanging from the left side of his lower lip. Ashes fell onto the door threshold. I kicked them outside, which was what I wanted to do to these guys standing in front of me. I kept my voice very soft and withheld all but the words I thought were necessary. "He's gone," I said.

The tall one, Eddy, spoke hoarsely. "Where? Where is he? We don't have time for games."

I froze as Eddy scratched his plaid Baker Boy hat and snarled. His shirt had a sweat spot under the armpits that looked a week old. Tony stared intently at me, without saying a word. I edged backward. Dew from the porch overhang dripped cold water onto Eddy's nose. This didn't make him happy.

"What the hell was that?" His huge hand swatted at his nose like a fly had landed. I tried to slam the door on them, but Eddy had his hand on it. Tony's black eyes burned a hole into my chest. That's when Pearl appeared. I hadn't even heard her approach. She stepped in front of me. She had on a skimpy, yellow and pink flowered Asian print robe and her hair was in curlers. It didn't look like she had anything else on. She was obviously groggy, probably from her night out on the town, but that didn't stop her from barking at Tony, the little guy, as he stared at her chest.

"Why are you staring at my bosoms, buster? What do you want?"

Obviously excited by her features, and oblivious to the curlers, Tony fell off his game. "Your baby sister is worthless," he said. "No help at all in helping us locate Solly, who just happens to owe us some money."

I muttered under my breathe. "I'm not worthless, you greasy pig."

His sweaty hand slipped off the front door and he stumbled. As he tried to balance himself, Pearl took advantage. "You're a real piece of work, mister," she said.

Eddy took control. "Enough talk, girls. Where's Solly?"

Pearl elbowed me, pushing me further back. I realized I should be out back, making sure Mama stayed outside, but I had completely forgotten Solly's instructions. No matter, Pearl was in charge now.

"My little sister told you once already, Solly's gone," she said. "He went to work. He left you a message. You'll get what you want tonight!"

Eddy stuck his head inside, eyeballed the place, and said, "You wouldn't be lying to me, would you?"

Tony kept eyeballing Pearl's chest. Eddy kicked the back of his leg. He grimaced but held his ground. "Knock it off, idiot. We've got a job to do." Cigarette ashes dropped on the porch again.

I was agitated. A slight breeze uplifted the loose ashes and blew them all over the porch. "That's twice you dropped your ashes. My mama will take a skillet to your head if you spoil her front porch." Mama had often threatened to do this to Solly and Pearl when they'd left their ashes scattered about.

Eddy, undeterred, rotated his neck and shoulders forward and stuck his face beyond the threshold. I was still standing behind Pearl. All I could see was his big, crusty red nose. "Tell your big brother," he said, "we will be by again tonight if we don't get what we want. Be sure to tell him that, will ya?"

Pearl puffed up her chest and moved within inches of Tony. "You boys go on home now. You look like you need some sleep." Several strands of her bobbed hair sprung loose from the curlers and formed bangs over her forehead.

"Just make sure that brother of yours gets our message," said Tony. Without another word, they turned and walked away, oblivious to the gesture Pearl made with her middle finger.

Oxygen returned to my lungs. The backdoor slammed and Mama reentered the house.

"Why were you girls at the front door?"

Pearl brushed Mama off. "It was nothing. A couple of boys were trying to sell us a pretty little miniature boat for the mantle. I told them we didn't have a mantle. You know how dense boys can be. They just wouldn't believe me."

I decided to let Pearl deal with Mama and went to my room to get dressed. Pearl came in a few minutes later and used my mirror because it was bigger. She plopped down in front of it and removed her curlers.

I heard Frieda skip up the steps just moments later. She always went out early on Sundays to visit Canter's delicatessen. Thank God she hadn't been around when those deadbeats were here.

"Girls, I've got Kaiser rolls and bagels. You better be grateful. I swear, the men on the streetcar hadn't bathed in months. They smelled to high heaven."

I was famished. By the time I reached the kitchen, Frieda had sliced the bagels. I smeared cream cheese on mine and pasted it with a few slices of the strawberries Mama had picked from her garden. I nervously chewed the hard bagel crust. Mama chided me for eating too fast.

"Slow down, girl, you'll choke if you're not careful." I finished eating just as Pearl, now dressed, joined us. I went back to my room to study. The grandfather clock in the living room slowly ticked off the hours as I tried to concentrate. *Solly get home already, will you,* I thought.

Two girls from school came by to say hello. Rudely, I sent them away. Talking with the girls was the last thing I wanted to do now. I was pathetically afraid I'd spill the beans about Solly's predicament.

By five o'clock that afternoon, the bright afternoon sunlight was fading. Pearl was singing with the crooners on the radio. I was back at my homework and her squealing didn't help my concentration a bit, so when she wandered outside to sit on the porch, I followed her.

"What do you think Solly will he do?" I asked Pearl.

"He better wise up and get us out of this disaster."

At five minutes past six, Solly turned the corner onto our street. Pearl and I watched him from our white rattan chairs on the front porch. He breezed past us, entering the house without a word. He offered no pleasantries as the front door slammed shut behind. I turned to Pearl. "Is he even interested in what happened?"

"He's just being Solly. The jerk is trying to throw us off the track. He may look like he doesn't care. Believe me, he does. He's plenty upset. He fakes it pretty good."

A few minutes later, Solly joined us, acting like he didn't have a care in the world.

"Were they here?"

I nodded yes. "They woke us up early."

He turned his back to me to look at his car. Pearl stood up and touched his shoulder, making him turn around and look at us. She managed to get his undivided attention. Suddenly, his calm turned to rage. He started to say something, but Pearl put her fingers over her lips. "Don't alarm Mama!" she said.

He looked at me. "Well, what happened?" he said.

"They were here," I said. "But we took care of them."

Solly started to pace. "What do you mean, 'you took care of them?'" An early evening wind blew magnolia tree leaves high in the air and onto the porch. "What'd they say?"

Pearl intervened. "Honey, go inside and make sure Mama doesn't hear us, would ya?" I did as I was told, but made sure I got up next to the living room window so I could follow what was happening. Pearl made sure Solly listened to her. She was emphatic. "They'll be back later tonight! The money … they want it. Do you have it? Solly, I'm scared! Do you have the money you owe them?"

"Yeah, yeah, I've got it. They must have scared the living daylights out of you! I don't like that!"

Pearl got in his face. "You deserve a long kick for getting into this mess. Solly, I'm telling you, in the most certain of terms, get these guys paid." I want them far away from me and the rest of the family!"

Solly started to pace rapidly back and forth on the porch. The shirttails of his carefully tucked white shirt broke loose from the waistline of his pants. He stomped on the porch deck with his left shoe so hard that he cracked a plank.

Pearl grabbed his collar. "Did you get the money?" When Solly didn't answer, Pearl lit a Camel and handed it to him. She pointed to the broken plank. "Why in the heck did you do that? You're in enough trouble with Pa as it is. You know how he feels about things breaking around here."

Solly inhaled and exhaled smoke rings as he turned tight circles around the porch. Pearl pointed through the window at me. "This isn't just about you anymore, Solly. Bella was scared to death."

I pounded on the glass. Pearl ignored me. My pigtails wiggled as I motioned to them. I ran out onto the porch. "I wasn't scared, not a bit."

Solly's face was beet red. Pearl waved her finger again. "Just give them the money and be done with it!"

"Okay, I hear what you're saying. I get it. I'll never bet with Harry again. What a *khazer*! The man is a pig. Screw him!" Solly turned away from Pearl and went inside. Pearl and I followed. The two of us sat down on the couch, waiting for something to happen. God knows what we were waiting for. I guess we were preparing for whatever would come next. From the bedroom Solly shared with Pearl, we could hear cursing, followed by pounding on the nightstand, which had taken beatings from Solly before. It was already cracked and close to falling apart from so many poundings. Mama had put a lace doily over it so Pa wouldn't notice. Solly's temper always got the best of him. I guess he'd forgotten about disturbing Mama.

Pearl went inside the bedroom and I could hear her talking to Solly. "Knock it off. Mama will hear. I know you're mad. That nightstand is about to splinter into a million pieces under your fist! I told you, don't make it worse."

Solly walked back into the living room, using his hands to straighten his tie, which still hung from his neck, unaffected by his tirade. He slouched into his favorite living room chair. Pearl was right behind. I heard, and then saw, Mama. She had to have heard us. She smiled and went straight to the kitchen.

I got up, thinking I would join her, make sure she stayed busy, when through the living room window, I saw Tony and Eddy walking up the front porch steps. I pulled myself away from the window, into the back of the living room, without losing sight of who was standing outside.

"They're at the door!"

Solly jumped up. He ran to the door and opened up. Eddy almost fell inside, his hand still poised to knock. They both wore newly-pressed black pinstripe suits with red shirts, matching ties, and red and white suspenders. Pearl leaned into me. "Jeez, I didn't recognize him this morning. That tall one's the bouncer at the Roses. Go back into the kitchen and keep Mama busy."

I glided into the kitchen like everything was fine. I dipped a ladle into Mama's split pea soup and took a sip. "It needs a little more salt," I said.

Taking my hand, she said, "I hope you love it. Who's at the door?"

I giggled and tried to ignore her question. "Of course I love it. It's your split pea."

I suspected Mama knew there was trouble and just wanted Solly to take care of it. She shouted from the kitchen. "Solly, tell your friends they can join us for dinner."

I made up an excuse for what I knew would not happen. "Solly's stupid friends think they have more important things to do. I'm sure Solly won't even ask them."

Mama had an all-knowing look on her face that I had seen before. Clearly, the guys at door were not friends of any of us. From the kitchen, I heard Solly snarl.

Pearl later told me that Solly had placed ten twenty-dollar bills in Eddy's sweaty palms and told him to get out and not come back. She said she could still see Tony's wingtips kick and break one of the wooden planks on the porch, matching the one that Solly had cracked earlier.

Chapter 3

Pa never found out about the skirmish. In those days, he was spending most of his time at *shul*, so he'd missed the action. He'd come home late Saturday night and left again early Sunday morning, before daybreak. The only evidence that we'd been visited by Solly's unfriendly friends were the two cracked planks on the front porch. Pa noticed these the following Monday morning.

"Who broke my front porch floor?" he yelled, loud enough to wake the neighborhood.

Pa was five feet, five inches tall, but always seemed taller to me. In his cream-colored, three-piece gabardine suit, which fit him like a glove, he was a powerful figure. Every day he wore a different silk tie, which hung perfectly. His brown and white oxfords were the swankiest thing about him. Pa *kvetched* endlessly. "Something new in this house fails every day. That man who built it was a thief. I pay good money to fix one thing and before it's repaired, something else breaks."

It wasn't difficult for Pa to find something to rant about, especially if it provided an opportunity to cite the downfalls of living on the West Coast. For Pa, building standards were only the beginning.

"No attics, no basements, no brick, no mortar! Nothing holds this house together. Nothing but vertical planks of flimsy wood keeps our home from collapsing like a house of cards in the wind."

Pa had bought our house in 1921, three years after the end of the first world war. Before the war, the house could have been built for $1,000. But Los Angeles became a construction zone after the war ended. Prices skyrocketed.

When Pa ranted, Mama would try to talk sense to him.

"Just last month, Jack, our friend the St. Louis cobbler, moved into the neighborhood. He says all the sun worshippers will be coming west."

When Mama fought back, which rarely happened, it was war. Pa would not stop until she agreed.

"Sure they'll come. They know no better. Most of us rushed west like there was still a gold rush out here. We should have stayed put. California is for the zany. High society seekers in fancy red touring cars gallivant to speakeasies in high hats and tails. They fox trot in polished spats and get *shiker* drinking whiskey 'til all hours of the night. Everyone wants to look respectable, but acts outrageous."

Mama would interrupt. "Pa, quiet, you'll scare the kids."

"Quiet, my rear end, they need to know about life. Soon they'll all be on their own. The hoodlums own this town. There are too many on our streets. The cops are all corrupt. I call LAPD and get a beat cop with his hand out. What's to do!"

Mama was responsible for keeping us safe at home. Pa was always trying to tell us about the world away from home. They fought over what we should hear and know. One thing they agreed upon was that we should know our family history.

Mama and Pa arrived in America on the Fourth of July, 1907.

"Coming to America was terrifying," Mama told us "I was nauseated constantly while on that ship. I lived day and night in the darkness of the ship's hull. The food was uneatable. A beautiful baked *challah*, never was there even a morsel. Every day I prayed that I would wake up back in a bed in Poland. Then, the nightmare ended. I remember like it was yesterday the way Moshe Kaufman screamed 'Look! It's the Statue of Liberty. She salutes America's newest immigrants.' I didn't understand English so good. I panicked at Kaufman's words. I turned to Pa. 'Frank, Frank, what's she mean? Does the Statue of Liberty shoot America's newest immigrants? Are there criminals here? Will the pogroms begin again?' Pa just got huffy. He said 'don't be a *schmendrick*, in America we are safe. Here it will be different.' I believed him. Pa spoke with authority."

For Mama, who already missed her home in Poland, this new freedom meant nothing. Pa craved it. From New York, they traveled to St. Louis. Immediately, Pa aimed to make himself wealthy. He found work the first day and worked seven days a week, twelve hours a day, even on *shabes*, for an entire year. He learned retail well from his boss.

"Pa saved every dime he earned," said Ma. "We ate like tramps. With our savings of $2,000, Pa bought out his boss, who got sick. For two more years, he worked without help, relentlessly. By 1920, he was not only prosperous; he was a well-respected St. Louis merchant."

Mama helped Pa with the business when asked, but generally, stayed away.

"I raised *mein kinder*. I despised the weather from the beginning. It was never good."

When Mama received a letter from her cousin Sophia, who lived in Los Angeles, she knew life might change. To Mama, Sophia's letter was like a breath of fresh air.

> *Dear Minnie, I've settled out West. In Los Angeles, the weather is like a dream. The growing fields are filled with golden yellow corn, green lettuce and red beets like St. Louis. But here we have something better. There are thousands of trees loaded with juicy oranges so sweet they taste like candy. One problem, we have winds that blow like the dickens. The dust goes everywhere. Not to worry, when the winds die, our sky is whisked broom clean. My garden at home is like my personal farmer's market. Everything grows. The sun joins us all year round. It's hot, but humid it's not. Even our new synagogue grows. Last year, my new husband Moshe, who now calls himself Morris, and the Rabbi Kumski, started a little congregation. Now there are twenty of us. We need more. Those who come will prosper. How could they not in this world, drenched by the sun and bordered by white water waves from the ocean. How is life in St. Louis? Love Sophia.*

Mama, whose arthritis was worsening in the St. Louis winters, worked on convincing Pa to move.

"Pa, I'm sick," she said. "It's not good. The doctor says we should go where it's warm. Cousin Sophia is in Los Angeles. It's a land of sweet fruit. They say streets are lined with gold."

Pa scratched his head. A few hairs in his eyebrows sprang loose. He asked Ma, the way a knife pries open a broken lock, "Do you want to take Sarah and Kate away from their friends?

By that time, Mama had five children. Sarah and Kate were the oldest. Solly, Pearl, and Frieda were still little. I was not yet born. Of course, Pa's words racked Mama with guilt.

"Do I want to take them away from their friends? Never! My joints, they tell another story. When it's cold, I am frozen. My fingers, my neck, my aching back, the pain, it never stops, not day or night."

This dialogue went on for months. Pa knew Mama was sick. She slowed to a crawl. Still, he stalled the inevitable to buy time so he could get a good price for his business. When his biggest competitor offered him more money than he expected, the deal was done. He told Ma that night, in the privacy of their bedroom, that the business was sold, and that with the pretty penny he got for it, they could retire in California. Ma puckered and kissed him right on the lips.

In January, 1921, Ma, Pa, Sarah, Kate, Solly, Pearl, and Frieda boarded the train for Los Angeles. Whenever the train screeched to a stop, the sound was like dynamite, and Mama had to put her fingers in Frieda's ears. Pa paid little attention to the kids. He was forever playing canasta with the other men. Sarah and Kate helped with Pearl. She liked being with her older sisters. Between Frieda's crying and Solly's restlessness, Mama was exhausted when they finally arrived at the Le Grande Station, the Santa Fe Railway's main passenger terminal in 1921.

As she rounded the troops onto the platform outside, Pa dragged all seven bags off the train, four at a time. Then he paid the porter a dime to roll them down the long ramp and into the station. Mama carried Frieda and Sarah. Kate carried Pearl. Solly stumbled along, trying to keep up with Pa.

Their eyes bulged at the new train station and the arriving hordes of new Californians. Mama was taken immediately by the sleek station's design. She couldn't believe her eyes. The floor was like a kaleidoscope, wild designs and shapes of Spanish tiles in all colors. Hundreds of waiting passengers sat in tall cushioned chairs under a high ceiling broken only by recessed panels and long beams of timber. Mama was constantly pushed forward by others anxious to get outside. The station was still new, built in 1918 after a big Los Angeles fire.

Mama's legs were tired from sitting so many days with babies on her lap that she slipped, with Frieda in her arms, twice. No one got hurt. Still, she felt unsteady in this new place.

"I knew California would be something new, something different even before I took a breath of its fresh air. My heartbeats knocked on my chest like the chimes of a bell. The girls ran ahead of Pa to get outside. It had been a long train ride. He screamed at them so we would all exit together as a family.

"We walked with the porter and our bags through wooden doors that must have been twenty feet tall. In the bright California sunlight, I covered my eyes with the back of my hand to keep them open. First thing outside, Sarah yells 'what's that smell?' Kate points at the dark-skinned people cooking skinny corn pancakes on a grill. Our noses brought hunger to our stomachs. The roasted corn aroma was wonderful! Then Pa says so loudly I want to duck behind some of the other people in the crowd, 'Is this California or Mexico? Who are these dark people?' I looked around to see who heard him.

"We were all starving. Pa made his feelings about the food clear. He barked 'oy *vey*, that food on the train was *treyf*.' When he spoke about the food or the noise, I always felt he was getting mad at me, not the food or kids. It made me want to jump out of my skin.

"He bought five hand-rolled sandwiches. The nice man standing in line with us said the sandwiches were called tacos. Pa paid a nickel and dime for our tacos. The servers, who spoke no English, pointed to something that looked like red and green tomato sauce. I looked at Pa. He nodded 'yes' and the servers spiced up the tacos with a dab of that sauce. The girls and I ate one and Pa had two. Neither Frieda nor Solly were allowed to try this new food. They were too young."

Mama said that, on the street, horses strutted and pooped in place while their buggy drivers waited for arriving passengers. A porter loaded the bags, and off the family went to Sophia's bungalow. Once everyone got inside, it didn't take long for Pa to start up.

"From the train, all I see is prickly cactus, yellow scrub grass, and lots of undeveloped dirt. What's so beautiful?"

Mama had been sitting three long days with crying babies and screeching train noise. Her head begged for silence, but Pa was just getting warmed up.

"Is the world still working? I haven't seen a newspaper since I left."

"Frank, here is the *Los Angeles Examiner*," said Sophie. "You can get acquainted with it."

"Thank you. I will look later. Now I am hungry. Can you imagine two days without as much as a piece of fruit to wet my mouth! The help told me we roared through the bountiful Midwest, America's breadbasket, but the train had nothing, nothing good at all! Could have starved before we got to California. Now, we're here. What is here for us? I haven't slept for two days."

Mama said that Sophia had fried up scrambled eggs and salami for the lot of them for their arrival. The eggs were all she had. Mama said the eggs with fresh *challah* tasted like it was right out of God's hands. But as soon as Pa was done eating, he was done socializing, too.

"No time to talk now. The family needs to get sleep," he said.

Mama said he barely even looked at Sophia when he spoke to her, that he complained the whole time they stayed with her. Mama was so embarrassed.

"We'll be out of your hair soon," said Pa. "I spoke to a man before I left about a house for sale on Marathon Street. Do you know it?"

"Yes, of course," said Sophia. "It's high on a hill near Chavez Ravine. Most of the Jews live in this neighborhood, though. Our shops, the ones with the Jewish deli and market, are nearby on Brooklyn. Wouldn't you rather be with your own kind?"

"Maybe looking down on the neighborhood would be a nice change. We'll see. I'll run first thing in the morning to see the man about buying his house. I don't need your kindness. I have money. I will buy something, so I can make my family a place to stay."

The next morning, Pa dressed before dawn. He went into the streets wearing his grey wool trench coat, black striped three-piece suit, and Hamburg hat. He left before the milkman came to Sophia. He was dressed for the Missouri winter.

When he got to the house on Marathon Street, he extended his hand and looked the owner straight in the eye. Pa wasn't used to doing business with *gentiles*. All his customers in St. Louis were Jewish. The two walked into the house. Pa said nothing until he had seen every square inch. Then he blurted, "How much?"

"I'm asking $1,350, but if you can pay cash I can do better. I've have another man coming from Pittsburg tomorrow."

Pa smiled. "I'm no *shnorer*. I pay you a good price, but $1,350 for this is ridiculous. Is there gold buried in the dirt that lies loose beneath the floor? I'll give you $600 and not a dime more. What's that awful noise?"

The owner remained calm. "That's the neighbor next door. He practices the trumpet this time of day."

Pa didn't know this man from Adam. "No deal. I have children who must sleep. The walls are paper thin.

The owner became animated. "Krawiec, don't be hasty. I rent to the trumpet. I have a buyer for his house. I told him to move Monday. He's going to a new community on the west side. They call it Beverly something or another."

Pa actually liked the house. Without the crazy jazz music, he was interested. "Good, I'm sure all the neighbors will be happy he will be gone. But this house of yours, it's missing rooms. No attic or basement, how can that be? Even more important, there is no fireplace. Can't live in the winter without heat!"

The owner laughed. "Over there, near the window, there's a floor heater. The thermostat never drops below fifty degrees. That heat will keep you plenty toasty. Don't need a basement. There's a shed outside. Your kids will love the front porch. You can grow your fruit and vegetables, no problem.

See that orange tree. Ever had fresh-squeezed orange juice? It's like drinking sugar. What business you in?"

"I owned the biggest dry goods store in all of St. Louis before coming here."

"Humm, sounds like you made a lot of money. No matter, you'll never go back. If you open a store here, you'll need a wheel barrel to cart your profits to the bank. This is boomtown. You saw all the newcomers getting off that train, didn't you? Every day, it's the same. I like you. You'll be good for the neighborhood. Not too many like you here. I'll take $1,050. There is no better view in all of downtown."

The owner took Pa into the backyard, where he pointed down the hill to a park. "Look at Echo Park! Do you see the boats smack in the middle?"

"We had plenty lakes in St Louis. Real lakes, not puddles, surrounded by Palm trees like what do you call it, Echo Park? My last offer is $900. Take it or leave it."

The owner reached into his coat pocket and pulled out a matchbook. He scribbled the figures on the back of a matchbox cover. He grabbed Pa's hand and slipped the matchbook cover inside. "You have a deal. Take it now. I'm done negotiating."

"Okay, okay, I'll bring cash tomorrow."

The family moved to Marathon Street on Tuesday, February 18th, 1921. It took weeks before the sofa, table, chairs, and beds arrived. Sarah and Kate were older and would have preferred the comfort of furniture, but Solly, Pearl, and Frieda could have cared less. They loved sleeping on the floor. They loved the warm morning air. Pa put up a swing first thing. Playing outside under the magnolia tree in winter was a dream come true for kids from Missouri.

The back yard was to be Mama's domain. She knew she wanted a vegetable garden but had her work in store. The yard was all scrub grass; no trees or flowers. It overlooked Echo Park and what was to become the city of Los Angeles. It also overlooked the biggest hole she'd ever seen. Pa told her it would become Los Angeles City Hall. He'd seen some sort of model of the new building in the lobby of the downtown bank. Pa said the model looked like a bullet pointing straight up in the sky and was destined to become the tallest building on the West Coast. He couldn't understand why they would build such a big sky rise in the L.A. wilderness. Never missing an opportunity to compare Los Angeles to St. Louis, he said there were plenty of tall brick buildings on the banks of the Mississippi, but there were also steam engines to bring commerce downstream on the river. Pa laughed and said the tiny Los Angeles River was not high enough for a rowboat to bring bananas.

Never one to dawdle, within weeks of moving, Pa went out and found a storefront to rent. The storefront was on Brooklyn Avenue in Boyle Heights, not far from where Sophia and the rest of the Jews lived. Pa built racks and shelves in the new location. He studied the catalogues and ordered his first shipment of merchandize."

When it arrived, he took Solly with him to receive the shipment. He told Solly that someday the store would be his. Solly was not yet four years old. He reacted by taking off like a bat out of hell and joyously running around in circles. Solly thought he had a wonderful new playground. Pa would run after him and scoop him up before he tripped on the boxes that spread out everywhere.

Within weeks, a shingle with six-inch white letters hung over the front door. It said West Coast Dry Goods. Pa had willingly, or unwillingly, moved to California, bought a new home, and started a new business.

Los Angeles may have been boomtown, but the other lots on Brooklyn Avenue were still vacant. Weeds grew from loose dirt that clumped into mud clots when it rained. Within five miles of where the family lived, there were huge fields of crops and vast stretches of empty space. Los Angeles was primed. It was a boomtown ready to suck money and the adventuresome out of the Midwest.

I was born in August, 1921, not long after the family arrived in Los Angeles. By that time, both Sarah and Kate had married and moved out of the house. Pa had made a match for Sarah before he moved the family to California. Sarah was headstrong, but not strong enough to say *nisht* to Pa. She adjusted and no complaints were heard after the wedding. Kate's husband came from the *shadkhn*, the matchmaker, in California. Mama always said Kate was not easy. Even before moving to California, she was a wild one, an unbroken stallion with whom Mama had to make peace for both to survive.

As the last of Mama's children, I always felt that I had to be the best. Maybe my birth was not meant to be. Sometimes I wondered about that. But I never had to wonder about Mama's love.

"Bella," she would say. "Your birth cry came when no one expected it. You almost crawled out. You were the fastest; small, but the most enthusiastic. You were the only member of the family born west of the Mississippi. More than a month premature, you barely weighed six pounds, two ounces. In St. Louis, I had friends to help with delivery when Pa wasn't around. In Los Angeles, there was no one but cousin Sophia. But she had her own life and spent little time with us after Pa was so rude. I hadn't planned on you're coming so soon. But you wouldn't wait. I called Pa at the store, then I called Sarah. I tried to hold on. You would have none of it. My water broke, and when Pa and Sarah didn't get home in time, you and I just worked it out. You were born on the kitchen table. You were the easiest delivery of all, even without help. I held you until Pa and Sarah arrived. Pearl, Frieda, and Solly just cowered nearby watching the two of us struggle into life.

Chapter 4

Born in Los Angeles, I knew nothing about freezing winters or harsh, humid summers. The only waterway I knew was the Pacific Ocean and the lake at Echo Park. The Mississippi for me was part of the Huck Finn adventure, only mine through books. I was an Angelino, and unlike my older sisters, Sarah and Kate, I thought like a Californian. Maybe that's why I couldn't fully understood Pa's endless rants about why things were so much better in St. Louis.

If Mama happened to mention how happy she was that her children did not have to endure the frigid Missouri winters, or that in Los Angeles, shovels were made for planting, not shoveling snow, and that the California storms were gentle, just the rain kissing the earth, that the skies were blue most of the time, Pa would retort:

"Blue skies, who cares? Back in St. Louis, the brick walls of our home kept us warm in winter and cooled us in the summer. That was a real house with a solid foundation, not like this ramshackle. Snow or not, I lived there like King Solomon."

Mama listened quietly. She'd heard his tirades many, many times. "Frank, blue brings God's spirituality into our home. With all that praying you do, I thought you would like that. Besides, King Solomon had servants. You have only me."

My sister Sarah added a different perspective to Pa's high opinion of St. Louis:

"In St. Louis, Pa was a *macher,*" she said. "You know, an important man. Here, not so important. No one worked harder or was smarter than Pa in all of St. Louis. He left home at dawn and came home after midnight. He might have been the most important merchant in all St. Louis. He brought home powerful businessmen for dinner from New York. Kate and I were always excited to see those well-manicured men from the garment industry. They brought us gifts, usually jewelry. They came to St. Louis just to do business with Pa.

"He never warned Mama they were coming until late in the afternoon. She'd just get a phone call letting her know they had guests for dinner. He was completely oblivious to the chaos he created. Kate and I would giggle when the phone rang at four in the afternoon and hear Mama's '*oy vey, you're bringing home guests*.' Mama told us Pa would go on like it was nothing to prepare for another at the dinner table. Pa would just go on how this one was a big New York banker ... or, a big manufacturer ... or, a big jobber. It didn't matter how big or what industry he was big in. Pa always made a *ganze megillah* about the man coming over for dinner.

"But here in California, things changed. There are no important visitors. Pa starts a little store just so he can give Solly a business. Pa lost his power, his prestige once he came to California. Here in Los Angeles, he is an outsider. An older man who gets no respect."

Sarah had probably nailed the underlying cause of Pa's discontent, but Pa would never have pointed the finger at himself, especially when there were so many easier targets, ones that offended his expertise, like the way people dressed in Los Angeles. He railed against the boys, their fathers, then worked his way through the rest of the population. According to Pa, if his store didn't attract business like his store in St. Louis, the problem was the poor taste of the Angelinos. He hated their casual attire.

"Shorts and no shirt, this looks good?" he would say. "What style is there when everyone runs naked? When men wear tailored overcoats, double-breasted pinstriped suits, vests, suspenders, and silk ties, that's when class oozes out. To be a *mensch*, a human, you act like man, not a *shnorer*, a mooch.

"My best suits at the store aren't even touched. Mr. Mortenson, my banker, you would think he would care how he looked. He dresses like an *alter kocker*, an old complaining man. I show him my finest. 'Feel the nap of our woolen suits and linen shirts. Run your fingers on the cool silk in these ties. Feel the softness of our cashmere jackets. Here, put this Trilby on, it's all the rage.'

"From behind him, I raise the jacket so he can sink his arms into the sleeves. 'Now that's how a jacket should fit, tight just like a glove,' I say. Mortenson scowls at me. 'Krawiec, it's not like a glove, more like a noose. The slacks are worse. My crotch is in a vice. The wool scratches. Show me something lighter weight, softer, more casual, something a little more Californian!'"

Pa was out of step. Tailored suits turned stale, gathering dust on the racks.

The girls didn't fare much better:

"They go sleeveless. Who wants to see those chubby little arms? Their low-cut necklines show too much breast. Why buy the cow it you already get the milk for free? They raise their hems so every Tom, Dick, and Harry can see their skinny legs. A lady comes to me the other day. 'Mrs.,' I say, 'you must be a model. You from New York?' She asks me if I'm flirting. 'Flirting, no,' I say, 'but I know a beautiful gal when I see her. This dress is real couture for half the price. It leaves something to the imagination. It is good, no? It rises and falls where it should. Add a snug corset and the figure underneath is to die for. You like it?' The lady, if you can call her that, gets insulted. Her dimples turn to jowls. 'I am a modern woman,' she says. 'You've got to show off what you've got. Corsets are so yesterday. A slip and one of those French braziers, that's all my figure requires. If you don't have what I want, then I'll go where they do.'"

Pa got on his soap box with the customer:

"I don't *schlep khazeray*, if that's what you want. I'm no poor *schlub*. I'm a merchant with decades in the business. Those fast-change artists who sell what's here today and gone tomorrow, that's not me. *Nisht*, I won't sell those braziers or the nothing-here-or-there dresses. Look what I have! *Mein* is a fashionable European clothing store, not the stuff of harlots."

The lady stormed out. Pa steamed on, striking out at the first thing that came to mind.

"Today, the world is full *meshugas*. The Christian Temperance League, they run rough shot on us. For what? Because we, the men like me, have a drink or two. Does that make us criminals? Those women, they make this *meshuge* prohibition. From the day we arrive, their damn 18th amendment rules the land. Does it stop one from drinking? No, of course not. It just changes where to get whiskey, not whether to drink. It makes the mobsters piles of money. Hollywood glamorizes them. The speakeasies serve illegal alcohol, but still manage to find respectable patrons. How wrong is that? Of course, I buy my schnapps from gangsters. How else can I get it? The boys who deliver it call it hooch and have bulges in their hip pocket for God knows what. I never liked doing business with them. Finally, prohibition finished. Good riddance! Maybe now the citizens in this town, in this country, will put their crazy casual styles aside and learn to dress. I hope all this nonsense ends before it puts me in my grave."

Unlike Pa, Mama really loved California. She could usually be found in her kitchen or tending her ever-changing garden. From the time I was old enough to notice, she was always making improvements to our home. She painted each room a different color. She said it gave them personality. The room I shared with Frieda was emerald green. Pearl and Solly shared the red room. She and Pa slept in the blue room upstairs.

Dark walnut wainscoting covered the wall of the living/dining area from floor to mid-wall, and from there to the ceiling, rich red velvet wallpaper took over. This matched well with our large walnut dining table and beautiful crystal chandelier that draped forty-three crystals over the dining table. A large window framed the grand old magnolia tree in the front yard. Even from the kitchen, Mama could hear the laughter and squabbling of her children playing outside.

Mama rarely complained. Instead, she worried. By the time I was eleven, Solly and Pearl were out of control. Frieda was too frightened for her own good. Since I was Mama's last baby, I was her last chance to make a perfect, respectable women. Mama was always after me to listen.

"Bella, don't go there, you'll hurt yourself. I want to know where you are. Stay close to home. Bring your friends over. They are no problem. I love having young girls at my house. We have a big, beautiful backyard. Show them my garden. Maybe they can coax my tomatoes to ripen. Pick a few delicious red apples. If you bring a bunch at the same time, we can bake. I'll show them how apple strudel was made in the old country. It will bring them to their knees begging for more. Don't you love my pies and cookies?

"Yes Mama, but sometimes we like to wander Brooklyn Avenue by ourselves. The dill pickles are wonderful. Then there's Currie's mile-high vanilla ice cream. It's to die for. It's fun to explore."

"I understand, you are young. How do they say it? You want to sow oats for a while. But you are my last baby. My *sheyna punim*. I love seeing you at home. How about I make some chocolate chip cookies with walnuts. Remember when you used to come home and steal them, still soft and gooey, not yet baked, out of my oven? I used to catch you with melted chocolate on your nose. You were so cute. Still are. Don't I have enough aggravation with Solly and Pearl? I wish you would keep company with me more often. Here in your home, you are safe. I worry about you and the rest."

I nodded when Mama said these things, but I no longer thought of our front fence, or my neighborhood, as a boundary. I wanted to explore Los Angeles. Besides, Mama had no idea how much there was to fear that was right on our street. Often we heard horses pulling buggies get spooked and they would stampede right past our house. Wild dogs, let go by owners who no longer could feed them, roamed the hillside nearby and would yelp into the echo chamber of our neighborhood at night. I no longer wanted Mama's protection. Pearl and Solly, who were teenagers, downright resented her warnings. Still Mama lived to keep us safe.

One night in late December, 1933, Pearl suggested that the three of us girls go downtown for the New Year's Eve party at the Biltmore Hotel. I was excited to be included. A lot of kids from school were going. Mama would have none of it. Knowing how combative Pearl could be, Mama craftily switched the subject from her real concern, boys and booze, and went on and on about horses and cars.

"Have you lost your minds?" she said. "Pearl and Frieda, I can understand, but you, Bella, I thought you knew better. Didn't you read about the fifteen-year-old girl who was stomped to death by a wild horse on Broadway? She was downtown shopping and the horse got loose. Next thing you know, she had a hoof on her head. You are forbidden to go downtown. I don't' want to hear another word."

The three of us girls ran to the front porch for a pow wow. Pearl was the first to speak up.

"Mama is telling a *bubbe-meise* again. No girl was stomped to death downtown. Besides, she doesn't care about the horses, all of us know that. Maybe she should tether us to the front porch or buy us chastity belts. What she really cares about is boys, not horses. If the world's so risky, then I better have some fun before something really bad happens. I'm not afraid of horses, dogs, or men"

The horses weren't nearly as dangerous as the "tin lizzies." They all had cocky men drivers like Solly, so dazzled by the car's fancy knobs, they watched everything but the road ahead. Mama was right about one thing. There was danger on the roads.

As we huddled together on the front porch, winding up our New Year's Eve conversation, a lime-green Pierce Arrow limousine drove by, and through the windows, we could see four men and three girls inside its all-black interior. It was sleek, huge, and powerful. It just sailed by. I was mesmerized by its lines. Frieda and Pearl saw something else.

"Now, would you look at that?" said Pearl. "That is the most expensive car on the road. It costs nearly $4,000. See that dark-eyed, mustached guy in the high hat, driving. He must be a real highbrow."

Frieda thought they looked like movie stars. "That platinum blonde in the back seat, she looks like Jean Harlow. She played Ruby in *Hold Your Man*. Could have been her. Can you imagine Clark Gable as your costar? Now those folks live the life."

We rushed the fence. Pearl was the first to say it. "Horses may be dangerous, but guys who look like that ring my bells." Pearl could no longer control herself. "Let's go girls, let's beat that guy to the corner."

Frieda scrunched up her nose. "Mama will be mad."

This didn't matter to Pearl. She was off. The front gate slammed behind her. Behind us, we could Mama shouting, "*Oy vey*, Pearl, you will be the death of me."

Pearl was fearless. I didn't like what she did so much, but I loved that she had nerve.

The following day, sometime after twelve noon, when Pearl finally got out of bed, she surprised us. "I went to third base last night."

"You did what?" said Frieda.

"I met a boy at the Biltmore. We were drinking. Malcolm, that was kid's name. He's a high school boy. Went to Jefferson High. Anyway, I stared at him from across the room. I could see his buddies pushing him at me. So he comes over and asks me to dance. After a few times around the floor, the band takes a break. He gives me a peek at his silver flask in his inside coat pocket. Then he grabs my hand and pulls me outside.

Frieda interrupted. "Weren't you afraid?"

"No, I knew Solly was outside smoking. I figured he could bail me out. I even stopped to introduce Malcolm to Solly as we walked by him. Of course, Solly just grunts. Next thing, we're in the kid's car sipping from his flask. He kisses me on the lips. I didn't resist. I thrilled. Got to start life sometime."

"Will you see him again?" asked Frieda.

"When we walked back inside, first thing he did was give his boys the high sign. I got really mad. Dropped his hand and just walked away."

"Did that make you sad?" said Frieda, who I could tell was jealous.

"No, not really, he was kind of fat. I just wanted to have fun."

Pearl never lacked nerve. On the other hand, Solly did everything he could to prove he had it. He wouldn't give Frieda or me the time of day. Getting older made him act like he was too good for us girls, even Mama. He came home late at night, and, in the mornings, when Mama tried to ask about his plans for the day, he'd spit out a few minor details and run out the front door.

Solly did as he pleased. Sometimes at school, I'd see him and some of the other boys slap each other around until someone begged off. Sometimes the vice principle would break it up and give someone the strap.

Once, I saw him at a table in the corner of the lunchroom. Mama's birthday was that coming Friday, and we planned to celebrate on Saturday, at dinner. I wanted to make sure he'd be there. I walked toward him, and when I reached his table, he didn't acknowledge my presence. He kept gabbing with his boys. When I didn't go away, he twisted his hand into a stop sign and gave me that what-the- heck-do-you-think-you-are-doing look. I turned and walked away. His buddies thought he was the cat's meow. I could hear them say, "You really swatted her away. Sisters are a pain."

My girlfriends were afraid of him and his gang. They told me he and the other boys were *tsuris*. "They'll make life miserable for us."

Another time, at Frieda's school play, I saw him and his friend Sammy sitting together. Sammy lifted a pistol out of his pocket and showed it to Solly. Later at home, when everyone else was asleep, I heard him come in. I was waiting.

"Why're you up? It's late for a kid."

"I saw you take that gun from Sammy today. Don't you think that's pretty stupid?"

"Who you calling stupid?"

"I know you're trying to change the subject. You're gonna get so deep into it, you'll never get out if you get caught with a gun."

"It's none of your business. Besides, it wasn't mine. But you know what, when I get enough money, I may just get myself a pistol for protection."

I feared that Solly would end up in jail. He wouldn't be the first one in the neighborhood to do so. What I never figured was that Pearl would pack her bags and move out in the middle of the night before she turned fifteen.

Chapter 5

I liked being around Pearl. She knew how to act around boys and she hated being a child. She loved painting up her face to look older. Her revealing clothes and dangling earrings caught the eye of every guy at school. She always changed her clothes into something low cut and tight once she was out of the house. Mama never saw or knew about those clothes.

But one Saturday afternoon, as Pa was leaving services, he saw Pearl on the street. She wore a low-cut, boob-showing, black, frilly blouse, a thigh-tight, above-the-knee gold dress, loads of rouge, and thick red lipstick. Pa caught up with her, grabbed her by the ear and earring and dragged her home. When they arrived, Frieda and I were helping Ma with dinner. Hearing the commotion, we came into the living room as Pa entered the front door with Pearl in tow. Her ear had a triangle-shaped bruise that looked exactly like her earring.

"Wash that gook off your face and go straight to your room without dinner!" screamed Pa. "Who bought that outfit? Take it off. You look like a *hur*." Even then, Pa thought Pearl had already gone to hell.

Later that night, in her room, she told us, "I despise him. I'm going get free of Pa if it's the last thing I do."

A few weeks later, she got a job singing at Smell the Roses, hers and Solly's favorite hangout. Solly told us the bandleader had looked down from the stage and noticed her long gams.

"Honey, you got stage fright? If not, there a spot behind the band for you. Smile, kick up your heels a bit and chime in with the harmony if you can. Can you sing?"

The next night she was in the chorus line. She snuck out and worked there for a couple of month without anyone knowing but Solly. Not too long after Pa's embarrassing tirade, she used her wages to rent herself a utility apartment. She was on her own. None of us but Solly knew where.

Mama told me later that Pa was hurt when Pearl moved out. Even though he'd fought with her, he assumed he was still in control. He turned his hurt into anger.

"Pearl can go to hell as far as I am concerned," he said. "She is no longer a member of my family."

For two dreadful weeks after Pearl left, Mama was a total mess. Her long, gray hair, her pride and joy, hung scraggily uncombed halfway down her body. She wore the same *schmatta* every day. Her eyes were beet red.

One night, while Mama and I were clearing the *shabes* dinner dishes, Sarah interrogated Solly about Pearl. First she glared at him. He didn't like it. You could tell from his slumping posture, she made him uncomfortable. "I'm sure you know where Pearl went."

He just shrugged his shoulders. From the tone of her voice, I thought Sarah was going to come out of her shoes. "I know you know. Don't give me that innocent look."

Solly kept his silence. Then Mama, who had become teary-eyed at the mention of Pearl's name, attacked Pa, who was sipping a schnapps. I had never seen Mama go unprovoked after Pa before. "Frank, you went *meshuge* at the *shul* because Pearl dressed up. Your words were like a knife in the heart. You made her unwelcome. *A klap fargait, a vort bashtai.* Look what you have done. Pearl, she is gone. Who knows where?"

"She was a *shande* to our family. It is better she's gone."

Mama threw his empty plate on the floor and stomped off into the kitchen.

Next morning, Mama confessed to Frieda and me. "I am not well! My hands shake so. Wet dishes slip from my hands. I am a half-a-century old. I miss Pearl. Life isn't so good. Thank God, I still have you two. Other than my children, all I have are my memories about the old country." Her lips widened. A smile dawned in her eyes. She walked over to her curio cabinet, where her treasured collection of finely dressed men and women filled the oak shelves behind beveled glass. She pointed at them. The phone rang. For a moment, it was clear Mama thought Pearl might be calling. Our phone rarely rang so early Sunday morning.

Frieda picked it up. "Hello, Miriam, yes, of course, I'm coming to play Majong. Have I ever missed?" Frieda began to tell Miriam about a book she'd seen with pictures of scenes from some movie. "Wait, I'll get it," she said. She put the phone down and ran across the room to get the book.

Mama, clearly disappointed that the caller was not Pearl, screamed at Frieda. "Walk, will you! The running makes the cabinet jiggle. You'll break what I have left, my porcelain ladies and gentlemen. Walk! You weren't raised like pigs!"

It seemed that everything and everyone at our house was broken or breakable. Mama's heart had already been broken, but her collectables, if they broke, *oy vey!* The Hummel porcelain figurines were her most prized possessions. Lady Ann had a heavy ruffled dress with petticoats. Mr. Jeffrey had a big red bow tie, a long tuxedo jacket, a vest, and long, fancy trousers. On top, he wore a black, high-top hat. On the bottom, of course, were his glistening black shoes.

I had known for a long time how much these figurines meant to Mama. Ever since I was a little girl, I'd watched her handle them, always so careful.

Mama raised both hands to her temples. "*Oy vey*, my loneliness. I miss my old St. Louis friends. Sarah and Kate, the grandkids, they come to me only on *shabes*. Pearl maybe never come home again. Pa is impossible, he never talks to me. He just gives orders. Solly, he's something else altogether. You know, you can be in a crowd, but still be alone."

Mama opened the door to the cabinet and took out one of the tiny figures. She turned to Frieda and me. "Girls, you know how much I love my figurines. They have a purity that doesn't exist in our world today. Women no longer dress like frosted wedding cakes. Today young women like you two are more independent. Someday you will each fall in love. I wish you nothing but *nachas*. Whatever happens, remember, your husband is your partner, not your boss. You don't need to rush. You don't' need to submit to all his wishes. My parents were potato farmers. I didn't have fancy dresses. I wore hand-me-downs. I stayed home. I waited for my father to tell me when it was time. When Pa came along, I had no choice. I was told he was the one. He was my ticket out of my parent's home. He was smart, the way he got my father's permission. I was already promised to another. Pa came into my life at a family party. He saw me and knew. Next day, he came back dressed to kill with a big thick wallet in his back pocket. Next thing I knew, my father said to go with him. I looked at your pa, all dressed up and handsome. I thought maybe now there would be fancy balls. I was naïve.

Chapter 6

No matter what, the family came together for *shabes* dinner. If anyone tried to get out of this obligation, Pa's behavior was so predictable that even Frieda would mimic him in the privacy of our bedroom. She would turn her already deep voice into Pa's brusque baritone, *"You'll be here for shabes dinner. You live in my house. You show respect for your elders. There will be no excuses!"*

Mama loved her *shabes* ritual and she insisted our festive meal take place on Saturday evening rather than Friday, when the final minutes before sunset signal the dawn of the Jewish Sabbath. She believed it was easier for the family to come together on this day. But there was a bittersweet quality about her preparations after Pearl left. She would often stop in the middle of chopping carrots or celery for *tsholnt,* her special *shabes* stew, and stare out the kitchen window. Or in the midst of arranging chopped herring and liver on a platter so the family would have something to *nosh* while we waited for Pa to get home from services, she'd let out long sighs that had a forlorn quality to them.

Sarah and Kate usually joined us on those evenings with their kids and husbands. Before Pa would get home, a train could have busted through the living room unheard for the yakking going on. Although I held my own, *kibitzing* with the girls, by the time I turned thirteen, I'd also developed more than a passing interest in what I liked to call "the bigger picture." Unlike the other Kraweic children, I loved school and learning. Even Solly, in kinder moments, had taken to calling me the "smart one." I would even sneak Pa's newspaper into the bedroom at night to figure out if there were bigger reasons for what was happening all around me.

At that time, it seemed every man in the neighborhood was either home all day with no job, no money, or both. Grown men who used to have good jobs now stood on street corners with cardboard signs that said, "Need work, please help." Entire families slept on old newspapers on the sidewalks near my school. After the kids went home for the day, the homeless stood in line in the schoolyard for soup made in the lunchroom. Crime was rampant. Newspaper boys, in Baker Boy hats, stood on the corner screaming the headlines, "Read all about it: J. J. Riordan grabs gun from teller and shoots himself to death."

Because Pa had come to California with enough capital to retire, and because the store he bought to ensure Solly's future flourished in its early years, the Krawiec family was secure, or so we thought. That's because Pa always knew what to do.

When times first got tough and business slowed, Pa had started a tradition of credit. He made it clear to Solly that a sale on credit was even better than a cash sale.

"This depression, it's good for us. We can make new customers with credit. When other stores can't sale what they have, we can buy them out. Now, cash is king. I'm one of the few in this town who have cash."

Pa and Solly followed that plan. A good part of the conversation that took place at *shabes* dinners during that time consisted of Pa bragging about his dealings.

"I offered thirty cents on the dollar for everything in Schwartz's store," said Pa. Schwartz has *bupkes,* no buyers and nothing in the cash register. He's a dead man."

Bupkes literally meant goat turds, but to Pa, it meant Schwartz was ready to be eaten. Schwartz had laughed when Pa made his offer. He told Pa that everything he carried would sell at market price. Then he walked Pa to the door and told him not to get carried away buying distressed merchandize. Schwartz patted Pa on the shoulder and told him that soon, he'd be over to Pa's store to say hello and make him an offer for all the crap he'd accumulated but would never sell. Pa knew too much to be bluffed. He waited a month and showed up again. "Schwartz, ready to sell? Now, I offer 10 percent less. Take it before my price drops again."

Schwartz pointed to the door.

The month after that, Pa was back. "Schwartz, today is my last offer. Now my offer is again 10 percent less. Stuff your pockets before there is nothing left to feed your family. All you have left is junk. Go home to your family. There is no reason to hang on. You are finished."

Mama usually kept her nose out of Pa's business. But once, when Pa was done bragging, she said, "Frank, why do you need all this stuff? Nobody buys it. What if you can't sell it?

Pa put the palm of his left hand up. She came no closer to him.

"It will sell. Money finds its rightful place. The dust bowl blows half the Midwest to California. These farmers arrive daily in their hillbilly cars. They have little, but need the credit I extend. They will buy even if they don't have ten cents in their pocket. They will be customers for life. When the depression ends, they will pay and we will be very rich. I've got a sign in the window. It says Liquidation Sale — 50 percent off. They look, and are hooked. The prices make them fill their baskets. The credit gets them past the cash register."

The gamble Pa started continued and grew. Customers stuck like flies on flypaper. Solly learned well. Although he always took time away from the store to go gamble with his friends, Pa constantly reminded him, "Do what you must to keep your client. Make a good price. No matter what, always smile. The customer is always right. Give credit when needed. Business is not a gamble. It is an investment. You have to be there for the client to make you rich."

As the depression wore on, more of the store's working capital was invested in customer credit. Pa's capital started to run low. He was also spending more and more time at *shul*. When the family gathered for *shabes* dinner in early January, 1935, shortly after I'd turned fourteen, Pa hit us with a bombshell. Instead of *shabes* prayer, Pa's words set a hush to the room.

"Solly, Mama, girls, my plan has failed. I am running out of money. At this rate, I'll be broke by the end of the year. Something must change and quickly."

It was so quiet in the room you could hear the flame of the *shabes* candle burning low. It was unimaginable that Pa would admit failure. Solly was only seventeen. He'd worked Sundays in the store since he was eleven years old. From ten to thirteen, he'd gone to *cheder* to study to be a Jewish man. Pa had given Solly no choice. He'd quit school at fifteen to work full time at the store. Even though at that point, Pa considered himself officially retired, he stayed in the background. Solly followed Pa's lead. He did what he could to make Pa's plan work. Now he would have to find a way to start paying the bills with his own ideas. Pa had taught him well. But was that enough?

When no one spoke, not even Solly, Pa made his second announcement.

"Now, I will dedicate the rest of my life to the Jewish community. I will serve." He looked at Solly. "I shall prayer every day for your success and the success of the family. *Tzdaka* is more than dropping *gelt* in a *pushke*. Serving the community is giving of yourself. In St. Louis, Cantor Wilensky begged me every week, 'Krawiec, join the men, we need one more for *shabes minyan*. Leave the store. *Kenehora*, your business will be here tomorrow. Take time. The men you pray with will help, not hurt the business.'"

Solly's jaw dropped open as Pa continued.

"Now, here in Los Angeles, we shall see if my prayers help or hurt. Retired, with my son in charge, I am free to join the *yeshive bokhers*. Most are not so good at business as I. Still, their ties in the community run deep. After fourteen years in the Los Angeles wilderness, it is time they get to know me. I will become a *bar mitzvah* in their eyes. You will see. I will be more than Mr. Krawiec, businessman. I will be Frank Krawiec, *balebatim*, community leader, a *tzadik*, a righteous man. Religion is our tradition. If a few choose to do business with my son, who will complain?"

Chapter 7

Mama was flabbergasted. "How can you leave Solly with this mess? The store, it's too much."

Pa ignored her. "Minnie, mind yourself and the girls, not my son or my business. He can, and will, make a success. Put food on the table, make clean clothes, teach the girls, those who are left to be wives. Solly is a man, and what he doesn't know, he'll learn. Business is not good now. It will get better. You watch, he will make our small fortune. I will not be with him, but I will be close, watching from afar like a hawk."

Even after Solly took over the store, Pa and Solly continued to argue about the business. Late at night, when Frieda and I were alone in our room, Frieda went on about Pa.

"He's running away. When the business fails, he'll blame Solly. We'll be in the street like the rest of the paupers."

I wanted to believe everything would be okay, but when I looked at Pa, I was worried. One night, I said to Frieda, "Did you look, really look, at his face at dinner? White stubbles on his unshaven face are the only hair on his head. You can't see his tiny eyes. There are dark bags under them, and his eyelids cover what is left. First he storms us with his tirades, then, after a few shots of *schnapps*, he collapses into his chair. Ashes from his Camels fall to the floor as he snores. He's become what he wished for his competitors, a finished man. It's for Solly to build or break now. He is our only chance."

Mama feared Solly would fail and Pa would be forced back in. The depression dragged on. Competitors fell from grace. Pa attacked every move Solly made, but never took back the reigns.

Every chance, Mama's questioned Solly. "So, how is business?"

"Good, no, great. I expect more soon. Goods, they fly out the door, but still nobody has cash to pay. It will change." Solly never acknowledged fear, just a need for the business to come back fast.

With Pa now spending all his time at *shul*, Mama complained. "I miss the noise. Pearl's gone, who knows where! Solly leaves early for work, then carouses with his *no-goodnik* friends. Bella, you are so quiet, reading and staring out the window all the time. I hardly know you're here. The house is too quiet."

Unlike Pearl, who'd endlessly chattered about boys and makeup and clothes, or Frieda, who could go on and on about the latest movie and its stars, I was Mama's quiet one. I could easily become lost in a book. For the most part, I was content to read and study. That all changed one Sunday morning, however, when I got up early and looked out my bedroom window. Outside, parked in front of our house, was the most beautiful car I'd ever seen, even more so than the Shiny Black Beast, which Solly had sold to cover some gambling debts.

I ran into the kitchen, where Mama was making sure Solly ate something before going to work.

"Hey Solly, who's car is that on the curb?"

"The Rod, it's mine now! Bet it's worth over $825. I made my first fortune at the game last night." He was so animated, Mama and I stopped and stared as he spoke.

Even in front of Mama, Solly didn't scrimp on the details of his big win.

"I had an ace-high full house," said Solly, "so I went all in. Big shot, bet up, or get out!"

Solly was talking about Jerry Jerome, the rich kid who owned the Rod. When Solly had challenged Jerry, he just scratched his head. He didn't look up, just eyeballed his cards "Your bluffing!" said Jerry.

"Thank you for the compliment, Mr. Jerry Jerome," said Solly. You think I have the guts to bluff with all my money on the table. Test me, would you?"

Jerry fanned his cards with the thumb of his right hand. "I'm $150 short," he said. "Cover me, I'm good for it."

"That's too easy! Every day, my customers claim they're good for it, but weeks later I'm still waiting."

"I know you're bluffing," said Jerry. "Just wait, I've got something here." He reached into his pocket and pulled out an official looking document. "Look, this is the pink slip for my new car. It's parked outside." Jerry threw the paper on top of the cash. "This will cover the bet. It's all I've got with me right now."

Solly tried to keep a straight face. He suspected that Jerry, the spoiled son of a big-deal L.A. lawyer, third in line to the Jerome fortune, didn't have a clue as to his car's true worth.

Solly tapped the table a few times, then looked at his cards once more, just to be certain of what he had. Now that the bet was made, he could hardly keep from grinning. Solly had seen the car and knew what was at stake.

"It'll give me *nakhes*," he said, "a really great pleasure to take your bet, Jerry. Just remember, there are no take-backs. Get it!"

"Yeah, I get it and you're still bluffing. Let's see what you've got."

Solly knew he had a hand not to be believed, but not impossible to beat. The game had been played without wild cards, so four of a kind would have been tough to come by. Still, Jerry could have had just that. Jerry would have crushed him with four of a kind.

Solly placed his cards on the table, one at a time. When the fifth card went face up, everyone could see his full boat, three kings and two aces.

Jerry screamed, "Crap, you *schmuck*, you really had it!" He threw his two aces and three queens across the table and stood up. Solly thought he was going to throw a punch.

"No reason to get angry, Jerry. You gambled, but it didn't work out. Life's like that. My pa always says that when you gamble, there's no guarantee you'll win." With these words, Solly scooped the cash across the table and crammed it in his pocket, along with the pink slip. "I'll need your signature on this, please."

Jerry hesitated, but with everyone's attention on the game, he really had no choice but to pull out his pen and sign.

"Can you pass me the keys," said Solly, unable to resist a final stab at Jerry. "I need them to get her home."

Jerry's hands fumbled in his jacket pocket until he found the key. He slammed it down and glared at Solly.

After Solly finished his story, Mama didn't say anything. I could tell she disapproved, even though the best poker pot of Solly's sixteen-year life had produced a 1929 Ford Motel T and about $200 in cash.

The car was a classic. All I could say was, "She's beautiful."

Solly left his prize possession parked out front all week, but on the following Sunday morning, he took her out for a spin. I heard the engine while still in bed and ran outside in my long cotton nightgown to gawk as he drove away. Near the corner, he honked so everyone within earshot would see him driving his lucky charm.

Soon after he won the Rod, Solly convinced his friend Mortie to watch the store on Sundays so he could take long drives into the countryside. Mortie needed a second job and was thrilled to help out. After that, the drives became a Sunday ritual. No matter how late Solly had been out the night before, he'd dress, plop on his Baker Boy hat and ready the Rod for its Sunday cruise.

I would run outside to watch. After a month, I knew I needed to join him. "Solly, where're you going? Take me, take me, will you, will you, please!"

"Hell no, I can't have my kid sister tagging along while I'm cruising for girls."

"Just this once. I won't ask again. I promise. Take me just this once!"

"You're right, you won't ask again 'cause I'll say no, No, No! See you later, kid."

That day, when he returned, I was reading on the porch. Solly got out of his car and walked up to where I was sitting. He loved talking about the Rod and I was available. "I love that Carson lift-off top," he said. "When it's hot, I take it off and remove the front windshield. The wind blows my hair and pushes my face around. She rolls thirty miles per hour, but feels faster."

As he spoke, I repeated to myself, *The Rod, the rod, how dreamy.*

Solly chattered like girl. "You should have seen me," he said. "I drove out Sunset Boulevard down through Boyle Heights and then south along Whittier. I stopped to pick a few walnuts from the groves along the way. I kid you not, those nuts were bigger than my fist." Solly made a fist to show me. "So I get back in the car, and start cruising. Before long, these gorgeous girls are walking down the street. One of them, a curly blonde, sees me, smiles, and struts away. Maybe I'll see her the next time. Man of man, the Rod is one jazzy ride."

What a fairy tale! I was in love with Solly's car. I couldn't wait to peek at her every morning. On Sundays, I started following Solly around like we were glued at the hip.

"Can I go, can I go? Come on, just around the corner, that's all I want."

"Cruising with my little sis' sitting in passenger seat will drain the hot right out."

"Come on, I'll do anything, just let me ride with you."

"No, I said. *Nisht betler*, no begging. You are bugging me. Keep your distance. I feel like you are tailing me or something."

The Rod was an oilaholic. Solly added oil after every drive. I watched him carefully, scribbling notes in cursive in the margins of a school paper that had already been graded. I had devised a plan.

After three weeks of observing Solly's Sunday routine with the car, I left the house before him one morning, grabbed the oil and grease cans and handed these to him before he stepped off the front porch.

"What's this?" Solly was stunned that I had already filled the cans.

"It's your oil can, silly. I just wanted to help."

"Well, ah … thank you. Now clear out so I can get out of here."

I followed him to the car. He poured in the oil, lubricated the front and rear springs on the axles, greased the steering gear, got into the car and took off.

I continued this routine for two weeks. Finally, Solly let me help. I wasn't afraid to get dirty. I liked the way the grease felt sliding from my fingers onto the car. Solly hated getting his own hands soiled.

Solly let me do more and more. Once, after he left for his poker game, I snatched the Model T manual he left in his room, reading it thoroughly and putting it back before he returned.

I thought my plan was going well. I got used to feeding the Rod oil and water, greasing the axles and filling up the gas tank. Solly would anxiously study Marathon Street as I worked. He wanted to be ready to grab the cans from me if one of his buddies drove by. But my work didn't move me any closer to the passenger or driver's seat. After I was done, Solly would jump inside the Rod, press on the gas pedal, engage the gears as I stood on the curb, empty cans in hand.

He would accelerate at a snail's pace. The Rod coughed for about twenty feet before he allowed the gears to fall back, allowing the Rod to pick up speed. I would run to the corner and watch as he disappeared. Solly, at the wheel of his horseless carriage, cruising down the street under his Baker Boy flat hat, was the most handsome boy I'd ever seen.

Finally, I got tired of waiting for Solly to ask me to join him, which had been my plan. On the Sunday following Yom Kippur, as Solly jumped into the driver's seat, I hopped into the passenger seat at the same time. I sat there quietly with my hands folded in my lap like I belonged. Solly leaned over and opened the passenger door. "Get out, kid."

I didn't budge. "Hey Solly, why not take me into Boyle Heights. Mama told me to pick up some almond mandel bread cookies at the bakery. I'll buy one of the fresh rye breads with caraway seeds while I'm there. Aren't you starving after all that fasting for Yom Kippur yesterday?"

I was fibbing. I knew that for Solly, sweet crusty mandel bread was something to die for. Solly stared angrily at me. Still inside, I closed the passenger door that he had just opened. He just started driving. He hadn't kicked me out. Electricity jolted through me. Unable to sit still, my feet tapped the floorboard. I pushed on my thumping heart to try to slow it down. The ride to Boyle Heights took twenty minutes. A grin spread over my face. Sitting beside Solly, I was unofficially on the crew.

As we drove, my pigtails bounced up and down from the wind. I saw a girlfriend of mine and strummed my fingers at her.

"Keep your damn hands inside this car. The last thing I want is anyone's attention."

We passed City Hall. It was a 27-story shining tower, a straight arrow piercing the low-lying clouds. The building owned the downtown skyline and had taken years to build. It proved what Mama always said about change. "Be patient, getting what you want takes time."

When Solly dropped me back home, I was convinced of one thing. I needed to drive the Rod. I decided to ask Mama for help. Maybe she could convince Solly to teach me to drive. She said I should be patient, wait until I was older.

"But Mama, I have to, I just have to learn to drive. I've been helping Solly with his car, but he's so selfish. Can't you talk to him?"

"Sure, I can talk to him, but first you have to show him you are ready."

The following Saturday, I went to the Los Angeles County Library and found a book on automotive racing called *Wall Smacker*. It was higher than my reach. When I finally nudged it out, it fell on my head and bounced into my two hands.

I was hooked by the cover, a picture of an Italian driver with a racing hat completely covering his head. The book was written by Peter DePaelo, who was an infamous driver of early European rally cars. Its pages were still crisp and untouched. It seemed that no one but me cared much about this story.

At home, after I had finished my homework and eaten dinner, I climbed into bed and read 212 pages without a break. I forgot to say goodnight to Mama. I ignored Frieda's typically tedious questions.

DePaelo told about the first days of car racing on the old Brighton Beach course. He wrote about the 250-mile rally course that required thirteen tire changes to finish the race. As I read, I imagined that I was driving his car, racing the clock through dust clouds and pounding rain. None of the other drivers could believe it! A girl behind the wheel, no way, it couldn't be! They gave me such a look. The road was covered with loose gravel. Fans, mostly handsome, skinny Italians wearing long jackets, flat hats, vests and suspenders, cheered as I passed. I was beside myself with excitement. Men I didn't know threw their hats in the air, laughed, jumped and waved their arms wildly for me. My ears buzzed at their cheers. I strained to see every inch of the road ahead, while preparing myself for turns that came out of nowhere. A dirt crust clung to my face. Goggles protected my eyes. A brown leather pilot's headgear kept my hair pasted in place. My hands were blackened with grease from the repair stops I had made in route. A glint of excitement, in my eye, spread into full-blown exhilaration when I saw the finish line 500 yards ahead. My boot smacked the gas petal. I accelerated for a big finish, thirty seconds ahead of all the other drivers. I was the last driver to start the race, but had the best time.

"Bella!" Mama's hand startled me! I must have jumped six inches. "Go to sleep!"

"Mama, I won!"

"Won what?"

"I won the rally."

"Go to sleep! You need your sleep. Tired young ladies can't win much of anything in this world."

Before I found that book, I simply wanted to know more about cars. Now, I knew my destiny. Less than twenty-four hours after being hit over the head by *Wall Smacker*, I knew that someday I wanted to be a rally driver. This meant one thing. I had to convince Solly to let me drive the Rod.

Chapter 8

I think Solly figured if he let me in his car once, I would stop bugging him. Of course, he was wrong. My campaign had just begun. I was fifteen years old and my racecar driving dreams became bigger and more demanding each day. I had hundreds of questions for my brother. "What happens when you press down on the gas petal on a curve? What do you do if she spins out of control?"

Solly was rarely in a mood to answer. "Another stupid question! Leave me alone! You annoy me, little sister. Go help Mama peel potatoes. Go! Go now!"

His refusal to answer my questions frustrated the heck out of me. I kept asking anyway. He was my only route to getting behind the steering wheel of the Rod.

Solly had other things on his mind. On the third day of Sukkot, the celebration of the harvest, we planned to eat dinner outside in the *sukkah*, a fragile structure covered in palm leaves to commemorate the pilgrimages of the harvest to Jerusalem. Traditionally, we ate dinner outside in the *sukkah* if the weather was good. Pa, as usual, cornered Solly and pummeled him with questions about the store.

Solly had his usual response. "Business is horrible. There are customers, but still no cash. I've done everything, including discounting for cash. No one has money.

I looked at Mama. She didn't like these confrontations between Pa and Solly. She winced and disappeared inside the house.

I knew money was short. More and more often, I'd hear Mama say, "I'm short. Barely have *gelt* to buy milk. Most of Pa's savings are gone. Solly brings nothing home. He pays no rent. What we have left goes as quick as the bills come in."

I liked living at home and going to school. I wanted to be the first in my family to go to college. Now, I feared that soon Pa would whisper into my ear, "Time to marry, my Jewish princess."

Getting married would be the end of my life. There would be no college in my future. I wanted to be the first in the family to finish high school. I wanted to be a rally driver someday. I had dreams. But times were tough, and the chances of making these dreams come true were falling like flies.

I knew I was smart, but not smart enough for an academic scholarship. There was only one of those given each year to the top student in the graduating class. I knew it was up to me. I had to find a way to save myself. I was athletic. Maybe I could blaze my own trail as an athlete. I was the fastest runner in my tenth grade class. Once, I raced a boy in the hundred-yard dash. Ten yards out, he veered into my lane, threw his left leg in front of me and caused me to trip. He was making sure he didn't lose to a girl.

I'd read about some of the exceptional women who excelled in sports. Gertrude Ederle was the first woman to swim the English Channel in 1926. Helen Willis Moody won a string of nineteen singles tennis championships at Wimbledon. Three Olympic gold medals had been awarded to figure skater Sonia Henie in the 1928 Paris Olympics.

I loved reading about these women's accomplishments. But my favorites were the women pilots. Ruth Nichols had set the transcontinental speed record, beating Charles Lindberg's time of thirteen hours and twenty-one minutes. Amy Johnson set the international speed record in 1930, flying from London to India in just thirteen days. In my mind, these women lived the life! They inspired me. I had to find a way to be like them.

Later that evening, while I was comfortably in bed reading *The Sign of the Twisted Candles*, a Nancy Drew mystery story, Frieda rushed in with a copy of *Screenland* magazine. "Can you believe how beautiful she is?"

"Who is?"

"Tallulah Bankhead is beautiful. Her hair is perfect. It certainly doesn't look like my steel wool! Look at that red lipstick she wears. Everything matches. She's dressed to kill, so exotic."

"Shush, I'm reading. I can't think with your jabbering all the time. Why are you always going on about your movie stars? Who cares really?" Frieda ignored me and tucked herself under the covers.

"Bella, do you think we're in trouble? I've never heard so much talk about money. My friends at school don't have money for lunch. Are we going loose our house?"

"How in the heck am I supposed to know? First, Pa quits the store. Then, Solly can't make a profit, and now, Mama says she doesn't have enough for milk. Yeah, I'm worried. Who wouldn't be?

Frieda tried being upbeat. "Solly thinks he can make money gambling until things turn around."

"Solly says a lot of things. You can believe what you want. You can't eat your dreams. I know those actors you adore on the screen go home every night to real problems. I'm not counting on Solly, Pa, or anyone else. I'm counting on me. I'm going to try to figure something out."

The next morning, I awoke in a glum mood. I had overslept. When I realized Solly was already out on his Sunday drive, my mood worsened. In the kitchen, Mama noticed. "My *sheyn meydl*, smile, you'll ruin your beautiful face."

I forced a smile. "I think I need some fresh air. Maybe I'll go for a walk around the block."

"Come, Bella, let's walk together in my garden. We'll find ourselves something for dinner. Tomatoes for stew, or cabbage for cold slaw, which is better for our dinner tonight?"

I decided I needed to at least put on an act of cheerfulness. No need to bring down Mama with my mood. "Will you make cold slaw with the corned beef?" I hated the texture of stewed tomatoes. They were too gushy for me. I liked cold slaw, especially when the vinegar was right.

In the garden, Mama instructed me. "Honey, pick a big a big head of cabbage from over there. While you're at it, pick six ripe tomatoes for a delicious stew."

As much as I loved Mama, I didn't want to be her. I wanted more from life than a kitchen, a garden, and children. My athlete ideas didn't fit Pa's image of me. For him, a woman had an important job in the world and that was in the home. He reminded all of us every *shabes* dinner that our people followed the teaching of the three fathers of Judaism. According to Pa, religion, business, politics, and sports were things men did. Women helped.

On the other hand, Solly was *bar mitzvah*. This meant he was a man and was subject to the laws of the Jewish faith. This wasn't something Solly wanted, but it was a ceremony he had gone through for Pa. There was never a question that Solly was the heir to the family business. Solly didn't take to that much, either. Nevertheless, Solly was the son. He was next in line to the throne.

Neither I, nor any my sisters, studied religion at *shul*. If we did go to High Holy Day events, we had to sit upstairs far away from the men. Once Sarah told me her husband had come to services after they started. He didn't want to make a fuss so he sat upstairs with the few women. Pa, who was on the *bema*, the stage which looked out to the congregation, looked up and saw Mike upstairs sitting with the women. Pa immediately ran right upstairs and shoed Mike out of the women's gallery. God forbid, a man should embarrass Pa.

Even long after Solly had taken over the business, he complained of the time he had wasted at *cheder*. He preferred hanging out with the neighborhood hoodlums. The rabbi's teachings meant nothing to him. Pa thought Solly was an ingrate.

We had moved to Echo Park because Pa wanted to appear better off than most of his Jewish friends, who lived in Boyle Heights. Boyle Heights was fine, but Echo Park, high on the hill above it all, was better.

Sunday summer picnics in Echo Park were the best of all times for the family. We ate hamburgers on Kaiser rolls with sour pickles and *kugl*, a noodle pudding. Palm trees swayed in the wind as their palm fronds waved like little fingers at the blue sky. Echo Park was near a big church, where the loud speaker blasted a message we couldn't ignore.

"With God, I can do all things! But with God and you, and the people who you can interest, by the grace of God, we're gonna cover the world! And my task, as I see it, is to interest you folks to help me, to help them, to join the line right around the whole world! Not only to help the heathen abroad, but to help the heathen in Los Angeles. By God's grace, if we can see our task and join hands and get together, we can spread the gospel around the world." The preacher was Amy Semple McPherson. Thousands came to hear her, and millions listened to her radio show.

Often, on the sidewalk near the edge of the park, a bearded man would speak to us as we walked toward the lake. He said things I didn't understand. Mama always told me to ignore him and to never look him in the eye. He invited all who passed to hear Minister Amy speak about the messiah, Jesus.

One afternoon, Frieda scrunched up her prominent nose. "Mama, do we know Jesus?"

"We don't believe Jesus was the messiah," said Mama. "We are still waiting for peace on Earth. We believe in many of the same values, but not that Jesus died for our sins. We believe we are completely responsible for our actions and must support the 5,000-year-old tradition of the Jews, which goes back 3,000 years before Jesus.

"Who is right?"

"It doesn't matter who is right. It only matters that we have the right to think for ourselves. Minister Amy believes her way is the only way. Pa says putting on *tallit*, the *tefilin*, the *kepot*, shows respect for God. He says *davening*, praying in the synagogue, makes him a good Jew, a *mensch*, a human being. He says the Christians should respect our ways and we should respect theirs. If we need comfort, we can pray in our own way."

We continued to walk as the man's voice faded behind us. Mama continued. "Pa and I left the old country to escape those who persecuted the Jews. Even here in Los Angeles, we are not accepted everywhere. We live in an area where they allow us to live. We are discouraged from going into gentile neighborhoods. Jews accept one another."

I laughed. "But Mama, everyone in our family fights. Sometimes we say disrespectful things. I see Jews in Boyle Heights who scream at each other. Is that respect?"

"They say put two Jews in a room and you'll get four opinions. Fighting is acceptable. We can respect each other's opinions even when we disagree."

"But Mama, Pa doesn't even want to *hear* our opinions. He fought so much with Pearl that she moved out. He doesn't listen to you most of the time."

"Sha! Don't disrespect your father with your rude comments. Pa has his reasons. He is older and wiser than his children. He is the provider in our house. We must learn from him, and when he is wrong, he has the right to be wrong. As Jews, it is good that we stick together, hold our ground, keep our beliefs. Some Jews marry the Christians. This is a terrible sin. Those who marry outside the faith loose the faith. There are so few of us. We cannot afford to lose any. There are Jews who would like to forget our 5,000-year history. When my children don't act like Jews, I worry. Being a Jew does not come easily. It is a big, big responsibility. The *goyim*, they have their beliefs. No matter where we live, they surround us. Their ministers are always inviting us to join them. I fear them. When you hear their persuasive words, be strong, resist. Keep to your own kind. Be a Jew. You have a lot to be proud of. Even now, as Minister McPherson's words echo throughout the park, understand this, that no one can say who is right."

Hundreds of happy churchgoers paraded outside after services. They laughed, shook friendly hands, lovingly slapped each other on the back, and seemed to walk on a cloud. Preacher Amy's voice was persuasive. It made me want to know more. There were so many that raved about her. She was very powerful. I didn't understand her words, but her followers seemed to adore her.

Mama said that some of the wealthiest people in Los Angeles belonged to her church. Some, who couldn't put food on their table, gave her money. In a way, I could understand why she was so powerful. Just hearing that voice come over the loud speaker gave me energy."

I tried to believe what Mama said about Pa. I wanted to adore him, too. He was hard, to be sure. He always pushed us away with his anger. These feelings made me want to go inside that church and listen. I wanted to. I really did.

Chapter 9

My sixteenth birthday approached. I earned honors in school. The mirror was kind to me. I found things that made me smile. Several school boys smiled back. I continued to dream, not about the boys, but about the car parked within eyesight of my bedroom window and how I could get Solly to let me drive it. I would fall asleep with that on my mind and wake up with no solution.

Frieda had already turned seventeen. Solly, now nineteen, continued to run the store and bet on his future. Every Sunday, he took a new girl for a ride. I wasn't one of those girls.

As little money as Solly made, his friends admired his paycheck. He earned $22 per week. He would take his cash in one dollar bills and small change. That way, his pockets always appeared full.

He was young, unmarried, and earning a living. But even though he still lived at home, he had expenses The ponies and pretty girls dug deep into the change he carried. If he ran short, he would find some way to close a sale. That way, he never left the store without his pockets jiggling.

Solly always had a wild streak. His *chutzpah* worked well in business, but got him in a lot of trouble, too. Every shuffle of the cards was an opportunity for an easy buck. Money was power, and the more he had, the more he wanted. There was a limit as to what he could take from the store.

His nightclub friends were very powerful — too powerful! He wasn't shy when talking about them and he found a good audience in Frieda and me. One night, he wandered into our bedroom after dinner and told us about a new club called the Keystone, where all the heavies hung out.

"So, guess what goes down the other night," he said.

"What?" said Frieda and I, in unison.

"I'm sitting at the bar, a few chairs down from Mickey Cohen. He starts pawing Mildred, the Lucky Strike girl. She was looking good! Cohen says to Mildred, 'what do you mean, you've got a boyfriend? I've got plenty of girlfriends. Who cares? We can spend the night together and no one else needs to know.' It's dark inside the bar, right, but I can see the whites of Mildred's eyes. They dart back and forth and land on this tall Italian guy with one of those pencil-thin mustaches. The Italian guy walks over and stands behind Mickey while he argues with Mildred. One of Mickey's thugs grabs the Italian's collar and presses his whole body to the wall. Cohen turns back to Mildred. Her already white face turns pasty. Cohen asks her if the Italian guy is her boy."

Solly leaned against the bedroom door, waiting for our reactions. I knew Mickey Cohen was a gangster.

"So what happened?" said Frieda.

"Mildred turns toward another customer. Any customer would do. She was trying to ignore Cohen. I can see the boss wasn't happy being ignored. Cohen raises the brim of his hat, pats down his hair. It's clearly a signal to get rid of Mr. Italiano. Next thing you know, her boy takes a fist to his gut, kneels over, and coughs. He says, 'what was that for?' Cohen's cohort leans down, looks right into the guy's face and says, 'Mr. Cohen was trying to have a conversation with Mildred, and you got in the way.' Two of Cohen's thugs cart the guy out. His heels never leave the ground. They make this funny squeaking sound as he gets dragged out the back door."

I'd heard of the Keystone Club but had no idea what could happen there. This guy, from what Solly had just said, did nothing wrong but show up. Worse yet, Solly said nobody, including himself, even bothered to put down their drink to help the poor guy out. Solly said he figured Mildred had ended up spending a warm, cozy night with Mr. Cohen. When I heard that, it made me feel queasy. Solly seemed to enjoy telling the story. What worried me was that I knew Solly admired Cohen's power. He said that Cohen knew how to get what he wanted. As much as I liked to hear Solly's stories, this one seemed darker than the rest. Solly had become so animated, with a big grin on his face, especially when telling about Cohen's goons. He didn't seem to care about Mildred at all.

I expected him to keep talking about the club, but instead he took a detour that surprised me. Solly started comparing Pa to Cohen. He said Pa had power inside the house. He also had power when he was running the store and chose who got credit.

"But what came of it?" Solly said. "Maybe a few 'yes sirs' from the customers who needed him. I'll tell you what came of it. Nothing! It comes down to this. You demand, you get. Pussy footing around gets you nowhere. Pa can be tough, but I'm tougher. I'm going to make truckloads of money. I'm not gambling. I'm *investing* when I play cards. Trying to squeeze juice out of the store in this economy is ridiculous. The real money is at the card table. Winning the Rod was fun. That was just the beginning. I'm going big-time soon." Solly grinned and left the room. I knew he thought he had made an impression on Frieda and me. We had listened intently.

All Solly's talk about gangsters made me wonder how Pearl was doing. We'd heard nothing for such a long time. We'd heard she had a room above some club and was singing there. I knew Frieda thought she was having the time of her life. To me, living alone in a small room above a noisy club and spending your nights with a bunch of two-bit jazz musicians didn't sound like much fun. If her club was anything like the Keystone Club, she too might have been forced to go off with someone like Cohen. I was afraid for her. I wished she was back home.

We did receive a letter from Pearl in February. It was addressed to Mama. In the letter, Pearl said she wanted to come home. There was a phone number at the bottom of the letter and Mama called it right away. "Pearl, it's your mama."

Later that evening, Mama told us that Pearl sobbed for twenty minutes before she could say a word. Mama said she told Pearl to write Pa a letter begging for forgiveness.

Pa never said a word about Pearl's letter. We knew he got it because Frieda discovered the crinkled envelope in the kitchen trash. She recognized Pearl's handwriting right away. The envelope had been opened, and inside was the letter, which looked like it had been pulled out and stuffed back inside. Had Pa read it? Or had he simply returned it to the envelope, unread, when he realized it was from Pearl? Frieda decided not to say anything to Mama about Pearl's letter to Pa, but later, at bedtime, when we were safely in our room, she read the letter by candlelight to me.

Dear Pa, I should never have left home. If Mama hasn't already told you, I fell in love with a guy in the band named Louie. We married. What a mistake. I broke it off before the end of our first week together. I was devastated. I would have come home then but I was too afraid. I know I was irresponsible and arrogant. Can you forgive me? I need you and Mama. I want to come home. I love you so much. I know I was wrong, storming out. I am done with these crazy musicians. I hate the club life. I miss Mama, Solly, and the girls. Please forgive me. I need you. Your loving daughter, Pearl.

"What do you think?" Frieda whispered. "Pa is hard like nails, but somewhere, deep inside, he must have a soft spot."

"But why was it in the trash?" I asked.

A few weeks later, on *shabes*, Pearl stood alone outside the Breed Street Shul and waited. When Papa came outside, he seemed preoccupied. Pearl was dressed in a long, dark blue, straight-laced outfit, which hung to her ankles. It wasn't hers. She had borrowed it for the occasion. She wore no jewelry, and the dress, which one of girls in the band had worn to a funeral, covered her chest right up to the neckline. Her hair, in a top knot, was inconspicuous under a simple black hat. She wore black flats. When Pa saw her, his face was without expression. Pearl took several steps toward him, got to within three feet and burst into tears. He stopped and seemed confused, then turned in his path as if to avoid a collision. He didn't even nod. One of the other men, a fellow board member of the *shul*, recognized Pearl and said to Pa, "Frank, isn't that Pearl, the beautiful daughter who wrote you that wonderful letter of apology that you just told me about?"

Pa turned and took a good look at Pearl for the first time. It was obvious he had not recognized her. Laying one hand on her shoulder, he kissed her. No smile emerged. Forgiveness was one thing. Letting go of his pride was another. Together, they walked to the trolley. His first question was about her marriage. "Who was this *nudnik* you married?"

"Oh Pa, he was such a jerk. Can't begin to explain how stupid I feel for having fallen. He was one of those enchanting musicians, who had no music left after the performance ended. Please, can't we talk about something else? How are Mama and the girls?"

Pa and Pearl arrived home together. I was in the kitchen with Mama, who rushed to Pearl like a bird flies to its nest. They hugged. Mama acted like Pearl had come home from an overnight with a girlfriend.

"I know Solly will squawk like a wounded duck, but your room is yours again, no matter what he says or does. Just be patient with him."

As expected, Solly acted like a *mamzer*, a son of a bitch, when he heard the news. "So, she comes back, and just plops her stuff down, just like that. Now, it's her room again. My God, I won't put up with it!"

Mama made sure Solly didn't turn Pearl back out. "She is your sister. If you don't like it, you can sleep in the living room, on the couch. I will have no more of this lunacy."

Pearl hadn't mentioned her new boyfriend, Jack, to Pa. Jack, who was Jewish, and in Pearl's eyes, a soon-to-be-successful businessman, would be something positive she could spring at the right time, which of course, was *shabes* dinner the following week. Knowing Pearl, we all guessed that Jack's looks were more compelling than his brains. It didn't matter. Pearl was back, and Pa accepted her return.

Soon, Pearl and Jack were dancing the night away at the finest of clubs in town. During the afternoons, once Frieda and I got home from school, Pearl told us tales of the high life on Sunset. She also filled us in on Jack.

He had inherited money from his grandfather, a big-time jeweler in New York City, and had invested most of it in his own business. He had worked as a salesman in the furniture business for years. Now he wanted to go out on his own.

We met Jack for the first time after *shabes* dinner.

"Hello, Mr. Krawiec," he said to Pa. "I've heard so much about you."

Pa got a skeptical look on his face and reached out tentatively to shake Jack's hand. Jack grabbed Pa's hand and shook it like he was cranking an engine.

"Jack, is that your name?" said Pa.

"Yes, Mr. Krawiec, I'm Jack Levy."

"You a member of the tribe?"

"Yes, of course I'm Jewish. Pearl told me how important it was to you that she date a Jewish man."

"What else did Pearl tell you about me?"

"Not so much, really. She did say you were a very successful merchant and that now you spend most of your time at the synagogue."

"Did she tell you anything else?"

Jack was smart enough to know what not to say. "She said I could learn a lot from you. I'm starting my business soon."

"Yes, I'd be happy to talk to you about that later. Now, I know you two have plans. Go out and enjoy. But get my daughter home by midnight. We have rules, you know."

"Yes, Mr. Krawiec, I'll be sure to take care of her. I know all families have rules. It's our way of protecting one another."

Since it was Friday night, Pearl and Jack were dressed in their formal best. Jack wore a tuxedo with tails, a black silk vest, black tie and a top hat. A white silk monogrammed handkerchief peeked out of his coat's top pocket. His shoes were mirror-shined black oxfords. Pearl wore a long strand of white pearls, a long red dress and red high heels. Careful not to anger Pa, her neckline was high and unrevealing.

Pearl and Jack pranced down our porch steps under the star-studded Los Angeles sky and glided into Jack's car. They drove off in a 1928 Model T sedan that Pearl told us he bought with a few dollars down and a big loan. She said Jack wasn't afraid to open his wallet. Later, we learned he was living off the money that was supposed to stock his store.

To Frieda and me, Jack and Pearl were the best looking couple in all of Los Angeles. Jack had light blonde hair, a well-manicured mustache, good skin and a tight torso. Pearl, standing next to him, was a knockout.

Solly, who sometimes went to the same clubs as Pearl and Jack, would tell us that on the dance floor, Pearl's three-inch heels never touched the floor as Jack twirled her as they fox trotted the night away. Solly would proudly say, "Saw Pearl and Jack last night. Man, there wasn't an eye in the place that wasn't glued to their every move."

With Pearl back home, I was all ears when she would tell Frieda and me about men. "Men," said Pearl, "want to believe they are attractive, and when a woman makes them feel that way, men became men."

While I wasn't so concerned about getting a man, I did enjoy finding out how to get what I wanted.

Chapter 10

T he key to a man's heart is his stomach." Mama repeated her advice daily. Pa didn't care what she cooked as long as it was ready on time. Solly, too, was oblivious to how good Mama's cooking was. Just like Pa, he was always in a hurry.

We were all waiting for Pa to arrive for *shabes* dinner. Outside, rain poured on Mama's roses. Inside, Solly was bragging, as usual.

"Girls, you should have seen my last shot. I caromed the white cue ball off the felt and drove the green six ball into the far right pocket. The pile of bills on the counter leaped into my hip pocket. It was like taking a baby from the candy. I mean taking candy from a baby."

Boasting about his gambling winnings came naturally to Solly. He never spoke about the times he lost. It dawned on me, as he spoke, that Solly needed gambling, that he couldn't do without it. That gave me an idea. *I'll just put myself into his gambling world,* I thought.

"Solly, can you set up a road rally? I could drive! You could make some real money. Those guys, your poker buddies, will never … never believe your little sister can outdrive them!"

"You're kidding! You, a girl rally driver! Ha? Those guys would laugh me right out of town if I proposed my little sis rally with them. Besides, there is no chance I'd ever let you drive, much less put my money in on you. Do I look like some sort of *shmegege*?"

The very next week, over *shabes* dinner, Pearl, Frieda, and I grinned throughout the meal. Frieda had never smiled like that before. It was wonderful to have Pearl back on the team. Solly gobbled down dinner and strutted for the exits. Before the front door slammed shut, he looked back at us. "What the heck are you girls smiling about? Is there green stuff stuck between my front teeth?" Solly put his hand on his crouch to check for an open fly. "I know I didn't let the cows out. Is there mustard on my lip?"

Our voices merged an emphatic Nope. We chuckled, pushed ourselves away from the table, and wandered off toward our room. "Knock it off would you!" he said, leaving.

The following week, once again, Pearl, Frieda, and I giggled throughout dinner, as if we had some secret. We didn't give Solly a single look. His face illuminated like a jack-o'-lantern as he glared at us. "Alright girls, what's going on?"

Pearl leaned over to me and whispered into my ear. "Does the giant awake? "He's so sure of himself. He doesn't have a clue."

Solly stood up like he going to throw something at us. Pa joined in. "Solly, sit down, they're just playing with you."

Solly did what Pa asked, but shook his head and said, "I don't have to put up with this crap."

I was ready for him. "You' re right, Solly, you don't have to put up with it, but when you hear what we have to say, you'll be glad you did."

Frieda joined the conversation. "Should we tell him how he can strike it rich?"

"Okay, okay, okay! Enough of your girling! What's up?"

I pointed to the porch. "I need five minutes on the porch!"

Solly's chest inflated and he puffed up like a peacock. "Get to it, I'm already late."

"Maybe we should wait until you have the time. Maybe your gambling buddies would like to hear first."

Solly looked into the living room, where Pa had retired with his schnapps, and walked slowly to my side of the table. He whispered into my ear. "When did you become a gambling expert?"

"Maybe I'm not an expert, but I know a sure thing. Sit and listen. This will take a few minutes! Do you have the time now?"

"Not now! I'm late." He walked out, slamming the door shut behind him. I let it go. In my mind, it was just a matter of time.

That night, Pearl, who considered herself an expert on men, joined Frieda and me in our bedroom. "Guys all have Achilles heels," she said. "Let them run after you. When you finally stop, they will fall into your lap. Once you get to them, they all shiver in the cold just like the rest of us." Pearl knew so much. As she opened up to us, Frieda got so nervous sipping her Mr. Brown's cream soda, she about choked.

In response to Pearl's talk about men, I explained what I had read about rally drivers. "They aren't like other guys. They're prize fighters who constantly pound the target. They go forty-eight hours straight, switching drivers every two hours. When they're exhausted, their instincts kick in. They are athletes because they never back off and never give up."

"You make it all sound too complicated," said Pearl. "Books and movies are fine, but they aren't real life."

She got up and walked to the door. "Come on, girls, I have an idea. Can you drive, Bella? I'd like to see you drive Solly's car now. What do you say? Are you ready?"

My body responded before I could open my mouth. I felt like I had the flu, hot, cold, hot and cold again, then cold all over. "You mean now? Right now?"

Look," said Pearl. "It comes down to this. Do you have any guts or are you all about talk? Life is more than those books you read."

I sat silently for a minute. I had never expected that Pearl would be the one to push me into the driver's seat.

"Let's get on the road," I said. "I'll drive. I can do it. I know the Rod like the back of my hand. I've worked on her. If you two are with me, I'm ready to roll."

Pearl grabbed my hand and her face came so close it was blurry. "Can you drive without cracking her up? He'll *kill* us if you do."

I rose slowly, then pointed through my bedroom window at the Rod. "No more gabbing, girls, let's go!" We tiptoed out the door. The last thing we wanted was to wake Mama. I was afraid Frieda might chicken out before we were outside. Pearl pulled the front door open carefully so as not to make a sound. When Pearl and Frieda reached the curb, they hoisted themselves off the running board and piled one on top of the other, into the passenger seat. Walking as quietly as I could to the side yard, I grabbed Solly's stash of gasoline. The night sky was black. I could barely see two feet in front of me as I made my way to the Rod and topped her off with gas. On the driver's side, I opened the door and shoved the gas can under the seat. Climbing inside, I plopped myself behind the steering wheel. I sat up as straight as I could so I could see the over the dashboard. My left foot pushed onto the floor starter, and when she purred, I pressed ever so slightly on the gas pedal. She was in neutral and I could hear her idle.

Pearl reminded Frieda, who was probably holding her breath, to relax. I turned on the headlamps. I couldn't shake the fear that Mama might wake up and catch us. I could only see about ten feet ahead. The rest of Marathon was dark and looked empty through the car's front window. Strangely enough, I felt right at home behind the wheel.

I popped the clutch into first gear, turned the steering wheel with both hands and stretched my right leg to engage the gas pedal. We rolled slowly forward and out from the curb. I muscled the driver's wheel to get her straight onto the road, pressing harder on the gas pedal. At first, I was scared, but then, the excitement of driving the Rod set in. I was soon making my first turn onto Waterloo. A minute later, I turned right onto Alvarado, then right again on Greenfield. As I started my last right turn, back onto the other end of Marathon, my headlamps shone directly onto the front porch of my neighbor and school chum, Mary Rogers, who was kissing a boy. The boy's hand fell away from Mary's shoulder as they both looked my way.

Frieda kicked my foot when she saw them. Thankfully, I didn't accelerate out of control.

"What now? I asked.

"Keep going," said Pearl. "Just get us home."

Reaching our house a few seconds later, I turned the steering wheel to the right, eased off the gas pedal, downshifted, and parked right where we started. I had mentally marked the car's parked position, relative to the front gate and the rose bushes, so that I would know where to park when we returned.

I took a deep breath. No accident! Pearl and I opened the car doors and lowered ourselves onto the sidewalk. Fried followed.

I reached under the seat and pulled up the gas can, careful not to spill a drop inside the car. Creeping quietly back into the side yard, I was careful to place the can where Solly had left it.

Rejoining Pearl and Frieda, we walked on our toes up the porch stairs, eased open the unlocked front door and headed for the bedroom. There, the three of us collapsed onto one bed, united by our successful stunt. Our mission was accomplished. No one knew. I visualized myself writing about this in a book someday.

Chapter 11

Next *shabes* dinner, Solly belched his way through the meal. I waited until he was done eating and said, "Solly, let's take a few minutes on the porch."

"Sure, but make it short. I don't want to hang around for long."

I hustled outside and settled in to my favorite porch chair and waited. I could see Pearl and Frieda by the window. Solly remained inside for what seemed like an eternity, talking to Pa about some business *hazarai*. When he finally joined me, he just stood there, snorting and belching like some sort of animal. I didn't say a word, just pointed to the Rod.

"Why are you pointing at my car?"

I conjured a half smile, then something took over. "I can drive the Rod," I said. "Just like a professional race car driver."

Saliva formed on Solly's bottom lip. He swept it away with his tongue. "I told you. You can't drive my car!"

"I already have."

Solly's face turned red. "You already have what?"

I ignored his question. "Look," I said, "I've figured out a way to make some cash for you. With the Rod." I took her out for a spin around the block a few nights ago. Pearl and Frieda were with me. Don't worry, nothing bad happened."

The palm of Solly's hand unfurled as I spoke. Mama, who had joined Pearl by the window, must have known it was time for a distraction.

"Hey, you two, I've got strawberry pie for dessert?"

"No, Mama, I'm full, can't eat a bit more."

Solly was surprisingly polite. "No, Mama, not now."

Glaring at me, Solly whispered so Mama wouldn't hear, "If Mama wasn't inside looking at us, I'd smack …!"

Solly towered over me. It was time to get up and look at him directly in the face. I popped up, feeling strength I didn't know I had. "Maybe you will, or maybe you won't, but if you don't want grief from Pa, I'd think twice about threatening me!"

Tiny beads of sweat appeared on his forehead. I was right. He knew it. If he hit me, he would become a pariah in Pa's house. The men in my family might scream, but they didn't smack. At least, they didn't smack girls.

The bun holding my hair knot unraveled, and my hair fell around my shoulders. I pushed it back with my hand. "Here's the deal! Your friends, the ones who gamble, they don't think girls can drive as well as they can. They'll never believe that your little sister could outdrive them in a road rally. You'll get — what do you call it — odds against me. If you bet, and I win, you'll make a fortune! I can beat those palookas and make you rich!"

Solly was visibly stunned. But he also looked thoughtful. "You're right," he said. "They'll never believe it. They'll laugh me halfway across the poker table." He looked toward the window, then back at me. "You know, driving the Rod is really no big deal. I could teach you. The Rod is fast. I know that. But driving in a race is not the same as driving around the corner." He turned to the street, looking up and down Marathon. "Bella, I'm going to let you drive. We can put those boys into the poor house. They're *shnorers* anyway, mooches to the end. We'll need to practice. This won't be a walk in the park. We'll need four or five hours every Sunday. I know you think I'm bossy now, but I'll get worse. You can either put up with me, or we can forget the whole thing. I'm warning you now. And one more thing. You will never, ever, ever drive without my permission again. Get it!" He turned on his heels, and before I could say a word, was gone. It didn't matter. We had a deal. I was about to become a rally car driver.

Dizzy with victory, I stumbled inside. The girls and Mama were still at the window. They must have known from the grin they had seen on Solly's face that he bought my story. Pearl and I jumped up and down, laughing hysterically. Mama just smiled.

Two days after Solly and I made our plans, I came home to a familiar sound. Pa was yelling. *"Bay tog zolstu hengen un bay nakht zolstu brenen."*

Pearl pulled me aside and explained that Pa had not been elected president of the congregation. He didn't seem to notice us as he ranted at Mama.

"May they hang by day and burn by night. They are imbeciles. How could they elect Shulman. He's a cobbler. Never made a living and can't lead!" Pa's fists pounded the kitchen counter. The pepper shaker crashed on one of his hands. That made him even angrier. He flung it onto the floor. Mama cowered in the corner.

Pa's campaign to be elected Breed Street Shul president had failed. His endless schmoozing had gotten him nowhere. Even raising hordes of money for the building fund had meant nothing.

Pa hollered at Mama, "Get my schnapps."

"Frank, please, lower your voice, the girls ..."

Pa scuffed the floor like a bull ready to attack. "Shut up. I'm in no mood. I'm starving. Why are you yakking? Get my dinner now!"

"Dinner is ready. Come, let's eat. The schnapps is all gone. Last night, you had some and then fell asleep in the living room chair, remember? You'll have to go without for now."

"But there was half a bottle! I drank it all?"

"Yes, all of it! I haven't had a chance to replace it yet." I knew Mama was lying. The rest of the bottle was safely hidden where Pa wouldn't know to look. Mama was desperate to keep him out of the bottle. He wasn't a *shiker*, but when things didn't go his way, a few shots were like poison. "I'll get you more tomorrow. Look, I've made one of your favorites, matzo balls chicken soup. The matzo balls are light as a feather, just the way you love them. Sit down, make yourself comfortable, you need to relax. I'll get the soup."

Pearl and I joined Mama in the kitchen to help serve. She broke into tears.

When dinner was ready, everybody but Mama sat down at the table. Frieda looked up at me as I spooned soup into Mama's china. I knew she thought it was time one of us set Pa straight. Maybe it wasn't time, but it was going to happen either way. Frieda nudged me with a pat on my leg under the table. Mama was still in the kitchen.

"Pa, Mama's crying, can't you be nicer to her?"

Pa didn't respond or even acknowledge what I had said. I decided to let it go. Antagonizing Pa wasn't going to change him, and I didn't want to risk anything getting in the way of my rally plans. Also, I was in no mood for his rage. I had other *dybbuks* to worry about. I hadn't even starting training yet. Solly hadn't even sprung our plan on his gambling buddies yet. And I was already being eaten alive by fear of failure. What if those boys pulled a trick on me while I was on the road? I might get hurt. I might die. Worse yet, I might lose.

The following Saturday night, before my first training session, I dreamt I was driving and talking to Solly at the same time. I turned my head to smile at a school friend standing on the roadside. I took my eyes off the road. A toddler ran out of nowhere. I jammed my foot on the brakes, but I had stepped on the wrong pedal. The Rod accelerated. I was supposed to throttle down, clutch into neutral, and brake. There was just no time! I did everything wrong. I ran over the child.

I awoke soaked. It took me five minutes to stop panting. I sat up in the pitch black of my room. I tried talking to myself. I was only half awake. It was a dream. But what if it had happened? What if it did happen?

Dream or not, it scared the living daylights out of me. But I was now committed. The rally would be my chance. My head throbbed. I forced myself to get dressed. I acted like I didn't have a care in the world while I ate my cereal. I measured my steps as I walked out the front door, down the porch steps, and to the curb where Solly stood waiting. I tried to look confident. I reassured myself that I was the luckiest girl in the world. Once I reached Solly, I smiled like I thought the luckiest girl in the world would smile.

Still tinkering, he ignored my smile and barked at me. "You sit there." He pointed to the passenger seat. He was making it clear who was in charge, and it certainly wasn't me. "I'll drive out. You sit there until we're out of the neighborhood."

I wasn't worried he'd change his mind. I was his ticket. I was just worried I'd screw up. I was glad when he started driving. It would be my turn soon enough. He leaned over to me. "No one, absolutely no one, can see you or hear about your driving. If they do, it's over. If the boys catch on, then our trick pony is dead." Then he added, "I believe in you."

Solly believed in me! I couldn't believe what I'd just heard.

"There'll be a big pot," said Solly. "I can't afford to lose. First, you're going to learn the road, every bump and every pothole. You'll have to accelerate on the straightaways. Then, you'll learn to take corners without slowing. It's all about momentum. Once you've got it, you have to keep it. There is no backing off. There's no turning back. Get it."

Solly knew the Rod performed well on dirt roads. He'd been taking Sunday country drives for months. I knew he was counting on the boys underestimating how well she would perform.

Once we were out of the neighborhood, I started to feel better. I had forgotten my nightmare. The morning air did me good. There were plenty of open fields and a lot of dirt roads, so I could practice where there were no children or cars to get in my way.

When we reached the open country roads, Solly pulled over, and we switched positions. From the passenger seat, he gave me directions. I started her up, and we moved forward. As I listened to Solly, my eyes stayed pasted to the road. I had all I could handle to keep the Rod moving over the bumps in the dirt roads and around corners. Solly went on and on, like there would be a test afterwards.

"She has 4 cylinders, manufactured of Vanadium steel, weighs 1500 pounds and has power of 22 horses. Max speed, that's want counts. She can go thirty miles per hour, faster than some of the newer cars, but not nearly as fast as most rally cars. Her weight and that vanadium steel will keep her steady on rough roads. That'll be important if it rains."

My head ached. I fought through it as I memorized every lever and pedal, trying not to lose concentration. Mistakes would not be an option during the rally. The open roads stretched onward, bordered on both sides by orange groves. Solly seemed to know all about these groves and the climate that made them productive. I'd never known him to talk like this. I suspected that driving the Rod on these country roads brought out something different in him.

"These fields produce one heck of a lot of juice," he said. The sun and dry air attract lots of people to California. Some say they come for the business climate. I think they come for the sun. There are so many immigrants. Someday, I'll bet these groves will be gone and there will be houses in their place. And it won't be just houses. There'll be factories and offices. Lawyers and doctors will live and work here. Universities will be built. It will be glorious for those of us who got here first, though, because we can take advantage of all this opportunity. All it takes is money. It takes *gelt* to be successful. That's why I want to be rich. This rally could be the start of something big for both us."

As I listened to Solly, I grew more comfortable behind the wheel. Then, out of nowhere, a produce truck barreled down the road from the opposite direction. It was bigger than half the divided road. I pulled and pushed the right levers, slowed down, and edged onto the roadside to avoid collision. The truck whizzed by. The Rod rocked in the gust of wind the truck blew at us. "Wow," I said. "I don't know how I did that, but it was sure a good thing I did! I thought we'd get hit. That truck was big, too!"

"You were cool as a cucumber, little sis. Good going!" On the way back, Solly tested me. "Let's see what you can do on this stretch."

I pressed down on the pedal, gassing her good. My arms were tired from holding onto the wheel. My right leg was exhausted. It was an effort just to reach the pedal. It was obvious to me that I would need a lot of time behind the wheel. There was more to driving the Rod than I had expected. Road divots and bumps jolted her up and down, jostling Solly and me in the seats. At one point, a jack rabbit crossed the road. It was impossible to stop. I sucked in so much air that it popped out of my nose involuntarily.

But I was able to keep my speed steady. Luckily, the rabbit scampered out of the way.

Once we approached the city, there was more traffic. A huge horse-drawn trailer, loaded with fresh-picked oranges, lumbered toward us. By that time, my muscles were moaning with fatigue. Instead of gently guiding the Rod off to the side, I tensed up, clenched the steering wheel, and speeded up. At the last minute, I twisted the Rod off the paved road and into a ditch. Solly and I lurched forward. Our sudden stop had nearly flipped us.

"What the hell are you doing!" yelled Solly. You trying to get us killed!" He got out of the car. While he pushed from behind, I accelerated. It did no good. The tires spun out of control and spewed mud onto Solly. After he wiped the mud off his face and uttered a few choice words, he walked into a nearby field and grabbed two fallen tree branches. He edged them under the tires for traction. I pumped the gas and the Rod popped out of the mud. Once again, we were on our way. As I urged the Rod homeward, Solly reminded me that he was the expert.

"The way you handled that truck was dead wrong. You've got to stay in control. If I gambled the way you just drove, I'd be dead broke."

I did feel bad, but thought Solly was being pompous. "Solly, aren't you dead broke *now*?" I asked.

He blew me off. "I meant *dead broke* as a way of making a point. As I was saying, you have to keep your impulses in control. If you do, the car will follow. Never squeeze that wheel. Hold it like you would a baby. Be gentle. If you choke up, you'll kill the car and the both of us. When something crazy comes down the road, take it easy, take it *real* easy."

I liked that phrase and repeated it several times before Solly started to instruct me again. "Turn the steering wheel gradually away from oncoming traffic. Don't yank it at the last second. Start turning early. Be prepared. Don't panic. Take it easy. Oh yeah, and slow the heck down!"

I sighed and took a few deep breaths. It wasn't long before my next test. An oil rig was coming from the opposite direction. It was huge like a freight train.

Solly calmly directed me. "There's room for the both of us. Hold your course. Remember to take it easy. If you need to, you can veer to the edge of the road. Now that we're in the city, the roads are wider.

I was convinced he was wrong. "Are you nuts! He'll mow us down!"

"Just hold the road and don't panic."

I did as he said, managing to stay on the road. Afterwards, I said, "You were right. There was room. It's a miracle. Even now, I can't imagine how that worked. We missed each other by inches. I steered her through the little window the truck left for me. This big hunk of steel responded perfectly."

The more I relaxed, the better I drove. Before we got to Boyle Heights, Solly made me pull over. We switched seats and he took the wheel. Within less than a half an hour, Solly parked the Rod on the curb in front of our house. I was tipsy with excitement. Our first day of practice was over. My good dreams were coming true.

Chapter 12

During those first Sunday drives, Solly barked endless commands. "Hold your speed on the straightaways. Accelerate on the turns. Keep your eyes on the road. Listen to me, I'm talking to you! Slow down, will you! You trying turn this buggy over!"

He could only scream so loud. It didn't give him more control. I was the one behind the wheel. By our first ride in March, we were both ready for whatever came our way. On our way home, we slid into a pothole on Sunset Boulevard. I hadn't even seen it. The passenger side of the chassis keeled down and the right bumper scraped the ground. I eased the Rod out of that rut. I felt like a pro.

Solly looked cross-eyed at me, but then caught me by surprise with his words. "That a gal. You rammed your way into the hole. That wasn't good. Then you finessed your way out. That was great. You really showed me how it's done! Don't let up! Winning is about taking chances. Don't ever let your nerves bog you down. Push to the limit. Then push beyond it. You'll make mistakes. Who doesn't."

The Rod and I became partners by the beginning of March. I wanted my partner to be in tiptop shape. "Solly, if you want to go to the limit, I'm going to need a mechanic to put her in shape. We need power. I've got my foot to the floorboards most of the time now."

I expected an argument, but he agreed right away. It was hard to believe that the man in the passenger seat was the Solly I knew. He *agreed*, didn't fight or belittle me. He simply agreed.

The need for a mechanic brought Morrie into our lives. A German immigrant, he had worked at the Mercedes manufacturing plant in Stuttgart before coming to America. He knew cars better than he knew English. His sister Louisa, who was a mail-order bride, came to Los Angeles first to escape the faltering German economy. Her American husband, Harry, worked in an auto-parts store. As more cars took to the roads, good mechanics like Morrie were in demand.

Morrie's mother and father were born in Berlin. Although they would never consider leaving their homeland, protecting their children was of great concern. They wanted Morrie and Louisa to be safe and to protect each other.

When Morrie's boat arrived in Los Angeles harbor, Louisa had cried with joy at his arrival. Immediately, he moved into her tiny bungalow just a few blocks from Brooklyn Avenue. Harry didn't want another man in the house. Louisa barely had room for him. As soon as Morrie found work at a different auto-parts store than the one where Harry worked, Morrie got his own place.

It wasn't long before he wandered into West Coast Dry Goods. Solly was stocking shelves when the bell in the stockroom rang. Solly climbed down the ladder and hustled up front.

"Welcome, friend. I'm Solly Krawiec. First time at West Coast Dry Goods?" Solly grinned his best "happy to meet you" grin.

At six feet, two inches, Morrie towered over Solly by half a foot. His typical Germanic reserve made an immediate impression on Solly.

"Mein name is Morrie Adelsdorfer. *Ich brache* unterwasche. How you say 'under, under trousers, need'"

"Drawers? You mean underwear?" said Solly.

Morrie's pale skin radiated embarrassment. He pulled under his trousers at his underwear.

"Sure, sure," said Solly. "I've got just what you need."

Solly walked back to the stock room and grabbed three pairs of underwear, a package of T-shirts, and a couple of cotton handkerchiefs. Returning to where Morrie stood, he handed him the underwear and lay the other clothing on the counter. "Is this what you want?"

Morrie nodded yes.

"Need a hanky? These T-shirts are on sale. Everything all together adds up to $2.29, plus tax. What do you think? Might as well save yourself another trip and get everything now."

Taking the T-shirts and handkerchiefs, Morrie nodded yes.

Solly pointed to a spot in Morrie's shirt. "You have a grease stain right there. Need another shirt so you can wash that one?"

Morrie coughed and rubbed his fingers together, indicating to Solly he didn't have much money. Solly could tell that Morrie worked with machines from the smudge on his face and the grease on his shirt. "What's kind of work do you do?" he asked.

"I work at auto-parts store. Yesterday, took night job to repair customer car. Learned mechanic in Stuttgart, Germany. You know Mercedes?"

"Humm," said Morrie. "You a trained mechanic?"

"Trained, what mean?"

Solly began to break up his own English to get through to Morrie. "You learned in Stuttgart at Mercedes, how long?"

"Mercedes in Deutschland, my homeland, teach me," said Morrie. "I fix any car *goot*."

"If you worked for Mercedes, you must know your stuff. You must be good."

Solly had never ridden in a Mercedes and wasn't sure if a Mercedes mechanic could even work on a ten-year-old American Model T Roadster like the Rod. "You know American car, the Model T. Roadster?" he asked Morrie. "I have one, and plan to race it. My kid sister's going to drive it in a road rally."

"Your sister driving?" said Morrie.

"Sure is," said Solly.

"Yes, I can work on your car," said Morrie. "I can work on Ford. Nice car, the Ford. "Why your sister racing? Why not you?"

"I gamble. That's how I won the car. My friends don't believe a girl can drive. They' re pigeons waiting to be plucked."

"Pigeons?"

"Never mind that. My sister can drive. Believe me, I've been out with her. She'll beat the pants off these guys if everything goes right. That's why I need you. They're going to bet big time against her when I spring this rally on them. They will give me odds"

"Odds?"

"Never mind. I want my Model T to drive like a German tank, unstoppable." Solly thought a minute. "Well, maybe faster than a tank, but you know what I mean? Can you help? Wait a second, you're not a Nazi, are you?"

"No, not Nazi, left Germany to get away from thugs. But I know German tank. It is very powerful. I fix Model T. When I start?"

"Sunday, you come Sunday to work. Here's my address on Marathon." Solly put a piece of paper in Morrie's hands.

"See you there, Mr. Krawiec. Is it a Jewish name, Krawiec?"

"Yeah, is that a problem?"

"No problem, I have friends in Stuttgart who are Jewish."

"Are they still there?

Don't know. Don't know what happened to them."

"Okay, Sunday then. See you, Morrie."

Morrie came to our house the following Sunday morning. There was a very light knock on the door. "Mama, is there someone at the door?" I said.

"I didn't hear a thing."

"Solly said he was sending someone over to work on the Rod. Maybe that's him. I'll get it." I had been cutting carrots and chopping onions with Mama. My eyes were still teary from the onions.

Solly had reached the door before me. "This is Morrie," he said. "He's here to see the car."

"Hi, nice to meet you, Morrie. I'm Bella." I extended my hand, saw that half the kitchen cuttings were on it, and pulled it back as Morrie put out his. He scrunched up his nose. Embarrassed, I said, "So you're the mechanic."

"Yes," said Morrie. " I'm German mechanic. Know cars. Solly told me you drive car in race, mean rally."

I nodded, looking into the bluest eyes I'd ever seen, and suddenly conscious of how I must look to him, covered with food.

As Solly, Morrie, and I walked out to the street to examine the Rod, Mama came out to the front porch. "Kids, come eat your breakfast. Hotcakes are getting cold. Tell that nice young man to join us."

"Will you join us, Morrie?" I said, repeating Mama's request.

"Me, eat here?"

"Yes, Mama insists."

Morrie followed me inside without a word. He sat down at the dining table and Mama placed a stack of blueberry pancakes before him. "Mama, this is Morrie," said Solly. "He's going to help us fix up the Rod for our rally."

"Nice to meet you, Morrie. Better eat those pancakes quickly before they go cold."

Morrie grinned at Mama. "She is beautiful, very, very beautiful."

Mama beamed. "Yes, she is. My daughter has a gorgeous face."

I flushed. "No Mama, Morrie was talking about the car. He thinks the Rod is beautiful."

As Morrie ate, I noticed his biceps bulging out of his T-shirt. Maybe the shirt was too small.

Morrie couldn't wait to start work. After breakfast, he and Solly went back outside. I helped Mama clear the dishes, then joined them. Morrie had opened the Rod's hood. He pointed at the transmission. "Problem not engine, it transmission."

Solly leaned over to me. "Go inside now. I need to talk to Morrie about his fee."

I walked inside and watched them through the living room window. Solly was animated. Morrie stood with both arms crossed. He just listened.

Solly wrote something on a piece of paper and showed it to Morrie. There was a handshake and that was it. Up to that point, I had not been that interested in boys, but found myself thinking that Morrie was very handsome.

Chapter 13

Morrie returned to our house at exactly six o'clock the following Tuesday evening. Solly wasn't home. As usual, he was playing cards. I answered the door.

"Is Solly home?" asked Morrie.

"I'm sorry, Solly isn't here."

Morrie seemed to be struggling with what to say. "Is … is he coming? Did he … change mind? Is tonight problem? I can go if … should I work on the car … the Rod?" He studied the floor as he spoke. I stepped out on the porch and told Morrie to follow me. I couldn't believe that Solly would have forgotten about asking Morrie to come over. Somebody needed to take charge. I was that somebody. At the curb, I pointed to the Rod.

Morrie went to his own car, pulled out wrenches, a flashlight, and a platform slider. He returned to the Rod, sat down on the slider, and rolled himself and his tools underneath her. I watched him. After a few minutes, he popped out from under the car. "Need parts for clutch. First, I replace bearings, then work on transmission. It take several day's work to get her in shape."

He put his tools back and rolled his shirt sleeves down. He looked ready to leave.

"Wait, you don't have to go yet," I said. I've driven her for more than a month. I can point out a few problems you need to look into. Let's take her once around the block, okay."

Morrie stammered. "Ah … ride … is alright without Solly?"

"Don't worry, I'm in charge now."

Morrie opened the driver's door for me, jogged around to the passenger side and jumped in. When I pressed on the gear shift, it fought back. I showed him, and he nodded that he understood. When I pressed the gas pedal, the Rod crept forward and then sputtered into a smooth roll.

"Cam worn," said Morrie.

I didn't know what he was talking about, but nodded my head anyway. Turning the corner, I shifted into a higher gear. Morrie crouched down and watched my foot on the pedal, then quickly returned to a sitting position. I made two right turns, and we were back on Marathon. After I parked, Morrie hopped out, mumbled something about all the parts he needed, and ran to his car.

The next morning at breakfast, I mentioned Morrie's visit to Solly. "Where were you?" I asked. "I showed him the car. He said he would come back Sunday with some parts." I didn't dare tell Solly that I had taken Morrie for a spin. He would have blown a gasket. He might even have fired Morrie, holding him responsible.

Solly gasped. "Oh man, I screwed up. I forgot that Morrie was coming. Did he go nuts?"

"Heck no. I took charge." Since I was worried that Morrie would show up with parts for problems he hadn't discussed with Solly, I added, "While he was here, I complained that the clutch always sticks and that it's hard to get into first gear. It didn't adjust right on my last drive. He said he'll bring parts Sunday. Will you remember to be here on Sunday, Solly?"

"Sure, I'll be here. Next Sunday and every Tuesday and Sunday from now on, I'll be here. I won't miss a day. I want to win this race. I want that car in winning condition."

Feeling more like a big sister than a little girl, I said, "Don't you worry, Solly. We're going to win. You, Morrie, and me, we're all on the same team."

By April, it was clear Morrie needed a long ride to test the Rod's performance. I convinced Solly to let me drive, with Morrie as a passenger. "I'm the one driving in this race," I said. "Morrie's the mechanic. He's got to get on the road with me. That makes sense, doesn't it?"

Solly said he wanted to get the Rod in race condition first, so over the next few weeks, Morrie adjusted the carburetor to increase the air intake and increase the fuel burn rate. He worked on the transmission so the gears meshed. He greased the bushings, the wheel hub, spindle end, and bearings. Solly worked alongside Morrie and got his hands greasier than he liked. I stood close by, ready to hand them the right tools. I listened to their car talk and piped in when I could. It was hard to understand Morrie, but I liked watching him work.

April turned to May. Summer came early. In Los Angeles, summer meant sunlight until after eight o'clock in the evening, with temperatures in the eighties. Mama would make fresh-squeezed lemonade to cool us down as we worked.

Solly and Morrie took their shirts off to beat the heat. Morrie was light skinned. His white stomach turned pink in the California sun. Sweat dripped down his chest. I asked Frieda and Pearl their thoughts about Morrie.

"He is strong," said Frieda, "a little too strong and muscled for me. I don't know about his freckly skin. He burns fast. Guys like that often have a temper. He's a foreigner, doesn't speak English well, really not one of us. Maybe he is not so smart. He's no Clark Gable." Then she would back pedal. "But he seems like a nice man. I like him."

Pearl's impression was more favorable. "Morrie is beautiful. If I weren't in love with Jack, I'd go for him. He's quiet. Don't know what's really behind that easy-going smirk of his. Frieda's right, he has a quite way. He'll never be a great talker, but he certainly is a hard worker. And those muscles! Poor speaker or not, at eighteen, he's a man, tall and built."

If it hadn't been for Jack, Pearl might have taken a shot at Morrie. But Jack offered all she needed, and, most important for Pearl, he was a lot of fun. "I love Jack," she would say. "I do. I really love him!" Pearl always repeated herself to make a point. She would then look at Frieda, and both of them, in unison, would say to me, "Don't go there! You're too young."

Summer turned to Fall, and Morrie and I finally got to take the Rod out for a drive. As I reached the countryside, Morrie opened up.

"Solly's car is a *wunderbar* !" he said. "Can't believe it! Mercedes built first and I always thinked they were the only great car. But Ford is *goot*. Shits well on the road.

I laughed. "Morrie do you mean to say *sits*, not *shits*?"

"My English not so *goot*, how you say it? Sits, yes, that's what I say."

"No you said *shits*. Never mind, maybe I misunderstood. I'll help you with English and you can help me with car talk, okay? Tell me about Germany. Why did you come here?"

Morrie wasn't exactly a chatterbox. Until that moment, Morrie hadn't said much to me beyond car talk. I thought that maybe he was self-conscious, afraid to make a mistake. Then the spigot opened. "Germany not so *goot* now! My *vater* used to own garage. Now he digs ditches. Mama used to work, but now women not allowed to work. *Der fuhrer*, Hitler, says he puts some people to work, but no one in neighborhood makes enough to eat. I send money home. My *mutter* writes back. She says it's *goot*. I think not! I am afraid for them. Afraid of Hitler."

I wanted to know more. I didn't' understand what Morrie had told me. Pa always said not to say bad things about our government, but Morrie said terrible things about his homeland. I could tell he was afraid.

I couldn't help but recall our last Passover Seder. That night, as was our tradition, Pa read from the *Haggadah*:

*The God of the Hebrews hath met with us; let us go, we pray thee, three days'
journey into the wilderness, and sacrifice unto the Lord our God, lest He fall upon
us with pestilence or with the sword.*

Then, he made the passage from the Passover story relevant. He said
there was talk at *shul* from those who had families in Germany of people
beaten with clubs by the gestapo, the security police. "German Jews are
today's Egyptian slaves," he said. "This Hitler hates the Jews. He wrote his
Mein Kamph with an assassin's pen."

He told us that, not two thousand years ago, but more recently at the
Nuremberg Rallies, how Nazi Party conventions stripped citizenship from
German Jews. Pa called Hitler a monster and said he not only took away
the citizenship of German Jewish families, but robbed them of their right
to work, their right to live freely in German society, and their right to marry
other Germans. Pa was screaming by the time he told us that German Jewish families were stripped of everything they had earned over hundreds of
years. He shook his head fanatically and yelled that some Jews even gave up
their Jewish identity, some married out of the faith, and some changed their
names just to survive. Some of those who had married Christians lost their
families. He said Hitler wanted to erase Jews forever.

When Pa finally calmed down, his voice softened and he took a deep
breath. He spoke solemnly, like he was praying. "*Gut in himmel*, they will
need another Moses."

Solly said Pa was telling another *bubbe-meise* to teach the lessons of Pass-
over. "It couldn't be. You're making this up, right? It's the twentieth century.
Are you telling me this German chancellor woke up one day and decreed
Jews had no more rights?"

Pa's face turned red when Solly said this. He seemed to enter his own
head as he spoke. "Solly, *nisht ein a piste kayleh*, a simpleton. It's worse.
Hitler, the *nisht good-nik*, grabbed all the power. He is now the supreme and
only power in Germany!"

Solly was angered by Pa's comment about being a simpleton. As usual,
he had another angle. "If it's that bad, why don't the Jews move to another
country?"

Pa cackled and spit flew from his lips. "You don't know what it is to
move the family around the corner, let alone to a new country! When your
mama and I came to America, many on the boat didn't survive. Your mama's parents sent her away. Tears puddled beneath their feet as she and I
walked out the door. You know how she gets when we talk about the homeland. Her parents wished for her a better life. They and their parents were

born and raised in Poland. They grew like Mama's garden out of the soil of Poland. Even if they wanted to leave, getting a visa would have been next to impossible. After days and days on that shipwreck, we arrived in New York. There it was no good, so we moved again, to St Louis. We had nothing but a few gold rubles in our pockets. Hardly enough for a *blintz*. I spoke but a few words of English. Who could I do business with? I stuck to my own kind. We helped each other. Worked our fingers to the bone. You don't know what it's like to, as you say, move to another country. You, who mill with lazy hooligans, drive fancy cars, and spend your nights gambling, you ask why not move! What do you know? Nothing, I say. You know nothing!"

Pa stood, nearly knocking over his chair. He continued to scream at Solly so loud, I think he woke the coyotes who slept in the hills. I feared he would have a stroke. "Life is not so easy," he said, his head shaking like a madman. "No matter how hard you work to get ahead, you never ..." Pa stopped in midsentence, turned on his heels and stomped upstairs. Solly scratched his head and walked out the front door without a word.

During our next drive, I asked Morrie if it were true that Jews couldn't be citizens in Germany.

"I shouldn't talk ... about German Jews."

"Do you have something against them?"

"No ... nothing against ... Jews. Some friends ... some family ... are Jewish."

"Are you were Christian?"

"Yes I am ... Christian ... now."

"*Now*. What does that mean? Why do you say *now*?"

"My *vater* and *mutter* told me not to talk about what was."

"Morrie, what are you afraid of?"

"I'm afraid for them. Don't want them hurt."

"Them? You mean your friends?"

"Ya ... no, I mean my parents."

"Who could hurt them? You can tell me. I can keep a secret."

"My *mutter* and *vater*, they still live in Germany. They are Jewish. I was born Jewish."

"You were?"

"We had no choice. My *vater* came home from work. As we ate *schnitzel* and *spaetzel*, my favorite, he tell us *der fuhrer*, Adolf Hitler, speak against Jews to big Nazi crowd. My family, like many other Jewish families, live long time in Berlin. Hitler say Jews no longer welcome in Berlin, no longer welcome in Germany. It make no sense. There are many German Jews. *Vater* afraid for Louisa and me. He sells garage to a gentile. We move outside of Stutgart, where no one know us. *Vater* look in the United States papers and find American who wants German bride. He send Louisa off to marry man none of us ever see. At first she says no. Then *Vater* tells her we have to change our names and go to church. Louisa goes before we change name. Mama cries for days. She just sit in chair, shake her head, and wail. I am told keep secret from everyone, even those I trust. *Vater* hoped Hitler and Nazi party be voted out. There was talk, but Hitler, he gets something passed that shut down Reichstag. He become leader of Germany. He build war machine. Say he make jobs for Germans by putting them in Army. It never get better while I there. I work for Mercedes in Stuttgart. Louisa sends money so we can come to Los Angeles. My *vater* no longer could work. Still he refuses to leave Germany. He sends me away to be with Louisa. Sometimes, even here, I think walls have ears. I am afraid what will happen to them if the Nazis find out. There are German spies here. When Solly tells me he is Jewish, I don't believe him. Thought it is trap. Louisa showed me letter from *Mutter*. She said *Vater* has gone *meshugas*. He acts like crazy man. Mama says she stays with him all day and night, hoping Hitler will go and *Vater* will get better. They never come now. I am afraid. I am so afraid."

I almost drove into a ditch, startled by the extent of Morrie's fear. "I'm sorry … I mean, that's horrible! You had to leave your family to get away because you are Jewish!"

Morrie stiffened in the seat beside me. I didn't' think he meant to spill the beans like that. I put my hand on his forearm, then quickly pulled it away.

The weather was warm when we started our drive, and I had put the top down. Now, a surprisingly cool breeze swept over my face. By the time we reached the country roads, it was downright cold. I had hung a woolen sweater on the back of Morrie's seat. "Can you hand me the sweater over there, please?" I asked him.

As he turned toward me to reach for the sweater, I hit a rut in the road, which jostled Morrie, causing him to reach toward my lap to regain his balance. Luckily, he didn't jar me too much. I was able to hold the car steady. Morrie looked embarrassed as he slid back into his seat.

"I sorry; try to get sweater and then knocked you. "I sorry. Forgive me?"

I could see he was uncomfortable. "Don't worry."

Within in a few minutes, the little wisps of white clouds that had trailed us all the way from home turned into black menacing clouds that crowded the sky. Rain drops fell on my head. Soon, it would pour. I slowed and pulled off the road under a huge walnut tree. Morrie and I jumped out of the car to get better protection from the thick green leaves that covered the tree's branches. No matter, rain now poured through the branches onto us. I was suddenly soaked and cold. "Morrie, you still have my sweater in your hand. Please give it to me." I shivered. "I can't stop shaking!" I said, through quivering lips. Morrie started to hand me my sweater, but it was soaked. He tried ringing it out, but in the pouring rain, it was no use. I was getting colder by the minute. I nudged closer to him. His arms surrounded me. I thought about pulling away. It was no use. I pulled closer. His long arms protected well. The chills I had been feeling turned to excitement.

For a moment, Morrie seemed surprised at my response. He started to pull away, but seeing clearly that I liked his hug, he tightened his awkward clutch. Strands of my wet hair fell against his chest. I reached up to brush the hair away, but ended up with my fingers on his lips. I could no longer resist the urge. We kissed, but immediately backed away from each other. The rain turned into a drizzle as we trudged through the mud, back to the car. He pulled a work rag from his pocket and placed it on my seat so I wouldn't have to sit in a puddle. I positioned myself behind the wheel. To keep the Rod from forming a ditch in the muddy ground, Morrie found a broken branch that lay near the tree. He used it as a lever. The Rod's tires swam back onto the road.

We didn't talk during the drive back home, When I pulled up in front of the house, the passenger door opened, and without saying a word, Morrie walked over to his bike. He turned and looked at me with puppy-dog eyes, then pedaled away.

The silence was eerie. I ran into the house in what felt like slow motion.

"Bella?" said Mama, walking out of the kitchen.

I didn't answer. Instead, I looked down at my muddy shoes, which I had forgotten to take off before coming inside. Then I ran to Mama. "I'm sorry! I … forgot to take my muddy shoes off … and … tracked mud inside. Morrie and I … we got caught in a rain storm."

Mama smiled. "*Kinahora*, you are dripping wet. Go now. Take those wet clothes off before you catch a death of cold." She looked over at my shoes. "Don't worry about the rug right now. Go dry off and get new clothes on."

Mama had been cooking dinner. She returned to the kitchen as I walked into my room. The bedroom window revealed a sky that was now crystal clear. I was amazed how clear everything had suddenly become. I took off my clothes and dried myself with a towel in front of the floor-length bedroom mirror. I stood there naked for a few minutes, staring at my body.

Mama's voice came from the kitchen. "Are you dry yet, Bella? Come and taste this hot matzo ball chicken soup I just made. It will fix you right up."

I dressed, walked into the kitchen and slurped up an entire bowl of Mama's soup. When I was done, Mama nudged me and asked me to follow her upstairs to her room. I wondered what was going on.

Once upstairs, she asked me to stand on her bed and pull down the ladder from the attic trap door. I did. She instructed me to climb up and grab the wooden crate marked with Polish writing. I did as she asked and lowered both myself and the crate to the bed. Inside the crate was a quilt. As Mama unfolded it, first a countryside, then an arrangement of tiny village scenes, were revealed in the weave. Mama told me this was the Polish village where she was born.

"Bella, it's Pa's birthday," she said. "You should wish him well on this birthday. He has done so much for us. It's my mama's birthday too. I'm homesick for her. That's why I made her famous soup. When we came to America, I wrapped many things in the *Dziennik Lodzki,* the local newspaper. There were many pictures of the town where I was born. I copied my favorite scenes into weavings and sewed them onto this quilt. I want you to have it so you never forget. Don't worry, I have other things for your sisters. You are the youngest, and I want you to remember what our lives were like before."

I held the quilt tight and kissed Mama's cheek. She walked me back downstairs to my room, where I placed it at the foot of my bed.

That night, I couldn't sleep. The scenes of Mama's hometown, sewn into her quilt, were so peaceful. I knew that Mama and Pa had left Poland to find a better life in America. Mama's quilt reminded me that I was a first generation American, lucky to be here.

The following Tuesday, when Morrie came back to work on the Rod, I kept out of his sight. After he left, when Frieda and I were in our beds, I told Frieda I needed to talk to her.

"Is it important? I'm tired."

"I think it's important, you may not. It's about the Rod."

Frieda stared. "Shouldn't you talk to Solly about that? I don't know how that thing works."

"No, I need some girl talk. You know what I mean."

She sat up in bed. "Is it Morrie?"

"Yes, that's it. On Sunday, I pulled over during our drive. I had to stop because it was raining. I brushed up against him and then there was a peck on the lips."

"He kissed you?"

"It didn't last long."

"Solly should fire him."

"Hold on, will you. It was a tiny kiss and I kissed him back."

"You … you kissed him back? How tiny a kiss was it?"

"Really, it was nothing. It ended before it began."

"If it was nothing, why are we talking?"

"Well … ah … even though … you know…"

"No, I don't know. Get it out! What the heck are you trying to say?"

"Well, it really was … I mean … not long. Oh heck, it felt like a lifetime!"

Frieda fidgeted. Older sister or not, I knew she had never been kissed. My face flushed like a beet.

Frieda's eyebrow arched "What else?"

"Nothing, I swear. We locked eyes, that's all. Then there was silence all the way home."

"And … in the car … what happened in the silence?"

"Nothing! I swear! Nothing. We didn't touch again. We sat apart."

"And?"

"I can't get him out of my mind."

"Well, you've sure spent a lot of time under your new quilt just staring at the walls lately."

"When he came over on Tuesday, he kept looking at my bedroom window while he worked. I could tell because I peeked out a few times."

"Now I understand why you didn't run out to help him. You're frightened of him, aren't you? Do you think he will hurt you?"

"No, of course not! Frieda, I kissed him first. We were face to face, about an inch apart. I touched his lips and then I kissed him. I was the one. It is my fault."

"Do you really, really want my advice?"

"I think so. It depends. Alright, what is it?"

"Stay the hell away from him. I told you already, you are too, too young and men … well … you know."

"I know you're right. But he comes here twice a week."

"I'm warning you, Bella, keep your distance. Does he need you to help?"

"Solly says he knows his stuff. He doesn't need me to tinker with him or the car." I bit my lip. I had already said too much. "Good night, Frieda."

Chapter 14

O n Monday morning, I awoke early enough to catch Solly before he left. "I want you to drive with me on Sunday," I said.

"Of course. I need to show you some things anyway. You aren't going to learn what you need to know from that mechanic. I can't go every Sunday. I have to work. So, you'll have to rely on him sometime. But time is ticking away. I can show you how to take those turns. I'll go with you as often as I can. You're going to have to be good, damn good!"

I couldn't stop thinking about the "mechanic," as Solly had put it. I was in love. Right or wrong, Cupid had touched me. I tried to stay busy with my schoolwork. I desperately needed the distraction. I heard Morrie had taken a third job working on another car. That meant his days were spent at AAA Auto Parts and Tuesday nights were reserved for the Rod. I was impressed by how hard he worked. I knew he was sending money to his parents back home.

Solly told Morrie that he wouldn't be needed on Sundays for a while. It felt strange having Solly beside me in the passenger seat again. It was hot that first Sunday, maybe ninety degrees, and the winds were howling by the time we reached the outskirts of downtown Los Angeles. In Southern California, these weather conditions were referred to as a *Santa Ana*, and I knew the winds could get treacherous, sometimes gusting at over fifty miles per hour.

By the time we were on the open country roads and headed east, I was swerving over the road like a drunken sailor. "I can't hold the road," I yelled at Solly. Although he was sitting right next to me, I could tell he couldn't hear me. The winds pounded. Instinctively, my grip tightened around the steering wheel. I tensed. Solly was shockingly silent. The Rod swerved across the divided highway. The wind flipped flying dirt and debris into our faces. I had goggles, but they weren't designed for the crosswinds, so my vision was clouded by whatever blew in from the sides. I jerked the steering wheel so as to keep my 1,500-pound monster on the straight and narrow. The wheels spun as I hit the sand piles. I couldn't gain traction. I muscled my way out several times. Then I hit a ditch. At first, I couldn't jerk out of it. My wheels squealed but remained stuck. Finally, the Rod lurched forward and out of the rut.

Down the road, the winds worsened. I lost sight of the road all together. Tiny tornados swirled. I nudged the throttle to reduce the gas flow, engaged the clutch, hit the brake and levered back into neutral. I stopped in the middle of the road. The Rod idled. Dust covered the windshield. It became an opaque wall. I coughed to expel the dirt that blocked my nose shut and clogged my throat. I gasped. It was impossible to talk, let alone breathe.

"What are we going to do?" I screamed at Solly. "I can't see. I can't hold the car. I can't drive this damn thing."

I could tell Solly was affected, too, maybe as scared as me. I wanted to be safely home, comfortable under my quilt. Finally, Solly was able to force the car door open after several tries. As he inched his way around the car's body, his jacket opened like wings of an airplane from the gusts. His hat blew off and sailed a hundred yards down road. When he reached the driver's side, he pried open the door against the gusts. It almost slammed shut on his fingers. I scooted over as he finally made it inside and got behind the wheel.

He shifted into first and made and U-turn. The road leading us back to downtown Los Angeles was littered with leaves, tumble weeds, trees twigs, and whatever other debris the winds had managed to capture along the way. When we reached the downtown area, it was shrouded in dust. Typically, we would have been able to see the peak of City Hall. Not only did we not see City Hall, we couldn't see any buildings. We were less than twenty miles from home. We took the southern route because the Santa Ana storms were blowing northwest.

The closer we got to the city; the more polluted the air became. My head was spinning. I thought I might pass out.

"You look horrible," said Solly.

I coughed. "I'll be okay. Just get us home."

After nearly an hour, Solly turned slowly onto Marathon from Waterloo. I couldn't stop coughing and it was hard to breathe through my nose. I wondered if I would suffocate. I couldn't help but be morbid.

When Solly parked the Rod in front of our house, I didn't think I had ever been so happy to be home. I had survived.

I fumbled with the passenger door. As I stepped out of the Rod, my knees caved as my feet hit the ground. My chest felt like all those twigs that were flying around had settled inside. I coughed. Rocks cracked themselves against my chest. Hunched over, I plodded up the front porch steps. As I entered the front room, Pearl and Jack were cooing at each other and didn't even notice me. I stumbled into the bathroom, wet a cloth and laid it onto my face. I cupped my hands several times, filling them with cold tap water and pouring it over my head. My coughing persisted. I wiped my face with a wet towel, which turned black from the sludge on my face. I caught a dollop of yellow phlegm with a tissue as it oozed out my nose.

Mama must have heard me because suddenly she was standing at the bathroom door. "*Gut in himmel*, what happened to you? *Nisht, nisht*, you need hot water, not the cold. Heat, you must use heat to clear the congestion. That yellow phlegm means infection. Here, honey, take my arm, I'll help you to bed."

Once I lay down, Mama placed her handkerchief on the nightstand. Still coughing, I sat up, grabbed the hanky and tried to catch what came up. I watched Mama wobble out of the room on her tiny feet. After a few minutes, she returned with Lipton tea and eucalyptus leaves in a steaming hot water bottle. "Drink this tea," she said. "It'll help break up the congestion."

Sitting up, I sipped, then sunk back on to my pillow.

"You're home now, sleep, *mein shayna maidel*."

"Thank you, Mama." I coughed again. More phlegm came up. I caught it just in time with Mama's hanky. "Hurts. It hurts!" My heart raced.

Mama put the back of her hand on my forehead. "You're burning hot. Lay back, rest." Mama wrapped a towel around the hot water bottle and placed it on my chest. "Breathe the eucalyptus. Take little breathes. Don't try too hard." She kissed my forehead. My nose puckered. My heartbeat slowed. Exhausted, my head fell deeper into my pillow as my eyes slid shut.

Chapter 15

I slept until noon on Tuesday, over thirty-six hours. It did me good. I got out of bed, dressed, grabbed a book and walked out to the front porch. I grinned. I had proved I could handle the Rod, even in near-blind conditions. I had held my own for most of trip. This must mean I had the gift.

Sitting down on the porch step, I opened my novel and read until the daylight started to fade. When I looked up, I saw Morrie pedaling toward the house on his bicycle. He had come to work.

He looked over at me. We hadn't spoken for days. None the less, I hadn't been able to stop thinking about him. "Hi Morrie!" I said, as he dismounted.

Morrie eyes sparkled at my friendliness. "It's been a while," he said. "Can we drive together on Sunday?"

I smiled. "I'd like that. I'd really like going with you." Mama called. "Got to go now. Mama needs my help in the kitchen. See you Sunday."

After Morrie finished his work and pedaled away, I approached Solly. "Morrie needs to see the results of his tinkering. He should ride with me this Sunday. You okay with that?"

Solly was no dummy. He knew I was hooked. "Okay, go with the *goy*. No hanky panky. I don't want to have to break you two up before the rally." Solly didn't know Morrie was Jewish. There was a lot I hadn't told him.

The following Sunday, Morrie came early and prepped the car. By nine o'clock, when I came outside, he was sitting in the passenger seat waiting for me. When he saw me, he scrambled out and sprinted to the driver's side to open my door. I got in.

Luckily, we escaped town before the Sunday traffic and were soon driving through wide-open spaces, filled with citrus and nut groves, east of Los Angeles. I stared at the road ahead, but couldn't help sensing Morrie's closeness.

"Sounds *goot*," said Morrie. "Clutch glides."

We approached the walnut tree that had inspired our kiss without comment. I strummed my fingers on the wheel and Morrie fidgeted in his seat as we passed. After a while, I stopped at a fruit stand along the side of the road. We bought strawberries there, which we ate while driving. When I turned back toward Los Angeles, it was mid-afternoon. A chill filled the air. I asked Morrie to hand me my sweater. When he passed it over to me, our fingers touched. I couldn't help myself. I turned off the main road and parked the car. Before I had turned to face him, he gently touched my cheek with his grease-stained fingertips. Then his lips were on top of mine. His arms stretched around me and I returned his embrace. We held each other tightly, kissing and touching. He began to unbutton my blouse. I resisted. He was gentler than I had imagined. He slid away. We were not ready, and we both knew it. Morrie settled back into the passenger seat. Neither of us spoke a word. I turned on the engine, pressed the gas pedal, shifted the throttle, and drove the Rod back onto the road. It was now dark, and I could barely see in front of me.

Morrie motioned to me. "Stop, must light headlamp candle." I pulled over and Morrie got out. As he got the headlamps working, I admired his bigger-than-life shadow on the road.

Once we were back on our way, I followed the light projecting from the lamps as I drove. The air was cool but fresh, very fresh. "Smell the strawberry fields, Morrie?" I said. "The fruit must be growing everywhere."

Morrie nodded. I felt his hand on my shoulder. I stiffened. "Morrie, please don't. Look, this has to be our secret, okay. If Solly finds out, he'll be furious. Do you get it?" I sounded just like Solly, so insensitive.

Morrie's face started to twitch. "Was I bad?" he said.

"No, you were wonderful. But I'm afraid of my brother, what he might do if he finds out. Don't even ask me about my Pa."

"Why?"

I didn't answer right away, but before we reached Marathon, pulled over once again. "Morrie, listen to me, you don't know Solly. Believe me, he is not nice. He takes after my Pa, who can be really awful."

When we pulled up to the house, Solly and Pa were on the front porch. Pa *never* sat on the front porch. They both stared at Morrie. Pa screamed as I opened the car door. "It's eight o'clock. Your Mama is upstairs, *meshuge* with fear. Where've you been? What no good has come to you? I don't want any *bubbe-meise* from you."

I tried to smile. "Pa, I'm so sorry. We had car trouble and were stuck on the roadside for over two hours. Not to worry. Morrie fixed it."

I could see that Solly didn't want to stir Pa further. Looking at Morrie, he sent the conversation on a detour. "Was it the engine?"

"Yes, engine got overheated," said Morrie. "I will work on radiator next Tuesday. Bella drove fast, maybe too fast. Had to let cool down. Had no extra water. My mistake. I am sorry. I should have water all the time. Must plan ahead. Maybe put in new engine with bigger valves. The Rod is *goot*, but not ready for all that speed."

Solly nodded. His car was safe, and so was his driver.

Pa appeared to believe our story. "Oh," he said. "Well, thanks, I'm glad you were with Bella. I wouldn't have known what to do. Will it cost much?"

"Will get parts from my store wholesale. I can fix cheap. Don't worry."

"Money, that's something you men can discuss. I'm tired and hungry." I walked up the porch steps to go inside, but turned at the front door and saw Solly walking toward Morrie. They spoke for a moment, then shook hands. I went to the window and watched Morrie get on his bike. He was whistling as he pedaled away.

I had missed dinner. Mama gave me split pea soup that was still hot.

"You should sell that car," Pa said to Solly, as they walked into the kitchen. "It's the store you should pay attention to, not car races."

"Pa, we have more business than Joseph the haberdasher and Marco the cobbler. My car is not the problem. It's that damn credit policy you started back when you thought this depression would be short-lived. I won my car fair and square and I'm going to keep it until I'm ready for something bigger. As far as the store is concerned, business will come back and so will the cash."

Pa pointed a finger at Solly. "Cash, what do you know from cash! You spend today what you expect to win tomorrow. If the cash doesn't come, we'll all be in trouble."

"Look Pa, I worry even more than you do. Believe me, I know we need cash to pay the bills."

Pa started to stomp out of the kitchen. I kept my eyes glued to my bowl of soup, eating slowly, relieved that Pa was leaving the room. Mama was toasting me a piece of rye bread, but jumped when Pa turned around and said, "Mama! Schnapps! I need a shot now!"

"Not now, Pa. I am making toast for Bella."

Pa's presence filled the room. Mama and I froze in place. Pa went off. "Sure as my name is Krawiec, my boy is going lose the business and everything I spent my life building. My God, woman! I need a drink now. Do you understand me?"

I knew I had given Mama a real scare already, being gone all day. She was in no mood for Pa's threats, too. "Just calm down," she said. "We're out of schnapps. Now that you're a man of religion, you are spending too much time with your head in the spirits. Solly will bring home schnapps after work. Now, go back to the living room and sit down."

I stood up, walked over to where Mama was standing, and hugged her. She was a saint. A wrinkled, hunched-over, constantly-getting-shorter saint, but a saint, still the same. She had raised six children with little money and no help from Pa. He was hardly ever home anymore, except for *shabes* dinner on Friday nights. Why couldn't he be a human being, a *mensch*, tonight? Mama looked like she had seen a ghost when I walked through the front door earlier. She hadn't said a nasty word, just asked, "Bella you must be starving. Can I get you some delicious pea soup?" She was the peacemaker. Her callused, gentle hands had rubbed the pain out of our necks when we were sick. Who had taken care of her?

For the next two weeks, Morrie worked on the Rod's engine. "Look, new valves and all new hoses to the radiator." Morrie turned on the engine and pressed down onto the pedal while she was in neutral. The Rod roared like never before. "The car ready, she runs *goot*."

Morrie asked Solly for $100. "I got parts wholesale. I don't even charge you for my work."

"A hundred dollars! I wasn't expecting it to be that much." Solly then turned the conversation in a direction I wasn't expecting. "Listen to me, Morrie. You're an immigrant, an escapee from Hitler's chaos. You're lucky to be here and luckier than most to have work. I'm an American Jew. Your people destroy my kind, and then you escape and come work for me. Imagine that. The money you spent on that trumped repair will have to wait. I don't want to hear any more about it. I don't have that kind of money. Why do you suppose I'm promoting this rally? I need the money. Bella has to win. Like it or not, your income, like mine, is now part of her victory. No victory and there will be no money!"

I was standing on the porch. I didn't think Morrie even noticed I was there. He stood his ground with Solly, but looked really confused. Then, he turned, got on his bike, and pedaled off.

"Why did you treat Morrie like that?" I said as Solly joined me on the porch. "He was just trying to help. He did the work. He should be paid."

"Paid with what, my good looks? Look, honey ... I mean Bella, you're going to have to win this rally for me for anyone to get paid. Besides, just so you know, I don't like Germans. You've heard what Pa says. What they are doing to our people in Germany is an abomination. Morrie's working class.

Those are the people, the working class, who think they deserve a paycheck. They put Hitler in office.

"Solly, but ..."

"No *buts* about it. I have to live with this dinosaur Pa calls a business and strung around my neck. Pa's brilliant strategy of extending credit has blown up in our faces. We're owed a lot of money and not one customer has a penny to their name. Not one. Can you believe it? We gave loans to a bunch of deadbeats. At this rate, our store will be long gone before we get any of our money back."

Desperate to raise cash, Solly put our scheme into play at his next poker game. Jerry, the guy who lost the Rod to Solly, had started betting again. "Solly, how's my car doing?" he had asked Solly.

"She's wonderful. I'm happy to be her owner. I've hired a top-notch German mechanic to push her to the limit."

"*Her!* You call that car a *her!*"

"Yep, she runs like a filly at Santa Anita. I named *her* the Rod. I'm sure *she* is much faster than when you owned *her*."

"Well," said Billy, "that's nice you've given *her* a name. But, the Rod, as you call it, is yesterday's news. Just so happens my dad got a big bonus at Kaiser Steel and the first thing he does is get me a better car. You should see it. It's lighter and faster than that *tin lizzy* you snaked from me. It can take your piece of junk any day."

"Ha! You're dreaming," said Solly. "I'll bet my little sister could drive the Rod and beat you."

"Solly, you're nuts," said Jerry. "Your little sister, what is she, a rally driver or something?"

"As a matter of fact," said Solly, "she wants to be the first women rally driver."

"Gee whiz," said Jerry, laughing. "She must be quite a gal. I suppose after she becomes a women rally driver, you're gonna run her for president of the United States."

At this point, the other players at the table were following the exchange with growing interest. One of Solly's friends, Frank, made a proposal. "Look here Solly, how about each of us take fifty bucks of that action and give you ten to one, just to be kind."

Jerry took the bait, as Solly had expected. "Look, I'll give you twenty to one on a hundred bucks, that is, if you've got a hundred bucks to bet."

Solly rocked in his chair like he was trapped and scared. "Okay, I mean, if you really want to bet against my sister. Oh heck, I'll take all comers. You're on! We'll rally!

Solly hadn't expected so much to be wagered on the rally. He also knew he needed a big win. The next day, he took $25 from the cash register at the store that he needed for that night's game. He won a few bucks that night, and in the weeks that followed. When he lost, he cooked the books. Then he would overcharge unsuspecting customers to make up the shortage. Of course, that only worked when they paid cash, which was rare. To cover his bet, Solly went to Harry, Mickey Cohen's enforcer, for a loan. Having dealt with Harry before, Solly did not consider failure to win the rally an option.

A couple of weeks before the rally was scheduled to take place, Solly suggested a route change to the other players. He'd upped the bet with money borrowed from Harry. The addition to the route included Turnbull Canyon, something he didn't bother to tell me until the following Sunday, before our final test drive. Turnbull terrified me. When Solly told me about the change, my lower lip about dropped off my face. I felt nauseous when I took my seat behind the wheel.

"Bella," said Solly, "you need to drive to Painter Street, then to Beverly, and take the hills into Turnbull Canyon."

"Why did you change the route?" I asked. "I've never been in Turnbull before."

"Look, Turnbull Canyon will set Jerry, the coward, on edge. Besides, the Rod travels better than other cars on dirt roads. Trust me, Jerry will turn into a nervous Nelly in that canyon. He'll either slow down, and you'll beat his time, or be stupid and speed through the turns. If he does, he'll lose control of his car and slide off the road. Believe me, he knows nothing about driving mountain roads. He's a city boy. You'll speed up on those turns 'cause you know how to take them."

I stared at Solly. Everything he said about Jerry was just as true about me.

"Look," said Solly, "let's talk about the route. You'll get onto Alvarado, then go past the cathedral on West Temple. You know the one. From there, you'll go through Boyle Heights. The Heights will be loaded with people running every which way across the street. You'll head southeast toward Whittier College. From there, you drive into the mountains to Turnbull Canyon. Look, Bella, I wouldn't have suggested this change if I didn't think you could handle it. Come on, prove to yourself there's nothing to fear. What do you say?"

The idea that Solly and I would see the canyon together made it *sorta* alright, or at least, that's what I told myself. I nodded and started the engine.

"That a girl," said Solly. He grinned, pointed ahead, and off we went.

The roads were clear and I was able to take advantage of the added power that had come about because of Morrie's work on the engine. I had her up to forty miles per hour on Sunset. "Hey, you're speeding," said Solly, "take it easy. I want you alive for next week."

I was definitely in control. A driver passed me. I pressed on the gas and passed him back. The look on his face was to die for. When a jack rabbit ran out, I crushed it with my front bumper.

Solly barked at me about messing his bumper. "Why'd you do that?"

"If I stopped at this speed, I would have hit it, then skidded right off the road. You can't stop a two-ton buggy in less than four hundred feet."

"How'd you know that?"

"It's in those books I've been reading, the ones about driving. Maybe turn a page or two. It'll do you good. I know plenty, buddy boy. I want to win. Don't you?" I was always amazed how driving the Rod boosted my confidence. Maybe Solly knew this, too. Maybe that's why he wasn't afraid of what I'd be able to do in Turnbull Canyon. Maybe Solly knew me better than I knew myself, at least when it came to the Rod.

"Win?" he said, answering my question. "Damn right I do! You're a smart little cookie, sis. You've got spunk! Can't wait to see you take out that rube, Jerry."

Secretly, I hated killing the rabbit, but I'd never let that secret be known. Besides, I liked how Solly responded to my attitude.

Solly had checked his old railroad pocket watch when we left the house. He counted the minutes to the cathedral, Boyle Heights, the Home of Peace Cemetery, and the train station. We passed Pio Pico State Historical Monument. We were moving. Solly didn't call out the time. I kept my nose to the wheel and eyes on the road. I was completely focused on the job I had to do. We passed Whittier College on our way into the Santa Monica Mountains, home of Turnbull Canyon.

As I started climbing, Solly asked how I was feeling.

"I feel fantastic. Never better! I'm ready. I'm really ready." I repeated something that I had written down to prepare myself for the rally. *I'm the driver. I'm the one. I'm the best. This is going to be real fun!* In the back of my mind, this little chant was becoming automatic. As I drove, I recalled Pearl telling me about an insane asylum for teenagers somewhere in Turnbull Canyon. She said they did something called electroshock treatments there.

I imagined kids sticking their fingers in electrical sockets and the hair on their head springing straight up like Alfalfa in the *Our Gang* movie. I continued to chant, *I'm the driver. I'm the one. I'm the best. This is going to be real fun!* Off the side of road, I thought I glimpsed some kind of building, maybe the holding tank for those kids. Didn't see any of them. Not a sole. *I'm the driver. I'm the one. I'm the best. This is going to be real fun!*

"What the ..." Something seemed to be caressing my hair. I shrieked at Solly. "Stop it!"

"Stop what!"

I glanced down and saw that his hands were in his lap. My imagination must be playing tricks on me, I thought. Ghosts don't come out in the morning. Ghosts! Pa called them *dybbuks*, demons that settled into the bodies of humans. Stop thinking so much! I told myself. *I'm the driver. I'm the one. I'm the best. This is going to be real fun!*

The road came to a dead end. I slowed and made a U-turn. I could see the steep canyon wall that extended beyond. Solly pulled his railroad watch from his back pocket. We'd been driving for two hours. *Not bad time, not bad at all.*

Now we were on our way back, descending out of the mountains. After about fifteen minutes, we were out of the canyon. I felt my chest loosen. I heard Solly take a deep breath. That brat, he was scared, too.

Exhausted, I eased off the gas pedal. "You okay?" I asked Solly.

"If I wasn't okay; do you think I would tell you?" Solly grinned. I don't' think I'd ever seen him look that happy. I grinned back. The rest of the route flew.

When I pulled in front of the house, Solly looked down at his watch. It lay on his lap between his legs. He bent over and studied it like I'd never seen him study anything before. "Two hours out to the dead end in Turnbull Canyon;" he said, "but less than four hours to complete the entire route. Pretty damn good, I'd say. Pretty damn good for a girl."

Sure enough, he was right. Making sure I was familiar with the course would prove to be a big advantage. Now all we had to do was wait.

I was very fidgety the next few days. I couldn't contain myself. Morrie came over for a final Tuesday engine check. He didn't talk about the money issue and seemed distant. I didn't say anything. Since our kiss, he had acted confused. Maybe he thought that once I completed the rally, I wouldn't need him anymore. I had other ideas.

Solly stayed home every night that week. It was funny having him around so much. Every night, like clockwork, he asked the same question. "How you doing tonight? Good, I hope. Not getting cold feet are you?"

I always gave him the same answer. "I am fine. Don't worry. I'm as solid as rock."

Jacob Pearlstein had been given the job as stakeholder. Solly and the other guys agreed that once the money was in, the rally would take place, rain or shine, starting at nine o'clock sharp on Sunday. Of course, Solly never asked what I thought. As agreed, Solly and Jerry had personally delivered the money to Pearlstein. Solly had marked the route on a Gillespie road map of Los Angeles.

The roads would accommodate only one driver at a time. The rally was to be a time trial, just like the ones in Europe. According to the rules, if either car broke down, or the driver quit, then the opposing driver was the winner by default.

The day before the rally, I was reading on the porch when Morrie came by. I hadn't seen him since Solly made such a fuss about the money Morrie spent fixing up the Rod. "Here to check on Rod," he said. "She has to be perfect, really perfect. How you doing? It's been a while since ..."

"I'm doing good, really good. Can't wait for tomorrow. You think everything will be okay? I mean ... really okay?"

"No worry, Bella, you're beautiful. Mean Rod is beautiful. Mean you're beautiful, really beautiful."

I laughed. I could tell Morrie was embarrassed. He tried to smile, but couldn't get his face right. He turned and went to work on the Rod. I watched him for a while, then went inside. I didn't want to get distracted, not now.

At dinner, that evening, Solly pulled me aside. "Are you ready?"

"Ready, never been more. Thank you. Thank you. Thank you. I really mean it. I'm so excited I could pee. Thank you for letting me drive your car. This rally is important. It's important to both of us. For me, it's a beginning. For you, it's a means to an end, cash to get ahead. I am ready! I'm ready. I'm so ready!"

Even though Solly was a gambler, he had no intention of leaving this particular gamble to mere chance. He had too much at stake. He winked at me and whispered into my ear. "I'm glad you're raring to go. If things don't go our way at first, don't worry, kiddo, I've got a few tricks up my sleeve."

I believed in myself. Still, I understood things could wrong. Rally cars often broke down. Engine issues, fuel and air-mixture problems while climbing, dust in the carburetor, broken axles, all and any of these could knock out a good driver. And then, there were road and weather hazards. It could rain. The roads could be slippery. I tried to put all this out of my mind. I wondered what trick Solly had planned. I didn't want to know. I wanted to drive. I couldn't wait.

Solly had bought me racing goggles and a leather racing helmet. That night, before I went to bed, I put on the goggles and headgear. In the bathroom mirror, I studied my face. I looked like the picture of DiPaelo. But the reflection in the mirror wasn't DiPaelo. It was me, Bella. I was the driver!

I removed the goggles and headgear and got into bed. I sat down and closed my eyes, trying to visualize every inch of the road, every turn, every rut, everything that mattered. I picked up the DiPaelo book by my bedside and read like it was a roadmap of my future life. It was chilly, but I didn't notice.

Chapter 16

I awoke race day morning with a start. I was ready. I was anxious. I couldn't wait for the day to begin. I tiptoed out of my room in my pajamas so as not to awake Frieda, who was snoring. Not even Mama was awake.

In the kitchen, I toasted a piece of rye bread and covered it with cream cheese and strawberry preserves. It was six in morning. I wandered onto the front porch. I could see the day was going to be clear. I paced back and forth. The porch moaned under my feet. I sat down, then got up again.

It wasn't long before Solly came out to join me. I told him I wanted to be alone. Surprisingly, he listened. He and the rest of the family had breakfast while I stood next to the porch railing staring at the Rod.

Jerry showed up at a quarter to nine, fifteen minutes before start time. He wasn't what I expected at all. He looked like a kid in tenth grade with short red hair and freckles. He walked right up to the foot of the porch steps. "So you're the skinny kid I'm racing." He had three other guys with him.

I was determined not to let him get to me. "You must be Jerry. Solly told me the Rod used to be yours. Too bad you lost it. She drives like a dream."

"Funny, I was thinking it would be your biggest nightmare," he said.

Jerry introduced the other guys, who crowded behind him like they were his gang or something. "This is Malcolm, Zack and Harry." They boys nodded, one at a time. I wanted to giggle but held back. Jerry said, "We're all poker buddies of Solly."

"Oh, I'll get Solly." I started to turn and walk inside. I wanted them to see how in control I was. But Solly was already in the doorway. He joined me on the porch and nodded at Jerry.

A few minutes later, Jacob, the stakeholder, pulled up on a bike. He would double as the starter. Jacob explained he had overslept. He sprinted over to Jerry and tapped him on the shoulder. Jerry turned around, as did the other guys. They gave Jacob a blank look. Jacob didn't look like he enjoyed facing all four of them. "It's … it's time. Are you ready to get started? I mean, we need to get started, okay.

Jerry looked at Jacob with contempt. "Are you kidding, I've got a date for lunch. You're late! I thought you'd never get here." Jerry turned and strutted to his car with the rest of his gang marching right behind him.

Jacob looked at his watch and screeched up at me on the porch like I was five hundred yards away. "How's about you, Bella, you ready?"

"I'm ready. I've can't wait to get on the road again. It's a beautiful route!"

Jerry craned his neck around. I was hoping that he would realize that I wasn't the novice I appeared to be. He and Solly had just drawn straws to determine who got to choose their starting position. "Honey, want to switch positions?" said Jerry.

Solly had won and he chose to start after Jerry. Hearing Jerry's proposition, Solly shook his head at me, warning that I shouldn't say a word. "What's your story, Jerry?" he said. "Trying to get the best of my little sis before the race?"

I walked down to Solly and the boys. "Don't worry. Nobody's going to get the best of me!" I turned and looked up at Jerry. He was about a foot taller than I was. I had a smirk on my face. "I am happy to follow you out. I'll catch up soon enough. Then you're welcome to follow me home, in case you get lost."

Jerry spit on the ground. Jacob stood in the center of Marathon and pulled up a pocket watch that hung from his suspenders by a chain. In his other hand were green and white flags. He raised the white flag five minutes before start time. "Prep your engine, Car 1."

Goose bumps rose on both my arms and I wrapped one around the other so no one would see me shiver. Jerry stepped up on his running board and plopped down into the driver's seat. His boys took care of all the preparation. I listened to his engine. It sounded loud, louder than the Rod. Jacob raised the green flag and began to count. After sixty seconds, the last minute of the countdown, he threw down that flag. "And, your off!"

Jerry rolled into the road, picked up speed by his first turn and was soon out of sight. I suddenly had a moment of doubt. My early-morning cream cheese and preserves rose up to my throat and found their way into my mouth. I thought I would wretch, but held it. Was Jerry's loud engine truly as powerful as it sounded? He did have a newer car. Would I remember everything I had learned, or go blank? What had happened to all my confidence?

I tried to pull myself together. With Jerry's fifteen-minute head start, I expected to be behind him for the entire race. I didn't have to finish in front of him, just in less time than it took him. With the possibility of other vehicles, pedestrians, and animals on the road, I did not want to add the hazard of the two of us jockeying for position.

I got into my car. Solly made sure she was ready. Five minutes before my start time, Jacob raised the white flag high above his head. "Car 2, prep your engine!"

Solly checked the fuel and kicked the tires. Then he leaned inside. "Bella," he said, "now's your chance. Show those guys what you've got."

Jacob raised the green flag and started the countdown.

I knew a good start was important. Before Jacob had finished saying, "Now you're off," I was in first gear. Before the flag hit the ground, I had rolled into higher gear.

I headed northeast to Sunset and made a sharp right turn southeast, toward the cathedral. I struggled to keep my eyes on the road. Thoughts about what I needed to do and what could go wrong filled my head. My eyes darted everywhere and nowhere. By the time I calmed, I had passed the cathedral. It was named after a lady saint.. I could have sworn she smiled at me.

Currents of wind, blowing in every direction, attacked the Rod. I was driving slower than on my practice run. Or at least, it seemed that way. I reached Boyle Heights. Down the center of Brooklyn Avenue, four guys had created a production line so as to pass huge sides of beef to a kosher Jewish deli. I came to a stop until their traffic guard let me pass. I wondered if Jerry had to stop, too. Finally, after two minutes, I was moving again, though seemingly at a crawl. The road was so crowded. I moved like a snail. One greasy-looking guy, with an ugly scar on his cheek, walked out in the road, stopped right in front of me, stared and winked. I ignored him. That was the last thing I needed was some ugly, old guy ogling me. I tried to slip through the opening on the other side of the street. When I jerked the steering wheel in that direction, a huge truck headed toward me. I swerved back to avoid a head-on collision.

Finally, after about five minutes, I was able to edge forward with the traffic until the road cleared, and I could accelerate out of the Heights. I had lost a lot of time.

As I turned right onto Alameda, someone screamed. "Jerry is thirteen minutes ahead." I didn't take time to look, but knew it was Morrie. Wow, I'd gained two minutes on Jerry. I guess he'd gotten caught even worse than me.

I steered south on Soto and then made a right turn toward Montebello. I was now in the countryside. The wind was behind me, and I picked up speed. My helmet and goggles were doing their job, keeping the sand and wind out of my eyes. Jerry had not been wearing goggles. If he was getting pounded by the wind like I was, he needed them. I realized something else. Jerry's car, a sedan, was lighter than mine. In these winds, the Rod's weight gave me an advantage.

Suddenly, I saw something that caught my attention. An old Chinese vegetable vendor, sporting a *Fu Manchu*, pressed his two horses into a gallop, coming toward me. His cart was empty. I pulled off to the side of the road, giving him room. He gave me a toothless grin.

As I approached Whittier College, Solly's current girlfriend, Sue Ann, dressed like she'd just left one of the clubs, ran into the street. I didn't like her much and saw no reason to stop. She screamed. "Jerry passed me ten minutes ago. You're gaining on him. Go girl!" As she pushed both arms up into the air to cheer me on, her skirt rose up to the top of her thighs.

I was thrilled at the news about Jerry. I made a sharp turn on Painter Street, causing the car to skid, its rear end sliding on the road as the engine pulled the back tires through the curve. *Wow! That was good!* If I'd eased off during the skid, I might have stalled. I never let up on the gas pedal. My hands remained loose on the wheel, just the way Solly coached me.

I was now surprisingly relaxed. At Turnbull Canyon, the road turned to dirt. About a mile into the canyon, I saw squash, lettuce, turnips, carrots, and cucumbers strewn all over the road. I was thrown off focus. It was too late to slow down and swerve to the side, so instead, I accelerated, never once touching the brake pedal as I smashed piles of green beneath my wheels.

I kept my eyes glued to the road, my confidence growing as I navigated every curve. At the turnaround point, I checked the pocket watch Solly had given me to gauge my rally time at this specific spot. During the trial run that Solly and I had made together, it had taken me two hours to get to the top of Turnbull. I was ahead of my previous trial time. I was holding my own. So was the Rod.

I thought about all the work Morrie had put in to make the Rod go faster. I imagined him cheering wildly for me as I turned onto Marathon, his long arms reaching out to me. I urged my thoughts back onto the road. It seemed I was out of the canyon in no time at all.

At Painter, there were a few girls who looked about my age, waving as I drove by. Sue Ann must have mentioned to them that I was in a rally against a boy. "Go Bella! Go! Go! Go!" Chills crept down my spine. Inadvertently, I gunned the engine. The Rod lurched forward. I scared myself half to death. For a moment, I thought the Rod might break down.

I passed Whittier College, heading west this time. The winds were behind me now. When I got to Pio Pico, I knew I was three quarters of the way home. It had only been thirty-five minutes since the turn at Turnbull. Boyle Height's Sunday traffic better not slow me. I'd done everything right. I couldn't lose now! I counted in my head. I was making good time, much better than my trail run.

I pushed the gas pedal to the floor all the way up the hill, on to Soto, then back into Boyle Heights, where hungry, mid-day crowds milled on the sidewalks eating pickled herring from barrels and pretzels hot off the grill. Traffic slowed again, but this time not so bad. I noticed a girl from school and her boyfriend sharing a pistachio ice cream cone, trying to keep the ice cream from dripping on them in the mid-day heat. It seemed like everybody was out, enjoying a lazy Sunday afternoon. The Russians, the Japanese, and even the Pachuca girls in their dresses, so tight they had to take baby steps to avoid tipping over. Their hair rose high above their foreheads. I liked looking at them as I slowed to a crawl. They were so different.

Street vendors with potato *knishes* and Canter's pickles ran right up to me. My stomach growled. I was starving. "Ready for a *nosh*?" they said.

I smelled the cheese in the *knishes*. "No, not now!" I said, realizing I needed to move faster. "Please get out of the way. I'll come back another day." Then I added, "I've got a race to win right now. Go away. Just go away!"

On the way out of Boyle Heights, I saw one of Solly's sleazy friends chuckling with the Chinese vegetable cart vendor at the end of Brooklyn. The vendor excitedly thrust his hands in the air as if he were telling a tall tale. What was one of Solly's friends doing with that guy? Was he the one who filled the road with vegetables? Where was Jerry? I should have caught up with him by now.

Chapter 17

As I turned toward into Echo Park, I saw Morrie five hundred yards ahead. He sprinted toward me, breathing hard. "Jerry off … off road … car broken … stuck edge of … cliff."

I pressed on the brakes, slowing to a sputter. "Was he hurt?" I asked.

Morrie grabbed onto my driver's door, swung himself around and ran slowly alongside me. "No, not hurt. Really mad! Skid on vegetables. Skid off the cliff. Car's a wreck. Caught rock that stopped his fall. Car stuck halfway over cliff.

"Oh my God. But he's not hurt? That's good!" I tried to stand up, forgetting I was still inside the Rod, which was still in gear. I quickly hit the brake and stopped in the middle of the road. There was a car behind me, which almost plowed into me. The driver started screaming, and Morrie yelled back at him. "My girl just won a race. You wait a minute. You just wait. She start again in minute."

I realized I still had to finish to win. I was smiling. Morrie had called me his girl. I pressed the starter button, and then the gas. Morrie started jogging alongside the Rod, then fell behind me. Within fifteen minutes, I saw the finish line. I had won!

Solly had a cocky smirk on his face as I reached home. I had finished three hours and ten minutes after I started. Not bad, considering I had come to a dead stop in the middle of Boyle Heights both ways. My pace had been faster than Jerry's before his car broke down. I parked and climbed down from the driver's seat with my arms raised high into the air. Solly hugged me first. Then, Mama, Pa, and the girls came up to me and I was in the center of my very proud family. I had no idea how tired I was. Mama ran her hands on the back of my neck, comforting me, as usual. As we stood there, hugging one another and talking, I saw Morrie come running toward us, gasping for air. I remembered how he had called me his girl, and ran over to him. He kissed my forehead and hugged me tightly, too tightly.

Solly wasted no time collecting his bet from Jacob and driving off in the Rod with Malcolm and Zack to help Jerry.

The next few hours were a blur. I sat on the porch with Frieda, who went on and on about how proud she was. "You beat that boy. Amazing!" By dusk, Solly, Billy, and the other boys were back. Billy's car had to be towed. At our celebratory dinner that evening, Solly fidgeted like a ten- year-old boy. Mama beamed. *"Altz iz gut.* It's good! You are the female maven of race car driving."

I was disappointed. I wanted to defeat Jerry, but Jerry had beaten himself. It didn't take long, or much food, to get over my disappointment. Once I saw the flame on Mama's bundt cake to celebrate my victory, I lit up. As soon as I blew out the candle, Solly got up from the table. "Sorry to break up the party. Got see a few friends before my date with Sue Ann."

After we had eaten, I offered to do the dishes, but Mama told me I had done enough. Pearl, Frieda, and I got up from the table and went to my room, still savoring Mama's cake. As the three of us *kibitzed*, Pearl turned the conversation to Morrie. She was blunt.

"You're in too deep. Morrie's a mechanic. He speaks broken English. He'll probably never have *bupkis.* He'll never have enough to take care of you. He's a grown man. You're still a young girl. He's is a *goy*, not one of us."

I felt my chest tighten as she spoke. "He doesn't *have* to be the one of us, but he is."

Pearl looked confused. "He's what?"

"He was born Jewish, and I care about — "

" — You'll get hurt," said Frieda. "Wait awhile. I'm afraid for you."

"What do you mean he was born Jewish?" said Pearl. "If he was born Jewish, then he is Jewish."

"What I mean to say is that he was afraid … of being Jewish … in Germany. It's a long story and I'm too tired now."

"He converted? Is that what you mean? He was Jewish and gave it up? That's worse than never having been. That means he's like those glassy-eyed people out front of the Amy Semple McPherson church near Echo Park. How could it be that he converted?"

I was truly exhausted and wanted the lecturing to stop. "He just did. Now stop talking about him, about me. I want to go to sleep."

"Look Bella, I still think you're in too deep," said Pearl. "Just slow down. Enjoy your victory. Bask in the glory. God knows, I enjoy being in the limelight. Right now, no girl in this town can match you. There will be many boys, and later men, who want you. You don't need Morrie. He's handsome, no doubt, but he's only a mechanic. You're smart. You've got potential.

Believe me, I know the consequences of getting caught up with the wrong people."

"Pearl's right," said Frieda. "You're smart. *Far vus*, why do you need the aggravation of this German? With war in Europe, who knows what will happen to him? Maybe his parents will make him fight for Germany. Who knows?"

"I know Morrie. He'll never go back. He told me he hates Germany and what Hitler has done." I grabbed Frieda's and Pearl's hands and held on tightly. "I need him. He is older. So what? Maybe it's wrong. I don't know. It's what I want. I go after what I want."

Pearl shook her head, got up from my bedside and walked to the door. Then she turned back. "We're not done with this. I'm not done with you, Bella."

Frieda lay down and buried her head in her pillow. She fell asleep, without another word. Soon, so did I.

The following Tuesday evening, around five, Morrie came by. I recognized his knock and was first to the door. My heart beat through my chest when I saw him standing there. "Hi Bella," he said. Solly home? I come for my money."

Solly wasn't home. He had left Morrie's money in an envelope with me. "Morrie," I said, "the Rod was perfect. What you did to it was fabulous. Wait here a second. Solly left you an envelope with the money. I'll go get it." Morrie smiled. I noticed that there was no grease under his fingernails and his hair was neatly combed. I'd never seen him so groomed before.

I went to get the money. When I handed him the envelope, he didn't open it to count the bills inside. His eyes avoided mine. "Can we take a little walk into the park?" he said.

"Sure," I said, finally getting him to look at me. "But it has to be quick. It's getting dark. I guess you deserve a few minutes of this famous rally driver's time." I giggled self-consciously.

No words were spoken until we turned the corner at Marathon. Once we reached the crest of the hill, we could see boys and girls paddling together in tiny row boats and the white swans gliding around the lake. Morrie pointed. "There's a lake not far from my home in Berlin that's pretty like this."

I turned my head toward his voice. Our eyes met. He took my hand. We walked down the hill toward the park. A crowd of people stood in front of Amy Semple McPherson's church. A tall, smiling man, about Morrie's age, came over to us. "Are you coming to hear Reverend McPherson preach?" he said.

Morrie looked down. I spoke up. I had too. "No, we didn't come to hear her speak. I am Jewish and Morrie is something else."

"A Jew and something else," said the man." Perfect, please join us. If not now, then soon. As a Jew, you certainly know Jesus. He was a good man. Reverend Amy will help you understand his teachings."

Morrie pulled my arm to urge me away, but I felt I needed to say something. "I don't believe as you do," I said. "I'm glad you have found a place that makes you happy."

The man wasn't giving up so easily. "Still, come next week," he said, "and see for yourself. Preacher Amy preaches peace of mind. Come. You will see."

Morrie pulled me to his side and looked the man straight in the eye. "Bella is a Jew. Her religion is enough. You believe Preacher Amy. Is *goot*. Bella no need your church to be happy. We leave now. Understand? We not come next Sunday. We not come at all. You go, be with your friends, but leave us alone."

We walked away. When we were some distance from the Preacher Amy's followers, Morrie turned to me, "Bella, your green eyes so bright, they glow. His electricity pulsed through my heart. I'd never felt like this before. He led me to the lake's edge, where a graceful white swan floated past us. Those crowding the sidewalk had gone inside the church. It was now dark. I was becoming concerned that Mama would be worried. I hadn't told her I was leaving. Then something else occurred to me. What if my friends at school saw me with Morrie? What would they think?

We turned and started to walk. As we approached the sidewalk leading out of the park, Morrie stopped and turned to look at me. I reached up and touched his earlobe. Morrie's lips separated and came down on mine. It seemed to be over too soon. "We need to go now, okay," I said.

Morrie nodded and we walked quickly up the hill, heading back to the house. As we walked, I heard words I had been waiting for. "Can we ride together on Sunday afternoon? I drive my car."

I nodded. When we got to Montrose, he turned, leaned over and gave me another kiss, this one longer than before. As his lips pressed against mine, I heard a noise, opened my eyes, and, in the distance, spied a silver coyote looking down at us from the hillside. He made a bloodcurdling cry. I had seen coyotes before in the neighborhood, but had never heard this frightening sound. I pulled away. "Morrie!"

I pointed toward the hills. He twisted around so he could see. The coyote was gone. Morrie took my hand. I realized how safe I felt with him beside me.

We continued walking toward the house. There were no more blood-curdling sounds. When we reached the front porch, I unclasped my fingers from Morrie's and turned to him. I touched his chest. My fingers slid down toward his belly, almost instinctively. Embarrassed, I looked up at him. "Sorry, I didn't mean to do that," I whispered. Can we go to Santa Monica beach next Sunday? If we leave by four o'clock and drive out Sunset, we'll see the sun before it falls."

"Sure," said Morrie. "I drive to beach with you." He placed his long arms over my shoulders and around the back of my neck. His large hands massaged my scalp.

"Morrie, that feels so good!"

Hearing a noise from inside the house, I moved away. Morrie dropped his hands. "I pick you up four in afternoon."

I danced my way up the porch steps.

Chapter 18

I waited until Saturday to let Mama know my plans. I pretended they had to do with becoming a better driver. "Morrie wants me to drive his car. I want to be experienced driving as many cars as possible. We're going out on Sunday."

"*Hitn sich far!* Spending time with that man is dangerous. He's German. Do you know about this *dybbuk*, Hitler? The mechanic's not for you. He fixed the car. You won. Now, he should stay away."

"But Mama, he's such a nice man. I can learn from him."

"You'll learn too much. A young girl should not learn too much from a man like that!"

"Mama, I'm going with him whether you approve or not!"

"*Mein kin*, I love you. I don't want you hurt. Let's see what Pa has to say."

At dinner that night, I tried to read Pa's face. I knew Mama must have brought up the subject of Morrie as soon as Pa got home from services.

Before the blessings, Pa drank his schnapps and turned only to Solly for conversation during the meal. Then, without warning, he leaned across the table in my direction. "I hear that crazy German boy wants you to drive his car."

Frieda played with the curls hanging over her ears. Pearl coughed loudly. I could tell Pa was tipsy. I smelled the alcohol on his breath and feared that he would forbid me to see Morrie.

"Morrie knows more about cars that I ever will," I said. "He offered to let me see how his car handles."

Pa wasn't buying. "Show you? He'll show you plenty! I know these young men."

Mama butted in. "Pa, *sha*, maybe this is not a good time to discuss — "

Pa bolted up. His chair fell to the ground with a thud. "Don't you dare give me directions! I am her father. I'll say what I damn well please! You … you let these girls go where they want and with whom they want. What am I, chopped liver? Everyone, the whole damn neighborhood, knows all about our Pearl. Behind my back, they call her a *hur.*. She and her Jack strut around town at all hours of the night. I still haven't lived down her marriage to the *goy*, let alone the divorce. At the synagogue, they murmur when I sit down. I hear what they say. I look like a *schlemiel,* a bungler and a fool. I mourned for her when she left. I took her back. Now … again … with this one."

His index finger pointed at me. The great actor, the king of the Maccabees, was on stage again. "She will not go! Never will I let her go with the mechanic. You … my Mrs. Krawiec … will not tell me how to run my family!"

He stomped out onto the porch. Tears ran down Mama's face. Her mascara smeared. A plate flew at Pa's head. It hit the wall and broke. *"Oy vey,"* she said to Pa, "look what you made me do." She turned and ran upstairs.

Pearl's cheeks, usually red with rouge, now glowed beet red without it. She grabbed her coonskin jacket, popped her flapper hat on top of her short black bob, and bounded out the door.

I was furious. Pa was behaving like a self-serving tyrant. He'd treated Mama like a nobody. He'd belittled me. He'd called Pearl a whore. I got up from the table and went upstairs to Mama. She sobbed, her face buried in a pillow. I put my hands on her shoulders "He should respect you. I hate him."

"Sha!" she said, turning to face me. "He is your Pa and my husband. What am I to do?"

"Mama, he has no right."

"He has every right. He is the provider. We live on his earnings, now his savings. I need him and so do you."

I could tell Mama believed Pa's tyranny and her temper would all be forgotten, like always. It wouldn't be talked about. Maybe I shouldn't have told Mama about seeing Morrie.

The following morning, I called my girlfriend Nina. She wrote down what I told her and delivered a note to Morrie. *Pa blew a gasket,* it said. *Our meeting must be kept secret. Meet me on the corner of Alvarado and Marathon at one this afternoon.*

Pa didn't need to know. Neither did Mama. When I left the house, I told her I'd canceled with Morrie, that I was going with Nina to the matinee at the Rialto.

At a quarter to one, I walked out the front door. The Rialto was a fifteen minute walk from the house. My plan was perfect. I waited until five minutes after one on the corner where we were to meet. A boy from school walked by. I looked away from him. I didn't want anyone to see me when Morrie drove up. My one-inch heels tapped on the cement. I almost turned and went home. Finally, he pulled up. The passenger door swung open. I slid into the seat next to him.

Morrie engaged the clutch and shifted into second gear. We traveled down Alvarado, then up Sunset toward the Coast Highway. I was happy, so happy. I slipped closer to him. He opened up. I listened.

"My *mutter* like your mama," he said. Never stops working. *Vater,* not like your Pa. *Vater,* he is quiet. After he sell garage, he get sick. I think he worry too much. After Hitler took the power, he worry more. Louisa, my sister, beg my parents to send me to America. By then, *Vater* too sick to leave. 'Morrie, go to America,' he tells me. 'Germany no *goot* anymore. Go with your sister in America before it is too late!' My *mutter* stood by him."

Tears filled Morrie's eyes as he spoke. He stared straight ahead, watching the road. "I miss her," he said. "She sweet lady like your mama. Pa knew. He knew I had to go."

We drove past the shanty houses of Chavez Ravine. By the time we reached Sunset, the subject changed and we marveled at the nightclubs we passed. I pointed to one of them. "Look, Morrie," I said. "Ella Fitzgerald and Louis Armstrong are performing tonight."

On the sidewalk, newspaper boys in Baker Boy hats screamed as we drove by. "Get your maps right here. See the homes of the stars!"

"Maybe we'll see Clark Gable or Susan Hayworth?" I said. Morrie had no idea what I was talking about.

Endless long fences protected mansions just south of Sunset in a newly developed area called Beverly Hills. I thought about the fancy parties that must take place in these homes, ladies in long gowns and men in pin-striped tuxedoes sipping martinis poolside. Solly had told me about one party he snuck into. "Everyone looked super!" he had said. "Even the servers, colored men dressed in tuxedos. Can you imagine dressing up just to give some dame a drink?"

We drove on. The temperature dropped. The afternoon wore on. We turned right onto Coast Highway. Suddenly our eyes soaked in ocean waves. The air filled with moisture. Morrie's car slowed as he pulled into the Will Rogers beach parking lot.

I had on a sleeveless summer dress. I thought it would be warmer. It was not. I was freezing. Morrie put his jacket on my shoulders. We got out of the car and raced to the sand. We took off our shoes and grains of unruffled white sand crushed under our feet as we ran to the water. The waves were magnificent. The sun hung low. The water glistened.

Morrie laid a blanket on the soft sand. We sat down beside each other, watching the waves. He pulled out a few black figs from a brown bag and peeled away strips of the dark skin. The stringy sweet insides gushed out. His hand, and a fig with half the skin hanging down, came toward my mouth. I smiled, but didn't part my lips. "Take it, it's so sweet," he said.

I was famished. I grabbed it with both hands, trying not to get its sticky juice all over myself as I bit into it. I handed the half-eaten fig back to Morrie.

"Goot?" He took what was left in one huge bite. What was left of the skin fell to the sand.

We ran to the water to wash off the stickiness. Then our hands clasped together. The crashing waves filled our ears. A melon-shaped sun flamed orange and disappeared into the sea. As we stumbled back to the blanket, I tripped and fell onto Morrie. My body fit into his. His strength pulled me closer. I could feel his heartbeat pounding against mine. The white foam closed in. Moisture settled on my brow.

I started to talk about Pa and found myself growing angry. "He'll never understand," I said to Morrie. "About us, he'll never understand."

Morrie listened intently. Then his lips closed mine. Interlocked, we lay kissing. Our legs intertwined like pretzels. We made love, oblivious to the crashing waves or the blackness that now covered us. The possibility that a passerby might see never crossed our minds. Afterward, we lay quietly in each other's arms. Gradually, I returned to my senses. I untangled our embrace, inhaled the salty air and stood up. The cool air awakened my senses. I was shaking. "We need to go now! Oh my God, it's pitch dark. Pa will kill me!"

Morrie stood. We were covered in wet sand. Quickly, we toweled each other off and walked back to the parking lot. Our lives were changed.

As Morrie drove onto Coast Highway, I fretted about what to say to Pa. "I'm so anxious," I said to Morrie.

Morrie tried to calm me down. "I will speak to your pa. No problem. We speak man to man."

"No! Never! He won't listen. He'll throw you out. I must speak for myself. I will ask Mama what to say. She'll know."

Morrie was not afraid for himself, but for me. "You talk to your mama. She knows best."

I nodded. I needed to talk about something else, anything. "Morrie, tell me what you dream about."

He kept his eyes on the road. "America is business. I want to own business. I want my own garage like my *vater*. Money like gasoline. It useless sitting around, but with it everything goes *goot*. You drive rally. I be mechanic. You be famous." Then he said something that scared me. "I want babies and family of my own."

I looked out the window. We had reached Beverly Hills. I realized I'd never really thought much about having children. I guessed I wanted them, but it was far off, in the future. What I did want was a life filled with something more than what Mama had. "Do not go to my house!" I instructed Morrie. "Drop me off on the corner. Pa must not see you!" I grabbed Morrie's arm. "Please, Morrie, you can't call me. When the time is right, I'll call you."

Morrie pulled to the curb. We lingered inside the car for a few moments. Finally, another car honked. Startled, I opened the door and jumped out without even a goodbye. When I got home, I noticed the lights were out. That meant nobody was home. I hurried through the living room, into my bedroom. I read for a while, then fell into a restless sleep.

Chapter 19

The summer sun burst through my bedroom window a few minutes after six the following morning, waking me from a restless sleep. I tried wrestling myself out of bed. I wasn't ready. I lay back down and thought about Frieda, who would turn seventeen in two days. I tried to focus on how she and I would celebrate. Thoughts about Morrie kept crowding her out. If Pa found about us, I would die. Thank goodness for Frieda's birthday. It will be a good distraction for the next few days.

I yawned. Frieda woke. "Hey girl, it's almost your birthday."

Frieda didn't look happy. "Seventeen, and never been kissed! It sucks. My life is passing by without me. I'll never meet a boy."

"Oh Frieda, don't be silly. Your time will come."

Frieda squinted. "What about you? Do you think Pa will let you see Morrie again? He made such a fuss. I don't know what the big deal is.

"I bit my lip. "Ah … humm … he's … a nice guy. But your birthday is coming up. Let's talk about you."

Frieda stood and walked over to the mirror. She tried running her fingers through her hair, but couldn't unravel it enough to set her fingers free. "Can you believe this rat's nest? Ugg-lee. It's time for a makeover. I think I should cut it short like Pearl. It's my birthday. That's what I want. I want a new do."

I laughed. We got dressed and joined Mama in the kitchen. She started the inquisition before I sat down. "How was the movie? What did you see?"

"I saw *Topper*, Mama. It's about this old codger who lives in a haunted house. Cary Grant stared. He's very handsome. I think Nina's in love with him. I'm meeting her and some other girls for lunch at the Farmer's Market. I've got to go now. Do you need anything? Sorry to eat and run. See you later. Thank you for breakfast."

"No, I've got what I need for dinner. Go, have a good time. I'm making brisket tonight so don't go filling your stomach with too many sweets, okay?

"Sure Mama, brisket, mumm, can't wait!"

I had no place to go, but didn't want to stay home. I decided to go to the downtown library. I needed some time to straighten out my head. I was in love and that was a problem. Pa would not allow it. Morrie was older and

Pa still thought of me as his baby. He didn't want me influenced by another man. And Morrie was new here. He could leave at any time. He was German and not well-liked because of it. Nobody knew he was Jewish.

When I got to the library, I thumbed through magazines, trying to find something to catch my interest, but I was too caught up in my thoughts about Morrie to pay attention. I must have fallen asleep, because it was closing time when the librarian tapped me on the shoulder.

On Wednesday, Frieda's birthday, Mama decided to make chicken-fat-fried liver and onions to celebrate. I walked in on her about four in the afternoon. She was cutting onions. Her eyes were watery.

"Something wrong, Mama? Why the tears?"

She chuckled. "It's the onions, silly. They make my eyes water."

I offered to take over. "Let me do it." Tears soon flowed from my eyes, too. We looked at each other and started laughing hysterically. I loved to see Mama laugh. She so rarely did.

I was famished and grabbed a piece of *challah* bread. I hadn't eaten lunch. After devouring the bread, I decided to read for a few minutes, so went out to the front porch. Pearl was just getting home from work. She gave me a look, and without a word, pointed to my bedroom. I closed my book and followed her inside. She sat down on Frieda's bed. I sat down on mine, next to Mama's quilt.

"Your eyes are so bright, honey," she said. "Have you been seeing Morrie?"

I knew I couldn't lie to Pearl. "You can't tell, not a soul, please promise!" I begged. "Please, please don't tell Pa. If he finds out, he'll kill me."

Pearl moved from Frieda's bed to mine, where she sat down next to me. I felt her hand on my cheek. She turned my face so we were looking directly at each other. She winked. Suddenly I realized that Pearl understood what I was going through in a way that Frieda could not. She reached up and ran her fingers through my bangs, sweeping them out of my eyes. "If you are going to be with men, you must do something about your hair," she said. "I'll take you to Leader's Beauty Salon. It's time you got your hair bobbed. You also need a cute flapper hat. All the girls are wearing them. I'll buy you a silky slip and a dress that shows a little of your figure." She got up and walked over to the bedroom door, but before leaving the room, looked at me and smiled. "I'm going out to the porch for a smoke. Don't worry, I'll explain your new look to the folks."

I walked into the bathroom and looked in the mirror, staring at my long auburn hair. It fell in waves past my shoulders, halfway to my waist. My hair was like Mama's. Hers fell to her waist. I'd never even thought about cutting mine short. Why would I? I had beautiful hair. It wasn't like Frieda's Brillo pad. Still, I wanted to be more beautiful for Morrie. If I were really going with Pearl to the beauty salon, I had to let Frieda know, since she'd already talked about a makeover. I didn't want mine to be a shock.

The following Saturday night, Frieda and I were home, as usual, trying to entertain ourselves. We turned on the radio and danced to Count Basie and the CBS studio band featuring Jimmy Rushing on the Saturday Night Swing show. Pearl had taught us the Lindy Hop. We twisted and kicked our heels back and forth to Basie's jazz beat.

Pearl was out with Jack, and Mama and Pa were next door at the Garfinkle's house, playing Canasta. Solly was probably somewhere he shouldn't be. By eight o'clock, Frieda and I were exhausted. Out of breath, we each fell back and lay on our beds. Frieda was glowing. There was something joyous about dancing, even if it was with your sister.

Thinking it would be a good time to tell Frieda about my plans, I said, "Pearl wants to take me to Leader's Salon on Wednesday to get my hair done in a bob."

"You're getting a bob! But you love your hair." Frieda stood up. "This is out of the blue, isn't it? Does it have to do with Morrie? Is that why you're getting your hair cut?"

She was onto me. "Well ... eh ... there is something I need to tell you."

Frieda was now paying strict attention to my every word. "Look," I said, "Pearl thinks if I change my appearance, Pa will see me as ... as ... older, like you."

Frieda frowned. "You snuck out with him, didn't you? Pa said no! Are you nuts?"

"I had too! He's a sweet guy. I told him I would."

Frieda's thumbnail went into her mouth. She chewed at her nails when she was nervous. "Sweet guy, okay, but what about Pa? No, what about you?"

I tried to stay calm. "I'm okay. We went to the beach. I enjoyed myself. Nothing special happened. Look, this doesn't have anything to do with the haircut. Pearl just thought it was time for a new me. Do you want to come with us?"

Frieda grimaced. "No, I'll wait. No telling what'll happen when Pa sees your new look. He'll know something's up. I'm worried. Aren't you?"

"I not worried about Pa. I can handle him. I'm excited about making a change. I'm kind of anxious too! I love my hair long and wavy. Pearl says I can grow it out again if I don't like it short."

On Wednesday, Pearl took me to Annie, her girl. At the sight of Annie's sharp scissors, I wanted to run. "Don't worry, honey," said Pearl. "Annie knows her stuff."

First, Annie washed my hair with warm peppermint shampoo. Then, at Pearl's urging, I shut my eyes as Annie clipped away. When I opened them, clumps of wavy hair lay on the floor, where I looked first, not having the courage to look at myself in the mirror. When I did, Annie was attacking my remaining stubs of hair with a hot curling iron. She then pulled a beautiful ivory comb from her utility belt. She combed me out and stood back to examine her handiwork. After a few moments, with a certain amount of pride in her voice, she said, "You're done."

"Oh my! I am cute." I studied myself. Short hair made my eyes and lips so big. My new hair framed my face. Before this trance of self-love had overwhelmed me, Pearl handed Annie a dollar bill, put her left arm around my shoulder and ushered me out the front door. We didn't go far. Right next door was Maxine's Ladies Apparel. It was filled with lingerie, skirts, dresses, hats, and silk stockings. Pearl instructed Maxine on what she wanted. A few minutes later, Maxine came out of the back room with her arms full.

"Try these on!" she said.

I picked half of what she brought out and took it to the back of the store, where a velvet curtain provided privacy to customers trying on the merchandise. The slip I had chosen was silk, and it felt cold against my bare skin as I slipped it over my head. The dress came next. I shimmied into it and pulled open the curtain. Through the window at the front of the story, I saw one of Solly's friends. He must have been walking past the store and turned to look in the window just as I walked out. He stopped for a moment, looking straight at me. I stepped back and closed the curtain, hoping to avoid his wandering eyes.

"What are you doing?" said Pearl. "Come out here right now. I want to see you."

I peeked out. He was gone. I opened the curtain and walked out.

"Twirl around," said Pearl.

I turned awkwardly.

"You are the gorgeous! Morrie will love it."

I looked in the three-way mirror. *Was it really me? Could I have changed so quickly?* Pearl stood behind me. I squeezed her hand. "Pearl, you've redone me," I said. "I love you. What will you tell Pa?"

Her eyes rose up toward the ceiling like she was thinking hard. "Don't worry, I'll take care of it. I'll just tell him that it was time for you to grow up."

We caught the street car at Brooklyn and took it to the Farnam exit. We walked up the hill with our bags of new clothes in hand. When we got home, Pa and Solly were in the front room. Pa had an empty glass on the floor in front of him. His eyes were red. Solly's arms were flailing out of control. Neither noticed us as we hurried past them into the bedroom.

Frieda was resting on her bed. She looked like she had lost her best friend. I wondered if she were trying to imitate some look from a scene in one of her movies. It turned out she was upset by all the arguing coming from the living room. She didn't even notice my new look.

"Pa and Solly have been at it for hours," she said. "Before Pa started in on Solly, he bellowed at Mama. She's upstairs crying. Now Pa and Solly just keep at each other. It's just not right! They act like children. They peck, peck, peck at each other, tearing like cocks fighting to the death. Real men don't fight like that. Pearl, you have to talk to him."

Pearl knew it was no use. She ignored Frieda and said she was going outside for a smoke. Frieda wanted to talk some more. I lay my head down and promised to listen, but couldn't concentrate on what she was saying.

The next morning, as I walked into the kitchen to get breakfast, Mama did a double take. "Bella, my *sheyn meydl*, look at your gorgeous face You growed up as I slept last night.

"Pearl took me to Leader's so Annie could bring me into the twentieth century."

Mama *kvelled*, marveling at me. "You are so beautiful. I hope your new face makes Pa smile too!"

I slept over at a friend's house that night to avoid Pa. I called Morrie from there. Hi Morrie, I need to talk to you."

His voice sounded worried. "Everything okay?"

"Yes, I think so." There was a moment of awkward silence. Neither of us seemed to know what to say next. We had been intimate. Now what? I took the lead. "Morrie, I like you, but I need time. I need a break. I need to think. It could be a while. Don't take it wrong. I do like you. I'm just confused. That's all."

"You okay, no problem, time I have."

We stayed apart for four weeks. Frieda and I went to the movies. We went to Hollywood Boulevard. We stood in front of Grauman's Chinese Theater for hours, hoping to see one of her idols. I spent hours at the library, trying to learn more about famous rally drivers. It was a great distraction, but I couldn't put Morrie out of mind.

I also was worried. My period hadn't come. It was usually right on time. I didn't want Frieda or Pearl to know I had missed. Waiting made me cranky.

As the month came to an end, Pearl couldn't figure out what was going on. "When are you going to see Morrie again? Are you embarrassed about your new look? Don't you like it?"

It had nothing to do with my look. I loved it. I just needed time. Each morning, I had *chalushes*, what Mama called nausea.

Solly and Pa left early every morning. Pa had gone back to work at the store to help stir up business. Morrie didn't call. Frieda, Pearl, and I yakked endlessly about dealing with Pa. We didn't ask Mama. We knew she what she would say. "Leave him alone. It's none of your business. He is a good man who gets his nose out of joint sometimes." Mama didn't think Pa could change.

Chapter 20

I felt my birthday dinner would be a good time to talk to Pa. Even Pa couldn't get mad at me on my birthday. Still, I wanted everything to be perfect.

Frieda and I awoke and had scrambled eggs with fried salami and onions for breakfast. We had a big day ahead. As Mama pulled her first batch of powdered cookies out of the oven, she told me she planned to prepare stuffed bell peppers, my favorite. She offered Frieda and me a cookie and we gratefully accepted one each to finish off our breakfast. Other than lemon meringue pie, there was no better desert.

Frieda and I giggled. The sugar had gone to our heads. We hatched our plot. To get Pa's attention, we had to first make him very comfortable. We left the house and hopped the streetcar to Boyle Heights to buy Pa his favorite *nosh*, a potato *knish* and *kishka* sausage. Pa loved knish. We bought the *kishka* sausage at Canter's. It had meat, meal, paprika, and carrots in brown sauce. I hated it, but Pa loved it. I wondered if his grumpy face would light up at sight of his favorite food.

Now that Pa was working again, sales rose, but still no one paid cash. Solly brought home nothing, not even a spare *shekel*. Pa heard at *shul* that Hitler had isolated the German Jews in ghettos. The few rights they had left were erased like they were slaved. Pa worried about what would happen next. His shots of schnapps at dinner increased. He flew off the handle at the slightest provocation.

Since it was *shabes*, Solly would get home from the store at noon. Pa wouldn't be home until well after sunset. During *shabes*, he didn't go to work with Solly. He prayed.

When Solly came through the front door, he looked at me and said, "Happy birthday, Bella. You're looking happy. What's the big grin for?"

"I have a plan for Pa tonight. Please see if you can avoid an argument until after I'm done. It's my birthday. Keeping quiet tonight is the least you can do."

"*Oy vey*, you think you can turn paper into gold!"

I didn't know anything about gold. I thought I knew Pa, though. Frieda and I had brought back Pa's favorite dishes from Boyle Heights. While I was putting them in the icebox for safekeeping, my stomach turned sour. I ran straight to the bathroom. Everything I had eaten went into the toilet. Dizzy, I splashed cold water on my face. This was no time to be sick. I convinced myself that all was well.

I came out of the bathroom, trying to look like nothing was wrong. Mama, who had seen me run to the toilet, wrinkled her nose. "You are okay?" she asked.

"Yep, fine." She came over and hugged me. I was worried she could smell my breath. If she did, she didn't mention it.

"Hope Pa will be pleasant," she said. "Tonight's your birthday dinner. It was so sweet of you to buy his favorite *noshes*. You're a good girl. Pa's been horrible lately. No matter what, don't let him throw you into a tizzy!"

Leaving Mama to finish dinner preparations, Frieda and I left the house again to go to the Poppy Seed and watch the new Marx Brothers movie. Harpo ran around without a word. He was a crackup. Sometimes silence could be more powerful than speaking.

We got home about five. "Mama, do you need help?" I asked.

"No honey, everything is under control."

Frieda and I sat down in the living room. Solly had gone to play his usual game of pool in the afternoon, but returned to the house at six thirty.

Frieda and I went to our room to dress. I wore one of the dresses Pearl had bought for me. It hung shorter and clung tighter than my other dresses. I had little breasts and showed a respectful smidgen of cleavage.

Frieda admired my figure. "You look so … so mature. I know you planned to talk to Pa tonight, but it is your birthday. Wouldn't you rather do it another time? You have such a gleam in your eye. I wouldn't want to see it disappear. How's he going to react to your new grown-up look? Pa doesn't like it when we grow fast."

"I'm not afraid. Our family is like the Marx house. There are lots of people who make noise, but none of us understands the others. Tonight, I'm going to change that. I'm going to make sure that Pa understands me. Pa may look mean, but I know he has a heart. I'm sure he does."

"Pa may have a heart, but he sure has a funny way of showing it. You know he has one way of seeing things and that's his way! Maybe you're going about this all wrong. Pearl and I talked and we know this is all about Morrie. Do you really think Pa's going to be fine with you seeing the mechanic just because you get a new haircut and wear a grown-up dress? Do you think putting his favorite foods on the table will make a difference? I'm telling you, you can't change Pa! You know what I think? I think that German mechanic has messed with your brain. Do you really think Pa will treat you any different than he treated Pearl?"

"Pearl's back home now. I think Pa's learned his lesson. You'll see."

Frieda shook her head. "Bella, what I think is that you're stubborn as Pa. Just mark my words! You're making a mistake."

Frieda and I were the first to sit down at the table. Then Pearl and rest of the family, including Sarah and Kate, their husbands and kids, joined us. Solly came running in from his bedroom before Pa's footsteps could be heard on the front porch. The adults quieted. The front door slammed shut behind him. Mama was laying cups of chopped liver and rye crisps on the table as he walked inside. Pa barked hello as he sat down in the tall walnut chair at the head of the table, frowning at the chattering grandkids.

Mama lit the *shabes* candles and recited prayers. *Barukh atah Adonai, Eloheinu, Vay'hi erev vay'hi voker yom hashish, vay'khal elohim bayom hash'vi'i m'la'kh'to asher asah.* All the girls and women recited the blessing together in English. *"Blessed are you, Lord, our God, sovereign of the universe who has sanctified us with His commandments and commanded us to light the lights of Shabbat Amen."*

Pa sat comfortably, listening. Even the grandchildren were quiet. Pa turned to look at me. For the first time, he seemed to notice my hair. Maybe the new dress accentuated the change. I shifted in my seat, catching his eyes with a respectful smile before he turned away.

Mama's *hadloke*, blessing over the candles, commanded total silence. Her *shabes* chanting was the only time peace and quiet filled our home. Immediately after she was done, Pa's stern voice bellowed. "Bella, who told you it was time to grow up? Who paid for your new hairdo? Where'd you get that dress?"

His words felt like a bear trap. If I responded at all, I feared the trap would snap shut around me. Had he somehow found out about my secret date with Morrie? Was he really going to throw a fit over my new look, which he hadn't even noticed for a month? I forced a grin, rising to my feet, looking over at Pearl to make sure she didn't interrupt. Walking around the table to where Pa was sitting, I whispered in his ear. "Pa, I love that you asked about my new look. I was afraid you wouldn't notice."

At that moment, Mama, who had gone into the kitchen, came out with a platter of glistening baked bell peppers. They were stuffed full with ground beef and topped with black olives and red pimentos. It was clear she had heard Pa's comments about my new look.

"Pa, it's Bella's birthday. Let's not make a fuss, okay."

She sat the platter down and returned to the kitchen. I followed her. She placed her index finger straight up over her lips to remind me that staying quiet was what I now needed to do. We walked back into the dining room, where I helped her serve. Then I returned to my chair. Everyone waited for Pa to start eating. I cut, bit, and chewed in slow motion.

Pearl took the hit for my dress and hair. "Our big-shot rally car driver needed a new look. Bobbed hair is all the rage behind the wheel and on the dance floor. She needed a new, shorter dress. Her hem grabbed the pedals of Solly's car. It wasn't safe. Certainly don't want her to get into an accident the next time she drives, do we?"

As Pearl spoke, Pa's right hand started to tremble. "Rubbish, she's still a baby. When I say she's ready, then, and only then, does she dress and act like a grownup."

Frieda's face flushed white. I thought she would pass out.

Pa continued. "God forbid, she should run off with some bit galoot like that German mechanic. I don't need anyone else around here like you, Pearl." He then turned in his seat to Mama. "Minnie, if you raised these girls properly, I wouldn't have to raise my voice. Of course I know it's Bella's birthday, and that's why I am bringing this up now. I don't want her getting any bad ideas. This family makes me *meshuge.*"

Kate and Sarah rolled their eyes like they thought Pa was nuts. Safely out of the house, with families of their own, they no longer had to take Pa seriously. Mama said nothing, returning to the kitchen for the stew. I assumed she would bring us the cookies too. Instead, she came out empty handed, and as all our mouths fell open, including Pa's, she said, "These girls and Solly were born in the new world. Stop brow beating them. Enough is enough! Be a *mensch.* Do you have a heart?"

Pa's white whiskers seemed to grow a quarter of an inch as he listened, then snarled at Mama. At least, the white stood out. We had all stopped talking. I heard every gulp and every chew made by the family. Pa pounded the table with his fist. The floor vibrated. Frieda started sobbing. Kate and Sarah sent their boys outside. Solly stretched his arms over the table in Pa's direction. Pearl patted down short waves of hair. I scooted my chair back, stood, and looked Pa straight in the eye. "Did you like the *knish*? I bought it special for you."

"For God sakes, Frank," said Mama." You scared us all half to death with your pounding."

Pa stood up, not far from where Mama now stood. He was only two inches taller than her, but might as well have been Hercules. "I will have none of this. All of you, shut up. I don't need your advice! This is my house." He touched his chest as he spoke. "Bella, I am ashamed of you. I don't care whose idea it was to make you something you are not. You think … you think you are now a women because you drive Solly's car against some boys? You are not! You are only as independent as I tell you, when and if I tell you. Go to your room now, Miss big-shot rally driver. Stay in your room until I tell you otherwise."

Looking Pa directly in the eyes, I said, "It's my birthday. Is this how you show your love? I will do and go as I please." As I spoke, my fear of Pa seemed to evaporate. I thought of Morrie, how I wanted to be with him. "I have a man in my life who knows how to show his love. He wants me. You apparently do not. I will not ask Morrie to stay away any longer. I will do and go as I please. You cannot change the way I feel. I am old enough to know what I want and who I am. My German mechanic, as you call him, treats me better than you treat Mama. How dare you scream at her! She works herself to the bone for you. Your only gift to her is grief."

Voices resonated around me. Pa looked like a hungry coyote. Solly's forearms flexed. I wondered if Pa would hit me. Would Solly smack him if he tried?

Pa pointed at me. He shouted loud enough for the Garfinkles next door to hear. "You are no longer my child! Get out! You are no longer welcome in my house! You get nothing more from me! Nothing!"

When he said this, when it became clear from Pa's words that my charm had failed, that I had earned no victory, my confidence left me. The silence in the room didn't seem warm and spiritual like I imagined it would be. It was deadly. Emotionally bruised, exhilaration turned to emptiness. I tumbled, and now teetered, on the edge. Morrie was all I could think of. I ran to my room. Frieda followed. For a moment, I said nothing. I looked at Ma's quilt, neatly folded at the foot of the bed. I remembered the story she had told me about coming to America, how hard the voyage had been. But she had survived. Looking down at my hands, I said, more to myself than to Frieda, "I am hurt. I am sad. But I'll get over it. I am not broken. I'll rally. I just need some time."

Frieda wiped a tear from her eye. "I never thought Pa would kick you out. I can't believe …! What kind of father throws his daughter into the street? What a brute! I can't take any more of it. You and I must move out together."

I sat up in bed. I never would have thought Frieda had the nerve. I started to think. Frieda now had a job at American Telephone and Telegraph as a bookkeeper. With her income and what I could earn, we could survive. We could do it. Morrie's boss had offered me a part-time job after school when he heard about the rally win. But now I needed fulltime work. I would need to quit school, but there was a rainbow in this storm. I would be able to see Morrie whenever I wanted. No more hiding. Would Frieda really move with me? She wasn't independent like Pearl. What if she waffled or decided to move back home? What would I do? I could never move home again!

As we were about to fall asleep, Solly barged into the bedroom. "I despise him! I can't work with him. I can't live with that man. The way he treats us is ridiculous. I should have grabbed that finger he was pointing and bent it around his neck!"

"Solly, stop! Stop now! The family needs you here. You are the other man in this house. Mama needs you here. Don't count on Pearl being around. She'll move out, it's only a matter of time. You just can't go around talking that way. Never let Pa know how you feel about him! He'll just take it out on Mama. Solly, look, you need to stay, because … Frieda and I … we're going to move out. Pa's different with us than with you because we're girls. He treats us like he treats Mama."

Frieda, who was listening, proved herself more practical than I imagined. "Listen, you two," she said. "When I went out to pick up Pa's gift, I noticed there's a For Rent sign in the duplex down the block. If we can rent it, we will not be far. Hopefully, it's not more than $25 a month. With my income, and if Bella can get a job, we'll have over $100 per month. We won't be rich, but we'll get by. Then Bella can see Morrie every day if she wants."

Solly's face was pale. "See Morrie every day! What about school? You can't drop out. You're the only one of us with a brain. Don't sacrifice your life for that tool belt, Bella. Look, with me it's different, I don't have a choice. Pa made the business for me and I took it when I could. I was no good in school, anyway. But you're different, really smart. Morrie's a nice guy. I like him, but he's not for you. He hardly speaks English and he's a mechanic. You can do better. We'll find another way."

I reached down at the foot of the bed and took Ma's quilt in my hands. "My mind is made up. I'll never speak to Pa again until he apologizes. He kicked me out and I need to be free of him. I'll survive. No looking back, that's not for me. Solly, remember when you told me to never look through the rearview, that you can't lead looking backwards. Well, tomorrow, Frieda and I will go to the owner of the duplex and rent that apartment. I will go to AAA Auto Parts and get a job. We may need $100 to get started. Can you help us?"

Solly's expression softened. He kissed my forehead. "Okay, whatever you need. I'll get it for you. I have friends."

My new life had begun.

Chapter 21

The following morning, as I awoke, I heard Mama calling my name. I thought I was dreaming, but when I opened my eyes, she was standing at the bedroom doorway. She was smiling, but it was a worried smile. I rubbed my eyes.

"Good morning sweetheart!" she said. Are you okay?"

"Hi Mama, did you say something?"

"Yes, I asked how you are feeling … after … well, after everything that happened last night with Pa."

"I'm tired, that's for sure. I'll be better once I get going. How long have you been up?"

"Me, I've been up since dawn. I couldn't sleep, not after Pa's outburst last night, and on your birthday, Bella. I thought I'd offer to speak with Pa for you. I think he'll calm down if I can get his attention. Lately, he listens to no one. It's not right. If I have to, I'll hit him over the head with a frying pan."

Frieda, now awake, giggled at Mama's comment. I smiled, but just barely. Mama looked strained, too tense for so early in the morning. I wondered if she was joking about the frying pan.

Frieda entered the conversation. "I don't' know, Mama. It won't be easy to change his mind this time."

I didn't want Frieda to have to tell Mama our plan. "Mama," I said, "you don't have to talk to Pa about this. Frieda says there's a duplex right down the street and we want to move there, the two of us."

Mama's face fell, but there was a look of resignation on her face, like she understood. "I saw that sign myself," she said. "The house is owned by Michael Clemenski. He's a hermit, and you never see him out in the daylight. I knew his mother. He's a strange one. You sure you want to move there? How can that be? Do you have money?

"Frieda has money saved from work," I said. "I can get a job." Mama came closer and rubbed the back of my neck with her calloused hands. "Please don't fret, Mama. Frieda and I will be okay."

Mama nodded. Without a word, she turned and shuffled off. Lying down, I pulled my quilt over my head. I just wasn't ready to get out of bed.

I slept until ten. I hadn't done that in years. Frieda was already up. Forcing myself out of bed, I walked over to the window and pulled the curtains from the bedroom window. Solly and Morrie were standing next to the Rod, talking. I blinked twice. Why was Morrie here? I threw a dress over my head and walked outside in my bare feet.

When Morrie saw me, he walked over. "Solly called me last night," he said. "He told me what happened with your Pa."

I looked over at Solly, who grinned and turned away.

Morrie came closer. "I will take care of you, Bella," he said. "You are strong, but I can help. Mathew, that's my boss, he will give you work on my say so. We will be okay."

Everything was happening all at once. When Morrie tried to kiss me again, I turned away. He looked confused. First, Solly had told him to take care of me. Now, I backed him off. He took a second look at me and walked off.

He mounted his bicycle, but before he could get away, I ran to him and hugged him again. "I don't want to hurt you. All this stuff with Pa makes me *meshuge*. I want to do this on my own. Don't be hurt. I care for you. I just need to do this on my own."

Morrie stepped back, taking both my hands in his. "You don't have to be alone," he said. I will go over to the AAA Auto Parts store later today. I'll make Matthew give you a job." He was off without another word.

Mama always made the best misery meals. After eating her fresh strawberries and a hearty blintz, Frieda and I packed. Haphazardly, I threw together white open-toed sandals, a pair of black and white oxfords, nice black paten heels, two skirts, a couple of white blouses, and my new dress. Misha, the thread-bare, brown teddy bear I got when I was six, ended up in the box with the clothes. I folded Mama's quilt on top. I thought about taking school books but then realized I wouldn't need them. I wouldn't be a schoolgirl anymore. I grabbed a silver hairbrush, my bristle-bent toothbrush and a stick of lipstick. I was done.

Frieda took more time. Her posters, which advertised the up-and-coming movies, would be perfect for the walls in our new place. She had one of mustached Clark Gable and another of Rudolf Valentino, hair slicked back.

Frieda told me she had dreamed about Clark Gable the night before. "Clark leaned over and kissed me. I was Claudette Colbert, sitting in the front seat of his car. His lips were soft and his mustache tickled. His arms stretched around me, holding me so tight I could barely breathe."

Busy packing, I hadn't heard the pitter pater on the roof. It was ten, and before we could move, we needed to be sure we could get the place. I wondered if we had jumped the gun by packing first.

Grabbing an umbrella, Frieda and I ran through the rain five houses down to Clemenski's Victorian. The front door was painted white, but peeling badly. The front yard was completely overgrown with brown weeds. I hoped the apartment would be better than the yard. There were lights on inside the unit to the left.

"Didn't Mama say this guy was always strange?" said Frieda. "Maybe we should have Mama come over here with us. Maybe he doesn't really want to rent it. It could be a ...."

I pointed to the section of cardboard propped up inside the dirty window. It definitely said For Rent. Grabbing hold of the copper lion's hoop nose that served as a knocker, I let it thump the door twice before pushing hard a third time.

"What'd you want?" The man's gruff voice didn't sound friendly.

Frieda looked ready to bolt. I grabbed her hand, making sure she couldn't pull away. We were both dripping wet from standing in the rain. I yelled as though he were half a block away. "Mr. Clemenski, I'm Bella. I'm here with my sister, Frieda Krawiec. We live down the street. Can we talk to you? We want to move out on our own and saw your For Rent sign. Can we see the apartment?"

The door opened. Clemenski was an older man, maybe thirty. His hair was straggly and he had a big red nose. He wore a wrinkled, white cotton shirt and grey slacks that were frayed at the hem where the cuff should have been.

Clemenski half smiled when he saw us. It didn't look like something he normally did. "You want to see my mother's apartment?"

Frieda gasped. "Does your mother live here, too? We thought ..."

"No, she's been dead for ten years. I just got up the gumption to rent the place last week. I can use the money. Didn't really expect anyone to be interested. Certainly not two pretty young girls. My papa built both sides forty years ago before anyone else lived on the block. He's been dead forever. I stick to myself. Don't like a lot of noise."

I smiled. "Mr. Clemenski — "

" — Call me Michael. Mr. Clemenski was my father. I'm just Michael."

"Okay, M ... Michael, we are very quiet girls. Sorry, we're both a mess. The rain dumped on us on the way down here. I'm Bella. This is Frieda. We've both lived just up the block our whole lives. We want to stay close to home, but need a place for ourselves. Mama's house has all the rosebushes out front. Frieda works. I've been promised a job and will be working soon."

Frieda, who was shocked by Michael's appearance, muttered with her chin tucked into her chest. "If it's already rented, or you've changed your mind about renting, we understand."

"I want to rent it alright. Sorry you had to get so wet to get a look at the place. Wait, just a minute, let me get the key."

We didn't have to wait long. It was obvious he was excited we were asking about the place. He returned with the key and led us to the rental. The room was larger than we had imagined. He pulled the For Rent sign out of the window to let some light inside. We started our tour. There was a little tiny kitchen. It wasn't actually a kitchen. It was a utility room with two gas burners. There was a small, rusty white sink and a teeny icebox that had no ice. Cobwebs owned the place. Once they were cleared out, and the floor was swept clean, there would be enough room for two small beds. One was already in place. The sink demanded elbow grease and a Brillo pad. Frieda looked over at me and nodded. I turned to Clemenski. "How much?"

"I wanted to rent it for $30 a month, but for you two girls, I'd be happy to rent for $25. I don't want any trouble. The walls are paper thin and I'm just next door. Don't want a bunch of rowdy boys around every night. I go to sleep no later than eight."

I stuck out my hand and we shook. I held a tight grip like Pa taught me so Clemenski would know I was honest. "Michael, thank you. We'll be back in the morning with the money. We have some stuff to bring over, too. We don't have much. See you soon."

Frieda and I walked home, hand in hand. She had seen the sign and I negotiated the deal. What a team we made. Since the rain had stopped, Mama was outside cutting flowers for the table.

"Did you get it?"

"Yes, we did! We'll be living just a few doors down." We walked inside, carrying Mama's freshly cut red roses. They smelled sweet.

Morrie had told me that AAA Auto Parts was closed on Sundays, but that Mathew would be there doing paperwork. I put on the dress that got me in so much trouble with Pa. I wanted to look good when I asked for a job. I kissed Mama goodbye, asked Frieda to wish me luck, and was out the door. The rain had swept the sidewalks clean. The Garfinkle's front garden sucked up the water and their plants stood tall, watching me as I skipped by. Red geraniums and perfectly purple tulips bloomed. The air was crisp and the powder-blue sky was dotted with white, puffy clouds. Maybe I'd never noticed all the color in our neighborhood before, but I sure noticed it on my walk to where I'd soon be working. One task down and one to go! I followed the route toward AAA Auto Parts. For the moment it seemed I was on the right road.

Chapter 22

I was happy to see Morrie through the glass door of AAA Auto Parts, but as I pulled it open, he turned and walked toward the back of the store. Mathew was standing at the counter, punching numbers on his calculator. His gray overalls read AAA Auto Parts. He looked up. "You must be Bella."

I was surprised he recognized me. "Oh hi, yes, that's me, Mr. ... ah, do you have a minute?" I didn't know his last name.

"Sorry, I didn't introduce myself. I'm Matthew Kandinsky. You can call me Matthew." He looked me up and down. "I do have a lot of work to do. I wouldn't be here on Sunday if I didn't. Then again, I guess that's why you're here. Heard you had some trouble at home. Looking for a job?"

"Trouble, no, not trouble, just a minor disagreement. Yes sir, Mr. Kandinsky, I'd like a job. I'm young but I'm dependable. I am ... I was the smartest kid in my class."

"Morrie mentioned you were coming. You're quitting school and getting your own apartment. Are you sure that's what you want?"

"Did Morrie tell you? I definitely want to work. I'm ambitious. I want to get ahead. Morrie said you offered to hire me part time. I would love to work here. Is full time a possibility?"

The smile on Kandinsky's face told me he knew more than he let on. "Morrie didn't tell me much. Just that you were moving out and needed work. I was impressed that you learned to drive and beat the bottom off your brother's friend in a road rally. You're a gutsy gal. Sure, I'd like you to join our team. As luck would have it, I just lost my stock clerk. I can use you full time. I can give you $25 a week to start, and if you work out, there could be more later. What do you think?"

I wanted to give him a hug but thought better and put my hand out to shake.

"Sounds spectacular to me! Tomorrow morning, I'm moving into my new place. Can I can come by in the afternoon after one o'clock to get started?"

"That'll be fine. See you tomorrow."

I turned to leave, but before I reached the door, he said, "Just one thing. You are young. This is your first job. Work is not a game. Can I depend on you to show up and be on time? Do you know what dependable means?"

"Sure do, Mr. Kandinsky. My pa owns a store. My brother runs it. I know how important a job is. You won't be disappointed." I smiled, opened the door, and slipped out. I jogged the entire eight blocks home. I forgot to say hello or goodbye to Morrie.

That night, Mama brought dinner to Frieda and me in our room before Pa got home. "No more fighting. Let's keep you two and Pa apart for the time being." She had made fried potato pancakes and a tender brisket. The brisket was moist and flaky. It melted like butter in my mouth. Ma stayed with the two us until Pa came home. When she heard him climbing the front porch steps, she put her finger to her lips, then kissed each of us on the forehead. "I know you girls will be fine. What has happened is a bad thing, a *shande*. It shouldn't happen in any family, especially this family."

Frieda whispered. "How can you stand his temper?"

"Your father is a good man, a hard-working family man. He loves me and he loves you." She left quickly.

Frieda and I spent the night whispering about our new apartment. Pa knew we were still home in our room. He ignored us. I think his pride got stuck in his throat.

Pearl had bought Frieda a new flapper hat. She showed it to us after she ate dinner with the family. Frieda loved it. It covered her tightly-wound Brillo-pad hair. Under the hat, all you could see on her face was her nose. After Pearl left, I tried to sleep, but thoughts about my new job and the new apartment assaulted me like those neon office signs that make you squint when you go downtown. I was on my own. I would never be a teenager again. I wanted to grow up, but wondered if this was too fast. Sometime after eleven, I finally dosed off. I slept most of the night, but awoke nauseous before daylight. On my way to the bathroom, I kicked the bedframe and screeched. I threw up once on the bedroom floor and twice in the toilet. Each time I thought I was done, the nausea came back up with a vengeance. I dragged a cold towel across my face and ran a comb through my hair. My screech had woken Frieda. "Must have eaten too many *latkes*," I said. She gave me a look and went back to sleep.

Frieda awoke at about seven. While she finished packing, I washed up. Together, we hauled boxes and luggage out the front door. I grabbed our old red wagon from the side yard where it held the gas and grease can. It was greasy and I tried to clean it up. We filled it.

Frieda had already written Clemenski a rent check. She handed it to him right away. "Good morning, Michael. Here's your check. Is there anything else we need to know?"

With his rusted key, he unlocked the door to our new place. He seemed to have taken to us and wanted to talk. We just wanted to be alone so we could tidy up and get organized.

He talked as we unloaded the wagon. "My mama wanted me to stay close. She was always lonely after my father died. I never moved away, not even after I was a grown man. I never made friends. Never had the time. Then when she died, I didn't know how."

Frieda gave me one of her looks. I smiled at Michael. "We're happy to be your friends. We can talk more later. Now we have to straighten up, you know, make this place livable." I walked him to the door and closed it behind him.

The two of us agreed to sleep together in the one bed until we could find twin beds to buy. The first thing Frieda did was unroll her posters and point to a spot on the wall to hang her favorite. A spot of grease from the red wagon was on Mr. Gable's face. I thought Frieda would have a cow. I wiped the grease off and she calmed down. "Now, that's better. Where should we put it?"

"There, above the bed. Clark Gable will be perfect there." We belly laughed at the irony of sleeping beneath the movie star's sly smile.

There was a big walnut vanity with six drawers in front of the window. We divided the drawers evenly. There was no closet. We organized our shoes in front of the vanity, Frieda's on the left and mine on the right. I laid Mama's quilt on my side of the bed, and together, the two of us rigged an old metal rod to one of the sidewalls so we could hang up our blouses and dresses. The room was small, but it was ours. There was a lamp near the bed, but it had no bulb, so light bulbs topped the list of things to buy at the local Piggly Wiggly the next day after work. Mama had given us old sheets, and together, we made the bed.

The next morning, we both got ready for work. We dressed without as much as good mirror or a wash cloth. When we were ready to leave, there was a knock on the door. Frieda about jumped a foot in the air at the sound. "Who knows we're here? I hope Michael hasn't come back for more conversation so soon."

I was scared too! But I didn't want to show it. I faked confidence. One of us had to at least act like an adult. "Who is it?"

"It's Pearl, the big bad wolf, let me in before I huff and puff and blow the door down."

Frieda and I ran to the door, almost tripping each other on the way. Pearl walked in like she owned the place. She walked around, wiped dust off the vanity with her forefinger, then raised it to show us all the dust. "Hey girls, how's your new place? Do you have room for one more?"

I wet a rag and wiped the dust off the vanity. "Oh sure, we have room for twenty more." Pearl was kidding and so was I. Our apartment was a size of a closet. With our dresses hanging every which way on the side wall, shoes scattered in front of the vanity, and the two of us bumping into each other, we barely had room for two. Pearl patted the bed and suggested I sit down beside her. "Bella, I need to speak with you privately."

"Okay, what's so private? I know I don't have the right clothes for work. Speaking of which, I have to get to my new job. Can it wait?"

"No, honey, we need to talk now!" She patted the spot next to her again. "Sit down."

Frieda wandered outside, closing the door behind her. I sat down on the bed next to Pearl, but when I looked at her face, I knew those big lips, painted burgundy red, were about to utter words I didn't want to hear. "You've been throwing up?"

"How'd you know that? It's nothing! I've always had a weak stomach. Sometimes I get sick when I eat too much."

"Bella, let me talk. Mama told me you got sick in the kitchen and Frieda said you've done the same in bathroom. She's heard you. She said you puked on the bedroom carpet, too."

"Oh, that. It must have been something I ate."

"Look Bella, I'm worried. Frieda is worried. So is Mama. You need to see a doctor."

"A doctor? Why? I'm fine. I just started this new job. I can't go gallivanting to the doctor every time my stomach gets upset." *Gallivanting* was a word Pearl liked to use. I thought it would throw her off.

Pearl reached for my hand. I could tell she meant business. "Bella, have you and Morrie …?"

"What do you mean?"

"You know what I mean. Did you protect yourself?"

"Protect from what?"

"Did you two make love?"

"Ah… well … I think so. But it was …"

"It doesn't take much."

"I didn't think…"

"Look, honey, it's probably just your stomach. It' can't hurt to go to the doctor. I'll make an appointment with Dr. Mendelbaum for Friday."

I was definitely *chalushes*. Could I be pregnant? That would ruin everything.

As soon as Pearl left, Frieda came back inside. "You're as white as a ghost!" she said.

I think Frieda already knew what Pearl told me. She looked down and I looked away. I had neither the time nor the inclination to get into this with her. "I have to leave now. We can talk another time. I can't be late. It's my first day at work. Goodbye."

The eight blocks to AAA Auto Parts should have been a joy walk for me. I was going to be with Morrie. I had my very own job. I was free of Pa. I should have felt like skipping. Instead, I had to will each leg forward. My exhilaration at the thought of seeing Morrie had turned to dread. Should I tell him what Pearl said? All I could think of was something Solly had told me when we driving together. "If the road gets tough, you can always steer through it." I stretched my mind around my problem. My throat tightened and I couldn't catch my breath. I let my shoulders drop back and rolled my neck to find comfort. I was running late. When I reached AAA, I forced a smile. Morrie had arrived at the same time and we walked inside together. He had just returned from lunch. He looked tired.

"How are you doing, Morrie?"

"Okay."

"It'll be good to work side by side, won't it?"

"Uh-huh." He didn't look directly at me. We were just inches apart.

"What's wrong?"

He blurted, "Do you like me?"

"Yes, of course. Why would you doubt that?"

"Yesterday, when you came here, you ignored me. You were so friendly to Matthew."

I was shocked. How could Morrie have confused my desire to be a dependable employee with ignoring him? Did shaking Matthew's hand and smiling mean more than thank you? Was Morrie jealous about such a small gesture? From day one, I had thought he was older, more mature. I thought he could teach me. Now, he was acting like such a child.

Matthew appeared and crowded between us. "Excuse me, you love birds. Bella has work to do." He led me to the back room. "You see those little cubbies," he said. "They house different parts. Get them mixed up and there will be a bunch of cars trying to get on the road with the wrong part. When the distribution truck pulls up to the shipping dock, you take the manifest from the driver and check off the boxes. You mark 'received' for the items delivered. You put the manifest up front in my payables basket. Then, when you have time, you unpack the boxes and store each part where it belongs. Any broken parts go over there in the corner marked 'returns'. Do you understand?"

There were literally hundreds of cubbyholes. Matthew threw me an inventory log. Several loose pages fell out as I caught the book with my right hand. There were over fifty pages. Twenty-two lines to a page. One line for each part. Next to each part was a number that described the quantity we needed in stock. "Yes, well, I have a lot to learn."

"That's right, you have a lot to learn. You must mark in the book every time we receive a part."

Matthew told me that each day I would need to count the parts on the shelves and compare these numbers with what we were supposed to have on hand. On Fridays, I would order those parts that were in short supply. Parts were stocked for individual car owners and dealerships, and hundreds of parts were moved every week. That was a whole lot of recordkeeping.

Morrie's job was to advise the customers which parts they needed. He had strong feelings about parts that were out of supply and hadn't been ordered. "Customer who wait more than a week for parts get angry. Their cars sit in parking lots or on the streets useless because somebody forgot to order missing part. I lose, too! Can't do my job when I don't have parts." Morrie was brilliant when it came to car mechanics.

On Wednesday night, Morrie and I left work together. It was dark and I didn't want to walk alone. Our little spat was over. We walked hand in hand under the light of a new moon. When we reached my new place, Morrie came in to see it. He noticed the loosely hinged rod holding our clothes.

"You need some shelves for your shoes and a better place to hang dresses. I'll come by Saturday and do some work for you, okay."

"I would love that, Morrie. I would really love for you to come by." I hadn't said anything to Morrie about seeing a doctor.

The next day, as I did cubbyhole entry, Matthew poked his head over my shoulder. He had been following me around all day. I could see Morrie out of the corner of my eye. At that moment, he wasn't with a customer. I began to understand that keeping Matthew from getting to close might be another part of my job.

On Friday, Pearl and I went to see Dr. Mendelbaum. I had never been to a gynecologist before and did not know what to expect.

"Honey, the doctor will touch you. It seems odd. He may need to do tests. He's a good man. Don't get riled up at anything he does or says."

The nurse was dressed in a white uniform, buttoned from the neck to the toe, a white cap on top of her platinum blond hair, and lace-up, white heelless shoes. She looked a lot like the nurse at school, except she was white. "Miss Krawiec."

I thought she wanted Pearl. Nobody called me Miss Krawiec. Pearl nudged me with her elbow. I followed the nurse to a little room. She weighed me and checked my blood pressure.

"Take your clothes off and lie down on the table over there. Put your feet up in the stirrups." She left. I disrobed. Lying naked in this strange office was not good, not good all. The window behind the doctor's desk was open but the Venetian blinds were down. Since his office was on the ground floor, I could see the silhouettes of business people walking by on the sidewalk outside. I wasn't sure if it was a fear of doctors or what this particular doctor might say, but I was shivering. I wanted to escape through the little window. I gave it more than a passing thought. Pearl's assurances had little effect on me. I really wanted to bolt.

I was uncomfortable on top of cold paper that stretched across the examining table. I tried to cover myself with my dress. There were blankets on a chair across the room, but I would have had to get up naked and walk over in front of that window to get them. My dress provided little shelter. The nurse had told me to put my feet in the stirrups. I wasn't ready for that. I was thinking about it when the doctor entered.

"Hello Miss Krawiec, I'm Dr. Mendelbaum." He had a thick German accent like Morrie. But he was older, about Pa's age, and looked a lot like him. He had a white beard and a few strands of curly white hair sticking on his head. It stood straight up from his scalp. He looked like he hadn't combed it in a week. "I know your sister, Pearl. I believe this is the first time I have had the pleasure of meeting you. How are you?"

"Pearl said I needed to come."

"Yes, of course, but why?"

"I've been nauseous lately. I'm sure it's nothing."

"Have you seen a gynecologist before?"

"No, I don't think anyone ever told me I needed to see a granologist before."

"Miss Krawiec, that's *gynecologist*. It's time to have a look. Please put your legs up and your feet in over here." He pointed to the stirrups. He pulled out a tool and removed my dress, which was loosely draped on top of me. I still had on my underwear and a slip.

"This may be uncomfortable but you'll need to take your undergarments off." I did as he asked. When he began his examination, I closed my eyes. He got under the hood like Morrie did when he worked on the Rod. He tinkered around, pushing and scraping, and after the five most disturbing minutes of my life, he was done. "Are you sexually active, Miss Krawiec?"

"I have a boyfriend. We've kissed."

"Did you have intercourse?"

"Intercourse?"

"Miss Krawiec, did you make love? Was he inside you with his penis?"

Being struck dead by lightening would have been perfect right then. Why did this old man need to know what Morrie and I did? What if he were a member of the synagogue? What if he knew Pa?

"Miss Krawiec, did you have sex? Please, it is important that I know."

"If I tell you, do you promise not to tell a soul? You can't tell my mama or pa. Do you promise?"

"Miss Krawiec, I am trying to understand why you are here. Please, did you have sex?"

"Yes, it was quick, nothing really. It was with my boyfriend."

"Okay, now we know you had sex. That's a start. I have a few more questions."

Actually, there were a lot of questions. I could barely keep them straight. Did I have allergies? What time of day did I vomit? When did it start? How did I feel after? Did the nausea stop or continue? Was there a particular food that made me vomit? I answered as best I could. The doctor made notes. Finally, he was finished.

"Miss Krawiec, I'll step out of the room now and be back in a few minutes. You can put your clothes back on. I am sorry if this was uncomfortable. Just want to keep you healthy."

When he returned, he told me that it was unlikely I had a digestive system problem. "I'd like to see you again next Friday, Miss Krawiec. I need to see the test results first. You may be pregnant."

Pregnant! The word echoed loudly.

Chapter 23

N*ot me! This can't be!* I hated Mendelbaum. I had felt like an animal in his stirrups. I was sobbing as Pearl and I left the office.

Pearl comforted as best she could. As I cried, she held me so tightly I thought I'd suffocate. Turning sixteen was not such a good thing! I'd quit school, and now motherhood might be on its way! At least I had Morrie. But what would he do when he found out he might be a father? What about money? Did Morrie make enough? Could I work after the baby was born? Mama never did. Yesterday, I was the baby of the family. Now, a mother! Morrie and I weren't even married. I'd already been shunned by my father. What would it be like as an unwed mother? I wouldn't be able to walk down the street without those horrible looks from the old *yentes*. They'd never stop talking about me. What would the men think? Guys like Solly's friends would be unbearable. As a thousand random thoughts raced through my head, I felt like my heart would burst. It didn't stop. It leaped. It gyrated. It rose in my chest and pounded me down. Every beat pounded up and down harder and harder until I thought I would pass out.

Pearl had been through so much. She knew what to do, what to say. "Slow down. Take a slow, deep breath. Morrie's an okay guy, just young. Solly will talk to him."

We arrived home. To this day, I don't remember the street car, the sidewalk, or even coming up Marathon. Frieda was out. Pearl came inside. She wet the nasty rag that lay in the sink and started to put it on my forehead.

"Don't! I wiped Clark Gable's mouth with that. It's disgusting!"

Pearl thought I had gone off the deep end. "You must be delirious. What are you talking? Clark Gable's mouth! Are you nuts? Lie down and rest. Relax. You can decide what to do when you have more information. Soon, we'll talk to the doctor again. Now you must rest."

Frieda came home. Pearl kissed me goodbye. Frieda didn't know what to say to me, which was fine. I didn't want to have to take care of her *and* her shock when she heard the news that I might be pregnant. She probably knew anyway. Women had a way of knowing these things.

She went out to Piggly Wiggly, brought home some food, and we sat without talking at the old pine kitchen table Michael had brought over. It had MC scratched into it with a knife. He must have done that when he was a kid. Kids did crazy things. I fell asleep at the table. I had no idea how I got into bed. Frieda must have carried me there. I fell asleep. Thank God.

The following morning, as I lay in bed with my eyes wide open and body glued to Mama's quilt, there was a knock on the door. "Who is it?"

"It's Morrie, you said come over. I have my tools to build your shelves."

"Hold on, I'll be there in a minute." Frieda and I jumped up. Our dresses were crumpled on the floor, having fallen off the rod we'd hung them on. We got dressed. Without a mirror, I had no idea how I looked. Worse yet, I didn't care.

I opened the door and there stood Morrie, ready to work. He had no idea what he was really getting into. I didn't say much. He worked for an hour. Frieda went out to get bagels and cream cheese. I was famished.

"That should hold you for now." Morrie proudly pointed to the hanging rod he had built on the side wall and then to the shelves above our vanity, which would hold our shoes.

When Frieda returned, she was amazed at what he had done. Solly couldn't even build a popsicle stick. "Wow, this is wonderful. Thank you so, so much for all your help."

Staying put in that tiny room with Morrie and Frieda all morning was enough to make me want to pull my hair out. I wanted to be alone with him. "What do you say to a drive in the country?" I said. "It's warm today. Once we get out of the city, there are plenty of oranges ripe for the picking."

Within minutes, we were in his car and off we went. I scooted close to Morrie. We found an orange grove where we could pick if we paid for the privilege. We also bought a container of drippy peanut butter, strawberry preserves, and a loaf of sliced rye bread. We drove a while longer, and then parked under a walnut tree not far from Whittier College. Morrie placed a blanket under the tree. I realized it was the same one we'd used that night on the beach and turned a deep shade of red. Morrie didn't seem to notice. He spread the peanut butter and preserves on four slices of rye and carefully fit the soggy bread together into a sandwich without dripping a bit on the ground. He was technical in every way I wasn't. With his Swiss army knife, he cut slices of an orange for desert. The weather was so perfect it gave me goose bumps. I was feeling human for the first time in twenty-four hours. Morrie asked if I wanted to drive.

"No, not now. I'm exhausted. I just want to relax." I wondered if being pregnant tired me out. That thought jangled my nerves.

The drive home was pleasant. Morrie parked in front of the apartment, opened my car door, and walked me to the front porch. He gave me a peck on the cheek. It was just a peck. I wanted to hold onto him for dear life. I held back all that churned inside. This was neither the time nor the place. It was still possible Mendelbaum's educated guess was dead wrong.

On Sunday, Morrie had a repair job. Frieda and I shopped and decorated. We scrubbed that sink clean, dusted, even painted one wall in the apartment. Michael came by, knocked, and when we opened the door for him, smiled like a pumpkin.

"Nice job! You girls cleaned this place up good. Frieda, you have white paint on the tip of your nose. It looks kind of cute."

Frieda touched her nose. She was happy to hear any man give her a compliment, but as usual, didn't know how to respond.

"Oh, forgive me," said Michael "I guess I shouldn't have said that."

I grinned and Frieda smiled. There was a spark in the room and it wasn't from the old gas stove in the corner.

Monday came and I was happy to have the distraction of work. I memorized where each part went. I needed order in my life. Tiny cubbyholes, one for each part. That was the order I needed.

Each morning, I awoke and threw up. Frieda was there with a cloth to wipe my face. She didn't' say a word. Just stared.

Although my mornings were bad, the days were good. Morrie and I would eat lunch together and make small talk. I avoided what was really on my mind. The nights were dark and frightening. My dreams were frightening. In one, I hit a baby while driving. In another, I was in the Rod with Morrie. I turned my head to kiss him, but he was no longer there. I woke up every night in a cold sweat. Frieda snored.

Friday finally came and I was at Dr. Mendelbaum's office again. I made up an excuse and left work early. Matthew was angry.

Waiting in the doctor's office, flipping through the pages of various magazines, I came across a picture in *Life* that was nothing less than painful. A kid, dressed in swimming trunks and not much younger than me, stood by a lake. The picture accompanied an article about summer camps. Summer camp was something I'd never experienced, and now, probably never would.

As I turned the pages of the magazine, Pearl blabbered on and on about Jack, nightclubs, and her exotic life. I almost screamed shut up. I held my tongue, but my mind went wild. Then the nurse called my name.

"Miss Krawiec, please." I jumped up and walked slowly into the doctor's office. He was reading a report as I entered. I stood silent. He looked up at me and smiled.

"Please sit, Miss Krawiec." He gestured to a seat across from his desk. I avoided his gaze, focusing instead on the photographs that covered the wall behind his desk. I guessed these were his grandchildren and adult children. His grandkids were cute, but a bit wild eyed. I realized I knew nothing about kids — that I was still a kid myself. If I was going to be a mother, how would I know what to do? I sat down.

Dr. Mendelbaum's stethoscope hung over a green lampshade at the top of his desk lamp, which didn't seem to emit enough light for reading such an important report. I almost laughed. This doctor was holding my future in his hands. And he was about to tell me what that future would hold. At that moment, as I sat there before him, Dr. Mendelbaum was the most powerful man in the world.

Everything was happening in slow motion. His lips opened and words formed. My head ached, my feet hurt, and stomach churned. I was listening underwater. Childhood experiences flashed before my eyes.

"Miss Krawiec, your tests are positive."

Positive? Did that mean I wasn't pregnant? Did it mean he was positive about the results?

"You are less than two months pregnant. There are a few things that you need to know now to assure a healthy baby."

I leaned forward. "Excuse me sir, can my sister Pearl come in?"

"Yes, of course. Just a second, my nurse will get her."

He arose and stepped out of the room. I heard muffled talk between him and his nurse. The doctor returned, followed by Pearl. I suspected she knew why she had been asked to join us. The doctor motioned for her to sit, and without hesitancy, started telling me what to do. "You must watch your diet. Some women let it get out of control and gain much more weight than they need. Contrary to myth, you really don't need to eat for two. Just stay conscious of your nutrition."

I stopped listening. I was crazed, could barely sit still, much less concentrate. I was glad Pearl was with me. She listened to everything the doctor was saying. She removed a pen and a notepad from her purse and scribbled notes. I'd never seen her write a word of cursive before. We got up. She held my arm. I felt like an invalid, weak and powerless. Before we left, she made another appointment with the nurse.

Next thing I knew, we were on the sidewalk out front. Pearl, who had always been the wild one, was now my mature advisor. How could that be? Was I dreaming? Wake up! Wake Up!

Pearl turned to face me. "Honey, you can abort."

"What? Did you say something?"

"It's not too late. You don't have to keep this baby. I know of people. You can also deliver and then put the baby up for adoption. You don't have to raise this child. You are so young. If you really want the baby, if you are ready, I can talk to Morrie for you."

I thought about what Pearl was saying. I knew she was offering a way out if I wanted it. But I also knew something else. There was no way I could reject this baby. It was my baby and I intended to keep it. If Morrie was not ready to be a father, I would take care of the baby myself. I would also be the one to talk with Morrie.

When Pearl and I got back to the apartment, I looked up the street and Mama was in her front garden. I waved at her. I knew I would need to tell her, but not yet. Frieda was just getting home from work. She waved at Mama as well. I whispered to Pearl, "I don't want to talk to Mama now." Together, Pearl, Frieda, and I walked inside. Frieda knew. Her forehead had wrinkled when she saw Pearl and me.

"What will you do?"

Pearl piped in. "She's too young. She should abort. She can also put it up for adoption. There are many young couples who would love a child."

Frieda probed. "What about Morrie? What does he want?"

Blood drained from me at that question. "I haven't told him. I will. He has the right to know."

"Does he love you?" asked Frieda.

Pearl, who was a seasoned skeptic, said, "Men, they love you until they don't."

"Morrie's not like that. He's from the old country. It's a long story. Just know he is different."

Pearl wasn't convinced. "But is he ready to a husband? What if he's like our brother? Men like Solly prefer playing to staying."

Frieda, the romantic, fantasized. "You two are perfect for each other. You make such a sweet couple. I will help you."

Exhaustion overcame me. I wouldn't see Morrie until Sunday. There was plenty of time. I needed to plan. "Girls, please leave me alone. I need to be by myself now."

Leaving work early on Friday turned out to be a much bigger problem than I expected. Matthew was furious. I had disappointed him just as he had warned me not to do. I had worked two weeks and missed half of two Fridays.

On Sunday morning, Morrie announced his arrival with a blast from his car's squawking duck horn. I was still at the toilet retching, practicing what I was going to say. Before I could clean the throw off my blouse, there was a knock at the door.

I screeched at Frieda. "Have him sit on the porch. I have to clean up!"

Frieda ran past me to the front door. She literally bounced into Morrie to bar his entrance. Then she pointed him onto our small front porch. I grabbed my brush and tried to turn terror into tame hair before joining Morrie.

"Bella, I worried about you. How you? Sick? I make chicken soup. It my mama's recipe.

Frieda hovered for a moment.

"I'm okay now. It's my stomach again. I can't eat right now. Frieda, can you put Morrie's soup in the sink with some ice to keep it from spoiling. I'll be sure to eat it later. Now, I just need some fresh air."

Frieda took the soup from Morrie. Rays of sunlight slid beyond our massive mushroom roof and marked dark shadows in the front yard.

"Why you miss work? Matthew furious! He want get rid of you. I told him no, he shouldn't. I say you have a good reason. You go to the doctor?"

My words, oft repeated in my head, but yet to be heard, came out like a fountain. "The doctor had good news! "I'm … ah … pregnant." The last word came out in slow motion.

Morrie's eyes zeroed in on my stomach. "A baby! My baby! You are pregnant with my baby?"

I didn't respond. "Ah … our baby. You are the only one I have ever loved. It was at the beach."

"Sure?"

"Sure, are you questioning … whose … baby it is?"

"No, are you sure you are pregnant?"

"Yes, I'm sorry, I didn't mean … yes … it's been nearly two months."

Morrie gave my nose a little peck. He was so gentle. He seemed afraid I might break. "Bella, I dreamed you were sick … I mean … like you had disease. My head pounded all night like piston in cylinder."

"Morrie, I'm not sick. But this is a big, big deal. Are you ready to be a father?"

His long fingers touched the top of my cheeks. They were cold. I pulled away. "Wow, why are your hands so cold?"

"Say cold fingers, warm heart. His eyes caught mine. "I happy. Very happy to be father. I love you. Not expect family so quick, but I …" He kneeled down. He eyes wetted. His black-and-white checkered German Hofbrauhaus hat was turned halfway around his head. There was a huge black grease smudge on his torn, gray woolen overalls. He looked up at me with puppy-dog eyes. His huge right hand smothered mine. I straightened his hat. His ears stood straight up in a point. "I want you marry me, he said."

I wasn't expecting that. Stunned, I couldn't respond. I had to be sure. I had important questions to ask. "I love you. But can you take care of me and a baby? You have a roommate and so do I. Where would we live? Mama will have to approve. Oh my God, how do I explain that you were Jewish, and now you are not Jewish!

"No worry. In my house, I have two thousand American dollars."

I was stunned. Had Morrie really saved that much money? Solly hadn't saved a dime his entire life.

"We live in my apartment. Roommate move. If you feel healthy, you work for a few months. We save more money. Then you no work more. Your mama, no problem. She likes me. What about your Pa? I will ask him to approve. I join Jewish again. I still worried about my family in Germany. No one can know they are Jewish. Too dangerous."

Pa would certainly say no. He would never understand converting from, or to, Judaism. Pa wouldn't sit for a second if he knew Morrie wanted to marry me, especially once he knew Morrie had given up the religion. I would not let Pa stand in our way. I was pregnant. I couldn't wait. I didn't need his approval. If he wanted to see his soon-to-be grandchild, he would have to apologize to me first.

"Your pa can make trouble. We must ask him. Can't ignore."

"We'll talk to Mama. Pa is a lost cause. Mama can deal with him if she wishes."

It was *shabes*. Pa was at *shul*. Thank God he wasn't home. He was the last one I wanted to see. Morrie and I walked up the street and onto the front porch. The door was unlocked. I knocked a few times. I couldn't just barge in. Mama opened the door and greeted us. She was making lemon meringue pie. She had flour on her fingertips and a bit of meringue on her nose. She motioned for us to come inside and sit down. I hadn't been in the house since moving out. It smelled lemony.

"Mrs. Krawiec, nice to see again. You make lemon meringue pie like my mama in Germany. It's my favorite."

Mama nodded. "Bella? What did the doctor say?"

"I'm fine. I have some news."

"What?"

I tried to smile. "Good news. I am going to have a baby. Morrie would like to ask your permission to marry me. May he?"

Mama's well-seasoned skin didn't peel off at my announcement. It did turn paler. She loosened her white apron strings and sat down. She looked like she was about to pass out.

"*Oy* Bella, pregnant!" She looked up at Morrie, who must have appeared ten feet tall to her. "You?"

I could tell Morrie was nervous. The combination of his broken English and fear made it difficult for him to get even a few words out of his throat and onto his lips. "Mrs. … never expect make of love to your beautiful Bella give us baby so quick. I careless. I sorry. I terribly sorry. She is important to me. I love … I work hard, not speak so *goot* English but make money with mechanic's hands. I save for Bella and baby. I be father. My parents in Germany, they married more than forty years. I want to marry your daughter. Is *goot*?"

The house was uncomfortably hot. I didn't feel well and cowered next to Mama as Morrie spoke.

Mama wasn't convinced we were doing the right thing. "Is this what you want?" she said to me. "Are you ready for a child and husband? You are just a baby yourself."

"Yes Mama, if God has seen fit to make me a mama, then I want it.

"What about your dreams, your education and your future?"

I knew Mama thought I was too young. Would she understand that I had made up my mind? Would she consider it disrespect?

"I will park my dreams for now," I said. "When I'm ready, I'll restart them."

Morrie did a double take. I knew he wanted me to be like Mama, like his own mama. He didn't want me to have dreams that might be beyond cooking, cleaning, and caring for his children.

"Listen to me," said Mama, speaking with more authority than I had heard from her before. "I have raised six children. Caring for a child is a fulltime job. Once you take responsibility, there is no retreating."

"Mama, I will manage. You will see I can do it." I put one hand inside Morrie's and another inside Mama's. Will you approve?"

She shrugged. "I want for you what makes you happy. All I want for you is much *mazel*. You know I don't speak for Pa. After all, Morrie is not Jewish.

Morrie was silent. I knew he was afraid to talk about why he had converted to Christianity. I decided to explain. "Morrie was born Jewish. His father tried to save the family by hiding it from the government. He sold his business, moved the family, converted to Christianity and moved away from his friends. Morrie is worried about his family in Germany. He says Jews are being prepared for slaughter by Hitler. He worries that if anyone knows his family is Jewish, even here in America, it might get back to the government officials in Germany. He thinks there are spies here. Please don't' mention this to anyone you know. He was, and is at heart, Jewish. It's all so complicated, Mama. I love you. You will come to love Morrie. He wants Pa's permission. I said no. I will not let Morrie ask the man who kicked me out. If I am out, Pa is out. He will not visit me or my baby. Our lives can't wait for Pa's approval."

Mama let out a huge sigh. I thought it might be her last breathe. "You must speak to your Pa!"

"I will not! Pa threw me out. He must apologize first." I turned my back to Mama.

Morrie swiveled me around to face Mama again. "Bella, kiss your mama goodbye."

I hugged her tightly. She stood up. Morrie kissed Mama's forehead.

Morrie drove us to his apartment. Once inside, he spoke in German to his recently immigrated roommate, Horst, who smiled at me and told Morrie he would move to the local YMCA the next day. Morrie's apartment place was smaller than the Clemenski place. It smelled like a garage. I opened a little window over the sink to let in some fresh air. Morrie straightened up as I looked around. His bed was unmade. Dirty, wrinkled sheets hung off the bed and onto the floor. The floor hadn't been swept and was stained with grease in places. Morrie must have worked on car parts right inside this room. Dishes were stacked inside the sink. I visualized myself with a baby in one arm and a mop in the other.

I started to sweep up. As I did so, Morrie clasped my belly from behind. He leaned into me and spoke quietly in my ear. "I love you."

I felt his warmth, but it was not a comforting feeling. Even though I wanted to have this baby, and even though I knew I loved Morrie, I was also angry with him. How could he have done this to me? I stood unresponsive. Then I broke his hold. "We need to go. Frieda has to be told.

When we arrived at the Clemenski place, I couldn't get my key to open the front door. Morrie had to muscle it open. Inside, we sat on the edge of the bed, waiting for Frieda. I was falling into a deep depression. This was the bed that Frieda and I shared. How ironic that I now sat with Morrie beneath the picture of Clark Gable. We were about as far from his movie star status as could be imagined.

When Frieda arrived, I announced, with as much joy as I could muster, that Morrie and I were to be married. She provided an appropriate half smile. Her dreams of making a life with me were dashed. Morrie, who needed to go to work, hugged Frieda and walked quietly out the door.

Chapter 24

Shortly after Morrie left, Pearl bounded in our door without bothering to knock. "How'd it go?" she asked. "What did Morrie say? Did he head for the exits?"

Upon hearing of his proposal, she suggested that we should marry in Las Vegas since Nevada had passed a law eliminating the waiting period for a marriage license. Also, parental approval was not required. The new law was intended to increase gambling revenue. Even though Pearl was excited about a trip to Las Vegas, she did have her doubts about its purpose. "I hope your marriage lasts longer than mine. High hopes can produce the most depressing results. On the other hand, Las Vegas is a splendid place to celebrate no matter what happens. We can go to the Pair-O-Dice, have some fun in the desert sun, and do some gambling to boot. If we can drive out Friday night, we can be back at work on Monday. You'll be long married before you start showing. Mama will want a rabbi in Los Angeles later. That is, if we can get one for the was-but-no-longer German Jew."

I did want to get married before I started showing. In no time at all, the three of us were able to get a hotel reservation and find a florist, piano player, and a tiny chapel across from the casino. Even though I didn't need parental consent, I wanted Ma's approval. Pearl convinced her to sign the necessary papers. I borrowed Solly's car to drive Mama to the bank to get the permission slip notarized.

That Friday evening, September 10, 1937, Morrie, Frieda, and I sat in the front seat of Morrie's car. Pearl, Jack, and Michael Clemenski sat in the back. Pearl had invited Michael to keep Frieda company. She thought Michael was perfect for Frieda. Frieda and Michael had no clue that Pearl thought they were meant for each other.

To save money, we all agreed to share the same room that first night. Morrie and I slept in the bed. Frieda slept on one side of the room, and Michael on the other. I think she was petrified to be in the same room with Michael. Pearl and Jack stayed up all night and gambled.

The next day, we went to the chapel, showed our identification, the permission slip signed by Mama, and paid our $35 fee. The service started at ten in the morning and was over by a quarter after ten.

"Morrie, do you take Bella as your lawfully wedded wife?"

"I do."

"Bella, do you take Morrie as your lawfully wedded husband."

"I do."

We did, and that was that.

"You may kiss the bride."

Kissing Morrie in front of my sisters was really odd, as if this simple act signified that I was no longer just Bella, a member of the Krawiec family, but Bella Adelsdorfer, wife and soon-to-be mother.

It was *shabes*. On top of that, it was *shabes* that fell between Rosh Hashanah and Yom Kippur, the holiest time of the Jewish year. The Jewish New Year had brought me a new life.

After our brief wedding ceremony, we returned to the hotel. The others were anxious to change into swimsuits and lounge by the pool, so Morrie and I only had the room to ourselves for a few minutes. In the room, I slipped out of my simple crocheted white dress and white, patent-leather three-inch heels. Pearl had insisted I wear the heels even though they weren't my cup of tea. So I had worn them. Morrie tore off his rented-at-the-casino tuxedo. "This bowtie chokes like noose around my neck," he said. We were thrilled to disrobe, but naked for the first time in the light of day, we avoided each other. Morrie pulled on his two-piece black swimming costume while I slipped into a one-piece, floral suit Pearl had bought for me at the casino.

We met the others downstairs. Jack had ordered happy hour vodka gimlets and everyone was already sloppy drunk. Morrie and I left our drinks on the bar and went to the pool while they went up to change. When they rejoined us, they stumbled out to the pool deck and jumped into the water hand in hand. Michael and Frieda were surprisingly game.

About five o'clock, we all went up to dress for dinner. The girls crowded into the bathroom while the guys played poker on the bed. After about forty-five minutes, Jack made it known that they wanted their turn.

"Come on girls, we need to get ready, too! Besides, I am losing my shirt in this game."

Pearl was not sympathetic. "Hold your horses. The bevy of beauty you expect to see doesn't come easily, you know."

All three of us strutted out of the bathroom twenty minutes later. The guys applauded. "Well, the wait was long, but you girls cleaned up good." Pearl had donned a long, red silky thing and a white pearl necklace. Frieda wore basic beige down to her ankles. Pearl tried to get Frieda to wear a gown with a plunging neck, but Frieda would have no part of it. I wore a dress that Pearl bought me. It was white with a slit up the side. It went with the black pearl necklace she had lent me for the evening. The guys dressed in the same outfits they had worn for the wedding.

Pearl insisted we go to the Oasis, the same club where she had fox trotted the night away with her previous husband. When we arrived, Nelson Riddle was leading a ten-piece brass section, and Gene Krupa banged away at the drums to keep the beat going.

In what seemed like the wee hours of the morning, we grabbed a cab back to the hotel. By that time, Pearl and Jack were so drunk they needed help to stand up.

For our special evening, Morrie had reserved a room for the two of us. Before herding my drunken sisters and their men upstairs, he handed me the key. I couldn't believe how late it was.

I located our room and stepped inside. Walking over to the queen-sized bed, I turned back the heavy spread and sheets. I couldn't help but think of Ma's quilt. It was part of my history and I suddenly missed something so familiar.

There was a knock on the door. When I opened it, Morrie stood next to a bellman, who was holding our bags. The bellman put the bags inside. As he pocketed his tip, he winked at Morrie, who motioned me outside. "We need do this right," he said. As the bellman walked away, Morrie swung his long arms under my bottom and cradled me into his chest. He stood there a moment before officially carrying me over the threshold. I giggled and then fell under his spell.

Inside, he gently lay me down on our bed. As he joined me, our bodies touched. I thought something should happen, but before it did, we promptly fell asleep. The party was over.

The following morning, we all stuffed ourselves at a Las Vegas all-you-can-eat buffet filled with bagels, lox, onions, cream cheese, tomatoes, kippers, and apple, pear, and orange slices. Then we piled into Morrie's car. Eight hours later, we arrived back in Los Angeles after dark.

Morrie dropped everyone off before we headed to our new home. Pearl had decided to move in with Frieda since Jack was still trying to save money and build his business during difficult times.

In the craziness of our wedding, I had completely failed to observe that the seed of friendship between Frieda and Michael had bloomed. Pearl had been right about the attraction. Michael was much older than Frieda and not particularly attractive. But he was a wonderful hoofer. Apparently, his mother had been a dance instructor and that was the one social skill she had taught him. As the last sister without a man, Frieda was ready to give up her fantasies about Clark Gable and settle into steady dates with Michael.

Married life for Morrie and me settled into a routine. I added feminine touches to the apartment and bought new flowers every day for the table. I shopped for and bought pretty heart-shaped pink soap for the bathroom, white towels, and a copper Jell-O mold, which hung on the wall. Mama's quilt was at the foot of our bed.

Morrie and I had returned to work on the Monday following our wedding. Matthew had already suspected I was pregnant. He didn't care. "How long do you expect to work?"

"We need the money. I will work until the day I deliver."

"Are you sure you will be able to?"

"Don't worry about me. Remember, I'm the tough little girl rally driver. I'll hang in through the finish line."

Matthew respected Morrie and accepted our situation. I mastered the organization of the automotive parts. Morrie worked two to three nights a week completing repairs for clients. I often tagged along, handing him tools as needed. The night usually ended with me fast asleep with a socket wrench in my hand. As Morrie's reputation as an auto mechanic grew, demand for his services increased. He had to turn work down.

On Sundays, I would go to the downtown library and borrow books on childbearing. I loved to read and knew I had a lot to learn. Pearl would visit me on the weekends when she wasn't working. She had a daytime job as a waitress, and at night, she worked at a poker parlor. Jack's furniture business was struggling, so he kept delaying marriage. With no marriage in sight, the economy sagging, and endless hours of work, she had put on weight. At one point, I thought she was pregnant and said something. I was embarrassed to find she was not.

I was set to deliver in mid-March. During the final months of my pregnancy, my stomach protruded like a torpedo. I was always off balance and had trouble standing erect for long periods. Morrie sensed my discomfort. He tried to keep my spirits up. "You look more beautiful every day."

I didn't believe a word of it. By the last month, I was a big *umpa lumpa* and constantly exhausted. I missed school and the challenge of learning. I couldn't drive because my belly pressed hard into the steering wheel of Morrie's car. My water broke on Wednesday, March 23, 1938. It was mid-morning. I was at work.

Matthew saw the puddle on the floor. "Morrie, get over here fast," he yelled.

My fingers were filthy from lifting parts. My hair, now long again, hung like a dry floor mop, and I felt like a dirigible. I sat in the AAA waiting area while Morrie got his car.

We had decided that if the baby was a boy, his name would be Rodney, or Rod for short. We hadn't considered a name for a girl. My contractions went from five minutes to one minute by the time we reached Kasper Cohn Hospital. I thought I might deliver in the car.

Our beautiful baby boy, Rodney Adelsdorfer, was born that afternoon. Wrapped warm in a little blanket, the nurse placed him on my chest. He weighed eight pounds, two ounces. He had strands of black hair and a pudgy little nose. While Rod looked a lot like Morrie, he had my dark complexion.

Outside the delivery room, Morrie had paced himself into a heap. Later, he told me he wept after I was taken inside, fearful of what might go wrong. He worried I would break.

I remained in the hospital that night and the following day. Morrie came to see me as soon as he got off work. I was breastfeeding Rod when I felt my trance interrupted by Morrie's lips on my forehead. Rod had fallen asleep while feeding.

"You okay?" said Morrie. "Is everything okay for him?"

"It's your son, Morrie. You can call him Rod."

"Yes, is Rod goot?"

"We are wonderful. Look at our son. He has big hands like you."

I was so hormonal. Tears filled my eyes. They were happy tears, but tears all the same. I lifted Rod up so he could bond with his father. Morrie pulled him closer without taking care to support Rod's head. "No, Morrie, not that way! Cradle him near your chest and hold his head. His neck isn't strong yet." Rod's body quivered with each breath. Morrie cradled him tensely. "Hey you, he's not a wrench. Relax, will you?"

Morrie's face reddened. He handed Rod back to me. "If you *goot*, I am happy. I try to hold the baby better in morning before I go to work. You sleep now. You rest. You and the boy rest." Rod had already fallen asleep on my chest.

Morrie came the next morning, but seemed anxious to leave. "What's the hurry?" I asked. "You have a streetcar to catch?" I laughed, but Morrie did not. He held Rod for a minute, but looked uncomfortable. I assumed it might take him a few days to bond with his son.

On the third day of Rod's life, Morrie took us home. He had never driven so cautiously. He slowed to a crawl over every rut in the road.

At home, I carried Rod inside and Morrie helped me get settled. The apartment was immaculate. It looked like he had cleaned it with a fine-tooth comb. After Morrie left for work, I busied myself with feeding, changing diapers, and getting Rod to sleep.

That night, Rod awoke three times for feeding and care. Each time I got up, I noticed that Morrie was wide awake. "Did you just wake up?"

"No, I not sleep goot since you go to hospital. I worry. Can't sleep."

"What are you worried about?"

"It's not so *goot* you can't bring baby to your Pa. It's not right that your family not know I Jewish. I worry about my parents. I make this baby with you, but maybe I not ready to be father. I want to be ready. I am scared." He had left for work the next time I got up. It wasn't even dawn.

Chapter 25

Morrie worked long hours and saved all his side-job earnings. We lived frugally. Night and day feedings, baby poops, diaper changes, fixing meals for Morrie, and breast feeding consumed my time. When I had a free moment, I read books on childrearing.

There was much about motherhood that frightened me. Morrie had childproofed the house, but I still found things to worry about. I didn't know what my baby needed. But over time, in the same way Morrie was able to provide proper repairs by listening to his cars, I learned how to care for Rod by listening to his cries. Morrie, on the other hand, didn't understand Rod at all. "How you know that means he pooped?"

"A mother knows."

"When does father know?"

"That's up to you. You have to listen and watch. Then you will know."

Rod and I played. I thought our son would be a restless baby. He was not. My books said infants didn't smile unless they had gas. Rod smiled every time he saw me. Believe me, it wasn't gas. I knew when he had gas or poop. When I held him, I was careful to support his neck. Morrie would often pick him up clumsily and I'd scream, "Hold his neck, he's only an infant." Each night, I sang "Edelweiss," Morrie's favorite song. Rod little eyes closed, and he fell asleep as I sang. In his fifth month, after I removed him from my breast, I heard him say *da da*.

At this sound, Morrie, who was tinkering with the faucet in the kitchen , ran over to his son. "Did he say *da, da*?"

"Yes, that's what I heard."

There was no repeat performance. No matter, Morrie was ecstatic. "My son say *da da*. He say *da da*." The following day, Morrie told everyone at work.

Happy or not, Morrie was very tight in the wallet. He saved every extra dime for his new business, his own garage. He gave me two dollars for groceries and fifty cents for odds and ends around the house. I tried to decorate our apartment, but on such a limited budget, it was tough.

Morrie did buy Rod a tiny soccer ball right after his utterance of *da, da*. I put it on a high shelf. "He'll choke. We must be careful!" Morrie immediately understood my concern. What he didn't understand was the kind of concern that extended beyond Rod's environment. Rod's development was not progressing as quickly as expected. At five months, he still could not raise his neck, let alone roll over. I knew that babies developed at their own pace. I had read that most babies gained strength by pushing up on their arms enough to roll over in their third or fourth month. Rod's shoulders were constantly retracted, his back arched, and he couldn't raise his head. As the months rolled forward, he still smiled when I looked at him, but left on his own, became increasingly cranky. I worried.

When Morrie came home from work, he would always ask the same question. "What new Rod do today?"

By that time, I had learned to talk around the question so as not to disappoint Morrie. "He changes every day. Look at him. Do you see anything new? He ate well and pooped perfectly. He napped twice without a fuss. He is, you know, a perfect baby."

As Rod approached six months, I could no longer ignore Morrie's expectation that Rod would sit up on his own. He clearly couldn't.

When the weather turned warmer, I would push Rod in a stroller to Echo Park. I set up the stroller so he could watch the children play. He'd be okay for a minute, then his head would roll over to one side. He wasn't able to turn it back. Then, he would get my attention with a cry.

Other mothers stared at him. I'd smile back. They made me really anxious. Guiltily, I'd hold him passively in my lap so he could at least know I was there. With his neck held tightly by my arms, the way I did the day he was born, he'd eyeball the other children. There was little more I could do for him.

We had a six-month birthday party. Mama and Solly came, along with all my sisters and their kids. Mama cornered me in the kitchen when I was trying to write Rod's name on his cake.

"Go see your doctor," she said. He will know what to do. In the old days, none of us had doctors. I don't think Sarah saw a doctor until she was two years old. The women helped one another. We usually knew what to do. Today, in America, you go to the professional, a doctor. They know much more than we ever did."

Dr. Herman Schmaltz was the pediatrician Kate and Sarah used. They told me to go to him. Kate raved about him. "He's the best there is. Better than good. He is such a sweet man."

Professional, the best, sweet or not, I didn't like what Dr. Schmaltz told me. "Rod requires therapy. He has a muscular problem we call cerebral palsy. It comes from lesions on the brain that choke oxygen during birth. This condition stops the brain from sending the muscles the information they need. The right side of Rod's brain withholds information to activate the left side of his body. His left arm and leg don't know what to do. It is a motor problem. *Motor* refers to the way the body, brain, and nervous system work together. Rod will struggle. Later, he may need a brace to keep his foot from turning out from his ankles. His lack of muscle control will likely worsen as he grows. You need to get him physical therapy. The first task is to help stabilize his head and neck."

The doctor gave me homework. There were things I could do to stimulate Rod in ways his brain did not. Rod's frustration grew. He was smart. He wanted to move, but there was a missing link. When he wasn't sleeping, I had to be with him every minute. I barely had time to make Morrie dinner, let alone to clean the house.

Dr. Schmaltz wanted a nurse to make home visits. He recommended Nurse Mary Anaston. He said she would train Rod and then train me on how better to work with him. When I tried to explain the doctor's recommendations to Morrie, he stopped listening at the word *motor*. I knew I shouldn't have used it. Morrie refused to believe that his son had a motor he couldn't fix. He claimed the doctor just wanted money. "We cannot afford."

I knew it was more than that. Morrie was embarrassed. He already carried so much guilt about his parents and my separation from Pa. I knew that in some strange way, he also felt responsible for Rod's delayed development. He refused to face up to these feelings, which made it impossible to talk about them. He distanced himself from the entire problem.

I tried to find other solutions. Even though my sisters and Mama offered to help with the money, Morrie rejected them out of hand. I brought up the subject but he wouldn't listen. His behavior became all too familiar. I didn't mention the possibility of their help a second time. I asked Morrie to come with me to the doctor. He refused. He wanted to do everything his own way. He didn't like to take direction from others.

The doctor said since I didn't have a therapist, I would need to do some things myself. I learned to bring Rod's arms toward the center point of his mouth. This helped strengthen his shoulders, but he had made little progress by his first birthday. He was falling farther behind other babies his age. I was beside myself. I read everything I could about cerebral palsy. I placed

Rod in a clean, small hamper and secured it to a wall. In this way, I was able to use the hamper to help him stand. I pulled him up inside the hamper and showed him how to place his arms on the sides to push himself up. I turned it into a game and cheered at the slightest sign of progress. I hated watching him struggle so. I began to doubt all the decisions I had made in my young life. Was it a big mistake having Rod? Maybe I was too young. No, of course not, he is the sweetest baby ever.

I forced myself to have hope. I wanted to believe my life with Morrie would improve and that Rod would show progress. I worked hard at keeping a smile on my face for both my boys. Rod needed to see happiness and Morrie needed to believe things would get better.

Morrie put all his energy into work. Some weeks, he worked six days and every night at AAA. He didn't get much sleep. We didn't talk.

At least I had most of my family around. Mama adored Rod. Even though she was always exhausted whenever she came over, at the first sight of Rod, she became a childlike grandma, throwing kisses, laughing and hugging her newest grandson. "*Shtik naches*. He gives me so much joy. If only I could hold up this baby's beautiful *punim* to my mother, his great grandmother. If only for one second, she would have *kvelled* to all her *yentes* in the old neighborhood. *If only*, but that is not to be. She is long gone and the old country is gone for me, too. *Mein kin* struggles, but will grow strong. Bella, you must be strong. You will see him grow up fast. You need to make time for yourself so you can grow up, too. You are not yet eighteen years old. You have so much living to do. Go, go out, shop, walk, meet with other girls your age. I can watch Rod. Just say the word. I'd love to be alone with him."

I wasn't ready to go out. I was afraid for Rod. I desperately wanted professional training so he could grow strong. I blamed Morrie. He stood in my way like a boulder in the middle of the road. He had money. He wouldn't give it to me. He saved for the Lord knows what. He fantasized about bringing his parents to America. This was ridiculous. He hadn't heard from them. He didn't even know where they were. They didn't respond to his or his sister's letters. Hiring a therapist was what we needed.

I tried talking to Morrie. "I can work. All the money I make will go for Rod's care. Frieda and Mama can help watch him."

"Mothers shouldn't work. My mommy, your mama, never worked. Stay home. I make enough. Soon, I open the garage and give you money to pay."

Morrie was single minded. I couldn't argue. He considered money his department. I had to keep peace at home. There was already enough *meshugas*. More craziness was no good. I gave in. "You want your garage, okay,

okay, you will have it. But understand this, when you have your success, it will be Rod's turn. I will work and Rod will have his braces. His struggles will not last one minute longer than the time it takes for you to make a big success."

Morrie looked down at the ground. Our rare conversations included little eye contact. Often, his only response was a shrug. He clearly was not happy with what he heard. In some ways, this was understandable. We were from different worlds. As restrictive as Pa was, my family encouraged risk in the pursuit of gain. Pa had made a conscious decision to immigrate. Morrie had been forced to come to America. In a sad way, he was forced to marry me. He worked on engines, something he understood. He was good with closed systems. He was comfortable at AAA. He liked being there. He liked the predictability of identifying a part that would fix the problem. He liked being under the hood. He wanted a garage because his father had a garage before everything fell apart in Germany. He knew owning a garage would not be a risk. He didn't like risk. In his eyes, ignoring Pa was risk. Facing up to Rod's problem, something that could not be solved with a single part or a day under the hood, was a risk. Rod's problem was complex. I didn't understand it fully myself. But I refused to consider failure. I was willing to try. I was optimistic that, together, Rod and I would succeed.

After Morrie shrugged, he muttered, "He grow out of it. My son won't need crutch. Where I grow up, children laugh at boy with crutch. No one laugh at my son."

I shook my head and went outside for a walk. I needed fresh air. Later that day, Morrie and I took Rod to the park. Morrie had taken the afternoon off, seeing my intense frustration. At the park, he stared vacantly at the toddlers who ran freely, while our son struggled to crawl.

I sat on the bench next to him. Rod was in my arms. I raised my voice. Not so loud that anyone could hear. Just loud enough for Morrie to get the point. "Damn it, you are a selfish man. Be a *mensch*. Rod is more important than a garage. Pitching dimes to bring your parents here is a waste. They won't come. You don't even know where they are. They haven't answered your letters. There is war in Germany. Who knows how they are. Rod is the problem we can solve now. There is nothing we can do about Germany. You are in America. For God's sake, live with me and Rod in America." Rod started to cry. The tone of my voice frightened him. I bounced him up and down on my lap.

Morrie looked crushed. I hadn't meant to speak about his parents that way. He found his only safety valve. "I am man. You will not tell me what to do. You will not work. It may be right in America but it is not right for my wife."

"Morrie, please listen to me. You work too much already. Come home some nights. Say hello to your son. He needs the man. He needs you." I spoke into deaf ears.

"Can't come home, go to Johnson's, fix car."

"Can't you cancel, just this time?"

"*Nisht, meis kiet n drai mit nir kain kot.* Didn't I already say no!"

Before Rod turned two, Morrie was taking night work every weekend. *Was I driving him away?* I saw Doctor Schmaltz at the end of each month. Appointments meant more money. My sisters gave me the money to see him. I had no place else to turn. The brace Rod needed cost a month's pay. Morrie said no.

Mama visited. I screamed myself hoarse about Morrie. "He won't listen. He is a mule. He closes his eyes, tries to make everything disappear. Since it won't, he stays away. Maybe he wants me to disappear."

Time flew. Rod was such a lovable baby. He was my teddy bear. He couldn't play with the other kids. His biggest smiles were when I came near. He had two favorite toys, a blanket that I made for him and a stuffed doggy named Hot Dog. He cried when he would drop his *blankee* or Hot Dog.

When I put his toys in his arms, he giggled. I encouraged independence. I had to. He needed to learn to make the best of his condition. I'd let him play alone. I didn't go far, just into another room of the apartment where he could not see me. At first, his cry of fear was shrill. Then, slowly, he amused himself. At three and half, he finally crawled. I cheered. He fell down. I got a bolster and dangled his toys in front of it. He stretched over the bolster for his toys. He was determined.

Morrie showed no signs of change. Every red cent went to savings. He was gone seven days and seven nights a week. Like so many immigrants, he believed in the American dream of ownership. He meant to live that dream.

Rod napped and I read more about cerebral palsy. One night, when Morrie got home, I grabbed my book and pointed to a section that shed some light on Rod's future. "Morrie, read this!"

"I tired. Don't like to read. My English is not *goot*. You are smart. You know best about Rod. You read it. I trust you."

Morrie struggled with trust. At least he trusted me. Rod's condition wasn't going to disappear. Having an active life required Rod to retrain his muscles and use both arms and legs. Rod's mind refused to tell his body what to do.

We struggled together. I had my disappointment and doubts. I made sure Rod never thought of me as disappointed.

One night, shortly before Rod's fourth birthday, when Morrie got home, I placed the evening newspaper, along with a letter that had come in the mail that morning, on the kitchen table. I explained to him that President Roosevelt had authorized the internment of Japanese citizens.

He stood next to me, staring at the headline. Then he saw the letter. "What's this?"

"It came this morning from England. I didn't open it. Do you know someone in England?"

"I have cousin there. His family fled to England when my sister come to America. Don't know why he write." He pierced the envelope with a fingernail and took out the letter inside. He read it quickly, then let it drop onto the floor.

"What is it? Is something wrong?"

"*Vater* and *mutter* have been found out. They have been moved to Auschwitz, a camp for war prisoners in Poland. My cousin learns this through what he calls British underground. That is all he knows. He fears they no longer alive. They are old and useless to Hitler. How can they survive in prison camp? I should not be here. I should be with them. I should go to Poland."

"Morrie, you can't go by yourself. The allies are fighting Hitler. You must stay here and take care of Rod and me."

He picked up the newspaper and threw it to me. "Look, look at what your Mr. FDR has done. He imprisons Japanese who are American citizens. What stops him from coming after Germans like me? I am not American. I am next! Then how safe will any of us be?"

"Morrie, he will not imprison Germans. The Japanese attacked Hawaii at Pearl Harbor, not the Germans."

"What's to stop him? Hitler takes my parents. Now Roosevelt will take me. I am no *goot*. I can't even make a strong child. It is God's punishment. I leave Germany, leave my religion, and leave my parents. I am no *goot* for parents, no *goot* for son, and no *goot* to you."

"Morrie, stop! Rod's condition is not from you. It is from me. I mean it is from my pregnancy. Don't blame yourself. Don't think of Rod as sick. He is loving, smart, and beautiful. Show him your love. He needs you. I need you!"

Morrie had already stopped listening. As I finished my sentence, I looked up and saw the front door slam behind him. He didn't hear a word I said.

I stayed up all night worrying. He must have walked the streets until dawn. When he finally returned, I tried to console him. He ignored me. I watched him dress and leave again without a word.

Rod's birthday party was the following Sunday. I had been planning it for days. Because Morrie was so upset, I thought about calling the family to cancel. I did not.

On the morning of the party, I tried to speak with Morrie. "Morrie, stop blaming yourself. Your parents sent you here. You didn't leave them. They left you. They chose to stay. They wanted you and your sister here safe from what they knew would harm you. Be grateful, not guilty. You are safe here with Rod and me. There is no prison for Germans here. This is not Hitler's Germany."

"I am one to blame. I am responsible. It's me. I make problem. I am *goot* for engines, not people. I touch you. Then you and your Pa break. I make Rod and he is broken. Better I stay away."

"Grow up! Stop whining! You are my husband and the father of our child. Act like a responsible adult. I cannot afford for you to blame yourself. Stop feeling sorry for yourself! Sometimes we must go on with our lives. That is our responsibility."

Rod heard us talking loudly. He got frightened and cried. It upset me to see how fearful Rod was of Morrie.

"Calm down," said Morrie. "You've frightened the boy."

Morrie bent down to take Rod in his arms. Rod fidgeted. Morrie put him down. I picked up him and Morrie stormed outside. I ran out after him. "Don't you dare leave now. I need you home. I need you for the party. I need you to be at your son's birthday. Can't you put your anguish aside long enough to be at your son's party?"

Morrie turned toward me, opening his hands. His shoulders slumped. Tears dripped down his face. Since work was what he knew best, I gave him a job. "Hang these streamers on the ceiling. I can't reach."

Like a zombie, Morrie went outside and returned with his tool box and a ladder. He hung the white and blue streamers from one end of the ceiling to the other. Then he inflated the red, white, and blue balloons, watching them rise. At least our apartment looked happy.

Everyone arrived by two o'clock. As usual, Morrie was quiet. It was Rod's time. In the kitchen, I told Solly what had happened. He tried talking to Morrie but was ignored. Morrie went to the kitchen three times to refill his mug with his favorite European coffee. His coffee was Pa's hooch. An hour into the party, after we all sang "Happy Birthday" to Rod, Morrie exploded.

Maybe it was the coffee or maybe something else. Normally the men, not even Solly, could get a word in edgewise when the girls started gabbing. Morrie spoke over us all. "I am going to prison! They are coming to get me. If American soldiers don't come first, then Germans will get me. I need to hide. I must hide."

Our party crashed into silence. The kids even stopped fighting. I wondered if Morrie was having a breakdown. As he ranted, all I could see was Pa standing in his shoes. Solly grabbed Morrie by the arm and escorted him outside. I don't know what was said. Morrie never told me. I wish I knew.

Once everyone left, I put Rod to bed and joined Morrie on the couch. He seemed calm. I hugged him. We didn't speak.

After that day, Morrie stopped taking new night jobs. He started coming home every night and gradually seemed to regain his self-confidence. I tried to keep busy and not worry.

Frieda visited twice a week. The It Girl, Clara Bow, or the cowboy, John Wayne, dominated her conversation. Hollywood was the universe where Frieda lived. She lived in the lives of stars she idolized. She really believed she was part of their world. They brought color to her life. She had married Michael Clemenski six months after my wedding. He rarely spoke and struggled to hear. His deafness came from the riveting sound of the telegraph early in his career at AT&T. At home, he blasted the radio to hear the RCA broadcast of the Los Angeles Angels in the Pacific Coast League team. He was born in Brooklyn and the Dodgers were his true love. He read the box scores every morning. He didn't like to go out, so he and Frieda no longer danced together. She got bored staying home all the time. On Saturday afternoons, before the birth or their first and only child, she'd sneak out dancing at the Biltmore, or go to the movies to catch a glimpse of the stars after Michael fell asleep to the blasting of the baseball announcer.

Frieda had gotten pregnant a month after marriage. She wanted a baby so our boys could grow up together. Donald was born when Rod was one and a half. Although the two boys tried to play, Rod was outmatched by his younger cousin.

Soon Rod was old enough to go to school. Although the first day was very exciting for both of us, his classmates quickly turned happiness to mental anguish. Rod sat alone and watched others play during recess.

His kindergarten teacher, Mrs. Adamson, gave up before she even tried to fit him into the classroom. "He will do better in a special school for children with disabilities."

I resisted. Instead of demanding other kids play with Rod, Mrs. Adamson went to the school principal to get him out of her class.

I refused to let Rod's teacher's insensitivity slow Rod's development. I worked with Rod every day to help him develop and to teach him how to hold his own. I devoted myself to him in ways I could never have imagined. "Rod, be strong. When the kids tease you, tell them something good about yourself. Better yet, say, 'sticks and stones will break my bones, but names can never hurt me.' Once they figure out they can't hurt you, they will respect you."

Morrie continued to dream of his own garage. Frieda fantasized about her movie stars. Michael followed his baseball stars. Pearl danced the night away. Jack dreamed of owning many stores. Solly risked it all at the track. My own dreams were fading and seemed distant, part of a different life. Late at night, when I had trouble sleeping, I read books about rally drivers to lull myself to sleep. Dreams of zooming by rally car drivers faded like the breezes in the heat of summer. I worried about what I was becoming. Had I become Mama?

Morrie continued to save money and bank it. Jack continued to pile on the debt. Pearl quit her day job and started working nights running poker and pan games. She and Jack had finally married, but she liked the excitement her job offered, and Jack worked late like Morrie. Playing over her head in her own games often turned her stake into losses. Still, she found the money to buy what pleased her. Pearl danced, drank, and dangled her long legs everywhere she went. I don't think she realized her teenage figure showed signs of fading. It would have killed Pearl to think she was no longer a living doll.

When she came to our place, she always sang to Rod. "Aunty Pearl is coming." Rod clapped and giggled and jumped for joy. Rod was the Pearl's best audience and she loved her nephew dearly. "He's amazing, so darn happy." She was always optimistic. "Doctors will come up with a fix. They just need a big payoff to their research. It's like playing ponies. Sooner or later your horse will come in." Struggling to keep my head above water, I loved her endlessly upbeat thoughts.

Mama also spent time with us. As usual, Pa was always at *shul*. She'd cook for days and bring me dinner for three nights at a time. She'd pick up the egg bread *challah* from Canter's. It pulled apart like cotton candy and tasted like butter. Her beef brisket, which simmered for a whole day on her stove, was my favorite. When I spooned the brisket gravy onto the *challah*,

Rod gushed, literally salivated while waiting for a bite. We often spoke of Pa.

"*Oy*, you can't believe, even in his sixties, he screams like a teenage hoodlum. '*Sha, sha!*' I tell him. 'Bring it down a notch.' He thinks he is a *gantser k'nacker*, such a big shot. The words that come out of his mouth. *Vey iz mir,* it's terrible. He just doesn't know how to be retired. Ever since we came to California, he acts not like an old cow put out to pasture, but an old bull running from slaughter."

"Mama, doesn't all his *dovening* in the temple make him more peaceful?"

"Peaceful, don't kid me! Every day he grows more self-righteous. I think he spends too much time at *shul*. The prayers are good. But we don't live in *Yisrael*. We live in Los Angeles with many gentiles. We live in difficult times. Pa *dovens*, then he drinks. This is not a peaceful combination. He comes home and *fresses* down his food like a man who hasn't eaten in days. I think he tries to fill the emptiness. I fear he will choke. The food and the shots of schnapps make him snore like a goat. He wakes in the middle of night in a cold sweat. God knows of what he dreams. Something, maybe death without redemption, scares him. In the morning, he's gone."

Mama was not aging well. Her arthritis and living with Pa had become a living hell. The eight blocks from her house to mine took it out of her. Solly walked with her. She stumbled when she climbed my stairs.

One Sunday, when the family had all gathered at my house, she shocked us all. "The doctors are worried about Pa. It's his ticker. He complained of heartburn. I forced him to Dr. Goldbloom. A few minutes after he goes in for an examination, the nurse calls me in. The doctor tells me Pa needs to change. So what's new? He needs to drink less whiskey. I laughed. Then I bring the doctor to his senses. 'From your mouth to God's ears. Sure I'd like him to stop. You think he listens to me?' Pa wriggles in his seat as I talk. He looks like he's ready to run. I tell the doctor I will try."

Solly piped up. "I'm glad this came up now. I've been meaning to talk to the family about Pa. Someone has to stop him before he destroys himself or one of us. Just last Tuesday, he bursts uninvited in the front door of the store and starts screaming, I mean *really screaming*, at a customer. '*Schmendrick*, don't just stand there, buy something. These prices are cheap, cheap, cheap. You waiting for Purim?'"

Solly continued as every ear pointed in his direction. "The customer looks at me. I want to *plotz* right on the spot. I apologize. I try to make amends. It doesn't matter, the customer walks."

We all waited for Solly to go on. That's when he sharpened his pencil and hit a bull's eye. "Pa's gone berserk! He's a menace to everyone around him. He attacked me, can you believe it! He attacked me after the customer left. His fists pounded my shoulder like I had kicked the poor customer out. What could I do? I couldn't hit him back. So Pa turns and walks out without as much as a word of apology. The doctor's right. We've got to stop him before it is too late."

I thought Mama might try to calm Solly down some, but instead, her next words were directed at me. "Bella, you never know. Please make amends. Go see your pa. Bring your Rod. Believe me, if you don't, you'll be sorry when he's gone."

The last thing, the very last thing, I needed in my life was another collision with Pa. "Mama, he kicked me out. He's the one that needs to apologize."

The conversation ended on those words. There was no anger. Rod and Donald had been playing in the other room. They were squabbling. It was time for everyone to go home. I put Rod down for a nap and started to clean up. Morrie went off to check on the garage. I sat down with a book and started to cry.

Later that night, when Morrie came home, he asked is something was wrong."

"Mama keeps demanding I go see Pa. I can't, I just can't!"

"Your mama is right, Bella. Go see your pa. You must go, first thing tomorrow."

"Damn it! Why do you always take her side? It's bad enough I get it from her. I don't deserve it from you. I can't. Rod has a doctor's appointment. Pa will have to wait. Morrie, I'm tired. Go kiss Rod goodnight."

"Do I have too? I so greasy. I scare him to death."

"Sometimes I don't know if you are the child or the father. Your son needs a father. Wash up and kiss him goodnight. He's probably already out. If he's scared, tell him to be strong. Be strong yourself. You are a good man and it's time to get over whatever is holding you back. You may not have your parents here in America. But you have your son. Go be a father! I mean it!"

He knew I was right about his relationship with Rod. I knew he was right about going to see Pa.

"You are a good mother. I am sorry. I wish I was *so goot*."

I knew Morrie wanted to do the right thing. "Rod thinks you are the greatest mechanic in the world. He always wants to fix things here at the house. At first I just laughed and told him that is Daddy's job. But he insists. 'Mama,' he says, 'I want to be fixer like daddy.'"

Morrie loved hearing that. Next thing, he washed up and spent more than an hour in Rod's room. When he came back to bed, I acted like I was asleep. He snuggled up to me. It had been a long time since we were that close.

Chapter 26

I n 1943, the day after Rod's fifth birthday, Solly pulled up in 1940 Cherry Red Chrysler Saratoga. It was a beauty.

"Go get Rod, let's take her for a spin."

The sun glistened off its domed roof. I climbed inside with Rod in my arms. He had never been in any car other than his daddy's. The upholstery was an amazing scotch plaid. Solly gunned it east on Sunset. "Please Solly, no heroics. Drive safely. I don't want Rod to be hurt." I clutched Rod's waist. Solly hadn't heard a word I said. Once we were out of the city, he speeded up.

"Mama, is this a rocket?"

No, honey, it's a Chrysler car."

"Sounds just like the rockets on Buck Roger's radio show."

Solly and I laughed. Rod grabbed a few locks of my hair, which had been tousled by the wind coming in through the open window. After a brief stop for lemonade, Solly put Rod in his lap behind the steering wheel. While still parked, Solly let Rod twist the steering as though he were driving.

"Look Mama, I'm driving."

If only Morrie could see this.

Solly must have seen my excitement. "Get behind the wheel, Bella. I know it's been a while but it'll be just like the old days."

"A while! How about six years?"

It was one thing to let Solly hold Rod while we were parked. It was another to get behind the wheel and leave my son in the hands of my brother. "Ah ... I shouldn't. No, maybe next time!"

"Come on, I know you can do it."

"Sure, I can do it. But can you handle Rod?"

"Are you kidding, we're old buddies. Aren't we old buddies, Rod?" Solly gave him a hug.

"Mama, we're buddies!"

"Heck, I'll give it a try. You hold onto him. Don't let go for a second. No telling what I'll do after all these years." I slid into the driver's seat as Solly carried Rod around to the passenger seat. I keyed the ignition and listened to the engine purr. My heart beat a rhythm. I was fifteen again. The steering wheel was like an old friend. My foot pressed and off we went. Another lady driver gave us a thumbs-up as she drove by. Solly raised Rod's right thumb to return the gesture.

While cruising back home, I felt a freedom I hadn't felt in years. I was on the open road again. Solly, Rod, and I were on the open road! Rod never stopped talking to Solly the whole time I was driving.

Back home, Rod ran around the apartment in circles. I started to prepare dinner. Then he picked up a baseball bat left behind by Donald. He held it with two hands in front of his chest. He pushed one side up and pulled the other side down. Then he moved the bat's angle in opposite directions. Soon I realized what he was doing.

"Let's go for a drive," I said. I grabbed a dish towel and made the same up-and-down motion he had been making. We were both driving cars. With Rod in front, and me in back, we sputtered around the house. Rod never took his eyes off the road. He was on his own. "Mama, I'm driving. I'm driving, just like you."

Chapter 27

On the Fourth of July, 1943, Mama, the girls, their kids, Morrie, Rod, and I gathered to watch the fireworks display at Echo Park. The lights in the sky came to a blazing finale. We made funny sounds of excitement as each light flamed up into the sky. Bob Bratten's brass band played "Star Spangled Banner." Morrie had been antsy the entire evening. Before we could gather our picnic basket and blanket, he stood up and motioned to get our attention. He spoke slowly, and I could tell he had practiced what he had to say, his sentences more well-formed than usual.

"It's been more than six years since I come to America. I have been blessed with my Bella and Rod. My dream has been to own a piece of this country, to have own garage. My *vater* owned garage in Germany. I learned to be mechanic from him. I wish I could hear what I have to say. Hopefully, I bring my parents here when war is over. It's no secret I save my earnings to buy business. Bella and Rod have suffered waiting for my dream to come. I have saved more than ten thousand American dollars. It is time to buy garage!"

Mama smiled. "He's worked like a dog. Now he will have his business."

Morrie found a struggling mechanic off Sunset and bought his shop. With so many fighting overseas, there was a shortage of skilled mechanics. Jack, the shop's former owner, agreed to stay on. He was getting a divorce and needed the money. Morrie told us he would name the shop after our son.

Rod was tickled pink with the new shop's name, The Hot Rod. Morrie invested $5,000 in the purchase and put aside the rest to run it. After working so many nights on different cars, his reputation in our part of town was unmatched. New customers lined up at his door as soon as he opened the shop. He hired a third mechanic. I took care of the books. Morrie continued to work day and night. Gradually, he shifted his clientele to professionals. They sought him out. They wanted the best.

Rod and I came into the garage every Friday afternoon after school was out. I completed payroll, deposited the cash receipts, and paid the bills. While I did the bookkeeping, Rod did his homework or played. By the time

Rod was in the second grade, at seven, he was the fastest reader in his class. During recess, he didn't play. He read. When the kids in his class realized he was smart, our phone rang off the hook.

"Hi Rod, I've got a question. Did you get the answer to number six on the homework? Oh, and just one more question? What is the name of the first mission in California?"

"Yep, that's easy. Father Junipero Serra founded Mission San Diego on July 16, 1769. After a few years, it was moved inland. In November, 1776, it was attacked by eight hundred Native Americans and burnt down. It was rebuilt in less than a year. There were twenty-one missions altogether."

"Okay, that's good, but all I needed to know was the name."

"It's all on page 30 of our history book. Can't think of the name without coming up with the history."

"Thanks Rod. See you at school."

Rod was at whiz at math, too!

"Hi Rod, can we study our multiplication tables together after school?"

"Sure, Mary, I know them. Need some help?"

"Yep, my mom works. She's not around most of the time. My dad's in the army fighting the Germans. I'd really love it if you'd help me."

Rod never hesitated. His group of friends grew. In the third grade, at Elysian Heights Elementary, he was elected president of his class. As part of a patriotism contest put on by the *Los Angeles Times* newspaper, all the kids wrote letters about the U.S military men in the war. Morrie helped Rod understand that not all Germans supported Hitler. The newspaper published Rod's essay. It was different from what the other kids wrote. I was thrilled to read my son's words. Before dawn, I ran out to buy ten copies for all the family to see. I wanted to be certain the newspaper boy on the street corner didn't sell out.

I am an American. My mother was born in Los Angeles and my father was born in Germany. My father works very hard. He bought a garage like his father and helps famous professional race drivers make their cars run superfast. I am lucky because he didn't have to go and fight the bad guys. I have never seen my grandparents in Germany. They were sent away by Hitler. They were Jewish. Now most of the kids in my school hate the Germans. That scares me. My daddy says many people in Germany do not like Hitler. Not all Germans are bad guys. My daddy is not a bad guy. It is sad when we have to fight for our rights. My daddy says you have to stand up for what you believe. I think maybe my grandparents spoke out against the government of Hitler and that's why Hitler sent them away. My daddy does not know where they are. I am sad for the kids whose fathers were sent to fight in the war. I hope they come back okay. I think the American Army will win the war. Then maybe, my grandparents can come to visit me. I hope nobody hates them, me, my mom, or my dad.

One anonymous person wrote an editorial that I did not show Rod, Morrie, or my family. Hopefully they will never see it.

It is disgusting that you published what that kid from Elysian Heights Elementary wrote. We are fighting the Germans. They want all of us dead. If it wasn't for the Jews, the Gypsies, the Catholics, and the homos, Hitler wouldn't be killing Americans. We've had to fight the Germans twice this century. Of course Germans are bad. Hitler is a monster. We put the Japs in this country in internment camps. We should put the Germans away too. That mechanic dad of the kid, he's probably a spy for the other side. As far as I concerned, all Germans are bad. Send the dad, the kid, and his whole family back to where they belong. Send them into the hands of the Fuhrer.

I was horrified by what I read. With people like *Anonymous* out there, it was no wonder that Morrie was constantly on edge.

One of Morrie's clients was Maximilian Spedanski. When Morrie told me that he was working with Spedanski, I couldn't believe it. Spedanski was a European rally-world idol. He had won nine major rallies in Europe, including the Rally Targa Florio, held in the mountains of Sicily. Morrie said there was talk about a rally in the United States and to keep an eye on the sports section of the newspaper. I had been doing this for weeks, but when I picked up the September 2nd, 1945, edition of the *Los Angeles Times* I didn't bother to look beyond the headlines. The Japanese had surrendered and World War II was finally over.

Germany had surrendered back on May 8, a week after Hitler committed suicide. American liberation troops found untold numbers of war prisoners, hideous gas chambers, and naked bodies in mass graves. There was no word from Morrie's parents. We feared the worst.

Celebratory events of all kinds were being planned throughout the country. I thought a cross-country rally by Europeans and American rally drivers would be a wonderful way to celebrate victory.

Morrie soon learned more about plans for a US rally. "Soon, Spedanski will make the first US cross-country rally from Los Angeles to Chicago. I am preparing two of his cars, including his Stutz Bearcat."

The drive in Solly's Chrysler had reignited something inside me. "I have to meet him. He's the best there ever was. When can I say hello?"

"Nishe goot. Don't want you in the way!"

"In the way! How can I be in the way! I'll just say hello. You know Rod is fascinated with racing. He'll be with me on Friday. Will Spedanski come in then?"

Morrie was still reeling from what he had been reading about those imprisoned in German concentration camps. He didn't answer right away.

"How about an introduction as a birthday present to me?" I had just celebrated my twenty-fourth birthday."

At first Morrie said no, Spedanski was a busy man, but after a week of harassing, he gave in. "Okay, Maximilian will come pick up his Stutz Friday morning. You and Rod come, and I will introduce."

It was mid- September and Rod was back in school. Morrie agreed to let Rod take the day off for the special meeting. To prepare, Rod and I read many books about rally racers. He wrote an essay at school about the Lucerne to Rome rally. It was brilliant. He not only reported on the winners, he wrote about those who almost didn't finish.

Rod and I arrived at Morrie's garage at ten Friday morning. We sat quietly waiting. Morrie worked on a pre-war BMW. Our world-famous driver was late. The clock ticked and we waited anxiously. By noon, Rod was hungry. There was nothing but black coffee at the shop. We were ready to go out for a bite. I wanted to wait a little longer.

"Mom, can we eat? Maybe he's not coming today. I want to see him, but I'm hungry."

"Let's wait another fifteen minutes, okay. If he doesn't come, we can go then."

At that moment, our man entered the garage with a flourish. His Panama hat shaded his face and a big cigar hung out of his mouth. His slight frame was covered in a three-piece white leather driving suit with a red winner medallion sewn on his vest. It was boiling outside. Maybe 85 degrees.

Spedanski walked up to Morrie, making no apology for being late. "What are you working on?"

Morrie was under the chassis of the BMW. "Mr. Spedanski, I so glad you're here. Finished your car. Now doing final repairs on an old BMW. It was made before the monster took over my country." Morrie came topside, ran to the Stutz Bearcat, got in the driver's seat and gunned the engine. "How does she sound, Max?"

"Sounds like a kitten. What did she need?"

Morrie got out of the car and asked Spedanski to come look under the hood. I couldn't see what they were looking at. Max smiled at Morrie like a

Cheshire cat. Morrie pointed his forefinger at the carburetor. "She is a beauty, Mr. Spedanski. I did some carburetor work, too!"

I smiled, listening to Morrie talk. His English was improving, especially when talking to customers. Morrie and Max went to the other side of the car. They were animated. When they were done, they came over to Rod and me.

"What do I owe, Morrie?"

For me, time stood still. Morrie motioned to the two of us. "Mr. Spedanski, this is my wife, Bella. This handsome young man is Rod, my son. They are great fans. I met Bella when she fifteen years old. Her brother had a 1926 T Rod Roadster. I had just arrived in America. He hired me to make his car perform for Bella. He had bet a lot of money that she would beat his buddies in a road race. She's not only a beauty and a good mother, she a great driver. Bella takes care of my accounting. She'll give you the bill. Rod is my pride and joy. He has cerebral palsy, but it doesn't hold him back. He's an *A* student in school."

Spedanski smiled and shook Rod's right hand. Rod grinned. "You are very famous, sir. I am proud to meet you. My mama and I have read about you in my books. My papa says your Stutz Bearcat is the fastest car ever."

"Happy to meet you, kid. I had a brother back in Russia who had cerebral palsy. It was tough. There was little that could be done then. Today, it's different. There is plenty that can be done to help. I love that you like race driving. For a kid, you've got one strong grip."

Rod beamed! Spedanski turned to me. "Bella, you are a lucky woman. Your husband is an excellent mechanic. I've never known a woman who liked to drive. You drove your brother's car in a race as a kid at fifteen! That is amazing! Gutsy, weren't you? What was it like for you?"

I opened my mouth, but was star struck. My cheeks must have turned dark red. Finally, I caught my breath. "Mr. Spedanski, it's been over eight years. It was pure exhilaration. Reaching the finish line was a rush of excitement. It was a moment in my life I will never forget! I don't drive much now, but when I do, the sensation is like that first time. It's always been my dream to be professional driver, but life happens. I am thrilled and proud to be Rod's mother and Morrie's wife. I don't need more right now."

"I know, I know, sometimes we lose our dreams. But have you completely given up on yours? Would you like to race again?"

"Well …" I turned away, befuddled for a second. "Yes, I would … someday." I wasn't sure where this was going. "I've always liked the thrill of competition. I love the battle." As I spoke, I realized how much I had given up.

I was so conflicted. The responsibility of motherhood and being a wife had overtaken me in ways I didn't fully grasp until Spedanski asked his question.

"Isn't Rod in school most of the day?"

"Yes, of course. But, I help him with his studies. We do homework."

"What does his doctor say?"

"There are some new therapies. We just don't have the money."

A summer rainstorm had blown in. The tin roof made a racket. Thunder exploded. Max turned to Morrie. "Morrie, you are a great mechanic. I'm a rally driver and a promoter. I have an opportunity for you, your wife, and your son that you cannot pass up. I'm promoting the first US cross-country rally from Los Angeles to Chicago along Route 66 next year in August. I think this country is ready for some fun. Some of the returning service men who went overseas have seen European rallies. I want to do something to celebrate the great victory of the Americans, Europeans, and Russians. I've got plenty of European men who will come here to promote the sport. I am sure there will be some American men who will participate. There's never been a woman rally driver. I'm concerned that we won't get much of a turnout or press coverage for our American rally. I would love to sponsor Bella as my driver. She could drive my Stutz Bearcat. That should give her an edge. You know better than I, you're the mechanic. I will pay her just to enter. I will cover all travel and hotel expenses for the three of you. If she wins, she will earn the winner's pot. I can pay the sponsorship money upfront in twelve monthly installments as long as she continues to train and perform. If you both accept my offer, and I'm sure you will, I'll make you the official mechanic for the race. I'll pay you a monthly stipend. We'll put a huge sign out front of your garage. You'll pick up many of the top European drivers and some new American upstarts. During the race, you can ride with Bella. That way, you can make sure the Bear doesn't break down and leave your wife stranded."

Max's proposal floored me! I melted into the chair behind me. Our world had just turned right side up.

Morrie's spoke quickly, with authority I never expected. His words echoed above the rain's patter on the roof. "Yes, we can do this! For my boy and my wife, this is something that can happen only in America."

Morrie reached out to Rod and me. We bear hugged. Then we added Max to make a foursome. He wasn't so comfortable with all this public hugging.

On the way home, Rod and I were like two kids, filled with enthusiasm that was impossible to contain. Life was on restart. Pearl had gotten it right.

Men are stubborn until they are not. Morrie had come around in his own time when he was ready.

Chapter 28

I didn't sleep well. I was too excited. When morning did come, I bounced out of bed full of energy. I ran around the house, straightening the pictures on the wall, washing dishes, reorganizing clothes in the closet, and finally making breakfast at six-thirty for Morrie and Rod. Rod was rubbing sleep out of his eyes. "Morning, Mom, how long have you been up?"

"Honey, I haven't been this excited in years. I woke up with the roosters. Made a special breakfast for my boys this morning."

I dished gobs of salami and eggs on each of their plates, spread orange marmalade on their toasted rye bread, and poured two small glasses of orange juice. After they finished eating, Morrie took Rod to his school bus stop.

Frieda called at ten. "Bella, I can't believe it! Been up all night."

Confused, I asked. "Who told you?"

"Solly was the first one to know. He's with the doctor now."

"Doctor? What are you talking about?"

"Pa had a stroke. Solly called the ambulance. Pa's in a coma at Cedars Hospital on Fountain. The doctor says he may not make it. Even if he rallies, he may never talk again."

"Oh, my God! How's Mama?"

"She's at the hospital. You know her. She's the Polish rock of Gibraltar."

My eyes welled with tears. "Frieda, what happened?"

Frieda sounded amazingly calm. "Didn't you know? Pa and Solly were battering each other yesterday. I guess Pa was giving him hell. Pa starts slurring his words and rubs his eyes like he has a headache. Then Pa just keels over. So Solly calls for an ambulance. He told me waiting for that ambulance to arrive was the longest seven minutes of his life. When they get there, an attendant hooks Pa up with an oxygen mask and some sort of intravenous solution. Once they get to the hospital, after the doctors in the emergency room finally get to him, they tell Solly that Pa has a massive brain hemorrhage. I don't really understand, but I know it's bad. Pearl took Mama there at midnight. She hasn't slept. They're all a mess."

Frieda started to sob. Now it was my turn to be the calm one. "I'm sure it's not as bad as it sounds. They always make it sound worse than it is. Don't worry, sis. He'll recover."

I needed to go to Mama. I rushed out the front door, remembered I was in my nightgown, and rushed back inside to change.

Pa was on the fifth floor of the hospital. When I arrived, Solly, Mama, and Pearl were sitting in the waiting area. I went immediately to Mama. She looked exhausted. We kissed.

"Go see him. Pay respects. You must."

I knew Mama was right this time. Gingerly, Solly took my hand. Together, we all walked toward the intensive care unit. The blood rushed out of my body. Solly was shockingly silent, none of his usual piss and vinegar on display. Before I entered Pa's room, Mama spoke to me. "God slowed him down. Now we must pray for his recovery."

I was shocked at how frail Pa looked. Bending beside his bed, I said, "Pa, it's Bella."

No response. His eyes were sunken, scalp bald, his face white with whiskers. He lay motionless under his oxygen mask with tubes hooked up to him for nutrition. Ironically, he looked peaceful.

I reached over and held his cold hand. Still no response. I couldn't hover over him for long. I couldn't take it. It was too painful. After a few minutes, Solly, whose face was stained with guilt, looked over to me. It was clear he wanted to be alone with Pa. I'd had enough for one day.

When I returned to the waiting room, Sarah, Kate, and Frieda were huddled together, deep in conversation. Now the whole family was gathered together, except for Pa. I don't remember what we said. Who knows the right words. The hospital smelled antiseptic. Solly soon joined us, slumping into the chair next to me, whimpering. Mama rubbed his shoulders as only a mama can do.

"It's my fault," said Solly. "I drove him to this." He threw up his hands. "It was about the cash register. It's always about that. He barrels into the store and about knocks over a customer. He grabs my collar. 'Where's my money? Where's my money?'" Solly looked at us, trying to take in his family in one desperate glace. "I'm no criminal. Why does he have to question me in front of a customer? He runs to the cash register, but there's nothing in it but small change. I'd cleaned it out the night before and forget to put the bills back in. The money I won at my game was still rolled up in a rubber band inside my pants pocket. So I pull the roll out of my pocket so he won't think we're dead broke. Then his rage turns to fury. He must have thought I was stealing. Crap, it's my store. I do all the work. It's none of his business where I keep the money. Sure, business is pretty damn slow. All this crazy rationing makes it impossible to buy any merchandize. We still have all that old junk Pa bought in the thirties. It's so old that nobody, and I mean *nobody*, wants it. Worse yet, those who buy that crap still can't afford to pay back their credit accounts. Cash sales hardly keep the doors open."

Solly took a breath. I could tell he was gauging our reactions. He went on, "So, when Pa starts slurring, I know something's up. I've seen him mad before, but he never loses it completely. This time, he starts shaking. He drops to the ground like a fallen tree." Once again, Solly stopped talking, trying to take us all in with one glance. He was sweating. We all just sat there. He went on. "He took me by surprise. I couldn't catch him. God, I wish I had stopped his fall. First, he knocks into the cabinet with tie tacks. After he hits the ground, hundreds of ties fall off the rack onto him. I brush them off, run and grab a wet rag for his forehead. He doesn't have a pulse. I'm pretty shook up. Never been that scared before. I hear the bell ring. A customer comes in. 'Call an ambulance,' I say. 'My Pa is sick.' After a horrible wait, I hear sirens. They're loud, and keep getting louder. Two guys come in. They put Pa on a gurney, and next thing, I'm talking to the doctors at Cedars. They tell me they've wired Pa up, that there's nothing to do but wait, that Pa's stable but very weak. That's when I called Mama. You know the rest."

There we were, huddled in the hospital lounge, helpless. Strange how things turn out. Pa always told us what to do, and we hated it, one and all. Now that he was unable to speak, we desperately wanted to hear his voice. His forcefulness had caused us to rebel. His silence forced us to return.

Mama sat in her chair, praying. The rest of us looked at one another, and then silently, without coaxing, prayed too. I had so much to say. "Let him live, dear God, even if we have all failed you, please give Pa a second chance."

The doctor entered the room. "We don't know how long his coma will last. If he awakes or worsens, we will call you. You should all go home."

Mama wanted to stay. We convinced her to come home with us.

"What if awakes? Who will be here to say hello?"

"Mama, the nurses will watch him."

"Nurses, what does he know from nurses? He'll be frightened to death of these *shiksehs* in their white uniforms with little hats on top."

"Mama, you need to rest. You're exhausted. Kate and Sarah will stay the night. Pearl will bring you back in the morning."

"How can they stay? What about their children?"

"Don't worry, they have husbands.

We took Mama home. It had been years since I set foot inside the house where I grew up. Mama refused to sit. "Hungry? I'll make banana bread. Would you like some?"

Solly didn't want her to cook. "For God's sake, Mama, sit down. We don't need banana bread now. You need you to rest."

Mama turned a deaf ear. I went to the kitchen with her. It was like the old days. She lit the light on the stove and pulled down the mixing bowls with stenciled cows on them. I crushed the bananas. She measured the baking soda, salt, flour, and brown sugar. I poured the mixture into baking tins. She stirred in the chunks of mashed bananas. In half an hour, she poured each of us a cup of milk and scooped strawberry preserves in her crystal dish, her Polish Rock of Gibraltar. It showed no signs of cracking.

Mama had stood strong during Pa's rampages. Why not during his silence. For the moment, until Pa returned to health, she would be the head of the family. Her eyes were bloodshot behind her round spectacles. Her white hair, thin and straight, hung to her waist. She wore her customary white blouse and black skirt. Her support hose covered the entire twelve inches between the hem of her skirt and her black oxford shoes. Mama was exhausted, but unchanged.

After cooking, serving, and washing dishes, she finally collapsed into the living room chair where Pa typically sat. I was the first to ask. "Mama, will you come and stay with me until Pa gets better?"

She turned in her chair, placed a tiny age-spotted hand on my shoulder, and looked directly into my eyes. "No, I'll be more comfortable at home. I need to be here to keep the place neat and tidy for when Pa comes home. I'll go to the hospital tomorrow. You come, too. We can visit there while we sit. I haven't seen Rod in a few days. Is he good?"

"He's fine, at school now. But I want you to stay with me and Rod."

"No, maybe later. Then I'll come and stay. Tomorrow, you'll come see Pa in the hospital, right?"

I wasn't going to change her mind. I was kind of happy that she was stubborn about staying. At least she had the strength to know what she wanted. "I'll pick you up, Mama. I need to see him." A pang of worry took hold of me. It had been so long. Would I ever hear Pa speak again? I was startled back to reality by Pearl's voice.

"Don't worry so much. There will be time. When he wakes, you two can talk. Now just get on with your life. Forget the past. God knows, I have lots to forget. Forgive yourself. You had no choice. Pa was tough, demanding, and unforgiving. Believe me, I know."

Mama was now on her knees in front a cabinet in the corner of the room. She reached into it and pulled out a bottle of schnapps. She poured it into tiny crystal shot glasses and handed one to each of us.

Solly led a toast to Pa. "May he live to see each of our smiling faces and those of all his grandchildren many times."

Mama spoke up. "There are things you may not know. He looked for purpose. He didn't much care about happiness. He didn't just *go* to the synagogue. He studied the Torah. The lessons he learned were certainly old school. He always felt betrayed by his children. He couldn't understand why you couldn't follow. The terror of the Jews in Europe didn't scare him, it made him more resolute. To you, Pa's rampages were *meshuge*, a crazy man ranting. To me, they were his desperate attempts to prove himself to his Temple friends. They became his family, followed the Torah, went to synagogue, but never really accepted of him. Yet, he never stopped trying to prove himself. He couldn't! We never saw eye to eye. I hated his rampages. But I understood."

As I took my sip of schnapps, I noticed the time. It was three in the afternoon.

"I have to run. Rod will be at the bus stop any minute." I flew out the door. I wanted to tell them, at least Frieda and Pearl, about my Spedanski miracle, but now was not the time.

Chapter 29

Hi Rod, I had such a day. I was worried you might get here before me."

"Why, is something wrong? Are we still in the rally?"

"Yes, of course we are. But I have a few things I need to think about before I discuss them with you. Can you be patient with me?"

"Patient? Sure. Is it Dad? Is he mad or something?"

"No, no, we'll talk later, okay?"

At home, I helped Rod with his homework, made dinner for the two of us, and put Morrie's meal in the icebox. Then I crawled into bed. Later, I woke up when I heard something hit the oven rack with a thud. I wriggled out of bed and went into the kitchen where Morrie was heating up the mac and cheese casserole I'd left for him. I gave him a big hug, which I held longer than normal. "I have bad news."

"What is it? Is Rod — ?

" — No, Rod is fine. It's Pa."

"Did you go to him, apologize?"

"Wish I had. He had a stroke and is in a coma. He may die. If he lives, he may not be able to speak again."

"How's your mama?"

"Holding up. She's tough."

"What happened?"

"Something broke in his brain. I don't really understand it all. It may be days before we know more."

"Did you tell them about Spedanski?"

"Couldn't. Wouldn't have been right. I will talk to Solly later. Now we must wait."

I struggled to get my words out. Morrie knew it. I felt feint. We held onto each other tightly for another moment. His body, next to mine, felt so good. He picked me up and carried me to bed. Yesterday, Morrie allowed me to take on the Spedanski challenge. Today, he consoled me. I fell asleep in his arms. It couldn't have been long before a dream filled my head.

I was driving Solly's new car. Pa was walking to work. I screamed for his attention. Rod was with me. "Rod, it's your grandpa." Rod did not recognize him. How could he? They'd never met. "Pa, it's me, Bella, and your grandson, Rod." Pa started walking faster, like he wanted to get away. I coasted at his speed. I spoke to him again. Pa started to jog. He'd never moved that fast before. "Pa, are you okay? Are you okay?" I screamed these last words in my sleep.

Morrie woke me. We both fell back asleep. This time, I dreamt Mama was trying to catch her breathe while climbing my stairs. I ran down to help her up. She would have none of it. She wanted to do it herself. "Don't need help. Did you see Pa today?" Her voice wasn't Mama's. It was Pa's. Her lips moved, but Pa's raspy, angry voice came out of her mouth. I awoke, this time in a cold sweat.

Morning came and Rod woke me out of a sound sleep. Morrie had left for work without breakfast. Rod readied himself for school without my help. Normally, I would have been up before him but I had overslept. I reached into my purse and handed him a quarter for lunch. I threw on an old dress and sandals and walked him to the bus. I was on the brink.

Back at the house, I called Frieda. "Any news?"

"No, Solly took Mama to the hospital early. Couldn't go myself."

"Okay, I'll stay home and wait to hear from Mama."

That afternoon, when Rod returned, I told him about Pa, explained how we had argued and become separated.

"Was Grandpa mean to you?"

"He was stubborn and could say some pretty mean things. He expected everyone to follows his rules, even when they weren't fair. He wasn't afraid to take it too us kids with a strap when he thought we needed it."

"A strap? You mean he hit you with a belt?"

"It didn't happen often. I might have deserved it. For Pa, it was his way or no way. Solly, my sisters, and I are all strong willed. You, too. Knowing what you want gives you character. Sometimes our strength becomes a weakness. We have our opinions. In the family, strong opinions sometimes create feuds. That's what happened with Pa and me. We had a terrible feud. We stopped talking before you were born. Your father and I fight. We don't feud. Sometimes, we stop talking for as long as a day. Then it's all good again. Feuding can be disastrous. It can go on for years. Everyone loses. The more we love, the tougher it is when love turns to hate. Hate happens too often within families."

"Fighting someone you love doesn't make sense."

"Emotions take charge. They shouldn't, but they do. My parents came from another time and another place. Pa and I damaged each other. I regret it now."

"Mama, I'm sorry you're sad."

"I'll get over it. He'll get better. Then I'll make amends."

After a week, Pa's condition was unchanged. I couldn't wait. I had to make plans for the rally. I had to speak to Solly. After I got Rod off to school and Morrie to work, I hopped the streetcar to the store. It had been years. I'd stayed away because I was afraid Pa would be there.

"We need to talk," I said to Solly. "Stop running around for a minute, will you."

"Okay, okay, what's so important?"

"I know this isn't the time, but I have good news."

"Is it about Pa?"

"No, I wish it were, but I have no news about him. It's about me. Something happened."

"Yeah?"

"It's like this. Morrie works on cars for a great European rally driver named Spedanski. He's promoting a big cross-country rally. He's asked me to drive for him. I'll be the first women rally driver in America. Morrie agreed to drive with me as my mechanic. I want you to join us, follow the rally to Chicago and drive Rod with you on the road. It will be an adventure."

Solly stopped dead in his tracks. "My God, you'll be the only woman driver in the first American cross-country rally! That's wonderful! I'm so happy for you. I mean it."

"Solly, I need your help. I can't leave Rod by himself. Can you come with us? Can you bring Rod across country in your car?"

"How can I go? Pa may die. There is no one to take care of Mama. The money to run the business is running out. I've got to get some of these deadbeats to pay up. Wartime rationing has ended. Soldiers are returning. There's opportunity to turn this business around. I can't go. I can't afford to pay someone to take care of it. I just can't."

"The race is nearly a year away. What if Pa gets better soon?"

"*What if?* I can't pay my bills with *what ifs*. That's how we got into trouble in the first place."

"Can't Kate take over while?"

"No, she has her own business and her children to watch out for. This store is mine. I'm part of this disaster. I'll find a way out, but it'll take time. Why not leave Rod here with me or with one of the girls."

"I can't do that. Rod is part of the dream. He has to come." I didn't like what I was hearing. I understood, but I didn't like it. I thanked Solly and let him know I would find a way to make things work.

"Bella, I know you better than you know yourself. I know you'll find a way.

That night, I told Morrie that Solly could not drive Rod. I already had a new plan "Rod can come with me in the Bear." You can drive a second car and be there with parts and solutions. What do you think?"

Morrie was determined to make everything work. He agreed. "Joey can take charge of the garage, and I'll bring Jack from the shop with me. That way we can follow you."

It was settled. I would have five glorious days with Rod at my side, traveling cross country in the rally of a lifetime. Now, if Pa would just rally.

Once I started training, time passed quickly. There was no change in Pa's condition. Every day, one of us took Mama to the hospital so she could sit at Pa's bedside.

Morrie started a new repair routine on the Bear to make sure Spedanski's car was in tiptop shape. Rod and I discussed the training I needed for the rally.

It was October 2nd, nearly ten days after Pa's stroke. Pa was still at the hospital, still speechless and in a coma. During each of those ten days, I had traced and retraced every inch of my practice route on an auto club map. I committed it to memory. Twice, I went to Morrie's garage and sat behind the wheel of Spedanski's pride and joy. Spedanski's car was faster and much more valuable than anything I had ever driven before. There was no room for error. Finally, I was ready to begin my training in earnest.

After leaving the hospital the morning of the eleventh day, I walked to Morrie's garage and told him I was ready to go.

"Okay, take it easy the first time out."

"No problem, I'll drive her like she's my own child." I sat behind the wheel, positioned myself so I could see perfectly, pressed upon the floor starter button, released the brake, and off I went. I drove her on a short route to Brooklyn Avenue and back. It was too late to take the long route and still get back in time to pick up Rod. It went well. She performed like no other car on the road. I returned to Morrie's garage, beaming. Life for me had begun anew.

After that, I drove the Bear for two hours on short training days and for four hours on days scheduled for longer training rides. I learned her flaws and strengths. I stopped on Brooklyn Avenue every day, at the end of my drive, for a phosphate vanilla soda before returning to Morrie's garage. I didn't have time for lunch. Once a week, I splurged at Canter's Deli, paying fifteen cents for a pastrami sandwich to share with Morrie at lunch. While we ate, I wrote down my concerns so he could work out the kinks. There were few problems, things I would have ignored if I was only driving for fun. But the Bear had to be perfect! Morrie and I would make her so.

After lunch, I would hop the streetcar down Brooklyn Avenue to get home. At home, I studied Route 66, learning every mile of the rally route that Spedanski had given us. If there was a dirt road, a pothole, a wind condition, or a lot of traffic, I marked it on my map. Spedenski sent monthly checks. Morrie gave them all to me to use as I chose. By spring, 1946, we had accumulated a lot of money. Some of it went to pay doctor's bills. I bought Rod swimming lessons. The doctors said it would help to strengthen his upper body. At first, he struggled to stay afloat. But by the end of May, as summer dawned, he was able to do the breaststroke and tread water in the shallow end of the pool.

Mama came to our house once a week. Even though she spent a good part of the day at the hospital, on Wednesday nights, she would make Rod her very own macaroni and cheese recipe. She refused to use the store-bought stuff. Mama had to make her specialty from scratch.

A month and a half before the rally, I made my list of provisions and discussed every problem imaginable with Morrie. It was a Wednesday night, so Mama came over at five in the evening, straight from the hospital. After coming up steps, her breathing seemed more labored than usual. I pulled a box of Kraft macaroni and cheese out of the cupboard. "Look Mama, you look tired. You don't have to trouble yourself making fresh pasta and that deli cheddar you bought last week. Rod can eat this.

She gave me a look like I was feeding him *treyf*. If looks could kill!

"A box! You want me to make his favorite from a box! Food requires love. They can't put love in a box. She opened it and unpacked the processed cheese. "This cheese here! It's made from chemicals!" She squeezed a piece of macaroni between thumb and forefinger. "Just look at this pasta! If you can even call it that! It's so old and hard you'll crack a tooth on it unless you boil it for days. For me, Rod will shred the fresh cheddar from the deli. For my grandson, this is a work of passion. Put your box away for a rainy day when I cannot come."

There was no change in Pa's condition. It had been more than nine months. The food they fed him through the tubes kept him bloated. His muscles turned to fat and he no longer looked right. I was about to start my rally with Rod and Morrie. I wanted in the worst way for Pa to wake up before we left.

Morrie received a ten-inch RCA 630TS television in trade for repairing a car. At eighty-five pounds, he placed it on a sturdy oak table that sat next to the couch.

"What's that?" I asked.

"It's television. Now, we watch people and hear their voices. You can see them like they are in our living room. On Wednesday night, Mr. Joe Louis fights Mr. William Conn in New York's Yankee Stadium and this box will broadcast the whole thing into our living room. You wait! Our TV will bring us a moving picture through thin air all the way from the other side of country."

I'd never seen a prize fight. I knew that Solly's hero, Mickey Cohen, had gotten his name, Gangster Mickey Cohen, in the boxing ring. Spilling blood that way didn't appeal to me.

When the big night came. Morrie came home early to watch the fight. Rod was so excited about our new toy, he could barely sit still during dinner. Mama kept telling him he needed to eat.

At exactly seven, Morrie walked to the box and turned the dial. Slowly, an image unfolded. Next thing we knew, the bruiser Joe Louis pummeled his opponent, the machine gun, Bill Conn. Louis must have outweighed Conn by at least fifty pounds. Rod and Morrie were glued to the screen. I turned away.

"Hit 'em with a left hook, you sissy! No, don't back away, go in for a knockout."

It wasn't Morrie or Rod screaming for blood. It was Mama. I thought she would hate the brutality but apparently she had gone to the prize fights with Pa early in their marriage. Rod was moving his little fists in tandem with Mama's screams. I was glad he didn't turn away from competition. He was about to be a participant in the biggest battle of our lives.

Chapter 30

Rod spent a lot of time with Morrie at the garage, learning from his dad. August had finally arrived and Morrie, Rod, and I joined Mama at the hospital to say our goodbyes before the rally, which was set for the next morning.

Night after night, I had dreamt Pa would awake, smile, and wish me good luck. It was not meant to be. Mama had sweet wine, *challah* bread, and *Shabbos* candles. She lit a single candle, said a prayer over it, and then we all said a prayer over the wine and *challah*. I held Pa's hand for more than five minutes.

Mama had moved our family dinners to Pa's hospital bed shortly after he got sick, now insisting that the meal be eaten on its customary Friday evening. Maybe she didn't want to risk even the slightest infringement on this Jewish tradition during Pa's illness. No one in the hospital was surprised to see our ritual. While I held Pa's hand, Morrie walked Rod down to the pediatric ward to look at the newborns. Morrie and Rod had their own ritual.

"Pa, can you hear me? If you can, wink or shake a finger at me." Nothing. "I am taking a car across country with Rod, your grandson. When I get back, please wake up and talk to me. Rod wants to meet his grandpa. I am sorry for all the trouble. I think you would be proud of Rod. Not only is he a smart boy, but Morrie … you know … the German mechanic, he's a successful businessman. He believes his parents were killed in the concentration camps. He is Jewish. You didn't know he was Jewish. Pa, I am going to be America's first female rally driver. Imagine that! I'm going to be famous. Please be proud. I don't know what else to say. Mama needs you. We all do. Don't die. Please don't die while we are gone." I had my say. I was ready for the rally.

Our route would take us onto Route 66, southeast from Los Angeles City Hall to Chicago's Buckingham Fountain. Each car was staggered about an hour apart. Our starting position was randomly drawn. We would be the eighteenth car to start. Rod, Morrie, and I got to City Hall three hours early. We found Cars 15, 16, and 17. Two of the drivers were from California and one was from Poland. We watched them warm up, then take off at the blast of the starter's horn. There would be thirty-two starters in all.

"When do we start?" Rod must have asked me this question ten times during our three-hour wait. He fidgeted as I checked our food and water. Morrie was dead serious as he gave me last-minute instructions. The first day's drive would be the longest and the toughest. It would wind through the desert and up into the mountains.

"If the car makes it through day one, you will finish," said Morrie. "You must drink plenty. Keep up strength. Experienced drivers often pass out from lack of water. I will carry extra water. Don't want to weigh down the Bear until after it gets through the mountains into New Mexico. Jack will meet you in Flagstaff, Arizona with water and spare parts. He's already left. He will be there when you arrive. Don't worry. We have a good team. Between Jack and me, we're loaded with fuel, water, fresh tires, oil, grease, and plenty of tools. I'll trail you by an hour, in case you break down. What do you have to eat?"

"I stocked water, bread, nuts, fruit, crackers, cookies, and pretzels."

"Don't be afraid to eat. Make sure you stop if you get tired. You need to stay alert. Don't worry about your time. This is endurance race."

I had never seen Morrie so serious. Our rally rules were very liberal since most of the drivers had not competed in a rally before. Spedanski wanted to avoid catastrophe. Under his rules, all drivers would be required to spend the evening at a hotel and sleep. The hotels also acted as checkpoints. After Flagstaff, the route would take us just beyond Albuquerque, New Mexico. We would eat dinner and sleep there for our first night. Morrie would catch up with us and work on our car while we slept.

"Most drivers will not make it out of the desert," said Morrie. "Last week, fifteen of the drivers tried to hire me for a last-minute tune-up on their cars. I had to turn them all down. I had no time. With our car, and the rest of my work schedule, I was full up. When you want to win, you have to plan ahead. These guys did not plan ahead."

Our starting time was perfect. We wouldn't hit the desert heat until after dark. We would have some late-afternoon city traffic. Our mountain climb would be after the night temperature had cooled, which would lighten demand on the carburetor.

The two stand-alone headlights Morrie put on the Bear were the best made. They also adjusted left or right with the direction of the steering wheel. This was extraordinarily important since I'd be driving with tired eyes through the pitch black on windy mountain roads. When we were finally up and the starter's blast burst into my eardrums. I was deaf for a few seconds. We were parked right underneath the horn. Solly, Frieda, and Pearl cheered loudly so I could hear them. All six cylinders of Bear purred smoothly as I pressed down on the gas pedal.

Solly didn't hold back a bit. "Whip their butts!"

Pearl belted out one of Rod's favorite songs. *"Bei Mir Bistu Shein ..."*

Frieda yelled as we went past. "Rod, make sure your mom doesn't fall asleep."

Rod was absolutely glowing. Hearing the starter's horn, the roaring crowd, and then the purr of our engine, he was beside himself. We headed east on Sunset through the San Gabriel Valley. On our left were vineyards, now barren, since the fall growing season and the spring picking season had passed. Two hours out, we arrived in Fontana. "I've got to pee, Mom."

"Can't you hold it?"

"No, I really need to go."

"You'll need to go in the bushes."

"In the bushes? Won't that be bad?"

"Nope, right now the bushes couldn't be more perfect."

I pulled off the side of the road. We walked out into the brush and Rod took his first outdoor pee "During this trip, we are going to break some rules. When we get back, the rules apply again, okay?"

"Okay, I get it. It's all about winning now."

Soon, we entered the desert. It was late afternoon and the thermometer I carried said 93 degrees. I pointed to the creosote bush. It was everywhere. "You see those yellow flowers. They grow on the world's oldest living plant. The stuff that looks like a wrinkled old man is called yucca cactus. Sometimes those arms grow twenty feet in the air." Rod stared at the cactus.

I had done my research. You never knew when you might break down and what you would need to survive. "Make sure you keep drinking, Rod. Make sure I do, too." We started climbing forty miles outside of Flagstaff, Arizona."

It was now dark, which would be a new test for us. It felt good to know that Morrie was probably only an hour behind us.

The temperature dropped into the high nineties as we climbed. In the town of Oatman, an oncoming train stared us down. I briefly veered off the road, then realized the train was far to our left where the Santa Fe Express train track paralleled the road. I turned on my headlamps. They were bright and added a hundred feet to my vision. The Bear's top was down and wind danced off our faces. The wind calmed and I felt relieved at the calm. When

I accelerated, the winds picked up again and rocked the car. Rod fidgeted in his seat. He looked frightened. I tightened my grip on the wheel.

"Rod, don't worry. I'm a great driver. A little wind can't hurt us." It was dark and I didn't realize he had put himself to sleep. I told myself to stay calm. We arrived safely in Kingman, Arizona. We had climbed 3,900 feet. The air temperature had dropped to 88 degrees.

Rod awoke. "What's that stinky garlic smell?"

"It's something called tellurium. They mine it around here. You can't see the huge zinc and lead mines out there because it's dark. I read in my books that the miners use a stinky compound that makes this putrid smell. Can you imagine living here?"

Rod curled up on his seat and fell asleep again. I was talking to myself. Thankfully, he slept through Kingman. The Bear moved forward without a hitch as we continued to climb.

Before we had left, Morrie had given me instructions about survival in the desert. "If she breaks down in the desert or on the climb, get out of the heat and crawl underneath until help arrives. Drink radiator water if you run out what you brought."

My mouth and nose were caked with dust. I ignored the grit in my mouth. I had throttled down on the climb to create more power, but less speed. When the grade flattened, I throttled up and increased speed. We were making progress very slowly. Broken-down competitors, with lanterns lighting their license plates, dotted the roadside. I did not want to join them.

Asphalt turned to loose gravel on the mountain road. Rod and I had worn leather driving helmets and goggles to protect us from any flying debris, but at the moment, I would have preferred the cooling effect of the desert wind through my hair. Rod woke up. "I'm hot! Can't I take this thing off?"

"No, keep it on. See, I have mine on. It'll protect your eyes. Use your eyes to look for stray animals."

"What animals? I don't see anything."

"Look carefully, honey. Their eyes will glow in the dark.

We headed east. I knew I needed to distract him. "Rod, these mountains are part of a dormant volcano. They are known as the San Francisco Mountains. They rise over twelve thousand feet."

"Are we going that high, Mom?"

"No. On our route, they don't rise above seven thousand. That's still plenty high. I'm glad they don't go higher because I think we'd get dizzy."

I had stopped in Oatman for gas and to adjust the carburetor. The adjustments I made increased the gasoline burn rate as we climbed. Being married to a hotrod mechanic gave me an edge. Morrie had trained me well. I saw two more race cars stranded on the side of the road. I wondered if these were the guys who had asked Morrie for help the week before the race.

"How come we're going so slow?" asked Rod.

"As we climb, the air gets thinner. It's harder for the engine to get the horsepower it needs without burning up. We have to protect the engine. It's our ticket to Chicago." A sign ahead said Flagstaff — 10 miles. The toughest part of our day was nearly over. I was tired, but knowing we were just ten miles out of Flagstaff dumped adrenalin into my veins. I was again fully awake. Rod was again fast asleep. I loved hearing his restful breathing as he sat beside me on this journey.

The smell of the Coconino pine trees replaced the dust in my nostrils. Rod awoke. "Where are we?"

"We're in the land of the Anasazi Indians. They lived here for centuries in cliff dwellings on the mountain side."

"I think I heard about them in my history class. Are there Indians with bows and arrows out there now?"

"Nope, they left mysteriously hundreds of years ago. Nobody really knows where they went or why they left. That's the deal, you know. If you hang in there, they all know who you are. If you win, even more people know you. If you give up, you are lost for all time."

"What are you talking about? You're not making any sense."

"Sorry, I'm just talking to myself, trying to stay awake."

"Look up there, Mama."

"Can't look up right now. I have to keep my eyes on the road. What'd you see?"

"The sky is filled with bright stars."

"Yes, it is. If you see the seven very bright stars that look like a measuring cup, that's what you call the Big Dipper. If you see them, you can find Polaris, the brightest star in the sky."

"Okay, I'll look. Mom, drive careful like Auntie Frieda said. Wow, there's a whole other world up here. Never seen anything like this at home."

"The night sky is beautiful. Can you imagine! Those Indians who disappeared lived off the land under these skies."

"Maybe they ran out of water. You have to have water to live."

"Maybe they did, son. Let's drink to the life."

"Here's your water, Mom. I wonder if five hundred years from now, some other people will wonder what happened to all the people who live in Los Angeles."

"Good question. There's a crater from a meteor about nine miles south of Flagstaff. It hit the earth at thousands of miles an hour and dug a deep canyon where it landed. It changed everything when it hit. Sometimes things change that we don't have any control over."

Rod fell back asleep .I started thinking about Pa and Mama as the breeze brushed through the trees. Ahead of us, our headlights silhouetted the higher peaks of the San Francisco Mountains against the sky. In the dark, the moonlight created a reddish hue from the copper inside them. It felt good to be behind the wheel. I cruised on, almost missing Jack, who was on the roadside waving me down. I pressed on my brakes and pulled over into a stop.

It took him close to fifteen minutes to replenish the car's fluids. I woke Rod. We stayed close to the car. I used a flashlight to see where we were. I stared down its beams into the darkness looking for mountain lions. Thankfully, no eyes shined back at me. When Jack was done, I helped Rod back inside the car and off we went. It was good that Jack completed his job so quickly. I was anxious to get the day's trip over.

We headed east through the Painted Desert. "I know you can't see them, but near us are jagged rocks worn down by wind and rain and painted by daylight. They've been adjusting to the world for thousands of years. Red clay rocks are streaked with cracks. Only the sturdiest creatures survive." My skin tightened on my face as the dry heat absorbed its natural moisture.

"My science teacher told me that fossils were found in this area. Can you believe it? This dry desert used to be a swamp! It was loaded with crocodiles thousands of years ago."

"A swamp, who would have thought? You know a lot, Rod. I am so proud of you."

"Heck, Mom, you're the driver out here, all by yourself, with just me here to protect you. I am proud of you, too!"

Up ahead, a bus on the opposite side of the road stopped to let a passenger off. With our headlamp, we saw an Indian man, woman, and two small children get off and walk into the desert.

"Where're they going?"

"Gosh, I don't know. Maybe their tribe lives out there behind those mountains. They probably wonder what *we're* doing out here.

Rod was perfect. He sat for extended periods and was filled with curiosity. It seemed as if the elements brought us even closer than we had been. He was growing up. I wished Morrie was riding with us.

"How do you think Papa's doing? Is he going to catch up to us?"

"I think he's doing fine. He likes being a loner."

"A loner, what's that?"

"It means he's most comfortable working alone. He's happy to be by himself." The scent of forest, the wind in my face, and the moonlight shining down from the azure blue sky dotted with bright stars made me think. Maybe Morrie didn't know how to be with us. Maybe his feelings of guilt — about his parents, my pregnancy, my feud with Pa, about Rod's condition — made him feel he was bad for Rod and me. Could that change? Everything changes. The night silence provided a backdrop for what was going through my mind. I wished Pa and Mama were with us. Maybe our lives wouldn't have been so crazy if Pa realized there was more to life than work and synagogue. Maybe God was his night sky.

"Are we there yet?"

"Open your eyes and look up."

The southwest sky grew larger as the mountains grew smaller. Strangely, it seemed to protect us. It opened us to new possibilities. Once, Morrie and I had taken Rod to Big Bear Mountain, about an hour-and-a-half drive from our house, so he could see snow. It was close, but still the trip had seemed like an adventure. None of us would have dreamed of these jagged mountain peaks that rose like a phoenix from the desert floor in Arizona.

"Hungry?"

"Heck yes, I forgot about eating. Now that you mention it, I'm starving."

Rod pulled out a cow-tongue sandwich, which we split. It had been packed in ice that was now melted. The bread was soggy. It didn't matter. We chomped into juicy tomatoes that surrounded a big hunk of tender meat. Tomato seeds dripped onto our laps.

"Hey Mom, there is so much dust on my lap and so many tomato seeds, I bet I can grow a plant if I just pour some water on it."

We were slaphappy from fatigue and elevation. We laughed so hysterically, it made our lungs hurt. The road was paved, but long weeks of spring rain and summer heat made the asphalt soft and loose. Dust from the roadside flew into our faces when the winds kicked up. The dust got into our throats and we coughed mercilessly. A mile outside of Flagstaff, a coyote ran into the road around two-hundred yards ahead of us. It stood for a moment until we got closer and then darted away. I glanced at Rod who once again had dozed off. He looked so peaceful. I couldn't help but feel we were kindred spirits on the journey of a lifetime.

Chapter 31

We entered New Mexico at Gallup, home of Red Rock State Park. The adrenalin I had at the start of the race had drained away. Now, only the white lines on the road kept me focused. The air temperature was a cool 72 degrees. Albuquerque was still a ways ahead. I pushed on. The Bear bounced, then rambled unstably. No, not now! I couldn't believe it. We had a flat.

My headlight beams lurched all over the road. I slammed on the brakes and stopped on the roadside. I knew how to fix a flat. The trouble was I couldn't see a darned thing. I knew I would be able to use my jack if I could find my flashlight. It was in the pack in the back of the car.

I sat for a moment, mentally rehearsing the steps necessary to change a tire. Without the hum of the car's engine, I expected an eerie silence. Instead, I heard voices somewhere off in the distance. They were getting closer. I thought I had seen something that might have been a campfire a few miles back. I'd been so exhausted, I wasn't sure. I wondered if some cowboy was camping. Maybe it was John Wayne. He'd come over and offer me a hand. I almost laughed. My imagination was going wild. I popped the car door and jumped down onto the dirt road. My right leg was asleep. I almost fell over when it hit the ground. I stumbled to the car's rear pack. Rod woke up.

"Mom, what happened? Where are we?"

"Don't worry, Rod, I'm right here. I'm getting the flashlight."

"Okay Mom, I can see you … sorta. You look like a ghost. I'm scared. Hurry up, will you."

I couldn't locate the tools I needed to change the tire. I couldn't imagine Morrie would have forgotten to pack them. I started to panic. Morrie would be here eventually, but I was losing time. Trying to stay calm, I fumbled through the large pack until I felt the cold metal of the tire iron and jack.

A horse whinnied. Could that be my cowboy or was it a stray? I pointed my flashlight at a faceless figure riding a horse. A stench clogged my nose. Fresh horse shit, I imagined. The figure wore a big brimmed cowboy hat. Behind the rider were silhouettes of a few head of longhorn cattle. "Rod, stay in the car. No matter what happens, stay in the car!"

"Who's out there, Mom? Is that a wild horse?"

A barbed wire fence separated cattle, horse, and the cowboy from us. "Howdy, you all stuck?" said a woman's voice.

A women! "Yes," I said. "I've got a flat. I can handle it."

"If you want, I can climb over this barbed wire and give you a hand."

"Me too, Mom," said a child's voice. "If you give me a lift, I'll help too."

"Jeez, a women on a horse and her son!

"Son," said the woman, "you stay there for now. Don't want you cutting yourself up."

"I'd love it if you could help," I said, relieved that my cowboy was a cowgirl. "This car is darn heavy. Don't think I can lift it in the dark and change the tire myself."

The woman dismounted. She slinked through an opening. Now, on my side of the fence, with my flashlight shined directly at her, I could see leather covered her head to toe. "Hi," she said. "I'm Trixie from Oklahoma City. Over there is my son, Brainerd. What's your name?"

"I'm Bella and this is my son, Rod. We're driving in a rally from Los Angeles to Chicago. Surprised to see you out riding so late."

"Wouldn't normally be out myself but Hank, my hubby, he's been drinking rye whiskey and we're missing a steer. He's on his ass. We're driving cattle to Tucson. I brought Brainerd because I don't like riding by myself. Funny to see a lady driving an automobile by herself."

"Up until now, I've loved the drive. This rally has been a dream come true. Rod is along for the ride. My husband, Morrie, is driving backend. He'll be along soon."

"Got to like that. Are all the drivers women?"

"No way. There are no other women. Just little old me."

"You beating the stuffing out of the menfolk? Well, fancy that! Let me give you a hand. So you don't lose any time."

Trixie stood six inches from my nose. I'd never seen a real cowboy before, let alone a cowgirl. She was the real McCoy. She towered almost foot above me. She was heaven sent.

With Trixie's help, we were able to jack up the car and use the tire iron to pry the rubber from the wheel. I glanced over to where Brainerd was getting to know Rod through the barbed wire fence.

"Where you all from?" said Brainerd.

"My mama and I are from Los Angeles. We are in a race to Chicago. She's driving all by herself. What're you doing out here?"

"I'm helping Ma bring in a stray steer. We're from Oklahoma."

"Oklahoma! That's where we're going. Tonight, we stop in Albie Turkey."

"Ha, ha, it's Albuquerque."

"Yeah, I'm kind of tired, that's what I meant. Are you a cowboy?"

"I go to school. This is my first drive. I love my pony. Say hello to Stray Eye." Stray Eye nodded his head up and down. Rod waved back. His arm moved like a windshield wiper gone crazy.

"How come your arm does that?"

"It just does. My arm is kind of like your pony's eye. It hasn't worked right since I was born. I'm working it out. Mom says everything works out in time with hard work. You probably had to teach Stray Eye to nod hello, didn't you?"

"It took me a whole week to teach him to nod like that."

"It takes me a long time to teach my arm to do stuff. Mama's getting help. I think she called it a *therapathis* ... I mean ... a therapist. I bet I'll be able to ride your pony in a year."

"That'd be mighty fine. Maybe you can come back. We can ride together."

"I'd like that."

As they talked, Trixie helped me get the spare tire on the wheel. The tire iron bent and was useless by the time we were done with it. "There's a terrible smell out here," I said.

Trixie broke into a hearty laugh. "I'm sorry. I must have stepped in some of it. Being around these cattle, you have to be real careful not to get it on you."

I was tired, but not too tired to join her laughter. It felt good to loosen up a little. Trixie threw the old tire over the fence.

"Wow, you've got a throwing arm," I said.

"Been shoeing horses my whole life. Muscles build where I don't want 'em."

I pumped the tire. Trixie loosened the jack and the frame came down on the tire with a thud. I grabbed the tire iron, jack, and a few loose bolts from the ground, then walked around back to put them away.

"Boys, we're ready to go. We got 'er done."

I gave Trixie a big hug and wrote her address on the back of my route sheet. "I'll send you a postcard from Chicago and let you know how it all works out. You're a life saver. I hope you'll come visit us in Los Angeles.

Rod had made a new friend in the strangest of places. "Hey Brainerd, I'll write you about our rally from Albie Turkey to Chicago. Then you can write back and tell me all about the drive to Tucson, okay."

The boys giggled. "Sure enough, partner," said Brainerd."

What amazing luck! It had to be *bashert*. Not a sole for miles, yet we broke down spitting distance from a friendly cowgirl and her son. If that wasn't destiny, I didn't know what was. Trixie and Brainerd rode off with the herd of cattle under the endless stars of the prairie.

Rod and I got back in the Bear. An hour later, we reached Albuquerque. I was more than ready to be done with the day's journey. We planned to sleep and eat at the Silver Moon Café and Motel a mile and half outside of town. I was exhausted. I even thought I saw monkeys hanging from trees as I drove the last few miles. Rod slept as we cruised on fumes into the dirt parking lot of the Silver Moon. As my left foot touched the ground, my body screamed *what are you doing to me?* I was stiff as a board. Both legs were asleep. I couldn't feel the earth beneath my feet.

Jack was waiting for us in the parking lot. Seeing me wobble, he offered to get Rod. Jack carried Rod's dangling body, still dead asleep, into the café. He had arrived an hour earlier. "You need some grub. Go eat in that shack. It's open all the time for the truck drivers that come through." He pointed to the little café with a flashing sign. "You'll need food in your belly for the morning. Don't miss those black beans."

I took Rod from Jack so he could go work on the Bear. I saw him wiggle a piece of paper out of his tight jeans. It must have been the checklist of repairs.

Rod woke up as I entered the café. "Smells good. Where are we?"

"We've arrived at the motel. First we eat. I think I smell spit-roasted corn on the cob."

Two Mexican ladies were making tortillas by hand. The place was empty except for two men who sat in a booth. The lone waitress, a short gal with dark, ruddy skin and long brown hair in a hairnet, walked over to where Rod and I sat. She placed two glasses of water on the table. I ordered the first thing on the menu that caught my eye, carne asada tacos.

"You want those with verde tomatillo salsa?" she asked.

"What is that?" I said, almost too tired to care. I didn't know the word *tomatillo*."

"It's a mild sauce with green tomatillo chili, oregano, garlic, and onions. It spices up your carne."

"Sure … sure," I said.

There were big green chili peppers and carrots in a little brown bowl on the table. They looked like dill pickles at Canter's. I bit into a pepper. It burned. "Rod, don't' touch that. It's not like home. It's hot." I downed the glass of cold water.

Rod ordered chicken and tortillas. "Mom, I just want the chicken, no bread or that crazy sauce."

When the food came, Rod dug in.

"Rod, slow down, you'll choke. Chew your food. It'll taste better."

He wouldn't slow down and as tired as I was, I matched him bite for bite. I hadn't realized how hungry I'd become. I smiled over at Rod. He ate fast and furious, then placed his head on the table and was instantaneously asleep. His lips were still open. When the waitress returned, I ordered Morrie some carne asada tacos, hoping they wouldn't be too cold by the time he arrived. He shouldn't be that far away. "How much?" I asked the waitress.

"That'll be a dollar."

I handed her a dollar and dime for a tip. A few minutes later, she gave me a brown paper bag with Morrie's tacos to go.

I tugged at Rod's feet to wake him. Then I dragged us both to our tiny motel room. We wouldn't get much sleep. We planned to rise at six.

The hot meal made me feel better. After tucking Rod into bed, I walked outside and stared at the New Mexico sky. There were a million stars that I had never seen. Back in the room, I began to worry. Where was Morrie? I wanted to see him before I fell asleep. As my head hit the pillow, there was a knock on the door. I jumped up, almost tripping as I ran to open it.

"Morrie, welcome to New Mexico!"

He was surprisingly energetic. I felt and looked awful. "How was your drive?" I asked, after he released me from a big hug.

"No problem," he said. "I hoped to be here earlier. You really made good time."

We walked outside, leaving the door ajar so I could hear Rod if he awoke. We kissed under the spectacular sky. Our lips touched like in the old days. There was heat in the kiss and I didn't think it was from the salsa. "Oh, I almost forgot," I said. "I bought you dinner." I ran back inside and grabbed the brown paper bag, which now had salsa stains all over it. "Hope this is enough. I know you'll love it. Watch out for the hot sauce."

"Thank you. How was the Bear?"

"I'll tell you, but first, go look at Rod. He's sleeping. Oh Morrie, he's was so good the entire day."

As I spoke, Morrie's salsa-stained mouth spread into an enormous grin and I could tell he was proud of our son. He turned toward the hotel room.

"Don't wake him. Quiet! He's so beat."

When Morrie came back outside, I started to tell him about my flat. Before I could get to the part about Trixie, he interrupted.

"You fixed it in the dark by yourself! You should have waited for me. If anything happened to you or Rod out there, I would never forgive myself. Damn it, Bella, why didn't you wait for me?"

"Didn't need to. Had the help of a cowgirl."

"Cowgirl?"

"Never you mind. Just get that spare fixed, okay. Anything happen to you?"

"I almost hit a coyote outside Gallup. It just stood in the road, staring. Couldn't have stopped if I wanted to. Then, just when I think I'm going to clip it, off it runs."

"I know that coyote. I think it's our lucky charm. I'll explain later. Now, get to work. I need some rest. Are you going to be okay? You won't have time to sleep."

He gave me a nod, a peck, and off he went. He was still the most handsome man I had ever seen. My alarm was set to ring at six in the morning.

Chapter 32

The next morning, eyes half shut, I dressed and helped Rod with his clothes. Inside the café, an all-too-cheery hostess greeted us with two menus and escorted us to the same table we had the night before. I begged for coffee. "Coffee, please, I really need something to wake up!"

When we finished eating, I paid the cashier and collected the eggs and tortillas I'd ordered for Morrie. I handed Rod a dime to leave as a tip.

Outside, Morrie was fast asleep in the driver's seat of the Bear. His hat covered his face. Rod laughed. "Dad looks really silly."

I noticed Morrie's boots beneath the car. "Look Rod, he doesn't have his shoes on. Why not tickle his feet to wake him up."

"Are you sure I should do that? He might get mad."

"Go ahead. I'll defend you." I opened the car and lifted Rod so he could reach Morrie's foot, which lay on the dashboard. Rod's hand barely touched the arch when the sleeping giant awoke, laughing. He smiled at Rod and me. I didn't think I'd ever seen Morrie so happy. I planted a kiss on his extra-dry lips. It was like kissing cardboard, but felt good anyway.

"Didn't get much sleep," he said. "How about you?"

"Slept like a log. Almost slept through my alarm's siren. Did you work on the car?"

"Was up until five working. I'm beat. Jack and me, we replaced the spare. She is *goot* as new. Jack is halfway to Wichita by now. He left at four. I'll trail you today by fifteen minutes, just in case there aren't any other cowgirls to help you out along the way." Morrie stood up and hoisted Rod over the driver's seat, and into the passenger side. I handed Morrie his breakfast, which he held onto for later.

At seven, with the blast of the horn, we were headed north towards the old Santa Fe River and onto the Old Santa Fe Trail. I noticed Car 12 was still in the parking lot. It looked like it had been towed in. We descended from 5,312 feet in Albuquerque without incident. As we leveled out, I noticed Car 4 smoking on the roadside. Morrie had told me nine drivers had already dropped out. The mountain roads had been a car killer. I had feared that Rod or I might get altitude sickness in Albuquerque. We were fine.

In the early morning daylight, we traveled through the Sandia Mountains. They surrounded Albuquerque with imposing red bluffs. Even in the middle of August, the highest peaks were snowcapped. I was afraid of the flat central plains of eastern New Mexico, Texas, and Oklahoma, which I had read produced roaring summer storms as the colder mountain air rushed down the slopes and bounced off the hot desert floor. Once we descended from the Sandias, we would travel on these plains 550 miles toward Oklahoma City. The winds there could be brutal. Rod and I had seen *The Wizard of Oz* for the second time a few weeks before we left Los Angeles. As we approached the plains, all I could think of were the whirling winds that swooped little Dorothy up into the Kansas skies.

The mountains looked monstrous though my windshield. The towns were tiny. We drove through two towns where not a soul was on the street.

"Where're all the people?"

"Maybe they're working in the mines."

"Will we see places here like Los Angeles, loaded with people and cars?"

"Not for some time."

"What do people up here do when they're not working?"

"Good question. I have no idea. They probably hunt, or fish, or whittle."

"Whittle, huh."

"Look at those puffs of white nothingness against the blue sky." I had taken the top off so Rod could see the sheer vastness of the plains. But as the first frigid winds soared up, I had to stop and hoist the top back up. Rod wanted to help. I told him stay put. He ducked down in his seat as I fought the wind. Car 23 passed us. I roped my waist to the bumper while I pushed the top back up over Rod's head. I struggled. "Honey, keep your head down. Don't want that top to knock you." I was finally able to get the top where I wanted it, so I undid the rope, ran to the front of the coupe, and latched it tightly down.

"Wow, Mom you're really tough. How'd you do that all by yourself?"

"I had to do it. Didn't have a choice. Did you see that driver whiz by? If I had sat around waiting for Papa, there might have been a whole bunch of cars passing us up. I did what was needed."

The winds accelerated. They were stinging cold. The Bear started to wobble. Within a mile, there was a sight I was not prepared to see. Car 9 — I think that was its number — was crumpled. It must have swerved and hit the oil rig off the roadside. I couldn't see the driver. Hopefully, he walked away. The car looked a bit like a stomped-down tin can. I was about to stop when I saw a sheriff's car coming from up ahead. Then I pressed down on my gas pedal to make up for lost time.

Stay loose, I told myself. *Hold that wheel lightly, like a bird*. When the winds first started, Rod had laughed, thinking it was fun. But now, he stiffened and fought off moodiness as they failed to relent. We weaved between both sides of the road. The dust made visibility almost impossible. Instinct took over. Rod was obviously scared.

"It'll be okay, honey. I've done this before. Just hold on. Let's have some fun. You count the number of times we swerve. Later, we'll see if we can get it into the book of Guinness World Records. Hold your seat with your right arm. Oops, that wasn't good!"

"Got it, Mom, I'm counting."

Up ahead, barely visible, something partially blocked the road. I saw it at the last minute and pumped the brakes, coming to a stop a few feet short of Car 24. The driver was beside his car, trying to steady himself in the wind. When he saw me, he pointed to a manzanita tree off the side of the road. "Ran smack into it," he said. "Stalled out and now I can't get her started again." He threw up his hands. "Looks like it's over for me."

"Don't worry, my husband will be along soon and he can help you get her off the road." I handed him a white rag to attach to his car's rear end.

"Hey, thanks, that's a good idea. "You're pretty smart, for a women."

The Bear rocked in the wind. Back in the driver's seat, I noticed Rod was green. "You okay, honey?"

"I guess."

"Let's get out of here right now. Sorry to make you sit there. You're a pretty tough young man, you know. If you've got to puke, just let me know. I can stop again."

"Don't worry, I'll be okay, Mom."

I started her up and off we went. "We got through that okay."

"Do you think that guy was hurt, Mom?"

"He's out of the race. His car will need fixing. Probably the only thing hurt is his feelings. He's probably embarrassed not to finish.

"Mom, is it time to turn around and go home?"

I took a big breath. "Can't quit now, honey. The toughest part is over. We've conquered California, Arizona, and New Mexico. We've got a job to do. Quitting just isn't an option. Trust me, we can get to Chicago safe and sound."

"I was worried about you, Mom. This wind is really scary. You don't have to prove anything to me, you know."

I grabbed Rod's hand. "I'll be okay. This wind is nothing." I said this as the gale-force air currents continued to turn the ride into a rocky adventure. "I'm sure it'll let up."

It was ten miles of utter hell before we hit the flatlands. Car 28 was right behind me. He'd tried to pass, but I wouldn't let him. I hogged the road. Before we hit the road sign that said Glen Rio, Texas, he stated to sputter. He must have run out of gas.

We drove into the tiny town of Adrian, the midway point of the rally. We gassed up at the Magnolia gas station. I was glad I had prepared a list of gas stations ahead of time. I was nearly on empty.

The attendant had an Oklahoma drawl. "Where ya'all going, ma'am?"

"We're part of the road rally. We're off to Chicago. Next stop is Amarillo. Have you seen many drivers this morning?"

"Yes ma'am, but they're all men. What're you doing in this here race?"

I grimaced. "Trying to win. Why, you think women can't drive as well as men?"

"Well, ma'am, I think you're a mighty brave gal. That's a real handsome boy you got there." My grimace turned into a grin. I paid, and we were back in the race.

"That man sounded funny. Didn't he like women?"

"It's not important. He's never seen a women rally driver before. That's no surprise, since there aren't any others."

Rod looked thoughtful. "Does that make you what they call a trailblazer, Mom?"

"I don't know what I am, Rod. But I do know what we're doing — you, me, your father — it means something. This rally is something we're always going to remember."

There were no signs of life for another hour down the road. We were buzzed by a biplane. Rod looked worried. "Hope we're not lost."

"No, Rod, he's up practicing. Wow, look, he's writing something with the stuff coming from his engine."

"Can you read what he wrote?"

"It's about us! I mean, about the rally! It says **WELCOME AMERICA'S RALLY**."

Once we got to Amarillo, we learned the pilot, Harold English, had formed a stunt pilot group, which was a big hit at county fairs throughout the Midwest. He stayed with us all the way into and out of Amarillo. Rod cocked his chin and watched the plane do flips. I couldn't see, but Rod gave me a blow-by-blow description. His eyes stayed glued to that plane. By half past eleven, the temperature had risen to 98 degrees. I was looking for, and nearly passed, the community swimming pool that had been designated as a checkpoint for the rally. I screeched to a stop.

"Why'd you do that? I almost went flying."

"Sorry, but we need to check in, and it's time for lunch. You're a swimmer now. You want to take a quick dip? We can clean up in the changing room next to the pool." I wiped a finger over my dust-covered forehead. "At least I can wash my face."

"A swim in a pool sounds good, really good."

Rod's swimming lessons had paid off. He looked perfectly comfortable. I hated to make him get out of the pool, but we needed to get some lunch.

The gal at the diner was sweet. She asked about the rally. I told her about the incident with Trixie and Brainerd. Turns out they'd picked up a sandwich in that very diner earlier in the week.

"She is a tough old gal. They come in on every trip. She'll keep Hank, the cattle, and Brainerd in line all the way out to Arizona. Old Hank, he thinks he's the boss. He just doesn't know who really calls the shots."

After lunch, and back in the car, we were clean and cool. As we pulled out onto the road, Car 21 pulled up for lunch. He was too close for comfort, but at least he was coming and we were going.

We arrived on schedule at five that afternoon. Jack was waiting at the hotel entrance. Our second leg was shorter and much easier than the first. Except for the stranded drivers, the only remaining competitor we had seen was Car 21.

Unlike the dusty little motel room in Albuquerque, Spedanski had arranged for us to stay the night at the glorious Skirven Hotel. The barren, hot and dry Oklahoma terrain housed, along with its cowboys, a surprisingly sophisticated group of wealthy eastern oil barons.

Our hotel was built to high Chicago standards. We wandered into the lobby through ornamental doors that were three times my size. Inside, our eyes fell upon the Art Deco floor tiles and then followed the Grecian columns upward to Baucus statues that sat prominently on top. Huge wooded columns dominated the room. I was counting them when Rod slipped on one of the tiles.

A formally dressed, three-foot-tall man, dressed in a red bellman's suit and a tall black hat, seemed to appear out of nowhere. He pulled Rod up by the armpits and said, "Sir, are you okay?" Rod grinned at the bellman and said he was just fine. The bellman performed a slight bow, grabbed our bags, and ushered us to the reception desk.

We had traveled in massive air currents through the desert, without a bath, for two days. Our driving suits were covered with tomato seeds and drippings from all we had eaten. Having removed our dark leather helmets, our faces were sunburned where our helmets didn't cover, and pasty white, where they did.

I was suddenly conscious of how Rod and I looked and felt embarrassed. I'd never seen a fine hotel, other than the Biltmore back home. People in the lobby were perfectly dressed. All the ladies wore fancy long dresses and hats. The gentlemen wore tailored East Coast suits. I noticed their stares.

The bellman had one bag in each hand. He was so short, they nearly dragged on the ground. "Do these people stare at everyone who comes in the door?" I asked.

He pointed to the sign in the front of the lobby. **WELCOME TO THE SKIRVEN, BELLA AND ROD KRAWIEC, WORLD FAMOUS RALLY DRIVERS**. "Miss Krawiec," said the bellman, you're famous. They're trying to get a look at you. The *Oklahoman,* the local newspaper, is all about you and your cross-country rally. A few of these folks may have placed a tidy little wager on you to win. The odds against you are huge. These are oil men and they love to gamble. They're not gawking, they're admiring."

A small crowd of men, smelling of cigars, and ladies reeking from that French perfume Pearl loved, came closer. They grinned at Rod and me, like we were in the zoo. I looked at the whole group, smiled, and curtseyed just the way Mama had taught me. They applauded loudly. The bellman walked toward the service elevator and pointed to another elevator with big glass doors. .Since everything we needed was in our bags, I shouted at the tiny bellman, who was loading bags into the service elevator. My voice echoed throughout the lobby. "You're bringing up our bags, aren't you?"

I couldn't hear his response because the doors to the glass elevator shut right after I screamed. I read the bellman's lips through the glass. "Don't worry, I'll bring everything to your room."

The elevator soared above the huge lobby below. The oil gentlemen and their ladies shrunk before our eyes. The elevator bounced to an abrupt stop. That bothered me more than all the rocking we had endured from the winds.

I unlocked the door to our room with the heavy brass key given to me at the front desk. Then I walked into Mama's living room! No! It was Mama's whole house! I'd never seen anything like it before. "Wow wee, will you look at this, Rod!"

"Whose house is this, Mom?"

"This is no house. It's our hotel room!"

The bellman knocked. I opened the door, very happy to see his tiny smiling face.

"Madam, where would you like your bags?"

"Over there in the corner, next to that little table."

He skillfully placed the bags on their side so it would be easy for Rod and me to open them. Then he went to the window, leaped up, caught the cord that controlled the plush satin drapes, and pulled it down. We didn't bother to look outside. By that time, we were so hungry we could have eaten the curtains.

"Where can we get some sandwiches?" I asked the bellman.

He led Rod and me back to the elevator. "Madam, two floors up is our Venetian room. You can dine there."

He left. We waited five minutes for the elevator. Rod had to pee, so I let him back in the room, waited for him, and went back to the elevator. By the time we came back out, the elevator had come and gone. We waited another five minutes and entered. The operator pushed the biggest button on the control panel. It said Venetian Room. We arrived within seconds.

"This is no delicatessen. Where do we sit?"

Every table was filled with more fancy suits and dresses. Near the entrance was a stand that read **Maître D'hotel**. A tall, handsome man, dressed in a black tuxedo with tails, spoke with a French accent. "May I help you, madam?"

"What are they eating on those little plates?"

"They are enjoying the rye crackers with beluga caviar, casaba melon, and aged Camembert cheese, madam. Most of the men drink Kentucky bourbon. The ladies drink Shirley Temples, usually. It's happy hour, you know."

Nobody looked that happy.

Unbathed and lacking clean clothes, I knew this place wasn't for us. "Never mind, we're not dressed. We'll order room service instead."

"As you like, madam."

The elevator was still on the restaurant floor, so we easily escaped. Once we returned to our room, I took off my shoes and found a gold-plated menu. "What do you want to eat, Rod?"

"It looks expensive."

"No matter, son, we deserve a good meal. Besides, Mr.Spedanski is footing the bill."

Rod loved that all I had to do was pick up the phone and say what we wanted.

"Wow, Mom, does someone take the order, cook the food, and then bring it up to us? Won't that take a long time? I'm really, really hungry."

"Don't worry. There are people in the kitchen. It'll arrive quickly."

Within twenty minutes, the waiters — yes — *two* waiters, rolled trays into our room. They removed the silver covers with such a flair I thought we were watching a stage show. The game hen I had ordered was a crisp golden brown. Rod's Texas-sized steak sizzled.

"Is that my dinner, Mom? What if I can't eat it all? Will I be in trouble with Mr. Spedanski?"

"No Rod, you won't be in trouble. I do, however, think that steak is about as big as you. Don't hurt yourself trying to get it eaten. Your dad will be along soon, and he would love to help you out."

I had never eaten a hen. It was so tender it fell apart like butter. Rod and I ate slowly. I savored every morsel. I loved Mama's food and had learned to cook casseroles and meatloaf. This was something else. I'd never tasted anything so delicious as the tiny scalloped potatoes and the asparagus drenched in the creamy hollandaise sauce.

The waiters milled inside our room as we ate. Standing there, they made me nervous. After stuffing myself, I walked over to the window and looked out, where I could see oil wells off in the distance, one after the other. They weren't pumping. I knew oil brought big bucks to this formerly dry and dusty town. I turned to one of waiters. "How's business?"

"Better now. The war pumped up oil demand. Business is improving again, and folks have returned after being away for more than a decade. We're rebuilding. In the thirties, hotel traffic dropped to nothing. We closed down for most of the decade. The Dust Bowl did a lot of damage to the farm community. It stopped raining for years when I was growing up in the twenties. Without rain, and with all the heavy winds, farmers lost their topsoil and their crops. No water, no topsoil, and no crops meant no money. Couldn't get through a day without someone saying the word bankruptcy. Half my friends piled into trucks and headed west with their families. Then the depression hit hard. Thank goodness for the war. Things are much better now."

I asked because I felt like I'd already met many of these Okies. They'd ended up in Los Angeles looking for credit at Pa's store. As bad as it was for city folks like Pa, the farmer's faces always showed more pain. People came west for lots of reasons. For Mama, it was the climate. For Morrie and his sister, it was safety and a new chance. For the Dust Bowl refugees and oil riggers, it was to find a new kind of work to do.

There was a loud knock on the door. I assumed it was Morrie and rushed to get it. Seeing his face at the door was the most wonderful view I could imagine.

"Hello there. Been playing in the mud?"

"No Morrie, been driving through prairie dust just like you."

Rod sat in the middle of the room with fine linen napkins hanging from his collar, a polished sterling silver fork in his hand, and a slice of potato on his lap. It had slipped off his fork. Rod hadn't made much of a dent in his steak. Morrie cut two thirds of what was left and edged it onto a small bread plate with some of my asparagus spears. The steak hung over the sides. We chatted for over an hour until Rod accidently pushed the fancy table on rollers away from us.

"Guess dinner's over."

Morrie and I moved to the couch and stared at the view.

"Go clean up in the bathtub, Rod, while your father and I get caught up."

There was bubble bath on the tub ledge. We heard Rod frolicking in the sudsy water, cackling as he splashed around. Morrie seemed anxious to tell me something.

"I have news."

"Don't stop now. I can't wait to hear. It's good news, isn't it?"

"For us, yes! More than half the cars dropped out during the first two days. These included the one that started ahead of you. Another fourteen drivers never got beyond Albuquerque. I know you almost ran over Car 21. I gave the driver a lift to the next town."

Morrie said that many of the novice drivers had not anticipated the wear and tear on their cars.

"Your time was good, Bella. You are in the top five now." Some of the drivers ran out of gasoline."

"Yeah, Car 28 ran out right before we got to Amarillo. Did he start again?"

"He did, but he lost two hours walking to that gas station and then back to his car."

"My God, Morrie, I can't believe it! We're doing so well."

"You got Spedanski's car and me. What more do you need?"

"I must be careful and not get over-confident. If I don't finish the last two legs, my current position won't add to squat."

"Help me! I can't get out of here!"

Morrie and I ran into the bathroom, where Rod was struggling to escape the slippery tub. Morrie scooped him out as I wrapped a towel around Rod's dripping body. He was exhausted. I dried him off and helped him into his pajamas. Morrie took him horsy-style to bed. He was asleep before his head hit the pillow.

It was time for Morrie to go to work on the Bear. Jack was waiting downstairs in the garage. Morrie was nearly out the door when he turned and said, "With this race money, the doctors will make Rod better."

Chapter 33

At a quarter to five the next morning, I awoke in a cold sweat. I couldn't have cut the humidity with a fork. I got out of bed and tried to locate the day's route sheet. I realized I must have left it in the car. I needed to get out and walk. After being glued inside the car for long hours at a time, I was stiff as a board. I called the front desk.

"Yes Mrs. Krawiec, can I help you?"

"Is it safe for my son and me to walk around here?"

"Ma'am, the Farmers Market opens in a few minutes at five. It's just on the other side of the garage. Restaurant owners go there in the morning to buy what they'll serve for the day. The Market is our pride and joy. You'll have no problem there."

"Rod, wake up, we're going to the market."

"It's dark outside, can't I sleep some more?"

"Son, you only live once and I'm sure you'll never see Oklahoma City again. You can sleep in the car later."

Downstairs, Morrie was dead asleep in the Bear. He must have worked for hours. Jack was already gone. Sunrise was still an hour ahead. "Hey mister, time to wake up."

Morrie half-opened his eyes and grinned when he saw Rod and me. "The sun's not up, why are you?"

"Going to the Farmers Market. Come on, we need some exercise."

Outside the backdoor of the Skirven Hotel garage, a neon sign blinked Oklahoma City Public Market. Sweet summer plums, apricots, and strawberries wafted into an aroma cloud of fresh baked molasses bread. We bagged a loaf and added a carton of strawberries. A few food hawkers down, we stuffed a brown bag with loose-leaf butter lettuce, two red heirloom tomatoes, and a can of Meredith's German brown mustard. Then we scooted past stinky, hanging cowhide rugs, piles of tiny Creek Indian beads, and an assortment of farm tools. There was even a place with a ten-foot backhoe for resale. At the exits, the smoked meats drew us in.

"What's in there?" Rod asked.

A cowboy in an ivory-snapped, grey plaid shirt and a mile-high, brown suede cowboy hat stood behind a smoker. He flipped up the hood and pointed to a seven-foot-long slab of deer carcass and four smoking rabbits. "That's Oklahoma's finest. Want a nibble, partner?"

Smoke filled my nose, Rod's eyes watered, and Morrie coughed.

"No thanks," I said. "Looks yummy, but we'll pass."

We poured fresh coffee into our thermoses, paid for everything, and headed back toward the hotel. Since we still had some time, instead of going back inside, all three of us squeezed into the Bear's front seat. I started her up and drove out into daylight. I parked near a field with yellow sunflowers. Rod and I munched strawberries as Morrie sliced the molasses bread unevenly with his knife. I sucked enough coffee to make my eyes pop out, and Rod sipped from the water jug stored in our tool bag. When we were done eating, Morrie snapped open the passenger door, jumped out, and Rod slid over where his dad had been sitting. I started her up and coasted onto the street where we were surprised by a cheering crowd of hotel staff.

We checked in with the starter for our appointed six o'clock start time. At the blast, we sped onto Route 66 east towards Galena, Kansas and Springfield, Missouri. Our final destination for the day would be St. Louis, Missouri. On the way out of town, we rolled over the steel-framed Lake Overholser Bridge. Steel cords provided the cable compression that held us high above the water. Rod held his breath as we crossed over.

"Those big old cables must be really strong to hold this car."

I laughed "Strong they are, son. Look behind us. That bridge looks kind of like the humps of a camel rising over the water."

Rod twisted to see. "Sure does. Oh yeah, I see a great big camel over the creek in the middle of the desert."

Morrie stayed close. Rod kept waving at his dad. We sped eastward toward St Louis. The drive along the banks of the Mississippi spurred talk about the mighty river, the dividing point between the eastern and western sides of the United States. I'd read plenty about the Mississippi in my Mark Twain books. After so many years, I would finally see it. It ran south from Canada across the Wisconsin border, into the Midwest and down through the southern states. The river was constant, and so were the boats that brought commerce down its river highway. Major cities like St Louis relied on its waters. Paddle wheelers carried people, and steamships carried raw materials, produce, and manufactured goods into the New Orleans Delta. Bigger ships were loaded there before heading off to Europe. Long before Route 66 and the automobile, the Mississippi connected the country.

Rod loved Mark Twain's tale of Tom Sawyer and his adventures on the old Mississippi. There was a big world out here and everywhere we went we saw how differently people lived. We stopped at Joplin, Missouri, a tiny mining town surrounded by gaping holes called open-pit mines. In 1933, a couple called Bonnie and Clyde had ravaged the local business community at gunpoint to steal a few dollars.

When I stopped for gas, there was a picture posted inside the station office of Bonnie, with one of her long legs stretched out across the fender of a car, pistol in hand, and a cigar hanging from her mouth. The picture had been taken nearby.

The gas station attendant ran out to pump gas, and seeing Rod and me, frowned. I could see he didn't think we should be out on our own.

"Where you going, ma'am?"

"We're heading for St. Louis, and then Chicago.

"Yes ma'am, but where's your hubby? Did he turn over the wheel so he could take a catnap?"

"No, he'll be pulling up shortly. I'm driving all the way myself. We're in that big cross-country rally. Have you seen any other drivers?"

"I've seen two or three. You must be with the leaders. Strange to see a women driver, going all the way across the country with her kid."

"I'm enjoying it a whole bunch. My husband's the mechanic. He's looking out for us, but he can't be in the rally. Just my boy and I are registered to rally."

"If you don't mind, ma'am, it doesn't seem right to me making a woman drive all by herself.

"I don't mind a bit. In fact, I think it's darn right. I never did anything so darn right in my whole life!"

After he walked to my side of car, I smiled and paid him $2.95 for twenty-two gallons of gas. I pressed on the starter button, gassed the pedal, and sped off.

I accelerated out of Joplin. I'd heard the miners could get pretty nasty in the late afternoon after a few shots at the local saloon. The wind kicked up. Dust devils and loose sand spat at us. I couldn't see much. Oppressed by the wind, I slowed to ten miles an hour.

When the wind finally died down, Rod caught sight of something I'd never seen. "Look at those ears."

"Can't look right now, Rod, I'm driving, remember."

"Oh yeah. But you won't believe what I am seeing. His face is so ugly. "Yuk!" Rod crouched down. I could see he was petrified. I looked up.

"Lord, what's a bat doing out in the daytime! They're nocturnal! It's alright, honey. It only eats ants and rodents."

"Are you sure? Look at its ears! They're half the size of its body and they point straight up." As I tried to stay focused on the road, a glob of bat poop landed square in Rod's lap. "Ooh, Mom, now what do I do?"

"Just leave it. Don't touch! Don't touch! I'll stop in a minute."

"Look at those wings. They look like spider webs! Look how big they are! Gosh, he's flying with his mouth wide open. Don't stop now! Let's get out of here, okay."

I tried to accelerate, but the gusts picked up again. At least we were able to leave the bat far behind. A billboard up ahead read Come and Get Your Wild Berries. I pulled over at the entrance to the orchard and tried to clean Rod up. All I did was smear bat poop down his leg. I wetted the rag from our drinking canteen and finally wiped him clean.

The blueberries and blackberries were three cents a pound. Rod asked to pick some, and I told him we would need to hurry. I didn't want to waste time or loose position. While we gathered up the berries, I noticed Car 32 cruise by. "Darn it, we've got to go. Come on, you can eat in the car."

Ten minutes back on the road, we heard a rifle shot. Racing alongside the road, I saw a cocker spaniel scouting a dead rabbit. The dog pointed to the rabbit, and the hunter picked it up by its hind legs. Then I saw Car28 with its hood up. The driver was looking under it. I waved as I drove past.

Rod had eaten his berries, but was still hungry. "We'll stop to eat at noon," I told him. "It's only eleven. I want to push forward. Can you wait?"

"You bet. I think we're winning, Mom!"

The Bear performed perfectly. Right before noon, Rod observed that Car 31 had been pulled over by the police. The driver was outside the car and looked a little wobbly.

"Is he okay?" asked Rod.

"He may have been drinking. That's stupid. You can't win a race drunk. I don't know what will happen next, but if he gets pulled into jail, he's another dead soldier."

"A dead soldier, is that a bad thing?"

"If he was really dead, that would be bad. But if he's knocked out of the race for drinking, sitting in the slammer for a few days is a good thing, a *real* good thing."

Just then, a logging truck barreled at us, carrying logs. I wrenched the steering wheel right, and we were able to get off the road just in time. The driver of the truck had been unable to stop. Safety was up to me.

"Good work, Mom!"

"Thanks, I was hoping he'd slow down. Can't depend on hope. Sometimes you have to act."

Fearing we were falling behind, I accelerated. We passed through Springfield, Missouri on our way to St. Louis. By dusk, up ahead, Rod saw the Chain of Rocks Bridge. It took us over the Mississippi and into the outskirts of St. Louis. It was supported by a series of pillars sunk deep into the river's bed. The Mississippi churned like an ocean beneath us. The river currents crashed onto shore. I never imagined currents so strong. We arrived in St. Louis. Our third driving day was done.

Chapter 34

Spedanski had arranged for us to stay at the beautiful Chase Park Plaza. On the way to the hotel, a team of Clydesdale horses could be seen from the road.

"Can you believe the size of those Clydesdales!" I said to Rod. "See those four trotting along together. They make me feel like that tiny bellhop back at the Skirven. Look at those piles of poo in the field. That's what I call horsepower!"

At the hotel, from our room on the tenth floor, we looked out upon Lake Forest Park, built for the St. Louis World's Fair. It lay directly beneath our room. It held the Barnes Jewish Hospital, where Solly and my sisters had been born. As I looked at the hospital and remembered Ma telling stories of those early days in St. Louis, I couldn't help but think of Pa. I felt I'd been away for a long time.

Famished, Rod and I decided to go into town for dinner. Stopping first at the front desk, I left a note for Morrie letting him know we'd gone to eat. I hadn't seen Jack, and wondered where we stood in the rally.

Tired of driving, I hailed a taxi to the Crown Candy restaurant, a local favorite Sarah always talked about back home. It was well known for its delicious desserts. When we entered, we heard Ella Fitzgerald, backed by Chuck Webb's band, streaming from the juke box.

St. Louis was bopping. At every table, diners were nodding and snapping their fingers to the beat. The place smelled like Mama's home cooking. The beef brisket sandwich I ordered was juicy. The meat flaked in my mouth. Rod said his hot dog hit the spot.

"To drink, let's share a chocolate phosphate," I said.

"Can I have whipped cream on top, Mom?"

"You bet. You've been such a good kid. What do you want for desert?"

"I'd like a chocolate sundae. The one that boy's slurping has fudge dripping all over it."

We had to chew the chocolate off the vanilla ice cream. Our noses ended up black and white from the sauce and ice cream. Morrie arrived as we finished. A couple in the corner turned up their noses as he walked past.

They could probably smell his three days on the road without a bath. He ordered a three-inch-high corned beef sandwich, and as soon as it arrived, inhaled it.

"Checked with the referee and the cars that started behind you are lagging by hours," he said. "Of the ones that started ahead, lots have dropped out. That leaves Car 23 and our 18. Car 23 is the one that passed you coming into the plains of Kansas. Many cars just didn't have the power to deal with the updraft between Oklahoma and Missouri. Once they fell behind, they turned back."

That meant there was but one leg to go and one car to beat.

"I can't believe it! We're in second place!"

"Bella, I'll change your tires and put on new brakes tonight. The traffic into Chicago will require you to use those brakes."

"Heck, I've driven in Los Angeles, what's the big deal about Chicago driving?"

Rod had fallen fast asleep at the table. I needed to get horizontal myself. Morrie drove us back to the hotel in his car. In our room, all the sugar from the sundae kicked in. Rod was wide awake.

"I'm not tired now. What can I do?"

"Go ahead and read about Chicago and the rest of Illinois in this hotel magazine. That'll certainly put you to sleep." I tucked myself in bed and left Rod reading in the armchair beside me. Room service woke us at four thirty the next morning. I had completely forgotten to call home. I felt guilty, but then again, I knew it would only be another day. The coffee was just what I needed. I went to wake Rod. He hadn't fallen asleep until the wee hours so was groggy. I gave him a tiny taste of my coffee.

"Jeez Mom, how can drink that stuff. It's awful."

"Glad you think so. You don't need to drink coffee until you need to drink coffee."

We ate scrambled eggs, crisp hash brown potatoes, and sour dough toast with apricot preserves. By a quarter past five, we were dressed in our crusty driving suits. I held both helmets in my hands.

Morrie met us in the lobby. After he'd finished working, he'd fallen asleep in one of the purple wing chairs there. Now, up and alert, he sliced away my confidence. "The shifter may not make it. It'll go at most another five hundred miles. Needs a new gasket. Jack was off before I knew I needed it. He had one in his car. I checked with the boy at the desk. The parts shops here won't be open for another hour, and then it could take me at least an hour to get everything working properly. "You'll have to risk it. If you break down, I'll be right behind you."

I was panicked. "What good will you be if you don't have the part?"

"Don't worry, I'll think of something. There's always something."

"We're on the verge of finishing and now this! Heck, if it breaks, I may lose my place."

"I'll get the part. Just go on ahead. Have a good time, son You're riding with the winner. I know it! You got to make sure your mom believes it, too."

Rod, the Bear, and I positioned ourselves for the six o'clock start. I heard the sounding blast and we were off.

Chapter 35

By seven thirty, we were soaked with humidity. We had reached Springfield, Illinois, the land of Lincoln. Rod had unknowingly mimicked Abraham Lincoln's late night study habits when he stayed up reading so late. For a brief second, I thought about Rod as a future president of the United States. Mama would have been happy if I had just finished high school. I wanted Rod to have much, much more than I had. Mr. Lincoln's story gave me hope.

To pass the time, and give Rod a sense of where we were, I mentioned Lincoln. I knew Rod had read a story in *Time* about Lincoln's rise to the presidency. Now, he reminded me of the impression that story had made on him.

"Can you believe it, Mom! He lost the election to the US Senate twice. He was ready to give up. Then the Lincoln Douglas debates got him the Republican nomination. He believed everyone was created equal and that slavery was wrong. There were a lot of people who didn't want to hear that. He was far from the favorite. Then several front runners fell apart at the last minute. They kind of canceled each other out. No one expected Mr. Lincoln to be president, not even Mr. Lincoln. Mom, you've got to keep trying even when you don't think you'll win. Papa told me to cheer you up. Did I do a good job?"

Rod understood more than I would have expected from an eight year old.

"You bet, Rod. Your timing is perfect. Timing means a lot in this world."

"Is today the right time for us to win this race? Do you think we still can?"

"We can do it if we stay determined. But we'll need some luck, just the way President Lincoln had some luck."

"Even with good luck, you have to fight for what you want."

I couldn't help but think of Pa. I really wished I'd called home last night. Now, I only wanted to finish quickly, without incident. I'd come this far. I realized I might win. But would winning justify leaving while Pa was still in a coma? Would he be proud on his grandson and me? I would call Mama tonight, no matter what.

We counted barns from St. Louis to Chicago to pass the time. There were red rectangles with peaked roofs, and round white-and-brown barns with large dormer windows. We were in Middle America. The barns made life look so simple. I couldn't help but think of the scenes of village life on Mama's quilt.

Rod scratched little dashes on the back of the route map every time he saw a barn. "I counted forty," he said. "Nineteen are red."

"Rod, you're brilliant. I only counted nine, and just two were red."

We arrived in Springfield. We had traveled about one hundred miles, which meant we had less than two hundred miles to Chicago. There was no sign of Car 23. He must still be ahead.

Along the way, a red cardinal flew over the deep blue-green grasses of Illinois. At several points, we saw huge yellow sunflowers standing four feet high at the end of large green stems. They looked like clowns, waving at us as we passed.

At Bill Shay's gasoline station, the attendant recognized us because our picture had been published in the *Springfield Gazette*. "Can I take a picture of the two of you in front of your car?"

"I guess so. Why do you want it?"

His pants were torn and he was missing teeth. I made sure I had the car keys in my pocket before Rod and I walked out front.

"Miss, you're famous. The whole town's talking about the lady rally driver and her kid."

Morrie pulled in as the attendant took our picture.

"Can I use your garage to do some repairs?" he asked. "I have to replace a gasket."

"It would be my pleasure, Mr. ..."

"Just Morrie. Bella's my wife, and this boy here is my son."

"You're the mechanic. Lucky guy!"

Morrie had stopped in Springfield, where he'd found the necessary part. He took care of the bad gasket in less than five minutes.

"That was fast!"

"We have no time to spare. Car 23 is ahead, but you may be able to catch him.

I wondered if I would be able to catch the other driver. We filled up, and Phil, the attendant, told us he would post our picture right next to the picture of Bonnie, the infamous bank robber. He had the same picture of her as the other gas station attendant.

We were off to Bloomington and Joliet, just outside Chicago. The air got hotter. It was obscenely humid. Then I saw him. Car 23 was just ahead of me. I accelerated. He did the same. I was on his tail. There was a stop sign ahead. He had to stop! And so did I! He did. I didn't. I rolled past him, keeping my foot on the pedal until I lost him in my rearview window. I knew it was wrong not to stop and wasn't sure what had come over me.

"Rod, never do what I just did, okay?"

"Did you break the law?"

"I did, and it was wrong. Don't ever do that when you learn to drive, okay?"

"If it was wrong, why didn't you stop?'

"I guess it's because I really want to win. Because … I just did. Just don't *you* do it!"

"I never thought you could lose, Mom. But you scared me. Did you really have to break that law?"

"No, but people do worse than running stop signs."

"What?"

We were now surrounded by Illinois corn fields as far as the eye could see. What could possibly stop us? It was dead of summer. All the corn was gone. All that was left were brown corn husks. I knew Car 23 wouldn't give up easily, not when we both were so close to the finish. I floored the gas pedal. I was pushing to the limit. Victory was within our grasp.

"Rod, you know what I'm thinking?"

"The finish line, Mom?"

"Nope, I thinking about how proud your grandpa, my pa, would be of you. Maybe he'll be awake when we get back home. We'll call as soon as we can. I want you to tell him all about our rally."

Everything was coming together. Morrie's business was booming. It looked as if I would be the first female rally driver in the USA. I might just have my career and two happy men at home. Life was looking grand!

"Rod, there is a terrible story in this town we're headed into now. I don't want to scare you, but I think this story puts everything in perspective. Back in 1924, Joliet Prison housed Nathan Leopold and Richard Loeb, wealthy Chicago students who murdered Bobby Franks to prove they could commit the perfect crime. They poured hydrochloric acid all over his body and left him on the roadside. They assumed he would be so disfigured he would not be identified. Incredibly, the murderers went immediately to a roadside stand and ate hotdogs for dinner, just like they were having a normal day. Crazy as it may sound, these guys weren't stupid. They were at the top of their class, highly intelligent, but very confused about right and wrong."

I wasn't sure why I was telling Rod this story. I was more tired than I thought. As I spoke, the car swerved across the divided highway several times.

"Are you okay, Mom?

"Yep, I'm fine, just a little tired."

"Those were bad guys, Mom?"

"They were as bad as could be."

"I guess going through a stop sign isn't so bad. I know I'll never do anything like what they've done. I guess breaking a few rules isn't the end of the world. Sometimes, not often, when people make fun of me, I want to say nasty things back."

My eyelids were heavy. I had to stay focused on the road. It was daylight. Why was I suddenly so tired? I couldn't help but think of Pa and his temper. Perhaps this had been on my mind more than I knew.

"Rod, losing your temper doesn't necessarily make you a terrible person but bad things can come from it. Sometimes you have to get mad to get someone's attention if they are hurting you. It's complicated."

"Mr. Cohn, my teacher, says it if you get mad, you're not very smart."

"Well, teachers don't like it when their students make trouble. You shouldn't make trouble in class. There is a time and place to make your feelings known. You have to understand that if you say things people don't want to hear, there are consequences. You have to expect someone like your teacher to discipline you if you say things in anger."

"Mom, why are you telling me all this stuff now?"

I didn't answer right away. I kept staring at the road, making sure I didn't lose control. I couldn't answer. It was if I hadn't explained things to myself until now, but when the words did come, I knew they were exactly right. "Rod, I'm trying to talk about your grandpa. I feel like he's been with us every second of this drive, even though I didn't know it until now. Maybe it's being on the road like this, moving from one place to the next, wanting to win this rally so bad, wanting things in the same way he wanted them. There were a lot of things he wanted that didn't come about, but not once did he stop trying, sometimes maybe to the point where he didn't pay attention to the people he was close to. I don't know why it's taken me so long to understand him better. This doesn't make him right, but right now I can say I wish I'd never fought with him. I didn't understand how important it was to him that I respected who he was. He was much older than me and had no tolerance for back talk. When I acted out in his house, he believed he had no choice but to kick me out."

"He kicked you out of your own house, away from your mom and everything?"

"He did. I was so angry I refused to ever talk to him again, even though it meant you would never get to know him. I was wrong. I was young. I didn't understand who he was, or who I was. I meant well. Sometimes you do things and mean well, but the results aren't good."

"You mean like those criminals."

"No, they're different. They meant to do harm and went to prison as a result. I mean sometimes good people like us think they have no choice."

"Did you have a choice?"

"I didn't think so. I was in love with your father. I either had to give up my father or yours. I'm glad I kept your father. He is a good man."

"I'm glad you kept Papa, too. I love him. Where is he now?"

"He should be coming up soon. We are nearly to Chicago."

I desperately wanted to call home. I wanted to talk to Pa. I wanted him to be awake. It was time to end our feud. My eyes welled up. Thinking about home made me sad. Funny how sad you can be in the middle of great happiness. The two emotions are not so far apart.

"Mom, are you crying about Grandpa?"

I didn't respond. I'd been so angry at Pa. All those years were lost to us. He'd rejected me. He'd attacked everything that made Pearl who she was. He'd berated Frieda as weak, and she was the only one of us who submitted. He'd battled Solly. He'd never given Mama the respect she deserved. Solly had no choice but to be the way he was. Pa would have crippled him psychologically if he hadn't fought back. I was too angry to apologize. I was hurt. Morrie chose me. I was young. I was in love, but learned that love didn't come so easy. Pa kicked me out of his house and then I barricaded him from my life. I gave up on him. Mama kept telling me to see him, but my anger got the best of me.

"Mom, are you sad because of Grandpa?"

"I'm sad because of you, Rod. I'm sad because your other grandpa in Europe has always been far, far away. You will probably never be able to know him. Your grandpa here may never be able to speak with you."

"Are you sad because I was born? Was I a mistake?"

"God no, both your father and I love you more than we can say. Your father struggles to show his love. Sometimes that's hard for him. He is getting better, though, isn't he?"

"Yeah, Mom. I like it that he's our mechanic and we're on this big trip together."

"We're lucky to have this experience together. But never forget how much we love you. Even if your father and I fight, or we tell you no, never forget how much we love you."

"Why do you and Papa fight?"

"I love him. But it doesn't matter how much you care, sometimes life gets in the way. You are so important to me, Rod. More important than this car, this drive, anything. You make me happy. Just your smile alone, that's all it takes. This trip with you has been a dream. Most people never get a chance to live their dream. I didn't always know how to get there, but deep in my heart I knew what I needed. Rod, I needed you and your dad to love each other and give me just a little freedom to find myself. Hope I get another chance to do that with Pa."

Morrie pulled up behind us, whistling. He'd taken a long time to accept my dreams. If it wasn't for Spedanski, I might still be waiting. The traffic crowded together on the road. There were tall buildings in the distance and billboards on the roadside. We were now five miles outside of Chicago. I accelerated so that we could end our journey with a flourish. The Bear shook, and continued to shake, until I pulled off to the side of the road.

"This can't be happening. We've broken down. Morrie stopped, got out of his car and opened the hood. "You're a ways ahead, don't worry."

"Don't worry! We can't lose now! We just can't!"

I got out while Morrie nervously examined underneath the hood, touching every connection he could reach short of pulling out the engine. Then he smiled. "It's fixed."

"Was it the transmission?"

"Nope, it's bad, but will work for another few miles."

"What then? You did little more than fiddle around. You didn't even pull out your tools. You're not kidding me, are you? I have no patience for kidding right now."

I noticed that Morrie had stopped chewing his gum. I looked down and saw a wad was on one of the hoses to the radiator. He had patched a little hole in the hose. The Bear had overheated because it was losing water. Morrie went to his car, pulled out a gallon can of water, and refilled the radiator. He grinned.

"Let's take her in, mechanic Morrie"

Rod piped up. "See Mom, everything worked out."

We got back in our purring cars and headed into Chicago. Our journey ended in Chicago at Buckingham Fountain. This massive man-made pool of water, with spouts shooting 150 feet in the air, was a modern marvel. There were hundreds of people waiting to see us — a tiny woman driver and her son Rod, who was challenged with cerebral palsy. We drove through the finish line in Spedanski's Stutz Bearcat. While not all the drivers had finished, our time was so much better than the next fastest car, we were un-officially declared the winner. As we drove a victory lap around the plaza, we saw a banner overhead on Congress Parkway that said **CONGRATULA-TIONS CROSS-COUNTRY RALLY DRIVERS.**

There were some boos from a couple of disgruntled men, hoping that one of their favorites had won the race. But compared to the loud ovation from the crowd, the disgruntled sounds were faint. Rod was the first to see another banner held by a couple of young girls who looked about his age. It said **GO BELLA, GO ROD**.

As we were announced winners, the crowd chanted, "Go Bella, Go Rod." Hundreds waved at us. Rod lifted his right arm and waved while bracing himself tightly on the car seat with the lower part of his body. As we finished our victory lap, the loud speaker blared, this time with the voice of Maximilian Spedanski. "Bella and Rod, in the Spedanski Stutz Bearcat, have won!"

As winners of the first rally in America, we owned a United States record. Morrie had followed us into Chicago, but stopped short of the finish line. He waited there for us to finish the victory lap. Spedanski darted out onto the roadway as I pulled to a stop. He snapped open my car door, and as I stepped onto the running board, he raised my arms high in the air. Together, we jumped in excitement.

Morrie ran to Rod's side of the car as Spedanski and I danced in the street. He hoisted Rod onto his shoulders and carried him back to me. Then Morrie carefully placed Rod on the driver's side car seat and handed me a dozen red roses he'd stopped to buy just outside of Chicago. As Spedanski handed me a check and a trophy, which was a statue of a wild coyote with his head cocked and his mouth open, he announced, "To be a winner, you must be independent. To be a winner and a woman, you must be daring and focused. You must keep you hopes high and your eyes on the sky. Our statue exemplifies the independence, focus, and hopes of all peoples. Bella, congratulations on your first-place finish. Rod, I know your mama made you proud. I'll bet she learned a few things from you along the way."

Morrie and I walked together with Rod to the fountain in the center of the plaza. The crowd, seeing our joy, followed us, some of them chanting my name, or Rod's, or both our names in unison. I was dirty and tired, but could not have been happier to be with my husband and son. Rod tapped Morrie on the shoulder. "Papa, Mom has an important phone call to make. Can we leave soon?"

About the Author

Michael Sedloff was born in 1949, a time when the postwar culture was defined by men in the workplace, earning a living; and women at home, raising a family. Bella, his mother, was such a women, and his father, Morris "Morrie" Sedloff, a depression-era baby, wanted nothing more than to be a good provider. In 1955, Morrie moved his family to Anaheim, California, to open his own business. This was the same year Walt Disney opened a business called Disneyland.

The move was an eye-opener for Michael. He witnessed the pace of change that accompanies a booming economy. Orange groves and fields laden with tumbleweed turned into tract homes, seemingly overnight. For Bella, however, Anaheim was awful. Away from her brothers and sisters, while her husband worked twelve hours a day, seven days a week, to make a success of himself, Bella was lonely. When she finally spoke up, Morrie listened and sold his business, moving the family back to Los Angeles.

The move provided Michael with the opportunity to become better acquainted with his eccentric aunts and uncles. Every Sunday, the family got together to play cards, eat lox and bagels, and tell stories about growing up in Boyle Heights. Once a month, Bella took Michael to the "old folks' home" in Boyle Heights to visit Grandpa Frank. In his nineties and deaf as a doormat, Frank would gruffly bark at Bella. Frank and Bella's relationship was based upon a foundation of love and disgust.

As a child, Michael clung to his mother's apron strings. He was a troubled speaker. In elementary school, he stuttered, but with therapy, turned his malady into success. His speech therapist convinced him to compete in an eighth-grade a poetry-reading contest. This experience paved the way to more performances, in which he recited poetry and read the essays that he had written. The confidence he gained eliminated his tendency to stutter. He had also discovered a wonderful means of self-expression.

Michael attended college near his home. Like many, although he loved learning, he didn't care much for tests. His passion was making things happen when others could not. He created an experimental college, leveraging the university's resources to serve thousands from the surrounding community.

After graduation, Michael traveled alone throughout Europe, then returned home to a job in publishing. He was unsure how he wanted to direct his future, and after a long illness, he returned to school to pursue his master's degree. Even then, he knew he had yet to discover what he wanted to do in life.

Eventually, he moved to San Diego, where he met Janice, the woman who was to become his beautiful wife. She and Michael raised their two children, Brandon and Erin, while building a successful business together.

A woman of the twenty-first century, Janice was confident, aggressive, and determined. Michael couldn't help but notice the contrast between his wife, who was able to make an exciting career for herself, and his mother, who suffered because the needs of those around her always outweighed her own.

This observation compelled Michael to write *Bella Will Rally*, his first novel. In it, he imbues his fictional Bella with both his mother's spirit and her struggles. His central character's relatives are marvelously similar to his own mother's family. The events and story are entirely a product of Michael's imagination.

www.ingramcontent.com/pod-product-compliance
Lightning Source LLC
Chambersburg PA
CBHW070556130626
46556CB00001B/178